1.50

A
BOTTLE
IN
THE
SMOKE

A BOTTLE IN THE SMOKE

A. N. WILSON

VIKING

VIKING
Published by the Penguin Group
Viking Penguin, a division of Penguin Books USA Inc.,
375 Hudson Street, New York, New York 10014, U.S.A.
Penguin Books Ltd, 27 Wrights Lane,
London W8 5TZ, England
Penguin Books Australia Ltd, Ringwood,
Victoria, Australia
Penguin Books Canada Ltd, 2801 John Street,
Markham, Ontario, Canada L3R 1B4
Penguin Books (N.Z.) Ltd, 182–190 Wairau Road,
Auckland 10, New Zealand

Penguin Books Ltd, Registered Offices:
Harmondsworth, Middlesex, England

First published in 1990 by Viking Penguin,
a division of Penguin Books USA Inc.

10 9 8 7 6 5 4 3 2 1

LIBRARY OF CONGRESS CATALOGING IN PUBLICATION DATA

Wilson, A. N., 1950–
    A bottle in the smoke/A.N. Wilson.
        p.   cm.
    Sequel to: Incline our hearts.
    ISBN 0-670-83211-9
    I. Title.
    PR6073.I439B6   1990
    823'.914—dc20   89–40686

Printed in the United States of America
Set in Sabon
Designed by Bernard Schleifer

A
BOTTLE
IN
THE
SMOKE

one

Killing Time. One spends more and more time doing it, I find. Sleep used to account for at least one-third of each twenty-four hours. Now I'm lucky if I get five hours of oblivion without a Mogadon. And I turn up early for everything. A luncheon date in Westminster at twelve-forty-five found me, not long ago, pacing about on the Embankment at eleven in the morning, and deciding to revisit old favourites at the Tate. I often go there, particularly to look at the Blake Room, and the modern sculpture, for which I have a weakness, and the Turners. Somehow, on that particular day, the minutes dragged past and I found that I had seen everything I wanted to see within three-quarters of an hour.

Coming down into the main hall, I decided to visit their special exhibition, and only then noticed that it was called "Mr. Pilbright at Home." Nothing could have been more calculated to bring before me Time's strange trick of long holding secrets in its bosom which are then, years later, trumpeted forth. Letters written in secret command high sums from the Sunday newspapers a generation later. Love affairs become a mere matter of serialisation rights. Spies who have handled information which, if disclosed, could ruin the lives of thousands are prepared, in time, to put the whole thing down on paper for in-flight entertainment.

Uncle Roy had a word for it in one of his church services—"when the secrets of all hearts shall be disclosed." Biographers like Hunter make such disclosures their stock in trade. Mr. Pilbright probably had no dramatic secrets to conceal except his genius—or his whatever it was, if it wasn't quite genius. If he had written any love letters they certainly did not survive. He appeared to have had no close relationships with women except that with his mother. The mysterious girl, variously called his "angel" or his "Magdalene," who appears so often in his pictures was thought by critics to have been a creature of his imagination, purely, but never knew, for all that she inspired his imagination for more than twenty-five years. She was not a model at any of the life classes he (to me surprisingly) turned out to have attended in the 1920s and 1930s. Yet again and again, she crops up in his work: as the angel telling the Fulham bus queue, "He is not here—He is risen!," or as the canvas nicknamed *The Woolworth Magdalene*, one of the Tate's finest Pilbrights, a moonfaced girl with her dark hair cut short, her skirt tight against her thighs as she kneels to empty a bottle of 4711 over the sandals of the slightly schoolmasterly, bearded figure, sitting in the pub with His friends. Critics admire the way she has kicked off one of her peep-toe stilettoes to reveal malformed feet with toenails, exuberant splashes of his vermilion brushwork.

The religious element in Mr. Pilbright's pictures does not always speak to me, and most of the comparisons with Blake seem pretty wide of the mark. There are paintings of his which I can enjoy—though not those with too overt a message. The enormous number of sketches and watercolours of people at work or simply going about their ordinary business in wartime or just post-wartime suburbia are the things to which I return. There's a lovely one called *Spring Comes to Balham* which I found once in the art gallery at Aberdeen. He seems to redeem the triviality of things by looking at them so lovingly. Plant pots. A woman walking her Scottie. Tulips in a window-box.

Some of the pictures of work recapture my own brief period of being his colleague at Tempest and Holmes during the year after I finished National Service. I have sometimes wondered whether I wasn't the model for *Boy in Accounts,* one in that series of sketches done in the mid-fifties which he worked up into that showy canvas, now in the Pompidou Centre, *Matthew Forsakes the Inland Revenue to Follow Christ.* Mr. Pilbright never sketched at work, of course. It was all done from memory. His existence as a painter was entirely unknown to me or to any of his colleagues at the time.

The special exhibition was extremely well done. You walked behind a large screen and immediately you were gazing into two perfectly constructed interiors, exact reproductions of the ground floor of Mr. Pilbright's Balham semi-detached. The front room (so designated, apparently by Mr. Pilbright himself, though I wondered whether he wouldn't have been a "lounge" man) was a perfectly respectable neat little interior, whose varnished oak furnishings dated mainly from the Edwardian period. The two-seater settee and the armchair were draped with antimacassars. The windows were concealed by lace curtains. On the vaguely 1909 neo-Tudor sideboard was a Bakelite wireless set. A small bookcase contained sentimental novels—one noted the names of Mrs. Henry Wood and Marie Corelli on the spines, but Day Muckley's *The Calderdale Saga* was also there. The gas fire was the old-fashioned sort, where the elements resemble false teeth. The pictures on the walls gave little clue to any artistic interest on the part of the inhabitant. There was a portrait of Mr. Gladstone, a couple of Arundel Society prints, and a large photograph of Mr. Pilbright's mother, hung up, it was conjectured, some time after that lady's demise during the Second World War.

The back room was in the greatest possible contrast. The orderliness, the bourgeois ordinariness of the front room was anonymous. If you thought long about it, perhaps there would have seemed something self-consciously old fashioned about it; but there must be many people, particularly the unmarried residing with parents, who live with inherited furniture and never bother to express their own taste by the purchase of contemporary fittings.

The back room was a chaos. A catalogue which I bought on my way out of the exhibition assured the visitor that the two rooms had been reconstructed with complete faithfulness. Certainly the difference between the two rooms fitted well with what I knew and did not know about Mr. Pilbright all those years ago. At the front he was the bourgeois suburban man, anonymous in his tedious, orderly acceptance of the conventions. Behind all this rioted his hidden artistic obsession.

The window of the back room had been boarded up. This had apparently been done long before the blackout. Mr. Pilbright preferred to work by the same even and unsatisfactory light dangling from the sixty-watt bulb (no shade) in the middle of the ceiling. The reason for this became clear as soon as you thought about it. Nearly all his work had to be done at night. He reached home by about six, ate a high tea, and then retreated to the studio for four or six hours' work. On Saturday and Sunday he would work a more or less full day in the back room. He was scarcely out of the place, a fact which accounted for that pasty prison complexion which I so well remember.

One wall of the back room was covered with his striking mural: *The Great Draught of Fishes at Kew Bridge*. Not one of his best. On the other hand, one saw his real merits, as an observer of the human scene if not exactly as a great artist, in the many half-finished paintings and drawings which littered this room. There were studies for *Morning 'Bus Ride*, and some of those memorable pen-and-ink sketches of ARP wardens after a raid. The room was crammed with these pictures, dozens of them—oils, charcoal sketches, watercolour studies. The room was carpeted, strewn with them. Palettes, jars of turps with brushes, paint tubes with no tops, were scattered all over the place, evidence that he worked in a frenzy, giving himself no time to tidy up afterwards, when exhausted after a solid spell of creativity, he would clamber into bed. A "voice over"—instantly recognisable as a replay of Raphael Hunter's television Arts programme, "Perspectives"—informed us that Pilbright worked each evening until he was so tired that the brush fell from his hand. Then he would remove his paint-stained overalls, go upstairs and sleep until the time came, a few hours later, to resume the persona of a manager in Accounts at Tempest and Holmes.

At this point in Hunter's narrative, Mr. Pilbright's own voice was heard. The content of what he had to say was not, when analysed, exactly interesting. I've often thought that, about the utterances of painters, sculptors or other non-verbal communicators; when they try to put into words what they have been up to in their art, it's not particularly impressive. But it was, from a personal point of view, truly extraordinary to hear that voice after nearly forty years, and in such a context. I had missed the original television programme, transmitted in the early sixties, which had "made" Pilbright's reputation. Hearing it for the first time in the gallery, it was almost as if Hunter and Pilbright, both in their different ways haunting figures, had been summoned up from the vasty deep. Hunter had just said to Pilbright that he enjoyed his canvases because of their sympathetic evocation of the lives of ordinary people.

"But there are no ordinary people!" said Pilbright. "Never heard of such a being! Ordinary! Jesus Christ was an ordinary person, if you are going to take that line. . . . No, in all my work, I've just tried to . . ."

"And religion has always been an important part of your inspiration?"

"Inspiration? Religion. Oh, dear, oh, dear!" In the cross scepticism and the cocknified twang of this retort I heard again *my* Mr. Pilbright. "Our watches must be set to different time scales," I remember his saying to me sarcastically when I arrived for work at ten past nine. "Mine's Greenwich Mean Time, what's yours?" "No," he was now saying to Hunter. "I've worked hard. Inspiration! I've lived by rule."

"You worked for many years in a shirt factory, I believe," wheedled Hunter.

"Look, I told you before you switched on all this equipment that I would only talk about art, about my work." Crossly, firmly, grandly, Mr. Pilbright's voice put Hunter down.

I couldn't blame him for not wishing to reminisce about life at Tempest and Holmes, which was tedious enough. There was probably nothing, imaginatively speaking, for him to remember. Life, properly defined, probably only happened for Pilbright in that back room in Balham beneath the naked sixty-watt bulb. Hunter, in his obvious way, discerning the fact that Pilbright's best pictures captured the qualities of workaday life, probably supposed that Pilbright would have something to say about it— as though painting were a substitute for talk. He might as well have assumed that Titian would have had more interesting things to say than the next man about classical mythology, or Winterhalter about Queen Victoria or Picasso about women.

What really astonished me, though, was how mistaken, how utterly mistaken, I had myself been about old Pilbright. I had known this for years. Pilbright became famous in the sixties, decades before I chanced upon this special exhibition at the Tate. But "Mr. Pilbright At Home" brought home to me the sheer crassness of a younger self, the crudity of my judgements, the simplicity of distinctions which I allowed to form in my mind between what was and wasn't boring, what did or didn't matter.

In the office, Pilbright had embodied everything which I considered uninspiring and unimportant. I despised him because I was so certain that he belonged to a world where art, literature, the theatre, music (my own imagined spheres) did not figure. If I had been more honest I should probably have admitted that social snobbery came into play, too. It usually does in England. My years with Aunt Deirdre and Uncle Roy had left their mark. I might wince at their talk of people being of "good" family or out of such and such a "drawer," but in fact with a large part of myself I had come to accept that the upper social reaches, or at least the cultivated classes, were inherently more estimable than the suburban sort of families from which we ourselves sprang, and to which Mr. Pilbright, all his life, unpretentiously belonged.

"Of course, I'm fond of Wagner," his cross voice, disembodied but now immortal, was saying through the loudspeakers, as visitors drifted through and peered at his reconstructed rooms, which were sealed off by plate glass. "Debussy, yes. Mainly composers who were working at the time my parents were married, I suppose you would say. Yes. César Franck, yes, yes. Did you say Elgar?"

Hunter, in the original interview, had apparently said Elgar.

"The choral music, are you trying to say?" said Pilbright's voice accusingly.

As he painted in the back room at Balham, Pilbright was apparently accustomed to play these composers on 78 recordings. Though at the period when I knew him, or didn't know him, I was almost completely ignorant of music, I would have been surprised that Pilbright knew these composers' names, let alone their work. If he had listened to anything, I should have conjectured that he would have been a Gilbert and Sullivan fan, or fond of "Music While You Work" on the wireless.

I don't exactly blame myself for failing to recognise at less than twenty-five-years old that people seldom reveal much of themselves at their place of employment. Pilbright was a studiedly dark horse. If the exhibition catalogue is right, he had been bitterly disappointed, during his own young manhood, by his failure to sell so much as one picture. It would seem as though he had doggedly, and in a spirit of self-immolation, thrown himself into the boring work at Tempest and Holmes. I now see that there was a strong element of self-parody in the way that he arrived each morning at two minutes to nine and left on the stroke of five. No one seemed to know where he lived. Since he never missed a day of work, it did not matter; there was no call to get in touch with him at home. Some of the typists giggled occasionally about the mystery of where he spent his dinner hour, always taken from half past twelve until half past one. What lay behind their fantasies was the shared assumption that Pilbright was so colourless that even the idea of his drinking half a pint of bitter in a pub, let alone seeing a woman, was so risqué as to be laughable. There is probably no bit of work done by Pilbright for Tempest and Holmes which could not nowadays be accomplished by a computer. His knowledge of the contents of the various ledgers and order books was encyclopaedic. He knew, for years back, all the transactions in which the firm had been involved, he knew the names of all the reps, all the retailers.

"Now let us *see*," he would say, with apparent relish; I now think there was irony, almost laughter, in this "enjoyment" taken in work. At the time, I thought that shirts were Pilbright's be all and end all. "Merrick and Son. Leicester. Yes, of course." First the town where the particular draper or men's outfitter was located. Having recited that, Mr. Pilbright liked to rehearse how many of a particular type of shirt they had, over the years, been able to sell. "Strangely enough, they've always been rather advanced in Leicester. What you would call avant-garde, young Ramsay."

This showed that he had sized me up as a person who would use the phrase and admire what it denoted. "Merricks were the first of our retailers to plump in a big way for collar-attacheds. Well, they all buy them now, of course, confounded inventions. You want to change your collar every day, I can see that, and your cuffs if you have that kind of work. But phew! A clean shirt every day!"

This was obviously out of the question. He seemed positively to relish being this sort of person, the sort who had a "bath night"—once a week?—and changed his sheets by rote once a fortnight. He did not belong, and still less wished to pretend to belong, to any world where the expression "avant-garde" could be used except in a humourous context.

It was entirely Mr. Pilbright's fault that I was working at Tempest and Holmes. My father had worked with him in Accounts there before the war. When Mummy and Daddy were killed in the air raid, Mr. Pilbright wrote a purely formulaic letter of condolence which touched my grandmother deeply. Subsequent communication had been limited to Christmas cards. Pilbright was quite a bit older than Daddy. I have no reason to suppose that my father was any closer to him than any of Pilbright's other colleagues had been. Granny, however, had for long had it in mind that I should follow in my father's footsteps. It was a joke proposition as far as I was concerned. But when National Service ended, and I was able to provide the family with no plausible alternative, events took their inevitable course.

There was naturally no question that Granny herself could write a letter. Apart from her eyes—suitable for reading, jaunts to the cinema in Norwich, and observing the passing scene but too frail for *writing*—there was all the "botheration," her word, of finding the wherewithal to write a letter. And then the further difficulty of posting the letter when it was complete. It must have been my aunt who was delegated to write the actual letters, one to Mr. Pilbright and another to the managing director. Much to my chagrin, I found myself not merely being interviewed, but offered a job. It is easy enough to say that I was not suited to the work, but since I had no money, and no "contacts" who could get me into drama school, or journalism, or any other exotic area, I found myself submitting. For the larger part of a year I did very little except study ledgers. I copied figures from one ledger into another ledger. I sorted certain bundles of the morning mail, and divided incoming settlements from the invoices. No wonder I remember no detail of the work. It was of a kind which did not occupy my imagination at all. One just did it, like a machine. Life was not enhanced by the fact that Aunt Deirdre had fixed me up with some "very suitable accommodation," as the lodger of a highly uncongenial family (friends of Aunt Deirdre's friend Bunty). For about six months, I was simply crushed by the experience, and felt too unhappy and disappointed to shake myself out of it. Until looking at those reconstructed rooms in the Tate and hearing again the voice of Mr. Pilbright, I had forgotten that feeling of desolation, the thought that life was never going to happen. It would simply be swallowed in work which I did not enjoy, meals which I did not like eating, company which afforded no kind of diversion. With the returning gloom, I felt a great envy of Mr. Pilbright. I remember telling one of my fellow clerks (whose name now escapes me) that I did not intend to be a drudge forever. I wanted to write—was indeed at work on a novel—and I wanted to act. Pilbright, coming along the row of desks at the moment when these ambitions were being aired, paused and looked into my face. How vividly I recall his expression; the sky-blue eyes behind steel-rimmed spectacles were laughing at me, I see that now. Was there not a clue in his curious hair-style—the silver hair *en brosse* cut so short as almost to be a crew-cut—that he was not quite the office automaton we all supposed? "Artistic ambitions, Ramsay? Wouldn't it be better to leave that as a hobby? Something to do with yourself in your spare time. Nice to have a hobby."

When he had gone, somebody spluttered an obscene suggestion as to Pilbright's chosen method of filling leisure hours. We all sniggered. Memory of that laughter increased my envy now. This was the right way round for fame and fortune to smile. The life which inspired that sniggering in Accounts had ended in a triumph—Hunter's "discovery" of Pilbright on "Perspectives," articles in the national press, exhibitions, interest from collectors, a belated ARA. For all his years of pure artistic activity he had the satisfaction of being able to work without the distractions of fame. To be a neglected genius (or whatever he was) for years and to be discovered at nearly sixty was a fairy-tale piece of good fortune which a true artist, in any sphere, would envy. Day Muckley's contrary fate—the Best Seller, as we so cruelly dubbed him in the Black Bottle—was much worse. He was prodigiously famous before the war for writing one book, *The Calderdale Saga*. The success could not be repeated. By middle age, however hard he tried to write books which would attract his old public, they resolutely refused to be interested. By the time I knew Muckley, he had sunk into an obscurity which was total.

Or seemed so. The television serialisation of *The Calderdale Saga* came too late for the Best Seller himself to enjoy it, but it showed that fame offers its bearers strange fortunes. Was it better to enjoy some posthumous fame, such as Muckley's, than to have none at all—to be like Fenella, dreaming all the time of the Big Break which would make her a celebrated actress, but having to live not only without recognition, but also without much money or, surely, without any confidence that she was really any good? The enviable, maddening thing about Pilbright is that he must have known that he was good—or good in his own way. Self-confidence sustained him for forty years of absolute obscurity. The house when he died was full of pictures, hundreds of them, many of which now hang in the most prestigious galleries and collections in the world. I do not suppose that Pilbright ever left London, unless for a day out by the sea at Brighton or Ramsgate. He had probably barely heard of the Museum of Modern Art in New York. He died before they built the Pompidou Centre in Paris. It probably did not give him any particular pleasure to read critics who said that he was better than Lowry or Stanley Spencer, a figure who lifted English Art out of its provincial confines, or that he deserved to be considered in the same league as Picasso and Pollock—a man who had recovered, as they had not, a new way forward for representational art. Whether or not he was a genius, he had the complete self-confidence which always accompanies genius. That was what sustained him for over forty years at Tempest and Holmes, that and the knowledge, when they presented him with his gold watch, at the time of his first "retrospective," that he had used up most of his waking hours in a pointless job, faultlessly executed. Not long after he retired, the factory itself closed down. Its few remaining buildings have since been transformed. On one floor there is a dance studio. On another, strangely enough, one of Vernon Lampitt's grand-daughters runs a thriving business which makes loose covers, festoon blinds, and huge profits out of upwardly mobile people uncertain of their own taste in interior design.

Probably Pilbright would have agreed with my grandmother's merciless assertion when insisting that I took the job that "you've got to do something with your life."

Unashamedly old-fashioned in her attitudes to the sexes, Granny appeared to think that this applied only to men. She could not be said to have done much herself, though the vehement tones in which she described her wholly passive role in things made it sound as though existence had been a constant drain on her reserves of energy. There was always the implication that having endured what she had done, it was unreasonable to expect any more of her.

"I did live through the 1930s," she'd say. "Ooh, they were

a worry. You never knew whether you were coming or going. First it was the Abdication, and then it was whether they were going to have a war. I ask you!"

Uncle Roy would flinch if she embarked on these sentiments, not because he disagreed, but because of the (to him) excruciating hints of a glottal stop when she said a word like *thirties*, the threat that the Abdication would become the Abdic-ie-shun. It is perfectly true that not everyone survived the 1930s. Granny's boast that she had done so, however, implied that after such a feat of endurance it was hardly feasible two decades later to expect her to go shopping or to help with the washing up. "I brought *two* boys into the world *and* I brought them up." The sentence was often on her lips, reminding hearers of the alarming fact that mothers do not necessarily do much for the care of their offspring. "*And* I brought them up." When she repeated the phrase, Granny would shut her eyes (a habitual gesture when on the verge of crossness) and her lips would close so firmly as to disappear altogether. Her expression announced that anyone wishing to hear more on that particular subject was going to be disappointed.

I had never questioned that, having brought Daddy and Uncle Roy into the world, Granny could not be expected to look after me when my parents were killed. Until I grew up, and she came to live with Uncle Roy and Aunt Deirdre, I only saw Granny at carefully spaced intervals. It was decreed by her protectress and close friend Mrs. Webb that you could hardly expect Thora to look after a child, not after what she'd been through. The phrase suggested something more ominous than existence itself. It made all the odder Granny's assertion (which she must have borrowed from the hyperactive Mrs. Webb) that "you've got to do something with life." Granny knew what I have discovered in later years, that it is possible to do absolutely nothing with life, simply let it go. "The things Thora has been *through*," Mrs. Webb would assert, with vehement shakings of the iron-hard perm. True, no doubt, just as Pilbright might have seemed, by those with more actively adventurous standards, to have had no life at all, but had, in his pictures, absorbed into his imagination a whole range of experience to which that artificial persona, Mr. Pilbright of Accounts, would have been a stranger.

I think I shared this idea—whether it came from Granny or from Mrs. Webb—not merely that one should do something with life, but that this doing was a matter of option or will. I thought that a series of infinitely extensible choices stretched ahead. All that was required was to try hard or to wait long enough. I was too young to know that very few wishes are ever fulfilled, or by the time they are, you have often stopped wishing them. I knew nothing about the strange part played in everything by chance. All I foresaw in the way of difficulty was the notorious trouble many creative people encounter in getting started. Thereafter, I should be able to fashion events. My ill-defined ambitions, and my only sporadically realistic sense of myself— a self which in any case was changing all the time—kept the perceptions of late middle age curtained from view. How trivial and empty and shapeless life for the most part is. I did not know that lives defined in terms of something durable (lives, as it turned out like Pilbright's) are very rare. The rest of us, crowds flowing over London Bridge into oblivion, leave no trace behind on this earth except offspring. Granny was right, perhaps, to make so much of her having brought two sons into the world. By some infinitesimal degree, evolutionary history had been changed by her. I was here, for example. And I must have inherited much of her passivity, else why should I have stayed so long in the routines imposed by my employment at Tempest and Holmes? If memory serves correctly, I worked truculently, but quite acceptingly. I rose early, and went to bed early, I travelled on a crowded bus at the beginning and end of each tedious day. I knew that the majority of Londoners lived like this, but I also knew that it was not what I regarded as "doing something with life." In fact, I saw Pilbright as the embodiment of what was wrong with this living death, his clean anonymous clothes, his grey suits and white shirts, his polite, industrious manner and his apparent non-existence after office hours. Even when the office routine began to wear me down with depression, I still did not fully believe myself to be a free agent. Held back by sheer lack of funds, my imagination did not allow itself to realise that I did not have to work at Tempest and Holmes. If I left there, no RSM would put me on a charge, no housemaster would gate me. I was to this extent free. It needed a friend to point this out to me, and for most of the time that I was working at Tempest and Holmes, I made no effort to keep in touch with the few friends I had. Then, completely by chance one Saturday, I met William Bloom, an old friend of army days, now a publisher. It was lunchtime and we were both looking round the same secondhand bookshop in the Charing Cross Road. It was only a matter of minutes before we were catching up on each other's lives, negotiating the traffic of the Soho streets, and settling ourselves in the saloon bar of the Black Bottle, my first visit to that pub.

No less simian, Bloom looked smarter, more prosperous, than when last seen in a demob suit. His thick hair, cut short, was greying at the temples, though he was only my age. His blue corduroy jacket spoke of a literary world, light years away from Pilbright.

"You're sure we want to go here?" I asked incredulously, as he pushed open the door of the Black Bottle. "It doesn't look much of a place to me." Later in the conversation, when I had bought the first round and explained my predicament, my hatred of Tempest and Holmes, my despondency about getting any sort of congenial work, it was Bloom's "Don't be so bloody wet!" which first stirred me to realise that my destiny in the short term was perfectly controllable.

"Live dangerously, my dear! Leave the awful job, carry on with the novel, go to auditions, act in the evenings."

"What do I do for money?"

I had the rather bitter belief, indefensible probably, that everyone I had met was much richer than I was. It was all right for Bloom, with his cosmopolitan background, to suggest giving up my job. What would I live on?

"You could get a part-time job in a bar. Pubs always take on extra staff. You could write your novel between the intervals of serving drinks. Thank God for the licensing hours. And you'd be in Soho—think of all the fascinating creatures who would come your way."

I looked through the cigarette haze of the saloon bar in the Black Bottle. Two old women were at a table drinking brandy and eating a packet of potato crisps. At the bar there was a blond young man with an iron contraption on one foot, and a man clad all in black, with a bowler hat on the back of his head. In that moment the place seemed a sort of Paradise from which work and Pilbrightery were excluding me. The Bottle was never by the wildest stretch of the imagination a fashionable pub, and it was hard to see any creatures who by Bloom's standards, or by mine, could be described as fascinating. Soho was Soho, though.

"And where are you living, for heaven's sake?"

When I explained about Bunty's friends the Murrays, Bloom exclaimed, "Darling, this really won't *do!* I can find you something so much more fun."

"I know what that would be like. No thanks."

"I assure you, Julian, your reputation would be quite unsullied. They're out-of-work actors, a man and his wife, and they're rather short of lodgers just now. It would be miles more amusing than where you're living at present."

"That wouldn't be difficult."

"Why not tell old Pillprick or whatever he's called that you are just going?"

"William, he's so awful, he's—oh, I suppose it's pathetic really, but he's a non-person."

"My dear, I can't bear it for you."

It was William's turn to buy drinks and he made his way to the bar. For a moment I had the extraordinary sensation of seeing T. S. Eliot dispense the drinks, in William's case a Bloody Mary, in mine a Winter Warmer in a straight glass. Of course I had only seen photographs of Eliot, but it was quite unmistakable. Not only the features of clerical cut, but the dark suit, the charming smile, the stoop. Mr. Eliot and Bloom seemed to be in conversation for some time before my friend returned with the drinks.

"He's persuadable," said William.

"Of what?"

"Of taking extra staff, part-time."

"Does it strike you that he looks like . . ."

"Yes—it's the only thing to be said for this pub. Surely you know about Cyril? He's one of the sights of London."

"I've not had time to go out much."

I don't remember whether it was on that very first occasion at the Bottle or whether it came later that Cyril offered me work there. The resemblance to St. Louis's most piously fastidious exile did not go beyond appearance. Neither in voice nor language was he markedly Eliotic.

"You a bum-boy? Not that I mind, see, only I don't want you bringing them all in here."

After a disavowal of any such inclinations and an acceptance of pitifully small wages, I was taken on as a barman.

Whether it was then or another time, Bloom raised his glass and drank to "Pillballs!"

"To Pillock!" I said.

My dislike of old Pilbright began before I ever went to Tempest and Holmes. Had it not been for his bloody Christmas cards my grandmother might have devised some other idea for how I should earn a living. Upon arrival at the office I had expected him at least to be friendly. He wasn't particularly. Beyond calling me "young Ramsay" with a bit of a smile which was half a leer, Pilbright showed me absolutely no preferential treatment. Being young, I was vain and I assumed that the almost-leer was suggestive of concealed sexual interest in myself. Did he get a bit too close, I wondered, when he said, "Oh, dear, oh, dear, oh, *dear!* Can't you draw a straighter line than *that,* young Ramsay?" And then he would lean over and take the metal rule from my hand and draw a straight line in my ledger for me. Yes, I have seen the hand of Pilbright clutch a pencil and draw, though it was only a straight line in my ledger. Was that the reason for his smile? Did he know that one day his secret would be out, and we would try to recall any detail which hinted at his talent? I can remember his large pink hands, clumsy hands in appearance, controlling the pencil and the rule. I remember the smell of his breath, too, oddly pleasing, like milk.

Looking round the "Mr. Pilbright at Home" exhibition, I realised that I still rather disliked the old man, perhaps disliked him more than ever. One of the secretaries—until that moment I had forgotten her existence; what was she called? May? June? A name redolent of summer or weather; her voice was immediately familiar—was now speaking. Her voice rang out to the visitors at the exhibition as it had once pealed down the row of desks in the accounts department, talking in those days of commonplace things, the price of clothes, the latest dance steps.

"We all knew he was an artist at heart. Oh, yes. Well, he had the real artistic temperament, like you might say. Oh, yes! You'd see him looking out of a window sometimes. For inspiration, I suppose you'd say. He was always looking, Mr. Pilbright was, you could see it in his eyes."

Hunter's voice took up the refrain. "He was always looking. Pilbright's eyes were open, all the time, the artist's eye, looking at the world. Even colleagues at work like Dawn Simmonds saw it . . ."

Dawn, that was it! She and Hunter were so wrong. We didn't know Pilbright was an artist, no one did; that was the point of Pilbright. I even believe now that after the initial disappointment of his early years, Pilbright came to enjoy his work at Tempest and Holmes. Work consoles. The more boring, the more pointless, the better. It removes us from all the things which cause pain—families, lovers, dreams. Pilbright knew it because he was of an age to know it. I was too young then. I wanted the relationships and the dreams to be front stage. I had not yet come to feel that life (if painfully short from some viewpoints) goes on the hell of a time, and you need something to fill it up. Granny was right. You need something to *do*. Aunt Deirdre had chosen the best, the most archetypally time-consuming occupation of them all: gardening. "Always something to do in a garden," she would rightly say. Only I didn't want to do it.

I wanted at that stage to cut a dash: writing, acting, anything would serve. Nor was perpetual, only occasionally fulfilled lust quite enough, either. I wanted to define existence in terms of some big relationship with a woman. Presumably, once I had left Tempest and Holmes, that was why everything happened so quickly, going to live with Rikko and Fenella, meeting Anne, getting married, writing that nondescript book—all the things which I crammed into that short period. Hearing Pilbright's voice brought it all back with painful vividness. I remembered the morning I told him that I was going to start a new way of life.

"What's the matter? Aren't we arty enough for you in accounts?"

Dawn Simmonds, fat, toothy, cackled with mirth.

"Wants to write a book, apparently," pursued Mr. Pilbright mercilessly. "Or a play."

"If its a nice comedy I'll come and see it," said Dawn. "Like Ben Travers. I like him."

Why was this funny? But we all laughed. It would have been rude not to.

"Got a part lined up? In a play?" Pilbright asked.

He had been through all these things in his own mind when he was a young man. He had opted for safety, anonymity, for keeping his art to himself. I now see how vulgar my choices must have seemed to him. At the time, I was determined not to admit to him the haphazard nature of the arrangements—half-board and lodging, arranged by Bloom, at Rikko and Fenella's, a part-time job as barman at the Black Bottle, time enough to write my novel and look about for theatrical work, perhaps attend some classes and think about drama school.

"There are quite a lot of possibilities," I said.

He looked at me closely.

"I just hope it won't be a decision you regret," he said. "Your father, now, he *liked* working here. We got on very well."

"He was lovely, your dad," said Dawn.

They had never spoken about Daddy before. It made the conversation all the more painful. As well as rejecting them and their harmless way of life, I appeared to be spitting on a dearly loved parent, setting myself above him.

So embarrassing did I find this conversation, which took place just before the dinner break, that I went straight out to a nearby pub and never returned to the Accounts Department. Presumably my cards were posted on to me at a later date, perhaps by Mr. Pilbright himself? I forget. How differently I view it all now. Mixed as my feelings about Pilbright and his pictures must remain, I think he was right. It is not an accident that human beings provide for themselves the narcotic of drudgery. Those of us who have opted out must pay the consequences.

At some turn of the painful conversation, he had said, "You need something to keep you going—I'm not just talking about money, of course."

The obviousness of this remark was not obvious to me then. I thought that just being me would keep me going, not realising that for much of the time this is precisely the thing one most needs to escape.

"I suppose painting's just a hobby," he said in one of those too-frequent newspaper interviews he gave. "Very rewarding, very satisfying, no doubt, but I don't regret having had a normal life like everyone else. What would I have had to paint, I wonder, if I'd just been an *artist,* and hung around in—what do you call it—a *coterie?*"

When one thought of the huge retrospective which set the seal on Pilbright's reputation—room after room at the Hayward Gallery, filled with his work, exhibiting, whatever one's doubts about it all, a confident exuberance, an ease with the medium, a sense of colour and dash which were all highly unusual—one felt he must have been lying when he said that it was just his hobby.

But it was only later that I saw the wisdom of his positive distaste for a way of life which was self-consciously artistic. Hanging around, being a bohemian, accepting a carefully fashioned, Rive Gauche manner of living was just what I wanted, in so far as such a thing could be achieved in London. Much good it did me.

But to see Pilbright's rooms! To hear his voice again in this strange, sanitised setting! He had become a bit of history. By extension, so had I, insofar as I could claim, for a very brief spell, to have known him. This exhibition, though, as a milestone in my own inner history was one of those deadening reminders of how much of life had gone, of how little I'd ever done with it, the advice of Pilbright and my grandmother notwithstanding. It had just *gone*. Inevitably, thoughts of Pilbright and that last conversation I'd had with him awoke a whole flood of other memories of that time. I thought of Anne's pony-tail of lustrous brown hair, and her pale slightly freckled face and her way of laughing which lit up not only her features, but the whole world around her.

In such a frame of mind, it was not quite possible to return to the outside world. Nor was the Pilbright Special Exhibition the right place to clear the head, wipe the memory clean, return to the present day with the painful old images of the past expunged. I wandered aimlessly through the ground-floor rooms, looking at the larger abstract paintings, and then back to the modern sculpture. But even there, reminders of the past were to be found. Among the Moores and the Frinks there was that stunning, swooping shape, reminiscent of a bird in flight, by Beryl Lewis.

How much I had been in love with her when I was a schoolboy, and she the art mistress at my private school. When love is completely unrequited (and in this case, undeclared, even) it never quite dies. I do not mean you go on feeling it at the same pitch; you'd go off your head if you did. Once reminded of it, though, as by the Beryl Lewis piece in the Tate, one recaptures the agonies and delights with much of their old intensity. Standing beside her work, I would hear her voice again, as it had been when I was just "Ramsay" and she was "Miss Beach." No Christian names. The recollection, happening inside my head, was more vivid than any reconstructed scene, such as the faked up rooms of "Mr. Pilbright at Home." And to think of Miss Beach was to think of Hunter and that dreadful afternoon, the first time I ever set eyes upon him, when I looked up at the window of her room and saw her in his arms.

Memory itself is a form of necromancy. Indulge it consciously and I find that strange things start to happen. The painful associations of Hunter and my marriage, and that whole year after I parted from Pilbright, might well have been triggered by some telepathic knowledge that Anne, not met for ages, was in fact nearby.

In younger days I should have caught sight of her sooner, but total concentration on the Beryl Lewis sculpture made all the middle distance of my vision into a fuzz. It was hearing her voice, older but unmistakable, which made me blink and focus on the other side of the gallery, where, with another woman of about her—our—age, she was staring at and holding forth on a Brancusi bronze.

It was the tone of Anne's voice which, during my brief and terrible period of hatred for her, had most annoyed me. It was pompous. About matters other than art, Anne was not in the least pompous. Get her talking about painting or sculpture though, and she could have been—even at twenty-five—Dame Ursula Lampitt, thirty-five years older than herself, lecturing to undergraduates at Oxford. There was free use of phrases like "as it were" and "one feels" and "it seems to me."

She was saying to her companion, "One feels as if Brancusi, as it were, has outsoared matter, and this, it seems to me, is a particularly successful piece. . . ."

Anne could not help being instructive when she talked about these things. Even when I was crazy about her, her art talk bored me, not because I was indifferent to the subject, but because of the way she . . . *spoilt* it. About all other matters, she could be as larky and as frivolous as everyone else known in those days.

"It's a pity we have no time," said Anne. "There's so much else I want to show you. We must spend half an hour with the Turners. I mustn't prejudge your reactions but it seems to me, as it were, that they've hung them in a manner—well, you'll see."

She had developed a nervous giggle. It had grown out of that infectious girlish laugh which first made me love her.

The friend said nothing at all. She seemed wonderfully patient. Perhaps she had asked Anne to show her the gallery.

I hid behind a large Henry Moore.

Feelings for those whom I had hardly known, Pilbright or Miss Beach, could be momentarily recaptured in something like their old forms. At least I could remember the feelings, even if they, like everything else, had been muted by Time's decay. With Anne, to whom I had been married, it was otherwise. I had known such a wide variety of feelings for her—an overexcited crush of much the same childish intensity I had felt for Miss Beach was the first thing. I had also found in her a hilarious friendship. We laughed so much in the early days; we found everything funny. Early, too, I had found that without any complications or guilt we seemed made for one another in bed, and this at the same time seemed like a joyous extension of the crush and the friendship and the laughter. When the other feelings entered in later on, the marital day-to-day irritation, the terrible feeling of disillusionment when I realised that she was not in love with me, my own guilt when I betrayed her, the hatred which flared up during our quarrels and our silences—when all these things had come upon us, I told myself that I had never really been in love with Anne at all, it had just been a juvenile mistake. But this wasn't true. I was in love with her certainly. Though silly and green, our younger self is worthy of our respect, deserves our truth telling, as much as soberer phases of existence.

This seemed hard to remember, looking at the sixty-year-old woman in the gallery. At that moment, I felt nothing for her, nothing. Just an embarrassed hope that she would not look up and see me and greet me in that perfectly poised manner which she adopted whenever we met. I knew her well enough still to know that this poise concealed feelings of awkwardness, probably as acute as my own. There was no bitterness or enmity between us any more, just a sad blank.

Why should feelings matter so much? Why have I spent such a very high proportion of my life considering what I feel about other people, or what they feel about me? Temperamentally, Anne and I should have been able to knock along together when the first difficulties had died down. We shared many of the same friends and interests. There was no physical incompatibility; the opposite right to the end. It was just this wretched matter of feelings which came between us. We no longer felt the same about each other. Anne felt, as she had never apparently felt about me, for Another. So we had to part. Would it not be better to cultivate indifference to feelings? Wouldn't life be more endurable, more civilised, if we decided to eschew feelings as we can, with enough effort, resist nicotine? Certainly it would be less painful. In a few rare individuals I have met such detachment. Like those many people devoid of aesthetic sense the non-feelers, or almost non-feelers, are probably likely to cause little emotional nuisance; perhaps on balance they are happier than the rest of us.

I remember a don at Oxford, a colleague of my cousin Felicity's, remarking in a slow voice after dinner one night, "I try not to make a distinction between liking and disliking people. In practice I find that I don't go in for liking or disliking. Does one have to?"

Shakespeare was impressed by such cold fishery, by those

> Who, moving others, are themselves as stone,
> Unmoved, cold, and to temptation slow.

The years have made me suspect "feelings." In their name, we seem to be able to inflict so much hurt on one another. But the chance sighting of Anne in the Tate made me recognise that even this suspicion itself took me no nearer the possession of wisdom. My acquired cold-fishery of late years was not a willed acquisition of detachment, but an atrophy of heart, a kind of death, like the failure of eyesight or trouble with teeth.

If I could choose, I should prefer to be that earlier self— impulsively able to feel, capable of foolish emotional adventures. The capacity to hurt, and to be hurt, does not depart when the capacity to love has been forgotten. In the end one returns gratefully to obvious truths, like Keats's "I am certain of nothing but of the holiness of the heart's affections." Treadmill, my old English master, had quoted the words to us in class long since. None of us had known who wrote them but I knew at once that this was my creed.

Anne looked dreadful. Her hair was short, grey, lank, swept back from the forehead defiantly as if she did not care any longer what she looked like. She was fat now. When I had been in love with her, she had the body of a lithe athletic boy. Her legs had now become a funny shape, the result, I suppose, of varicose veins. There were bulges where there shouldn't have been and one ankle had a bandage beneath the stocking.

I managed to get out of her line of vision and hide in the Gents until she and her companion had moved on. The face that looked back at me when I stared into the glass over the wash basins would probably have excited her embarrassed pity, just as she had done in me. She had gone to fat, I to scrawn. At some point, just past fifty, the whites of my eyes had turned yellowish and they were often, as today, rather bloodshot. The bony skull—how recognisably work for an undertaker now— was half bald and when I grinned, the teeth were appalling. I've no idea how I managed to develop so many lines on my face. If, like so many people I have known, I am doomed to go on until eighty, then the work of dilapidation is only three-quarters done.

"I am certain of nothing but of the holiness of the heart's affections."

A young man's words. Good words. If we did not accept that love was ennobling and even in some cases durable, what else could redeem death of its horror, and before death, this relentless destruction of the flesh? Perhaps, in seeking redemption, we were seeking sham consolations.

Children would change everything; I see that now. One's own collapse into nothingness, the blotting out of all memory and desire by the sheer process of bodily decay, ending in oblivion a non-being which rendered every second of being itself trivial, all this would be quite different with children and grandchildren; for through them, people defy time, and their own death. Then one would view in a different light the horrible mystery tour down the Senility Line (stopping posts at Bad Breath Halt, Incontinence Junction and Amnesia Whatsit; Arthritis served throughout the journey). It would be different with children. I have no children.

Another way, granted only to the few, was the artist's life. To write or paint or compose something which would endure— this surely would be a blow against the Enemy? Was my ego always rebelliously conscious of the enemy, long before I became conscious of him myself? Was it that which prompted my rash decision to be, in Pilbright's word, "arty"? In leaving Tempest and Holmes, I was only aware of reacting against precisely such a death-in-life as Pilbright of Accounts appeared to represent. But he had been deceiving us, and he was now at one with the Immortals.

As I left the gallery and came down the steps into Millbank, there was a rainbow over the other side of the Thames reminiscent of Pilbright's *God Gives a Token at Battersea That He Will Bring No More Destruction Upon the Earth.* (Another broken promise?) In Pilbright's big self-confident canvas the sky was a thick splashy mass of greys but sun shone through light rain and the bow was naively bright. The real rainbow at which I now looked was even brighter, and the whole arc was visible, casting an implausible nimbus over the Power Station. The waters of the river were high, like boiling gravy. Old Pilbright had won immortality, all right. Who would have thought it? Well, well.

two

I met Anne a few months after the final parting with Pilbright. Cutting loose from the office routine had all been perfectly easy. I had half imagined that someone might come running after me, compel me to go back, make me get up early in the mornings and wear a suit and tie. But who in the world cared?

Aunt Deirdre in one of her regular letters said that she thought it was a "bit of a pity" that I no longer had regular work. In my shamefully rare letters to her and Uncle Roy I had rather played down, in fact, to the extent of not mentioning it at all, my job at the Bottle. I had emphasized the literary side of things, and the fact that I was doing a tremendous amount of acting and theatre work—a number of temporary stagehand jobs at small West End theatres, drama classes, and some amateur work. The chance of a Part had begun to seem real to me. Neither in life nor in my professional aspirations had I the smallest inkling of what the great Casting Director had in mind for me—the smallest of walk-on parts, little more than an extra in the "crowd flows over London Bridge" sequence. If we knew these things, perhaps we wouldn't attend the auditions.

Aunt Deirdre and Uncle Roy were snobbishly quite pleased that I had extricated myself from the world of sale and manufacture. From my uncle's point of view, the desire to be a writer placed me (in an infinitely junior capacity) in the good company of the various Lampitts who had found their way into print. Not everyone reads Sargie Lampitt's book on the House of Lords, nor his cousin Ursula's *Anglo-Norman Literature: The First Decade*. James Petworth Lampitt is in a different league. His books have made a comeback ever since Hunter's first scandalous volume of biography of the man appeared. There was even a TV series (fronted by Hunter) based on Lampitt's Victorian sketches. Uncle Roy never mentioned Hunter, nor would he have stooped to the purchase of a television. But such was his general obsession with the whole tribe of Lampitts that he could only be pleased that the paperback-buying public were now enjoying such classics by Jimbo (as he was always known in the family) as *Prince Albert* and *Swinburne*.

"I always said Jimbo would last," my uncle had remarked when we last met.

Perfectly true. Anything my uncle said about the Lampitts was something which he "always said." Since Roy's disastrous quarrel with Sargie, Jimbo's brother, one might have supposed that he would have found another family to talk about, but this was not the case. The less he saw of any member of the Lampitt family the more he apparently needed to talk about them, rehearse their names and deeds and dates. Blessed are those who have not seen and yet have believed.

My aunt, who had had a surfeit of Lampitt talk, seldom responded when he was in full flood, but occasionally even she was prepared to allude to my uncle's enthusiasm, particularly if, as on some rare occasion, he found something new to say.

"Talking of Lampitts," she had written in her last, "your uncle"—When had he done anything else? My childhood was the story of my uncle talking of Lampitts.—"wonders if you'll come across Orlando Lampitt. Rather a black sheep, we gather!!! A cousin of Jimbo's and Sargie's who went on the *stage* in 1928 . . ."

My uncle did not often write me a letter, but he sometimes added marginalia to my aunt's small blue leaves of Basildon Bond. In his thick, florid italic, the ink blacker than I have ever seen, he had added at the bottom of my aunt's letter, "I must ask Sibs about Orlando. Do call on Sibs, by the way. I'll let you have the address if you have forgotten it."

Since my first going to live with Uncle Roy I had heard him recite the names and addresses of the Lampitts—Jimbo, 19 Hinde House, Manchester Square; Sargie (when in town, which I now gathered he was all the time), 14 Kensington Square, W.8; Vernon, 11 Lord North Street; Ursula, The Principal's Lodgings, Rawlinson College, Oxford. How could I ever forget the address of Sargie's youngest sibling? *108 Cadogan Square.*

I had no desire to visit Lady Starling, none whatever. If there was anything which I wished to escape more than the world of Pilbright and Accounts, it was the Lampitts and all their breed, who had obsessed my uncle and dominated all my childhood and adolescence, not by their physical presence, but by the fact that we talked about them at almost every meal. Besides, Lady Starling, though a magnificent-looking person, and in her way an amusing talker, was not someone with whom I had exactly hit it off in the past. It would have been impossible to drop in on her in Cadogan Square without in some infinitesimal degree reconstructing the obsequious spirit in which my uncle had called on the Lampitts at Timplingham Place in our village. The very idea of calling suggested a hint of deference. I much preferred the squalor of Wetherby Gardens, the house full of lodgers, myself now one, the stench of dogs and Camels, the raffish hours, the overpowering sense that one was in a house where Art mattered more than Life.

Bloom had fixed it that I should have a room *chez* Rikko and Fenella. In spite of a successful life as a young publisher Bloom always had time to boss about his friends, and he took a benign interest in Rikko and Fenella, who had been his landlords once upon a time. Most of their income derived from the rooms, rather than their art. One paid cash. All transactions with Fenella were for cash. It was some years since her last bust-up with a bank manager. No clearing-bank could be found who would allow either of them a chequebook—not since the last time, when Rikko, with less than nine pounds in the current account, had impulsively bought a yacht from a man in a pub.

"He didn't realise who we *were*," croaked Fenella, flicking Camel ash into the gas fire as she recalled the incident. "I told him, we're theatrical."

This—by some definitions—was self-evident.

"The fact that I don't put 'The Lady Fenella Kempe' on my chequebook doesn't mean a thing. You don't go crowing about titles. I don't have it on my Equity card either."

The fact that she did not put "The Lady Fenella" on her cheques, in the days when she had cheques, was best explained by her not being entitled to do so. In spite of frequent hints that she was the daughter of some ancient and distinguished lineage, there was in fact no evidence for this at all. If anyone were cruel enough to suggest that they had been unable to find a reference to Fenella in any of the usual books she would rumble, "Irish peerages are a bit different, darling," as though anyone with the slightest social pretensions would not have been seen dead in *Debrett*.

Her voice was deeper than most men's and sounded as though she were suffering from appallingly painful laryngitis. Emaciated to the point of being stringy, she made gallant efforts to recall her prime with scarlet lipstick and a blond hair dye which hinted of a less subtle, more innocent era than our own. Her very even dentures, slightly smeared with lipstick usually, gave the winsome smiles a ghoulish air, which she tempered by holding her head on one side and shaking her marigold tresses first on to one shoulder and then on to another.

"I told him," she would say, of the man who had sold Rikko the yacht, watched the cheque bounce, come round to remonstrate, "it's only *middle*-class people who keep money in current accounts. People like us have trusts, we have *land*."

When her claims, either to former triumphs on stage or screen, or to high birth, became too fantastical, Rikko would take his thumb and forefinger and squeeze the flesh of his brow just above the bridge of his nose. He would close his eyes and wait until the worst of the embarrassment was over. If Fenella persisted . . .

("I told him, my father was a marquess, I've acted in Hollywood, I'm a friend of Lauren Bacall's and I'd no more think of paying his cheque than I'd think of saying *toilet* . . .")

. . . then Rikko, in his precise and well-modulated voice would say, "Shut up Fenella, shut up, shut up."

If it got worse, her boasting, he would arise, still clutching his brow, and announce that he could bear it no longer.

"I'm taking Irving and Terry down the Gloucester Road."

Zipping his wind-jammer and muttering something about how he didn't know how he could stand living with Fenella, he would mince off, an Afghan hound pulling at each gloved and beautifully manicured hand.

How anyone survives life with anyone else is a bit of a mystery—not one to which, at that age, I'd given much thought. Bloom used to say that Fenella and Rikko had nothing in common except their hair dye! Certainly it was hard to understand why such a handsome (if mildly overweight) man, not much more than forty, should have chosen to make his hair the same violent yellow as his wife's. But perhaps there all mystery ended. Perhaps instead of trying to explain Fenella as a mother-substitute for Rikko (she must have been a good twenty years older than he) one should have accepted the fact that for some, perhaps much, of the time they simply liked each other.

The household, with its ever-changing population of lodgers, provided both of them with doubtless necessary variants to their sole companionship. The actors (in and out of work), painters (ditto), students and layabouts who stayed in Wetherby Gardens, some for a few nights and some, on and off, for years, provided Rikko and Fenella with something to love, beyond each other and the Afghans. I never heard of either of them being *in love* with any of the lodgers though that might have happened. They had an extraordinary capacity, though (in this respect like parents who love their children), to see virtues and talents in their lodgers which were far from apparent to anyone else.

"What people never see about Donald," Fenella would say about the morose unshaven young man in her attic, seldom up before two in the afternoon, by no means unsmelly, "is that he is multitalented. He can *act*, he can *paint*, he can *sing*."

It was true; people never saw it.

"He's got a beautiful voice," Rikko agreed.

For some reason, casting directors, theatrical agents, art schools, all failed to spot it. The Royal School of Ballet had been similarly myopic about redheaded Briony, and her flat feet. If you had believed Fenella's version of things, it would have been incomprehensible that Melissa (a near genius by the sound of it, and an Honourable) kept failing her A-levels.

This was the sort of person who crowded into that house, paid the quite modest rents, and ate Fenella's meals, which were hit-and-miss affairs depending for their palatability on how sober she was when meat or vegetables found their way into the oven. She served what I would think of as being Good English Food—lots of roasts—but always spoke of it as if it were traditional French cooking.

If by some aberration of a casting director Fenella had ever found herself in what she called work, I think she would have missed being a landlady. Bloom said, rather cruelly, that her career had been destroyed by the coming of the talkies.

"She really was in the movies once. But sound did for her, my dear. Not only was she far too stupid to learn the lines but her voice was so deep! People would assume she was just some old drag queen. Rikko, now! He could have done a nice falsetto and acted Marilyn Monroe off the screen."

As so often when Bloom made these remarks, he opened his mouth wide and almost put out his tongue as he guffawed at his own jokes.

Without resorting to female impersonation, Rikko had managed in a very minor way to keep afloat. Though most of his tiny trickles of money had been earned as a waiter or a teacher of English to foreigners, it was still not a complete mockery of the truth to put "actor" on his passport. He usually found several weeks' work a year in rep, and there was now the exciting new outlet of television. That, indeed, was why we were all huddled around the set in the drawing room on that particular evening.

Their drawing room told its own story. It was a Noël Coward set in the midst of which a furniture remover had apparently left a load of old junk for a few days before consigning it to the knacker's yard. There was a large white grand piano. On either side of the fireplace a gilded putto supported a lamp. All the lampshades, stools, marble ash-trays and festoons made gallant efforts to give off a 1930s rococo air of the gin-and-ostrich-feather school. But amid what Bloom called the all-too-predictable splendour of white and gold ("Ionian, darling? It's Edgware Road!") there were such objects as the lumpy old boardinghouse sofa, bursting springs and stuffing from its floral loose covers. A wobbly standard lamp, vaguely Chinese, gave you a slight electric shock every time you tried to switch it on. A heavy chintz armchair. This mingled assemblage of rubbish mingled oddly with the Louis Seize piano stools (circa 1934) or the tiger-skin rug near the hearth.

Several inches of dust resting over all the furniture gave a Sleeping Beauty air to many parts of the house. Fenella only intermittently employed charwomen and never herself cleaned the place up even if, as sometimes happened, Irving or Terry, unable to resist the calls of nature, had deposited turds on the frayed Oriental carpets.

It was on such a carpet that most of us sat round that evening, Fenella, Rikko and a handful of lodgers. We were all squeezed in to watch the wooden-framed set which was plugged in on the other side of the fireplace. Television in those days was enough of a novelty for one to be willing to watch absolutely anything which appeared on the screen. I forget what particular gibberish was being churned out on that occasion. It stopped eventually. And it was then, with her concentration so fixed on the screen that an inch of ash grew on the end of her Camel without being flicked, that Fenella said, "Now hush, darlings, this is Rikko."

Sure enough, there on the screen he was. First, you saw him smartly dressed in a suit, seated at a large office desk. Then his face was contorted with agony. A voice then said, "Acid indigestion, it can catch you unawares, anywhere." The screen was then filled with a diagram depicting a human silhouette. Rays of pain throbbed around the intestinal regions. A pill of the kind recommended made its swift passage through the lips of the silhouette down to the trouble spot. We then cut to Rikko once more, whose painstruck features relaxed and became wreathed in a smile. Within seconds, the thing was over, to be followed by one for washing powder.

It wasn't *Hamlet*, but I suppose it was work. I was disappointed that Rikko was not able actually to speak in the course of his film. The man recommending the washing powder in the ad which followed was given quite a lot to say about its detersive properties. All Rikko had to do was to look as though he was being tortured, and then act an expression of profound relief.

He was a good actor—made for television, really, since he had such a variety of facial expressions. The relief of the man with acid indigestion was in its way a masterpiece.

"Pity they made you wear that tie."

"Fenella!" He pursed his lips and wriggled his shoulders. He had obviously been proud of his performance.

"Probably they give you a tie to wear," I said.

"Of course," said Rikko.

"I wanted you to wear that Old Harrovian one that Hamish"—some lodger who may or may not have been to Harrow—"left behind in his drawer before he buggered off."

"I did wear it, since you made such a thing of it. The advertising people said it looked greasy."

"But the tie they gave you was all wrong for the part." Fenella was settling down to a thorough post-mortem on the piece. There were frequent reshowings throughout the season so she had plenty of time over the next few months to analyse the shortcomings of producer, wardrobe mistress and cameraman.

"You see, darling, they never understand upper-class people."

"I'm not upper class," said Rikko.

At this Fenella grinned coquettishly. Her smile suggested a conspiracy with her company not to take any such disavowal seriously.

"And anyway," said Rikko, "there was no need for the man with the bellyache to be upper class. They needed someone with whom the viewers could identify."

"Nonsense, he was a company director."

"That's not upper class!"

During this conversation, one sensed Rikko and Fenella becoming really angry with each other, one of those marital exchanges where the apparent subject under discussion could not possibly explain the heatedness with which it was being conducted. Most of the other young people were milling about, talking, hugging the dogs. The television pursued its own silly life in the corner. The adverts were over and "Perspectives" had begun, an arts programme, set up to rival a similar one broadcast by the BBC, and compered on this channel by Raphael Hunter.

He was already a familiar face on the television screen, so it was no longer a shock to me to see his bland, apparently ageless features smiling out from the cathode-ray tube. The impenetrable questions posed by that face were just the same on screen as off. Was he as insipid as he seemed? If so, how had he managed to advance himself so forcefully in his career, break the hearts of so many women, achieve that enviable combination of admiration and notoriety which Volume One of his *Petworth Lampitt* had brought on all sides? (Those who deprecated the indiscretions of the book were often those who were most in awe of Hunter's perspicacity, detective work, and his sheer industry in producing a volume so large.) The TV persona was just another string to Hunter's bow. This "Perspectives" programme was wide-ranging, consisting mainly of studio interviews, conducted by Hunter himself, with various practitioners of the arts. It was on this programme, about five or six years after the time I am describing, that Pilbright's reputation was made. As it happened, another of Hunter's more famous interviews was in progress that very evening, but hardly anyone in Fenella's room was watching. My eyes, naturally enough, were glued to the set. I felt I had been looking at Hunter's face all my life; now it had a power to hypnotise me, recalling already so many phases of existence that he had become a sort of Guardian Angel, witnessing, if not presiding over, some of the key moments in my life. But I was also watching so intently because the second face on the screen—that of the man being interviewed—was also familiar to me, though I could not place it at first. Working in a pub, you see any number of faces, some of them on a regular basis, without ever putting a name to them. It slowly dawned on me that the man being interviewed by Hunter was a "regular" at the Black Bottle, and I then realised who it was.

He usually sat on his own on a bar-stool drinking beer in pints. He had a huge white fleshy face. Horn-rimmed specs depended from elephantine ears and bridged a wide nose. A bruiser's face, but a highly intelligent bruiser. The lips, in the pub, were always wet, blubbery almost. He was accustomed to slurp as he drank, and as he did so he liked to talk. Cyril, my employer, nicknamed him the Best Seller, but I had hitherto taken the sobriquet in the scornful spirit in which it was meant.

My very first day at the Black Bottle, the Best Seller had surprised me, before ordering his pint, by speaking his name, something I never knew any other customer to do.

"Day Muckley," he said firmly, raspingly, almost threateningly.

The name meant almost nothing to me. The books for which, before the war, he had been famous—*Valley of Folk, That Tender Last Farewell*, but above all, *The Calderdale Saga*—were precisely of the kind I never read, broadly speaking, family sagas and love stories set in the district of Yorkshire where Muckley had grown up. Granny and Mrs. Webb had been very fond of *The Calderdale Saga*, but until I met him, I should have been hard-pressed to remember the name of the author. No wonder my blank expression when the Best Seller announced his name caused such a slyly belligerent look to pass over his face. He smiled contemptuously as though not to know the name was a mark of complete idiocy. When I knew him better I came to feel that the smile concealed a great hurt. He was always saying his name to people, bartenders, shopkeepers, waiters, barbers, bookies; and if they were under the age of fifty, he always got the same blank response. On first meeting, and on the few other subsequent occasions before the television programme, I thought of him as just another "character" of the sort you might expect to meet in a pub in central London.

Inviting Muckley on to the programme was entirely typical

behaviour on Hunter's part. One of the many things which made Hunter widely liked was his desire to rehabilitate lost reputations, set up new ones. It must in part have been simple kindness which motivated him; in part, power mania must have come into it, the thought that he could control Fame itself, and determine that unknown names should suddenly become household words.

Just when everyone had forgotten Jimbo's books, Hunter published *Petworth Lampitt: The Hidden Years*. In the entirely unknown Pilbright he discovered one of the most interesting representational painters of the century. The interview with the Best Seller was obviously designed to be just such a refurbishment job. It was always noticeable to my unsympathetic eye that Hunter's tastes were conservative and middle-brow. He liked the sort of art of which the Binker, headmaster of the private school which Hunter and I at very different stages had attended, would have approved.

In his effort to make Day Muckley into a Best Seller indeed, Hunter had not reckoned on the dangers of attempting a conversation with him after six in the evening. I myself tended to do lunchtime stints at the Bottle and I had not quite realised until the broadcast (which like most broadcasting then were live) Day's pattern of drinking; nor had I quite realised that his three or four pints put away between eleven in the morning and two in the afternoon, only intermittently fortified with whisky chasers, were merely his way of dealing with the hangover of the night before. It was some time after five that the spirit-drinking began in earnest. It was now perhaps half past eight or nine in the evening. I didn't hear Raphael Hunter's opening *spiel*. Rikko and Fenella were talking too loud. But I caught the odd phrase: "not ashamed to tell a good story . . . that much undervalued quality characterisation . . . literary reputations have their ups and downs . . ."

The camera now began to focus on the Best Seller, who looked at first sight his usual smiling frog-like self. It was only when Muckley attempted speech that the flickerings of anxiety in Hunter's face became explicable.

"The point is . . . Raphael . . . the point is this." Muckley spoke as if he had all the time in the world to make his point. You could almost hear the cameras turning over in the long pause which followed. He fumbled. He lit up one of his cigarettes—he smoked an Irish brand called Sweet Afton—and then he smiled, the first part of his sentence forgotten.

"Your novels stand very much in the realist tradition," Hunter said. "Names like Galsworthy, Priestley, Hugh Walpole."

"Sod Hugh Walpole," said Day Muckley.

"Sod," except as a way of defining a piece of turf, was not a word which was used on British television in those days. The actual phrase uttered was all the less acceptable because it had a kind of biographical plausibility; just some such conjunction had indeed been hinted at by Hunter himself between Walpole and Petworth Lampitt, an incident alleged to have occurred in a Turkish bath near the Elephant and Castle.

"No, Raphael, the point is, the point is this."

Whatever the point was, the Best Seller was the devil of a time coming to it. The extremely broad Yorkshire accent, though I'm sure genuine, was almost comically emphasised as if he were afraid that anyone would forget the northernness on which his literary reputation had been built.

"No, the point about a writer . . ."

"Arnold Bennett is another writer who has been mentioned," said Hunter briskly, trying to retrieve a hopeless situation by giving the TV audience a boring lecture on the realist tradition. "We might call it the English branch of the Balzacian—"

"Let me finish, Raph, Raphael, will you." The Best Seller lurched angrily in his chair and gestured jerkily with the cigarette. "I'm asking a serious question. The point is . . . this. Is a writer . . . *readable*? That's all the, sorry, that's all the book-buying public, that's all they want to know. When they pick up a book . . ."

"Your readability," said Hunter, "has always been one of your most—"

"They don't want to know is it modern, is it *avant-garde*, for Christ's sakes . . ." (That again! Echoes of Pilbrightery.) "Or is it exist- exis . . ."

"Existentialist." Hunter was mopping his brow.

"Sarter."

As I discovered when I knew him, the Best Seller always Anglicised foreign names. The Joe Blunt manner on which he prided himself did not prevent him from being familiar with a wide range of foreign literature. In fact, I think it quite likely that he had never read Bennett, Galsworthy, or any of the other English authors named by Hunter. But he had read Dostoyevsky, Proust, Flaubert . . .

"I mean, *La Nausée*. They want something wholesome. People. Wholesome. They want something for Christ's sakes that is *readable*. They don't need to be existentialised, bloody cheek. I mean *La Nausée*, to my mind, Raphael, does literally—"

At that moment a girl burst into the room and screamed with laughter.

"My God! There's a man . . . I can't believe it, *look!* There's a man on the television, being sick!"

Everybody turned to the set. What she said was undeniably true. The whole scene was momentarily obscured by a smudge of liquid, grey to our sight, which hit the lens of the camera as Muckley looked towards his public. I cannot say for certain what this grey smudge was, but if it was a normal day the mixture might well have included some fish and chips, some brown sauce, beer, cheese sandwiches, chutney, possibly a few pickled onions and, by nine in the evening, the best part of a bottle of whisky.

One heard the Best Seller's voice saying, "I'm very, very, sorry, feeling slightly off colour today" before the scene switched to the next item of the programme. Hunter, considerably ruffled, his suit a bit stained, announced that we would have a few minutes while a classical guitarist, visiting London from Madrid, displayed his soothing skills. By the time this performance was over Day Muckley had been trundled out of sight.

"Did you ever *see* such a thing?" said the girl. When she spoke her voice rose to a squeal which made everyone who heard it join in the laughter. I immediately started to laugh, laughter which lasted on and off for about a year.

"This is Robin," said my old school friend Darnley, whom I saw there for the first time.

I'd written to Darnley, telling him my new address, suggesting he drop in on me one evening and tell me his news. We'd been rather out of touch. When last heard of he was still an undergraduate. The melancholy of his grown-up appearance, lank floppy hair, heavy eyelids, thick sad lips, was increased by being muffled up in a dark, hooded duffel coat, Black Watch tartan scarf, black trousers. His features, as he watched the scene of Hunter trying to cope with being puked at on live television, recalled to me the miraculous way in which, during side-splitting episodes at school, Darnley always managed to keep a completely straight face, particularly when he himself was responsible for the chaos or comedy being enacted.

Not so his companions. They were two girls, guffawing with uncontrollable amusement. One of them, who looked a bit like Darnley, only pretty, I rightly took to be his sister. The other one, the one he called Robin, was Anne, the girl I was destined to marry. I assumed she was Darnley's girlfriend, and felt immediate envy of them both.

I introduced my friends to each other.

"Miles, this is Rikko, Rikko and Fenella, Fenella Kempe."

"This is Elizabeth, my sister. I forget if you've met before."

"Miles, I told you I'd never met Julian," said Elizabeth. For some reason this was so funny that she could hardly say it without laughing.

"This is Robin," said Darnley, almost as if showing Anne off.

Robin apparently lacked a surname. One was not mentioned, anyway. She looked as if the sight of Fenella might set her off again, unless she was very carefully handled.

"Darling!" Fenella instructed her husband with an imperious gesture, sending Camel ash everywhere. "Open a bottle of really good Burgundy." (Her usual way of describing the Algerian red of which she kept a modest supply in her kitchen.)

"We can't stay," said Darnley. "We've come to take Julian out."

"Well, at least you can take your coat off," wheedled Fenella.

Why was this so funny? Both Darnley's companions positively whooped.

"That's what I can't do, remove my coat," said Darnley.

" 'Course you can," said Fenella.

It was perfectly warm in that room. Darnley nevertheless continued to hold the scarf to his throat and clutch the duffel to his person. I began to wonder if he had no shirt on.

"Go on!" Robin spoke, her face absolutely full of mischief. "Take your coat off. I'm going to powder my nose."

"Up the stairs and turn right on to the half landing," recommended Fenella. Rikko came back with a corkscrew, a bottle and some glasses. While these things were happening, Fenella did manage to divest Darnley of his duffel.

His attire underneath the coat came as a great shock to me, but it confirmed something which I had long begun to fear about Darnley, ever since, after a gap, we met up during army days: that is, that he had his serious side. As a young child, when we were closest to each other, he had shown no seriousness at all. I looked at him now.

A high Roman collar, of the kind Uncle Roy never wore, encircled Darnley's throat. He wore a jet-black jacket and black corduroy trousers. We had been out of touch too long. It occurred to me that in our last few communications, he had been vague about what he was going to do with himself when studies were complete. Now all was revealed. In spite of growing up in a rectory (more likely, because of that fact), I belong to that huge proportion of the English population who are embarrassed by the clergy, unable to suppress in their presence the feeling that something unwholesome, not quite right, has prompted this individual to take the cloth. Usually if pressed for an explanation of this reaction, one would fall back on the individual's semi-successful attempt at repression of some not necessarily homo-erotic proclivity which was "coming out in other ways." Such cheap explanations probably fail to explain the shivers one gets down the spine with parsons. Much more obviously, the sight of the clerical collar arouses the embarrassing sense that the individual concerned has been prepared to subscribe to a number of metaphysical propositions which it does not seem quite sane to think about, still less to believe. If the clergyman is also, as in this case, a friend, there is the further embarrassment of wondering how could *they* have swallowed all *that*? Or, if we suspect them of having swallowed less than they should have done, how could they be so cynical as to pretend?

Rikko and Fenella's attitude to the whole thing was much more practical; an immediate fear that they would be asked to do something, attend a religious ceremony, part with some money or provide "jumble."

"You're a Catholic?" croaked Fenella.

"Just C of E," said Darnley sanctimoniously.

"Only, we're Catholics," said Fenella.

Rikko, dispensing drinks, twitched as he could not help doing when Fenella told one of her whoppers. Afterwards, she explained it as a matter of policy. Not only was Fenella one of those people who imagine (for reasons which have always been lost on me) that Roman Catholicism had more *chic* than other forms of Christianity, but she had discovered that to claim membership in the largest Christian church had a sobering effect on paid-up members of what our sergeant major in the army called the A.O.D.s, whether a vicar begging money for the church roof, or a Jehovah's Witness talking gibberish on your doorstep. Apparently, if you were only prepared to say that you were a Catholic, these different individuals knew that they were beaten and made a polite retreat.

"You do drink, though?" said Fenella.

"Just a very little." Darnley never in fact drank much. Since his ordination, his voice had become ostentatiously parsonical. And he had been such an amusing person when we were boys. No doubt he would be one of those witty clergymen you read about, but he would still be a clergyman, damn it, with all the creepy things which that implied.

"When we lived in Paris, I always liked to go into the Sacré Coeur to light candles for friends on their first nights. You know. One always wants it to be a success for them, and believe me, first nights are hell. I've had enough of them in my time."

"Do you mean honeymoons?" asked Darnley with a solemn sniff. "I hope you don't approve of premarital relations between the sexes."

"First *nights*, darling. We're theatrical," said Fenella.

When Anne came back from the loo and saw Darnley revealed in all his clerical clobber, her face instantly told me that I'd been a complete fool, and that he had no more right to be wearing such a collar than I did.

The premature unveiling of his fancy dress had now plunged him into the awkward position of having fooled Fenella. Never quick on the uptake, she would find it hard to grasp that Darnley had adopted this rig as a joke. It would be hard to reveal that he had done so without implying that he had deliberately set out to gull her. Rikko, I could see, had already begun to smell a rat, but when you meet someone for the first time dressed as Darnley was that night, you cannot easily accuse them of being impostors.

Wine in hand, cigarette alight, however, and pleased to have a new audience, Fenella was perfectly happy to dream her dreams aloud into Darnley's ears. Though on one level it was bad manners to allow her to continue thinking that he was a clergyman, on the other it did not really matter. With Fenella, it hardly made sense to distinguish between reality and falsehood.

"If I hadn't come from a very old Catholic family, there's no knowing who I might have married!"

Rikko's thumb and forefinger automatically went up to his brow when he heard these words, and he took a pinch of agonised flesh while the rest of us sipped our plonk.

"Of course it's just ridiculous," said Fenella, "that Catholics can't marry a member of the Royal Family." She switched on a flirtatious flash of the dentures and kittenishly hung her head sideways. "Now I've gone and blurted it out," she said.

With his eyes shut and his lips taut, Rikko said, "You never knew any member of the Royal Family."

"Darling, you don't know what you're *talking* about! I knew David Windsor terribly well in those days, long before Wallis Simpson came on the scene. If they don't keep up with me anymore, that's hardly surprising."

Fenella did not quite state that were it not for her religious affiliations, she might have been the Queen of England. Instead, she launched into one of her favourite anecdotes. It concerned an incident when she was working as an usherette at one of the larger cinemas in Leicester Square. The world première of some film was being shown; naturally, she knew all the stars. The Duke and Duchess of Gloucester were in attendance. Rikko squirmed in his seat, swigged his wine, swore at the bottle for being empty, turned it absolutely upside down and shook it over his glass, as if it concealed hidden reserves of alcohol. We were all drinking fast, anxious not to be hearing any more of this stuff.

Glasses were all more or less empty by the time the Duke of Gloucester was saying, "Fenella, darling! What the hell are you holding that torch for as if you were a bloody usherette."

"I told him, 'Harry, we've all got to live.' "

" 'Well, at least come and have dinner with us afterwards.' "

"I think the dogs need a walk," Rikko announced.

"Did you go and have the dinner?" Anne asked. She was always, and I am sure still is, wholly literal in her approach to things.

There being no more wine, Darnley proposed that he take me off to the pub, with "Robin" and his sister. "Robin" surprised me, as we were going down the stairs, by saying, "I've heard so much about you. I want to hear all about the old days."

I, too, had a duffel, only camel-coloured, not dark like Darnley's. "About me?" I asked her the question as I put on my coat in the hall. Rikko and Fenella, standing on the landing, were having such a row about the untruth of her Duke-in-the-cinema story that they did not say goodbye.

"No one is denying you were an usherette . . . All right, in the bloody Gaumont. Did I deny that? You might even have been there during some Royal Premiere . . ."

"That woman still thinks I'm the vicar," said Darnley gloomily.

"We were going to surprise you," said Robin. "Miles was going to take his coat off in the pub quite casually and you were meant to think."

"It would never have worked," said Darnley. "Julian has known me too long."

"I was fooled for a minute," I confessed. "It wasn't such a strange idea as you think. . . ."

"What!" exclaimed his sister. "Miles, a priest?"

"Is this pub all right?" I asked. "It's not spectacular, but it's near."

The Strathcona, just off Hereford Square, was a solid Edwardian place, with fine engraved glass and oak panelling around the bar. There were still booths to sit in if you wanted to be private in the public bar, though there was a saloon with a few semi-upholstered chairs, and button-backed benches in red velvet. Though the furnishing and look of the place suggested an era of self-confident pleasure-loving people of the sort who might have been painted by Sickert, the clientèle of the Strathcona was nondescript. Rather than kept women, moustachioed military types or red-faced roués in bookmaker's tweeds, the customers were chiefly drawn from the bedsit brigade, who had come to the pub not because they wished to drink or be convivial but just as an alternative to putting another shilling in the meter.

I got the first round while the others found somewhere to sit. Standing at the bar waiting for drinks, all kinds of thoughts raced through my head, most of them prompted by the fact that, more or less instantly, I had fallen in love with "Robin." Was she Darnley's girlfriend? If so, one had to rule out the idea of becoming involved.

From whom had she "heard so much about me"? From Darnley, presumably. What old days? I came back to their table with the cider, which was what we were all having. By the time I reached them, I could see that Darnley's collar was having a satisfying effect on a group at the next table, some perky young men, about five years older than us, who might have been commercial travellers.

"You can't fool me, vicar! Choir outing is it? And two lovely birds in tow!"

"Don't mind him, vic," said a friend, attempting to pour oil. "Nice to see a gentleman of the cloth."

"Nice to see one who likes girls for a change."

"Cut it out, Len."

"The first time he wore that thing," "Robin" said as I put the glasses down, "was coming to see Mummy. Can you imagine? He took his coat off in our hall, and I *just* didn't know what to *do*. As you can imagine, she was totally fooled, and as you can also imagine, she was completely furious when she found out that she had been tricked."

Gigglingly, "Robin" lit up a Woodbine.

"Mummy sends you her regards by the way," she said between puffs.

Darnley and his sister began to have a boring conversation about the Morris they apparently shared; something to do with one of them having to take it to the garage in the morning.

"Your *mother* sent me her regards?" I was completely puzzled that this angel from another planet to whom I already felt my destiny linked should turn out in some sense to know me. I was under the impression that I did not know anyone, and certainly did not know their mothers. Could she be some relation of Bunty or her awful friends the Murrays?

"She wondered if you and I might go and see Sargie, who, as usual, is feeling sorry for himself. Mummy says you are good with Sargie."

"I haven't seen him for ages."

"Mummy wants him and your uncle to patch up this quarrel they've had."

Do call on Sibs by the way—my uncle's postscript.

This girl's mother was Sybil Starling. It came as a shock to discover that such a pretty, animated being had not, as I supposed, burst into my life by accident, but had come as an emissary of the Lampitts. Uncle Roy had almost certainly written to Sibs and told her I was lonely and would value a visit. I felt a yank on the strings; I was a marionette after all. My sense of independence which had built up since leaving Tempest and Holmes now felt illusory.

"Robin was at school with Elizabeth. We were round at their place the other day and they were all talking about, would it be your uncle?"

"Roy sounds so *sweet!*" said "Robin."

I admitted that there were those who found him so, myself included really.

"It wasn't long after you'd written. I was coming to see you anyway, and then Lady Vulture said we ought to take you in hand and send you on errands."

"Roy writes Lady Vulture such super letters," said Robin. "And he really knows more about the family than we do, it's incredible."

"I know."

"Julian's uncle and my uncle were really, really close friends," Robin explained to Darnley and his sister.

Like a good catechumen I rehearsed in my mind Lady Starling's relationship with all the other Lampitts. She was the youngest sister of Sargie, Jimbo (James Petworth) and the other "Timplingham" Lampitts, a cousin to the Labour peer Vernon Lampitt, and also a cousin, in a way I momentarily forgot, to such worthies as Dame Ursula Lampitt, the principal of Rawlinson College, Oxford, or Sir Antony Lampitt, our man in Abu Dhabi.

Lady Starling was married to a man who was an *éminence grise* at the Treasury. She had three children—two sons, Gavin and Michael, both in the City and both I should guess already in their thirties, and a much younger daughter, Anne, whom I remembered, not quite accurately, to be an art student.

"I've just finished at the Courtauld," she said. "I want to do a thesis." Even at that moment the disappointingly solemn, incipiently pompous tone came upon her, and I felt my mind drifting as she said that she wanted to write about the iconography of Winterhalter.

It was one of those moments in life when any sense of freedom which you might have been entertaining gets abandoned. Existence seems instead to be a foreordained drama in which your part has already been written. My feeling that I was striking out on my own was completely removed by the discovery that Darnley's friend "Robin" was in fact Anne Starling, whose name I had heard so often on Uncle Roy's lips.

"Extraordinarily sweet child."

"How do you know—you've hardly met her."

"She came to old Mrs. Lampitt's eightieth."

"When she was about three."

"Everyone says she has come on *extraordinarily well.*"

"Robin" was a school nickname based on an obvious free flow of ornithological association. Darnley had picked it up from Elizabeth who had known Anne and been having her to stay in the Darnley household since she was about fourteen. The further extensions of bird names—Lady Vulture, or, for Robin's brothers, the Storks—were Darnley's own elaborations. It was typical of him that he should hold on to Anne's school name when everyone else had abandoned it. (Elizabeth called her Annie.) Darnley's acts of rebellion were seemingly anarchic but in fact they were reassuring and conservative. The desire to dress as a clergyman, for example, suggested a world in which people took the clergy seriously—else what would be the point of the joke? These were all aspects of Darnley's character which I pieced together later over the years rather than being things which I considered that evening in the pub.

I more thought then of my uncle Roy and his interest (His interest? His consuming obsession and love) for the Lampitts. In childhood, this was something which had seemed like a joke. When going to stay at the rectory one Christmas, when I was about six, I can remember Mummy saying, "I do hope we don't have too much of the Lampitt family."

Daddy, leaning forward in the railway carriage, had done a meanly accurate imitation of his brother Roy saying, "Lady Starling—Sibs to the family—is an extraoooooordinarily nice woman." When meditating anything truly serious like the Lampitts, Uncle Roy's vowels became deliberately elongated; perhaps the pleasure of uttering Lampitt names and addresses was so intense that he could not bear to allow the sounds to escape his larynx without caressing them. The syllables "Cadogan Square" in the lady's address were always enunciated with a solemnity which would not have been out of place when celebrating the Eucharist.

But then Mummy and Daddy died, and I grew up with Uncle

Roy, and Lampitt mania shaped my days, my mind. I now saw that this was no mere episode of childhood. Act One was over. What was about to begin? Not, as I supposed, a new play, but Act Two. My days and days and days of listening to Uncle Roy recount his conversations and outings with Sargent Lampitt had just been prep for life with Anne. The difference between falling in love with Anne and any previous attachment resided in this strange inner certainty, which might not have dawned at once, but which had certainly established itself in the pub by the time that Darnley was buying more cider, that our fortunes had already been forged.

At children's parties your partner in a game is allotted to you by the hostess or master of ceremonies. It's just pot luck who you get. A similar feeling came over me as we sat there in the Strathcona on the window seat. Although Darnley and Elizabeth were there, and over at the other table the perky travellers were drinking beer and eating peanuts, and around us there must have been sixty people in varying stages of intoxication, it felt as if Anne and I were quite alone together. And it was not, as on other occasions when feeling suddenly keen on a girl, a case of "Will she have me?" but much more, "Here is my partner, who has been assigned to me." At the same time, I felt that simply by being there I was betraying Darnley.

What was the partner like, who had been assigned to me in this particular round of party games? I could not believe my luck. Not only was she extremely pretty—she had such a nice face. I could never imagine, then or now, her ever saying a truly mean thing, even though she found so much in the human scene absurd.

"How is Sargie these days?" I asked.

"Well, when did you last see him?"

"And when did you last see your Lampitt? As I say, it's been a long time. More like years than months."

"Mummy says she never quite worked out what the row with your uncle was about. Partly Sargie pulling down Timplingham Place; partly that really ghastly book the man wrote about Uncle Jimbo."

"The ghastly book, by the way, was written by the man we've just seen on television."

"Not the one who threw up? God, that was funny."

She started to laugh again and—a gesture which I found instantly captivating—she tried to suppress the laughter coyly with the back of her hand, as though keeping back a cough.

"Not that one, the other one," I said.

"Oh, the really handsome interviewer-person. Mummy saw a lot of him when he was writing the book. Said he had a specious sort of charm. See what she means, now."

From that very early moment onwards, it became one of our shared jokes that Anne was crazy about Raphael Hunter, found him irresistible, slept with his photograph under her pillow. It was a bit of banter which surfaced several times a week in all our time together.

When Darnley came back from the bar with more cider, he asked me, "How did you manage to find yourself such a very distinctive landlady?"

"I thought she was a man!" said Elizabeth Darnley.

"I didn't find her," I said. "William Bloom did."

"Not the pansy you used to hang around with in the army?"

"Guilty secrets!" Anne laughed.

She wasn't one of those Englishwomen who positively prefer their men to be homosexual, but she assumed (not surprisingly, considering her Lampitt inheritance) that there would always be a fair spoonful of this sort of thing in the mixture.

"Not at all," said Darnley. "You think everyone's queer. This is just one of Julian's unsuitable friends. I entirely see now that he would go for your landlady, and even more for Mr. Afghan Hound."

"Bloom's rather a successful publisher already," I interrupted. "Odd isn't it? His having grown up, settled down, whatever the word would be, before the rest of us have got started?"

We talked a bit about our lives. Darnley did not want to do any of the normal jobs. He was eating dinners at some Inn of Court, but had no intention of becoming a barrister. Journalism in some form tempted him.

Anne's sense of her own career was much more determined. She was going to be, already considered that she was, an art historian. It all seemed reassuringly far from the world of Pilbright, the world where people may convincingly be said to earn their livings. When closing time came, the four of us walked once or twice round Hereford Square before saying goodbye. Darnley and Elizabeth walked ahead, I was paired with Anne. Then, without much ceremony, I parted from the three of them and let myself into the house in Wetherby Gardens.

That evening changed my life. Up to that point, my solitariness in London had been nearly crushing. I knew a tiny handful of people, none of them precisely my cup, but I clung to them with a kind of desperation for fear of having nothing and no one. The resurfacing of Darnley in my life changed all that. It was not so much that all of a sudden I made new friends. Rather, I now felt as if I were part of a group, however loosely constituted that group may have been. This resulted almost immediately from falling in love with Anne. I was no longer alone in the world. It seemed then that I had been lonely not merely since coming to live in London, but all my life, since that horrible day when a train pulled out of Paddington Station and for the last time I saw my mother standing there, waving. From that moment of goodbye to the moment when I met Anne had been an era, an interregnum. It was over now, finished, as I thought, forever.

I could not make out, still, in what sense Anne and Darnley were together. Was he just an old family friend? Or was it more complicated? Did he love her, and she not love him? I was in the state of mind where it was not really imaginable that anyone could know Anne and not be in love with her. I wanted her so much, and yet I so little wanted to behave like a shit to my oldest friend.

These thoughts, and the indigestible mixture of Fenella's Algerian red with the pub cider, guaranteed that I should not sleep much that night. A new life was beginning. But Anne's appearance, and all the talk about her family, had summoned up remembrance of things past with such poignancy that, even if

I were not so riotously in love, I think I might still have lain sleepless, and haunted by a thousand scenes which had gone by forever.

Arising at three-thirty A.M. to make extensive use of the toilet on the half-landing not far from Rikko and Fenella's bedroom, I could not avoid hearing the rhythmic groan of bedsprings in their old four-poster, and the rumbling bass tones of Fenella. She sounded very happy. It was embarrassing to overhear it, yet in a strange way reassuring, a harbinger of existence determined by marriage and its funny old routines.

three

"Take my word for it." The man drinking gin-and-lime was called Peter. "It happens bloody faster than you'd think possible."

"Don't you have any say in the matter at all?" I was polishing glasses as he spoke.

He was usually the first in. I had noticed him on my very first visit to the Black Bottle. Short blond hair, swept back from a smooth brow, a well-formed strong-boned face: in features, he could easily have been one of those Battle of Britain heroes or cricketers who used to appear on cigarette cards. In fact he had been a jockey, and promised well, until that calamitous Cesarovich when his horse Pride and Joy collapsed beneath him in their final furlong, and destroyed Peter's left foot. No one knew if the iron which he still wore was medically necessary, or whether he put it on as a painful sort of talisman, a visible token of why he had nothing better to do than sit around all day in the Bottle.

He usually wore a blazer, and I don't suppose he was much more than forty, if that. His most striking features were the bright blue eyes whose whites at this hour of the day were a faint pink. His hands shook violently as he fumbled for a Park Drive.

"Women," he pronounced when the fag was alight, "make

all the choices in life. Don't fool yourself about that. They choose when you get laid, they choose when to tie the wedding knot, they choose when to throw you out which, if they've got any sense, they do quite early on. Mercifully, almost no women have any sense."

"You married, then?" I asked as casually as possible. I genuinely wanted to know, but I did not want to ask questions which, in my employer's ears, would sound ridiculous or naif.

Unfortunately, Cyril heard my enquiry.

"Him? What d'you think, cod's cunt? Peter's been married more often than you've been sick."

"Eating your hot dinners, I suppose," retorted Peter.

"You boring little arsehole," said Cyril, I think to Peter rather than to myself.

Cyril's way of addressing colleagues and customers came as a sharp surprise, given his appearance. There was nothing of T. S. Eliot in his manner, except in so far as he was a good judge of a bit of cheese. Cyril's rudeness had something to do with Style. He had his style all worked out; perhaps he had been born with it. Mine was still at the planning stage.

Peter ignored the landlord and continued talking to me.

"You want to watch out," he said. "Along she'll come, some nice girl who's decided for her own stupid reasons that you're Mr. Right and that'll be it. You'll have no say in the matter at all."

"Three times, he's been married, stupid cunt," Cyril, not to be ignored, put in.

"Doesn't it take two to tango?" I asked.

Silently, Pete held out his glass and I refilled it from the upside-down bottle with the Gilbey's label. Pushing the tumbler against the teat of the bottle to get a double measure felt as if one were milking some cow which gave out gin, not milk.

("Plenty of those, dear, in the pubs I like to go to," Bloom would have to chip in.)

It was eleven-twenty-five A.M.

"A bit more lime as well?" I asked.

"Not so much as you gave me last time."

By the time he stubbed out the Park Drive, his hand was shaking less.

"It might take two to tango," he said. "It takes less than two to arrange a wedding. You just wouldn't believe the sheer fucking speed with which they operate."

"Why?" I asked. "What's in it for them? Particularly if they're going to throw you out again."

Cyril put his hand on my shoulder and smiled seraphically at Pete.

"Take this baby in hand, shortie. Educate him a bit."

"We do our best," said Pete.

By mid-day the bar had filled up. The old man who never spoke to anyone and who could make half a pint of bitter last over an hour was occupying his accustomed seat by the dusty grey window. His trilby-hatted head was a silhouette against the pane, framed by the semi-circular letters иооɹᴀƨ. Peter had turned aside to talk about racing (never a subject on which I have been able to concentrate) to a man with a very red face who looked like an old-fashioned lawyer's clerk—a black bowler hat on the back of his scarlet nut, an old black fustian coat and waistcoat, a winged collar. Known to Cyril as Mr. Porn, he made his living by composing scrofulous tales, obtainable from some shop in Frith Street where he also worked as an assistant.

Most of the tables (Cyril was a passable cook) were now full. The Kempes were there. Rikko was anxiously consulting the gold watch buried in hair on his left wrist. There was a decided contrast between the dark hair on his arms and the arresting blond on the top of his head. He wore blue corduroy trousers, yachting shoes and the sort of jumper then denominated a Sloppy Joe. The sleeves of this garment were pulled up to the elbow. One forearm was held in mid-air.

"They're a couple," said Cyril. "Go and see what he wants to eat or we'll have Special Branch down on us. You can't have blokes waving their arms like that; looks as if he's soliciting."

"Cyril wondered if you were ready to order," I said to them when I got to their table.

"This man from the BBC's over half an hour late," said Rikko, holding up the watch and the decoratively furry forearm to emphasise the point. An arrangement had been made to meet a wireless producer in the pub. "A really big part in radio drama," was how Fenella envisaged the possible outcome of the interview.

"It just could be Rikko's break," she said.

Her hair had been redyed for the occasion, the lips were brighter than ever. In spite of these superficial touches of glamour, the two of them sitting there put you in mind of a mother and son on the child's first day at school. Rikko obviously wanted her to be there. Her bright lips, yellow hair and jangling bracelets probably seemed as beautiful to him as his did to her. Fenella's fur coat, which to a dispassionate eye might have seemed like a suitable prop for Flanagan and Allan's "Underneath the Arches" routine to Rikko probably seemed as glamorous as a new one in Hollywood.

Was their marriage to be explained in the simple terms outlined an hour earlier by Peter? Had Fenella just decided to swoop down on Rikko and take him over? Or was life more complex than Peter supposed? Or, not more complex. Rather, were Peter's matrimonial failures based on his absolute refusal to live with saving illusions? Were happy marriages (Rikko and Fenella's, for all their interminable bickering could surely be so described) based on shared fantasy? These weren't questions I'd been sent over by Cyril to answer.

"Do you want lamb chops?" I asked.

They agreed that they did.

"We mustn't drink too much," said Rikko.

"Two cutlets!" I called back to Cyril.

"I'm not fucking deaf," he replied from behind the bar. This was simply Cyrilese for "message understood." He went backstage to prepare the grill and his wife, Brenda, came to help me serve behind the bar. By the time the chops were done, I could see Rikko and Fenella making contact with the wireless producer who had come down that morning from Birmingham. When I carried over their chops, they introduced me to the man briefly.

He was in the middle of a long, unconvincing-sounding rig-marole about why he was so late. He had hoped to bring down one of the temporary scriptwriters—Val—to discuss the part with Rikko. At the last minute, Val had been overpowered by some digestive disorder, a suspected appendicitis, and the pro-ducer, whose name was Rodney Jones, had caught a later train. By the time I came back and gave him his sausages with fried potatoes, and a glass of ginger beer shandy, it seemed as though the interview with Fenella and Rikko was proceeding amicably.

Between serving other customers I was keeping half an ear open to the Best Seller who, perched on a stool at the end of the bar opposite to Peter and Mr. Porn, was talking relentlessly to anyone who cared to listen and continued to talk even when his audience got up and walked away.

I had been far too embarrassed to allude to his misfortune on the television, now several weeks in the past. Nevertheless, in the course of not discussing it, we had somehow or another become friends. I can't quite explain how, but I now felt an affection for the old blighter even though there was little in his speech or manners which one would single out as obviously congenial. Liking and disliking, quite as much as more reckless forms of love, are totally arbitrary in my experience. Niceness (where could you find a nicer man than Hunter?) was not always lovable.

"No, Julian," said the Best Seller as I took the money for other people's beer and continued to fill their glasses. "The thing about England today is this. It's *decadent*. Look at those two." With a nod of his head he indicated Pete and Porn. "They're both intelligent men, or anyway not positively moronic, for Christ's sakes. And they've nothing better to do with their time than sit around in the middle of the day drinking."

I handed him the second pint of the morning and he smiled his frog-like grin.

"Discipline is what they need, lad."

"What are you gassing about—hanging, I shouldn't wonder." It was the pornographer who shouted this, adding a jest, which he was not quite articulate enough to make neat, about being well hung. It would probably have been funnier before his third glass of whisky and ginger. It was true that it took very little to start Day Muckley off on the matter of capital punishment. The execution of Ruth Ellis, the last woman to be hanged for murder in England, had particularly captured his imagination.

"Why do people suppose I'm such a cruel bugger?" he asked.

"Because you are," said Peter, coming down the bar and jabbing the air crossly with his Park Drive. "It was downright uncivilised, hanging a kid like that. Twenty-eight years of age she was."

I was familiar with the feelings on each side of the argument. Peter was an out-and-out abolitionist who considered that the death penalty was on a level with murder. The Best Seller was a law-and-order man; but more than that, he derived an obvious delight from baiting people, and had learnt that the expression of reactionary views in a public place was as good a way as any of making people like Peter get overexcited.

"What in Christ's name does her age matter or, come to that"—he paused to spit out a bit of loose tobacco which had stuck to his lips from the Sweet Afton—"come to that, her sex. She gunned down a man in cold blood. On Good Friday, I might add."

"I suppose you think that makes it worse." By Peter's third or fourth large gimlet of the day he was capable of quite passionate fury, though for some reason he did not usually get violent until the evenings.

"As a matter of fact," said Day Muckley, "I do think it makes it worse. A lot worse."

"Jesus was hanged," said Peter intensely. "Jesus was a victim of capital punishment. You're on the side of the people who murdered Jesus, I suppose."

"That sort of argument is beneath contempt," said the Best Seller, trying to keep his dignity in spite of rather an audible fart which he let out at this juncture. "Quite despicable, as a matter of fact."

"Why is everything a matter of fact," asked Peter, "and why can't you answer me? I asked you a question about your religion.

You're supposed to be on the same side as Jesus, aren't you?"

"Tell you one thing," said Cyril, who clearly thought the conversation nasty and needed a change of direction. "That pub where she did in her man—the Magnolia in Hampstead."

"The Magnolia," repeated the Best Seller, in a tone which suggested that Cyril had said otherwise and needed correction. "I've had more than one drink in the Magnolia, lad. It's not far from where my mistress lives."

"Well, that's just it," said Cyril.

"If I was your mistress," said Peter to the B.S., "and I had a shotgun . . ."

"Ever since Ruth shot her man outside that place," said Cyril, "the place has been packed to the doors. Good for business see, murder."

"Ghouls," said Peter with complete seriousness, all irony gone from his tone. "People disgust me sometimes."

"You want to watch out I don't have one of you monkey's pricks shot on your way out of here one day," said Cyril. "Multiply my trade by ten that would."

While these interesting matters were being aired, I looked across the smoky saloon and saw that Rikko was leaving with the producer chap, Rodney. Fenella, smiling triumphantly, advanced towards the bar and informed me, "They're off to BH! He's going to have a voice test."

"Just so long as he doesn't have to have a hormone test," said Cyril.

"What's BH?" I asked.

"Broadcasting House, catshit, and serve some customers, please. I don't pay you money for asking fucking ignorant questions."

"I'm going to have a gin-and-tonic to celebrate," said Fenella. "They're obviously desperate to get someone for the part and it looks as if at last that agent of ours has found Rikko his break."

"He hasn't got the part yet," I said, putting ice and lemon into a glass before squeezing on the Gilbey teat.

"What part is it anyway?" asked Cyril, who took an interest

in most aspects of the drama. Fenella put her head on one side and grinned.

"It's one of the main parts in 'The Mulberrys,' actually."

"Oh, yeah?"

For a moment, Cyril was stuck for an insult. I could tell he was quite impressed. Like about half the population of the British Isles he was addicted to this wireless serial, broadcast in daily episodes, claiming to be a realistic glimpse into the life of a small village of indeterminate region. I'd been "brought up" on "The Mulberrys." Aunt Deirdre was another addict. In later years, I had got out of the way of listening.

"It's not to replace Stan, is it?" asked Cyril.

"Well, it is, as a matter of fact," Fenella simpered modestly. It was as though Rikko had inherited a dukedom, but we were all to continue calling her by her first name.

"Well, well," said Cyril, and he began to whistle the "Mulberrys" theme tune. Now he really *was* impressed.

Out of touch as I might have been, I could yet remember that Stan Mulberry, heir to the largest farm in Barleybrook and son of Dick and Elsie, played a major role in the drama. Having been a bit of a lad, Stan had recently settled down and married. I now remembered having seen some item in a newspaper about the actor playing Stan. He had died, but the producer of the series had decided to replace the actor, rather than "phase out" the character of Stan. Hence, presumably, the hurry for a new Stan.

"Fancy that," said Cyril. "To think I've been selling Babychams to Stan Mulberry."

"He's always been brilliant at accents," said Fenella, quite truthfully. "It was obvious that Rodney was terribly impressed. Who knows? We might *all* get parts in the series now."

I hoped Cyril would hold his tongue, and luckily he did. I had begun to feel protective towards Fenella, as though she were some tiresome but much loved relative. If she really imagined that she might get a part in radio drama, it was obvious that she did not realise what her voice sounded like. All kinds of Cyrilese answers were imaginable. "You? A part? What as?

A fucking corncrake?" But he said nothing. Heart of gold, that man.

By the time she left the pub, Fenella was cock-a-hoop. She said she was going to the Italian butchers in Old Compton Street, promising a sumptuous dinner of osso bucco, Rikko's favourite, later that evening.

The bar was beginning to empty. The scene with its empty glasses and its almost numinous nicotine haze resembled a picture I had not yet seen, but was to admire in later years, Pilbright's *Marriage Feast at Canonbury*, now hanging in the National Gallery in Washington, D.C.

The little old man by the window had drunk his second half pint and tiptoed in and out of the Gents. Mr. Porn, too, had departed. He said that he had one of his "swish and bond" romances to complete before the afternoon was out. Evidently his literary productions flowed from the pen with much greater ease than my own novel, which obstinately refused to get to its conclusion. Peter, who had simmered down, was apologising to the Best Seller.

"I shouldn't have attacked your religion, Day. Actually I have a great respect for Catholics, in spite of the fact that my second wife became one, silly cow."

"It's a rock, lad," the Best Seller asserted, "something to hold on to when all the rest of life is pulling you down the bloody sink. Anyway, that's the way I'm made. My mistress, she doesn't understand it any better than you do. 'Look at you, you hypocritical old sod!' She really will say that to me, Julian."

"I can believe it," said Peter, who was holding out his glass for more medicine.

"But I always make an act of perfect contrition, you know, every time I make love, in case I have a bloody heart attack at the moment of climax."

He paused so that we could all take in his capability in this regard. I'd already begun to observe that older people (the Best Seller at around sixty struck me as positively antique) liked to keep you informed of their continued genital interests and attainments, though not everyone did so as blatantly as he did.

"Oh, yes," said Day Muckley, "I love it every single time. But I always make an act of perfect contrition before getting into bed to have my wicked way with her, Julian. Come to that, I make an act of perfect contrition if I'm getting into bed on my own, which I do from time to time, and if I'm just so bloody tired, for Christ's sakes, that all I want to do is sleep."

"Do you really suppose God gets upset when you've been having it away?" asks Peter. "That's one of the things I don't understand about religion. Why should God worry Himself about people having a spot of How's Our Father? I'm perfectly happy, sitting down here and downing the occasional glass of the Gilbey's, to know that all around us, in knocking shops all over Soho, they are playing the beast with two backs. It is even a positively cheering thought to me. It keeps them out of mischief. It momentarily stops them being unkind to one another."

"Except for the Swish and Bond merchants," said Cyril.

"Even they are only doing it for pleasure, and pleasure is in short supply in this world which God has so graciously filled with tears and disease. But God. He's different from me. He gets so angry every time you so much as toss off that He needs to be placated with these acts of perfect something or other. That's what finished religion for me at school. Once I'd had my first bird, that was it as far as God was concerned. I said to God, 'If you're so fucking jealous, or inquisitive or intolerant that you mind me having some crumpet, then you needn't expect me to turn up and sing you to sleep every Sunday morning.' Never thought about religion since, not seriously, not for myself."

"What you don't understand about God, Peter, is this." The Best Seller spoke with absolute authority on the matter. "God is a dictator. As a matter of fact He is very like old Stalin used to be. He doesn't really like cringers and whingers. He has a lot of rough rules, but He really prefers the rogues. He has a very soft spot for rogues. I'd even go so far as to say He has His favourites. Look at the Bible if you don't believe me. There's King David behaving like a complete and utter shit and God rewards him, even though he has stolen another man's wife, and sent that man off to certain death in battle. But along come the virtuous bloody characters and they say, 'O Lord, we worship Thee, we have kept thy statutes, O Lord.' And what does He do? He smites the buggers with plague and murrain and exile and makes their temple a smouldering ruin."

Day Muckley sipped his beer and smiled. This wholesale programme of destruction obviously seemed to him quite reasonable, all in a day's work as far as the Deity was concerned.

"No," he repeated, "God has his favourites just as old Joe Stalin used to have. You might have some perfectly virtuous man, who never smoked, a teetotaller from birth perhaps, never fornicated—and what happens to him? He gets smitten down with cancer. And then you get one of God's favourites, like King David—or like me. Take me. I smoke. I drink. I fornicate. And God looks down and He laughs. 'Eee, it's only old Day Muckley, having his little bit of fun.' "

God, in this version of theology, spoke with a Yorkshire accent even more pronounced than Day Muckley's itself. The Best Seller smiled seraphically as he contemplated his intimacy with the Mind behind the Universe.

For myself there was something hard to puzzle out about the Best Seller. I couldn't catch his tone. If this God-as-Stalin theory was a joke, it was surely, from the RC point of view, profane and possibly blasphemous. But if he genuinely believed this cosmic horror story, it was a puzzle to me how he could derive such evident comfort from the practice of his faith. He was forever lurching into St. Patrick's Church in Soho Square to catch the tail end of a Mass or to light, with the same fumbling fingers which ignited his forty a day, a candle to the Sacred Heart or to the Little Flower.

Perhaps because I was self-confident enough to disapprove of the Best Seller's attitudes, he was the first person whose religion I positively envied. Having been brought up in a parsonage, Anglicanism was in my blood. Whole chunks of the Book of Common Prayer and Coverdale's Psalter have remained in my head and provided me with a sort of mental furniture. But the C of E, as hitherto encountered, was relentlessly respectable. I was not looking for a religion to believe in. What I envied the Best Seller in his (wholly incredible) religion was the possession of a place, an institution, an inner world, where he could take himself and relate his own messy character to a universe of values outside himself.

"Within that household," as he liked to quote from a favourite author, "the human spirit has roof and hearth. Outside it, is the night."

"That's perfectly true, the last bit," Peter had replied from his neighbouring bar-stool. And then, after a long silence, "What you don't seem to realise is that inside, it is the night as well. What you call the night is just the condition of things."

"I go to Mass to lay down my burdens," said Muckley, shifting tack. "Not to be made better, for Christ's sakes." He must have regarded moral improvement as something like piles or influenza; it might, in the ordinary course of things, happen to anyone, but only a lunatic would seek it out.

Although Anglicanism provided an analogous "roof and hearth" for me, I found that it could not possibly provide what the Best Seller got from St. Patrick's. The thought of shuffling into, say, choral matins at Westminster Abbey half tight and then only staying for ten minutes of the service would have embarrassed me. Muckley was somehow able to behave in church as if he were at home. By paradox, my inability to do so had to do less with some innate Anglican stuffiness than with the fact that church was indelibly connected in my mind with childhood, with growing up in the rectory at Timplingham, with Uncle Roy and Aunt Deirdre. Though religious belief had been abandoned, church doggedly remained; not "church" in any nebulous sense, certainly not a theological concept, but as an actual place, Timplingham Parish Church, its cold perpendicular aisles, its vast rood screen. Beyond the screen stood the high altar, the riddel posts introduced by Roy and paid for by Sargie, who never went near the place. And before you reached the altar was the choir, with misericords carved with bucolic representations of late medieval life, and hidden by garish hassocks gros-pointed by the Mothers' Union. And above were the carved beams of the aisle, each boss supporting a figure: twenty-three Carmelite friars, and one maiden with a naked chest.

It was not just as a piece of architecture that I thought of Timplingham Church, as I might think of Timplingham Place, the handsome Palladian manor-house, now demolished, where Sargie and my uncle Roy had spent so many evenings together. When I thought of the church, it was of a phenomenon with which I had not yet been able to come to terms. At that period of life, when working at the Bottle, I should have said it was a phenomenon which was neither interesting nor important to me. Inside myself, I knew it to be both, in fact. Five hundred years earlier, the smaller priory church of Timplingham had been rebuilt, like so many others in East Anglia. Wool money had provided an airy, spindly house of light with tall clear windows and narrow fluted columns. And it was not quite enough to say that this beautiful building had been put up in the middle of a field in Norfolk to appease the guilt of some wool merchant. For all over the world they have been building shrines for time out of mind. It merely happens that Timplingham Church is the one I know and to which I will always continue to make an emotional response.

What one *thinks* about such places, rather than how one feels, perhaps doesn't matter very much. But I knew, even in my early twenties, that an England without its churches is unimaginable, even if everyone stopped believing. A life, to me, is unimaginable without recognising that impulse which led to churches first being built. Ultraorthodox churchmen would probably say that the churches were built just to embody rituals and doctrines, to house the Mass; but this is not true, for very often the first churches were built on the sites of older shrines and groves and altars to the "false" gods of paganism. Nor do I really like the superior humanist's idea that churches are only important because we have brought to them so many grave or serious moments of our lives, such as the funerals of those we love, or baptisms and weddings. In an awkward clumsy way, whether signing the visitors' book at the back of the building or making gros-point, or arranging flowers, those who enter these buildings are doing much more than wishing to solemnise their own experiences. At the heart of experience is a bottomless hole of irrationality. Any attempts to explain it, or to explain it away, will always fail. Any language which tries to tell us why there is no God, or why there is one and what He is like, are bound to fail; just as any system of psychological theory which thinks it can plumb our crazy and impulsive natures is bound to fail. The caveman who instinctively turned towards the rising sun and sacrificed his wild beast, the Druid who erected a ring of stones, the Christian founders who placed stone on stone in Timplingham were not guided by any such cerebral considerations. They followed impulse, not argument; what we respond to in such buildings we respond to imaginatively, and not intellectually.

Our ancestors had the half-articulated belief that material existence only makes sense when seen in an eternal glass, and that humankind cannot be defined or understood other than as children of God. But this was something which we lost, entirely, a hundred years ago or more, when Matthew Arnold heard the sea of faith withdrawing from Dover Beach, so that though we are homesick for our shrines and know that we need them, we are afraid of saying things which are untrue or indulging in nonsense. So we stay away, which is a pity, and leave the churches to those who have narrower ideas but probably have no more reason or right to be there than we do.

Even if it had not been for Matthew Arnold, and Doubt and all of that, I think I should have had to boot out religion from my life at that point, as a way of coming to terms with Aunt Deirdre and Uncle Roy. They were intimately connected in my mind with God; so much so that now, as Day Muckley talked nonsense about religion, I was instinctively conscious of Uncle Roy, two hundred miles away in Norfolk, smoking his pipe in his study and writing short letters to far-flung members of the Lampitt family, or reading the newspaper. ("Don't disturb your uncle, he's very busy in the study." How often that sentence of Aunt Deirdre's was repeated during my boyhood.) And now I thought of Aunt Deirdre herself, working for six or eight hours a day in the garden and returning to the house at intervals to concoct execrably dull meals, or to comment on the usually no less dull "news" of village life, gathered that morning in the queue at the post office.

I suppose that ever since I had been to live with them, I had walked a knife edge, feeling that almost any course of action would earn the disapproval of my uncle and aunt. There was no particular justification for this theory. When their daughter Felicity got into a scrape, for example, they were remarkably free of moralism. But neither did they radiate, in their daily conversation, much of that easy warmth and toleration of human weakness which would normally be associated with the forgiveness of sins. I could not explain why *my* religion failed to provide me with the sort of hearth and home which the Best Seller's gave to him. But if I were forced to explain it, or at least to realise it imaginatively, I only had to imagine an unthinkable meeting, Day Muckley and Aunt Deirdre herself. Instead of seeing him, as I had so often done in real life, staggering into St. Patrick's, Soho Square, I had to place him in my mind's eye making the same tottering and uncertain steps up the aisles of the parish church at Timplingham, and finding my aunt crossly arranging cotoneasters and foliage beneath her husband's pulpit. "Yes?" she would say, and as she looked at the Best Seller, she would draw in her breath. By those short, almost violent inhalations my aunt indicated disapproval of almost any form of human behaviour which she deemed "silly"; and this was a wide category.

Certainly the Black Bottle at any hour of day contained a high proportion of individuals who were by Aunt Deirdre's severe definitions very silly indeed. Soho, by Aunt Deirdre's view of things, was altogether a very silly place; she would have seen no point in it whatsoever.

I think he was still talking about God, old Day Muckley, when Cyril rang the bell for time. When we finally locked him out, the Best Seller would presumably go for a snooze at the back of St. Patrick's. The only alternatives were an afternoon with his mistress (he looked a little far gone for that, and did she in any case exist?) or the option of a total anaesthetic—two or three hours drinking spirits at the Concord Club, a dingy pair of rooms up a staircase in Dean Street, which somehow managed to get round the licensing laws and was able to dispense alcohol throughout the afternoon. I polished glasses and watched the Best Seller's face. The question of where he was to pass the next few hours did not look as if it were troubling him. Somewhere between the fourth and fifth drink, his features lost their animation and his eyes began to stare without focussing. His huge fleshy face, still quite pale, looked terribly, terribly sad. Peter on his nearby stool had managed to buy one more snort of gin-and-lime before Cyril called last orders, and he also looked sad. He did not have the unfocussed look, though. His face had turned red, and he had an expression of passion; his red eyes looked downwards and sideways with alarming fury. What he appeared to be looking at were the rows of fruit juices, bottled stouts and "mixers" which we kept on a lower shelf behind the bar, but from his face you might have guessed that Peter had seen his worst enemy and was planning a karate chop. Perhaps he too was thinking of God, and imagining what he would say to Him if they ever met.

There weren't many people left in the saloon, when Cyril shouted in the direction of the door (paradoxically, since it was opening), "We're fucking closed, can't you read a watch or something?"

But it was Anne, who was already perfectly used to Cyril's conversational mode. Taking no notice, she came up to see me at the bar. Most days now, she came to see me when work was finishing. Sometimes we'd see a film or "do something with the afternoon." As often as not, though, we'd just loaf about, smoking or talking, or going for walks arm in arm. It was strange, the speed with which we had "clicked," the way it seemed we were meant for each other.

Catching sight of the Best Seller at the bar, Anne brought out a wild shriek of laughter, and said, by way of introducing herself, "You're the man who was sick on the telly-box!"

This was the one sentence which no one, not even Cyril, had

been able to utter to Day Muckley. It was too humiliating. Reference to his television appearance had been minimal even among the regulars in the Bottle, most of whom never watched TV anyway. The fact that Fenella and Rikko had their eight-inch set was a sign of their extraordinary extravagance and rather vulgar desire to be up to the minute.

Muckley blinked, his face at that moment recalling some old seal floating just above the surface of the ocean.

"Who's this delectably nubile young beauty?"

I introduced them.

"And do you"—he assumed a mock-lecherous leer—"do you, you decadent young . . . have your evil way, you . . ."

"You were though," insisted Anne, "the man who was sick?"

The Best Seller sobered up by about four drinks at this call to order (disconcertingly reminiscent of Sibs's way of speaking).

"Oh, you mean that television programme?"

"That's what I said. It must have been terribly embarrassing. I was sick during a chemistry lesson at school once. It went everywhere. You feel so ashamed."

He smiled.

"I did hear that the *other* Day Muckley was up to his tricks again that night."

In time I came to think that this was one of the Best Seller's heavier jokes. Later still, as so often when thinking about my friends, I came radically to revise the judgement and to believe that he was a genuinely divided self, the right hand which wrote *The Calderdale Saga* and defended simple old-fashioned "morality" in occasional contributions to the *Yorkshire Post* scarcely aware of how much booze the left hand was pouring down Day's throat, or of the anarchic views of God and man thereby stimulated.

"I keep hearing about old Day Muckley, lass," he said. "That night you mention when, as usual, I was tucked up in bed at half past nine with my mug of Horlicks and my Dorothy L. Sayers mystery . . ." He paused. This was obviously an image of a perfect evening for him, an image which night after night the other Day Muckley smashed up and destroyed.

"Of course, I don't have a television set. For one thing I could never afford it. For another, I consider it to be decadent bloody rubbish. American rubbish, too, which is worse. But I gather old Day had no such scruples. He went on the television, and made a bit of a nuisance of himself as usual."

"You were sick all over the camera," said Anne. No trace of fantasy, no desire or need to lie, existed for her.

"Could you give me just, just a . . ." Being confronted with himself in this uncompromising manner diminished the Best Seller's ability to be articulate. "Just a little more . . . another drop of . . ."

"You heard me call time," said Cyril. "You've had your lot."

Peter, still perched on his bar stool, was staring at his empty glass with the air of a man who could not imagine what had happened to its contents. He shook an empty packet of Park Drive and leaned over the bar.

"And does the law forbid the sale of cigarettes after two-thirty P.M.?" He spat out the words.

"The law doesn't. I do. I'm fed up with you piss artists. Can't you sod off for a few hours and give us all a rest?"

In some moods Peter would have started a row at this point, but he merely turned to Day Muckley and said, "Let's go to the Concord."

"Well, Peter, I think that's a very, very . . ."

By the time Day had repeated "very" and negotiated the words "good idea," Cyril had taken pity on Pete and slapped down a packet of Park Drive on the bar.

"Here you are, dog dirt, and don't come back till we open again."

"Thanks."

Peter handed over the one-and-six.

When he and the Best Seller had swayed off to Dean Street Cyril turned to me with a quiet smile, removed his spectacles, huffed and puffed on the lenses and began to polish them with an immaculate white handkerchief.

"You've done enough work," he said with the quiet tones of the bank manager. "Why don't you both go and leave me in peace? Eh? Go on. Scram. Sod off."

Hand in hand, Anne and I walked through the afternoon

sunshine of Soho, I in my not-quite-winklepickers, tight blue jeans and sloppy jersey, she in a tight-waisted pleated skirt and a blouse. There was a coffee bar we both liked in Greek Street. Lonnie Donnegan was emitting his nasal, jerky noises from the juke-box. I carried the frothy coffees to the Formica-topped table where she already had two Woodbines alight, one for herself, one for me.

"Sargie's broken his toe," she said. "He's in some little hospital he's discovered in Bryanston Square. Mummy said he'd like a visit."

"O.K."

It was certainly not how I'd planned to spend the afternoon. Though I now felt fairly certain that Anne and I would be married, I had not allowed my mind to concentrate on her Lampitt connections. There had been one rather tricky dinner with her family during which I'd confirmed the impression made many years earlier that Lady Vulture didn't much like me. I still wanted to hold at arm's length any notion that in marrying Anne, I might in fact be doing the one thing that Uncle Roy most desired. Accompanying her to Sargie's hospital bed would bring together the two worlds of childhood and manhood with uncomfortable violence. Though it was only a few years since I had seen Sargie, it was, imaginatively speaking, a whole lifetime.

"I'm nearly seventy, my dear," he told me that afternoon in his small private hospital room. Sargie would have been nauseated by the Black Bottle, but he got through life with the same sustenance as Pete, Day Muckley and Mr. Porn. A Gold Flake was alight in Sargie's bone cigarette holder and the tooth mug in his right hand contained a dry martini, with gin, replenished from time to time from a cocktail shaker on his bedside locker. His foot, in plaster, was suspended from a pulley which he said was the sort of farcical arrangement which put one in mind of the Marx Brothers.

"At any moment, I expect the bed to roll away while I'm left here screaming in agony," he laughed. "Perhaps in the arms of Margaret Dumont. Harpo playing a serenade perhaps. Ha!"

He was in a beneficent mood. Being hospitalised suited him. It guaranteed not only that he was the centre of attention, but also the centre of sympathy. Ever since I knew of Sargie's existence, he had been trying to persuade someone, usually Uncle Roy, that he needed special treatment. His whole life, indeed, had been dominated by the need to make people feel sorry for him. The broken toe (consequence of an unwise attempt to lift a crate of gin which had been delivered to his flat off Kensington High Street) had cheered him up. He laughed a lot as Anne told him about her encounter with the Best Seller.

"Didn't he write something rather good before the war?"

"The Calderdale Saga."

"Something about these mill-owners in Yorkshire who'd been Catholics ever since penal times. Mama read it and thought it was rather good, I seem to remember."

"That's the man."

"Not my kind of thing. I can never believe in novels—can you? Still, my dears. You are moving in literary worlds. Such a pity Jimbo's dead. How he'd have liked hearing about it all. Not to go, there, of course, not this pub of yours. Don't suppose that Jimbo ever darkened the doors of a pub. Rather a prude in many ways. You never really knew him well, did you, Julian?"

"Sargie, he died before we were tiny!" Anne said.

"No, I was twelve when he died," I said. "I never actually met him, though he did call on Uncle Roy once to talk about the Archbishop Benson book."

I introduced this reference to my uncle as a measure of how the land lay. I might have been mentioning the name of Trotsky to Stalin's Politburo. Sargie showed no awareness in his features that the previous nineteen syllables had been voiced.

"I can actually just remember him," said Anne. "He gave me lovely presents when I was a little girl. My Arthur Rackham's Hans Andersen one Christmas, and another time, that musical box in the shape of a gondola—you know," she said to me, "the one I showed you the other evening."

"Lor! I remember buying that with him before the war," said Sargie. "We had a jaunt to Venice. Not a very happy one. The place is bloody depressing—ever been there? And we stayed at an absolutely godforsaken hotel."

"You should have stayed at one of the grand ones like the Gritti." Anne spoke with the authority of one who had written undergraduate essays on Titian, Tintoretto, Ruskin.

"Gritti! That's the place. God Almighty! My room overlooked this dreary sludge of water . . ."

"The Grand Canal," said Anne.

"I hate looking at water from a bedroom. And the stink. It made me ill. I had to get them to change my room, of course. Couldn't look out on that brown sludge. Like being in the back streets of Manchester or some God-awful place. And damp sheets, and boring food. All macaroni kind of stuff and fried fish galore. Thought I might actually die of constipation. They don't eat proper Italian food at all there, you know. You never so much as see a tomato."

"Your brother's Venice book is surely due for some kind of revival," I said.

"Have you been talking to Lover Boy? I notice that no publisher has actually reprinted the bloody thing."

"Who's Lover Boy?" asked Anne.

"Jimbo's biographer. Wows all the girls. Working like billy-o to get all Jimbo's books back into print. Can't tell what he has to gain from it—perhaps nothing; perhaps it's just altruism."

I had never asked Sargie's opinion of Hunter's book about his brother Jimbo. The publication had caused fury in the Lampitt family by its implied disclosures of a promiscuous homosexual life on the part of its subject.

"Your darling mother, Annie, thought we should have stopped Lover Boy writing the bloody book."

"Anne's one of Lover Boy's conquests," I chipped in. "Mad about him since seeing him on television. Careful what you say about him, Sargie."

"You wouldn't be the first, my dear." He drew on his bone holder and was silent apace. "No—but—family solicitor, threats, I said, 'Sibs, you *can't* stop a man writing a book. We could, I suppose, have withheld permission to quote from Jimbo's work, but it would only have tempted Lover Boy to write a book which was even more exciting for the Great British Public—the I.P., as I call them. To think of the *time* we've wasted in our dear old Party trying to better the lot of the I.P. and look at them now, all guzzling like hogs, earning more money than I do, most of them, all with inside *topos* and these bloody television things."

"I suppose Lady Starling thought Hunter's book would hurt people," I said.

"Well, it did. Of course it hurt people. But the only alternative is censorship, and that isn't an alternative."

"I don't know."

"Oh, for God's sake, Julian! Grow up! Read some Milton or something! If a man wants to publish a book saying Jimbo was queer, then you've got to let him do so. The only redress you would ever have lies in your own freedom to write a book saying he wasn't. Funny thing is, I don't think he was exactly, not old Jimbo. I never got the slightest whiff of it in his company. And of course he was terribly fastidious, a real old woman, you know. That Venice trip we made together—it was like going abroad with a maiden aunt. Smelling salts, Malvern water. It is simply unimaginable to me that Jimbo would ever have wandered off down some stinking alley and dropped his pants for a gondolier. Totally unthinkable. But young people think everyone's having sex all the time. They aren't, you know, my dears, they just aren't. I know that families get things wrong but I just don't think that Jimbo had a sexual nature."

"What about this diary he kept?" I asked. "It seems to have implied that he went to bed with almost everyone."

"Hardly bed. There seems to have been a lot of visits to the *topos* and other larks in the most unlikely places. Do you remember that supposed incident with the Duke of Albany in the tea tent during a Buckingham Palace garden party? I mean, I ask you! No, Julian, the operative words in your question are "seems" and "implied." Lover Boy very seldom gives a direct quote from those diaries of Jimbo's. Now it may have been as an insurance in case Sibs or I served a writ on him and prevented direct quotation—there's hardly any direct quotation in his book. The other explanation is that the diaries are not so specific as Lover Boy says."

"Are you saying"—I remembered a theory of my cousin Felicity, who had done a bit of work on the Lampitt Papers when they were still deposited at Timplingham Place—"that your brother wrote the diary as a sort of fiction, a fantasy?"

"You mean wrote things down which weren't true?" Anne asked with a puzzled tone. "Why would anyone wish to do that?"

"Most of us live in fantasy of one sort or another," I puddingly advanced. "A writer such as your uncle might have decided to lead a vicarious fantasy life which he had just made up."

"Yes, but if it isn't true and you know it isn't true," said Anne, "how could it possibly be consoling?" Darling Anne, how unlike the majority of the human race she was, and indubitably still is.

"As a matter of fact, my dears," said Sargie, who reached up and heaved himself into a more comfortable position in the bed by means of a winch, "I shouldn't mind your advice about Lover Boy. You see, he's still sitting on all Jimbo's papers and I'm vaguely worried about it. Foolish of me to lend them to him, I suppose, but I did." I wondered at this point if Sargie would allude to Uncle Roy, who had been delegated by Sibs to "disentangle Sargie from that horrible little man"—meaning Hunter. But nothing was said about Roy. Their friendship had been not merely important, but all-important to my uncle. I am sure that he thought of Sargie all the time. Perhaps Sargie was so solely occupied with his own concerns, and for much of the time with purely bodily sensations, that he did not think about it at all. Who could tell?

"Is Hunter ever going to write the second volume of your brother's life?" I asked.

"Well, that's what I shouldn't mind finding out," said Sargie. "Easier for you than for me—you're both more his sort of age."

(Hunter was, at this date, what? Forty-odd? I was in my early to mid twenties.) "Besides, I've got this wretched toe."

"Poor Sargie." Anne got up from her canvas chair and planted a kiss on her uncle's brow.

"You see," I joked relentlessly, "she's desperate to meet Lover Boy."

"It was a bit off, don't you think—putting it around that Jimbo was some sort of Oscar Wilde or Tom What's'isname?"

Anne reminded him of the name of the Labour MP whose adventures, always mysteriously kept out of the newspapers, were a bit of a byword.

"I've met him once or twice with Vernon, who likes him a lot. You know my cousin Vernon, don't you?"

"Heard a lot about him," I said. "Never actually met him."

"You must get Anne to introduce you."

"Mummy's so silly about Vernon. Says he's a red."

"Is now, practically," said Sargie. "There's been a real lurch to the left since Gaitskell beat him to the Chancellorship. Inheriting his father's title and all that money didn't help either. If you're of leftish persuasion, the richer you become the redder you get. Don't know why it should be, but it's an infallible rule."

"Mummy says that Vernon's the only serious Lampitt left," said Anne. "A couple of generations ago they were all serious."

Old Joseph Lampitt, who made money brewing in the 1760s, had been a serious man; a philosopher by bent, Unitarian, republican, pro-American. He had come William Blake's way, and once promised to buy some engravings from Blake's *America*. His large progeny had risen in the intellectual and political world. The eldest son Jo had been a radical MP. Another son, a friend of the Godwins, had been a pioneer feminist. Most of that generation had married well. Thence had sprung that tribe of Lampitts who became professors of science and philosophy, social reformers, and pillars of the *bien-pensant* Victorian intellectual hierarchy, intermarried with Sidgwicks, Wedgwoods, Stracheys, Potters, Bensons and Darwins, as well as with landed money.

"Old Joseph"—always Sargie's way of referring to the founding father of this dynasty—"is mentioned in Gilchrist, you know."

"Gilchrist?"

"Don't you know Gilchrist's *Life of Blake*? Oh, you're missing out." I made a mental note to look for the book when next in a second-hand bookshop.

It was not the first time that I had admired Sargie's method of getting his own way. In the midst of an apparently incoherent ramble about his family, he had had a very clear objective. We were to be delegated ambassadors to Hunter. We were to find out if he was contemplating writing any more of his biography of James Petworth Lampitt; we were to broach with him the extremely embarrassing question of the diaries, and if possible, get them back into Sargie's possession.

"Thing is," said Sargie, "I think it would be better coming from someone of Lover Boy's kind of age. You could be so much more casual about it all. But you remember all that hullaballoo when the first volume appeared. We don't want that all over again—your mother having the Dalalie Taps."

We all agreed that almost anything was preferable to an emotional disturbance in the bosom of Lady Vulture.

"He seemed really cheered up by our visit," said Anne, squeezing me as we came out again into Bryanston Square.

"Yes."

"Well, that's a good thing, isn't it?" She shook my arm, sensing my reservations.

I said, "I just wonder what we've let ourselves in for, that's all."

four

The question of whether Hunter was making progress with the biography of James Petworth Lampitt was completely peripheral to my interests and concerns. Uppermost in my mind was the question of what I was going to do with life, or life with me. Would the novel ever be finished, and if finished, published? Would the theatrical ambitions, instead, take over? A thousand times more important than either question, would Anne and I be married? Only later would I come to see that the Hunter question was closely linked to all the others, a good example of how seldom life gives any clue as to what is or isn't going to be important.

Hunter had first come my way as an object of sexual jealousy, then as a sort of predator making havoc, chiefly among Anne's Lampitt relations, but also among my own. The passage of a number of years, while not obliterating these images of Hunter from my mind, has allowed me, in common with most television viewers and readers of the highbrow Sunday newspapers, to be aware of Hunter the public man. I remember a sermon of Uncle Roy's in which Saint Augustine was quoted, describing his own career as a rhetorician as "so much smoke and wind." Hunter, in terms of tangible achievement at this date, was exhaling prodigious evanescent signals that he was there: a regular reviewing slot in some Sunday paper, frequent appearances on television (though none so memorable as the attempted conversation with Day Muckley); as well as all the usual appurtenances of such literary celebrity—membership of committees, a judge of various prestigious literary prizes. Giving out such quantities of smoke and wind must have been a very satisfying substitute for the rigours of literary composition, and it was not surprising that Volume Two of *Petworth Lampitt* had so far not made its appearance in the bookshops.

I know that it was around this point that I bumped into Hunter; but here is a good instance of how unreliable a narrative account of things can be. There were at this stage so many things going on. Had I, for example, already been auditioned for a fortnight's rep in King's Lynn? I think I had. I assume the novel was done, or knocked into some sort of shape. Was I still working at the Bottle regularly, or had it become a more casual arrangement? I simply can't remember, and since my diary of the period was not a daily chronicle so much as a sporadic outburst of thoughts—sometimes about reading, sometimes about life in general—I have no clues about the more mundane but interesting questions which now haunt me.

I know that Anne and I had by now taken to visiting Sargie fairly regularly. The toe had long healed and he was cheerfully installed at home with a newish cat, a bad-tempered Siamese called Eden with the habit of running up the curtains if you tried to stroke it. Frequent exposure to Sargie's concerns prompted me, when quite by chance I met Hunter in St. James's Square, to bring up the subject of the Lampitt papers.

"Sargie was asking after you the other day," I said.

A grin passed over Hunter's face. It was a flirtatious parody of "sheepish." It seemed to say, "You and I know more than the rest of the world about what lies behind that remark; we both like each other so much that we regard it as rather a joke." The odd thing, which I am sure most readers of this narrative would find it hard to believe, is that I did actually quite like Hunter. In that conspiratorial moment in the square I liked him very much. I felt as though he were drawing me into a very friendly conspiracy.

"I'm sure it's the same for you," he remarked, and for a

moment the smile deserted his boyish face. "One takes on too much. Sargie is probably anxiously wondering what has happened to Volume Two."

"On the contrary, I think he was wondering what had happened to the Lampitt papers."

This looks rather a threatening remark when written down. I said it smilingly, however, in a manner which fitted Hunter's own, and as soon as the words were out of my mouth, we both laughed.

"I promised Madge"—his publisher—"that I'd submit last Christmas." (Raised eyebrows said, "Aren't I awful?") I quite understood what he meant by "submit"—that is, "submit a typescript of my next book." He was sufficiently confident of himself not to need to supply such nouns. It was taken for granted by all who crossed Hunter's path that he was uppermost in their minds—his books, his career, the meetings he had to attend. It was probably a condescending awareness of this which inspired his kindness to writers less successful than himself; it was perhaps analogous to Sargie's theory that the richer left-wing people become, the redder in politics.

"But what are *you* writing?" he asked.

I began the usual mock-modest remarks about my novel's defects.

"I suppose you wouldn't let me read it?" he said. "If it's . . ." He paused for a split second and I could see him finding a polite synonym for "no bloody good." "If it's Madge Cruden's kind of book—she's my publisher, you know Madge, I expect, and she's always only too glad to have good stuff pushed in her direction."

"That would be awfully . . ."

I had not shown my book to Bloom, who was the only publisher I knew. He told me not to, said that however much I thought I wouldn't mind if he rejected it, I *would* mind. Instinct presumably told him at a hundred yards that the book was no good. Hunter's offer seemed all the more welcome.

"Not a bit," he said. "Look, we ought to have lunch one day."

Before I had time to return to the question of the Lampitt

papers or to pay homage to Hunter's increasing skill as a tel-
evisionary, he was consulting his wristwatch.

"Good heavens! And I'm having lunch with the great man
before this afternoon's meeting of the London Library
Committee."

"Which great man?"

As so often when I have asked Hunter a straight question, he
smiled, as if one's only motive in asking must have been some
frivolous and unexplained desire to tease. The syllables "Tom
Eliot" were murmured. I have since wondered whether he did
not intend to write Eliot's biography. The knowledge that there
was an embargo on such an enterprise would no doubt act as
a stimulus to Hunter's pen.

I was not lunching with T. S. Eliot's double at the Black Bottle,
though it would have been neat if I had been. In fact I had
agreed to meet Anne and her mother at Simpson's in the Strand.
On arrival, I blurted out a version of my conversation with
Hunter, partly to explain my own lateness at the restaurant.

"He just wanted to get you off the subject of Jimbo's diaries,"
said Sibs.

She looked no older than when I had first met her a decade
or so earlier; the long Lampitt face, the hooded eyes and strong
bones in cheek and nose, all of which gave something comic to
Sargie's appearance, were in his sister elegant and beautiful. She
had lovely, soft, very pale skin and terrifyingly sharp eyes. I
never did know how my uncle had formed the unshakable
impression that Sibs was the downtrodden member of the Lampitt family. It is *just* possible that during her childhood at Timplingham Place when Mrs. Lampitt had much favoured the older
boys, had taken little interest in the longed-for daughter when
she had been born, that my uncle had heard of some scene in
which little Sybil had been made to know her place, as the
youngest member of a family of egoists. Conceivably, he had
even seen her, as a young woman, demonstrating her unques-
tioned domestic skills about the Place, perhaps by tidying up
after Sargie or another brother. To the end of his days, Uncle
Roy would refer to Sibs as "a complete doormat." It meant that

on the occasions when he met anyone else who knew Sibs there would be a moment of confusion, while the other speaker felt it necessary to protest that if a doormat were under discussion this could not possibly be *their* Lady Starling. My uncle, for whom all Lampitts existed more as imaginative projections than people he saw much of, would take no notice of such contradictions and usually repeat the metaphor, or add, "Extraordinarily nice woman, Sibs."

Spirited, strong-willed and—I have to confess it, though she was thirty years older than me and I was in love with her daughter—sexually attractive to me, was Sibs, nice, either ordinarily, or extraordinarily?

"Really, Julian, you are a twerp," she said when she heard all she wanted to hear of my Hunter story. "You really had your opportunity there. You should have made a specific date with Mr. Hunter to go to his flat and pick up Jimbo's diaries."

"I don't know where he lives. He's a bit of a mystery man."

"Instead of which you let yourself be flattered by his remarks about this story you've written."

"Poor Julian! Mummy, leave him alone!"

Anne's voice rose an octave when arguing with her mother.

"How could he have got hold of Jimbo's silly old diaries? Anyway, you have to admit that Mr. Hunter is a bit of a dish."

Sibs stared across the table at me. For some reason the moisture of someone's eyes is one of the first things I notice when I find them physically appealing. Sibs's eyes were large, turquoise, as bright with moisture as could have been without actually weeping.

"Don't be silly, darling," she said. "Ah, at last!"

She immediately transferred her commanding-officer manner to the waiter who had arrived with the meat trolley. At his side another young man in a tall white hat sharpened and brandished the carving irons.

The two young men, who smiled at Anne as a pretty girl and largely ignored me, danced attendance on Sibs. She enchanted them. The boy carving the meat in particular was affected by her. He put down his knife on the trolley and made a little bow to her, raising his chef's hat to reveal a Brylcreamed ted's coif. She did not in the least object to this little bit of obeisance.

"The veal is always good," she asserted.

"It's what I would have chosen for you myself, madam," said the carver, who had a pronounced squint.

When we all had meat set before us—I dithered about the possibility of choosing lamb, but Sibs flatly vetoed any such idea ("Much easier for this young man to give us all the same!")— she fell to reminiscing about Jimbo, and her other brothers, and life in Timplingham before they were all scattered.

"I am a survivor, really. Oh, those Timplingham Christmases when Mama was alive! You can't quite imagine what family life was like in those days, a whole table full of interesting grown-up people, and all one's brothers and lots of cousins. We just didn't need the world outside us. I think that was Jimbo's trouble in some ways, and Sargie's now. They have never got used to living without that large supportive, innocent society of which we were all members as of right, and for which there is no substitute in the world. Yes, you know, that's what's so wicked about Mr. Hunter's book. It doesn't matter that he gets all the social details wrong; you'd expect that from someone like that."

"Mummy!" protested egalitarian Anne.

"You know what I *mean*, darling."

"Yes, and I don't like it!"

"You're forgetting Anne's crush on Mr. Hunter, Sibs," I prompted.

Her mother lifted a forefinger towards her daughter.

"Don't you *dare*," she said with great fierceness. "Don't you *dare!* As I say, you would expect him to get everything wrong. Whenever I appear in the book, which mercifully isn't often, I'm called Lady Sybil Starling."

"Mummy, people don't mind about those things anymore."

"And he's so horrid about Mama, who wasn't a dragon a bit in the way he suggests. It is true that early on she very much wanted a daughter and Jimbo had to wear girls' clothes for a bit."

"Till he was ten," I said.

"I think many boys did in those days."

The squint-eyed one appeared again, offering us second help-ings, which we all accepted.

"But of all the men I ever knew, Jimbo was in some ways the most innocent. He was kind, too—and you don't get any of that in the Hunter book. He was *so* kind to us when we first got married. He lent us his flat in Manchester Square because our house was all haywire with decorators, and he really was a very good uncle to your brothers. I'm only sorry you were too young to know him well, darling."

"But I *can* remember him," said Anne. "I came to some of the readings."

"After early supper in our house, Jimbo would often read aloud to the children. *Great Expectations* and *David Copper-field*, we had both those, and *Huckleberry Finn* and *Vice Versa*."

"One of my favourite novels," I said. "Perhaps the truest novel ever written about what it is like to go away to school."

Sibs had no interest in what I thought of books. She continued with memories of Jimbo and her other brothers. It interested me as a purely academic issue that Hunter's *Petworth Lampitt*, which at the time I took to be a lifeless but authoritative version of the man's life, should bear so little resemblance to Jimbo Lampitt as he was actually remembered by his family. I saw this, I can't remember why, as an inevitability: that Sargie and Sibs could not bear to read "the truth" about Jimbo. The notion that their actual memories of a real man might be authentic, possibly more so than Hunter's written narrative, did not strike me as even worth considering, until that luncheon. As Sibs spoke I began to have a glimmering awareness that things might be otherwise. Part of the difficulty was that the Lampitts were, for me, already semi-fictionalised beings before they began to cross my path in person. As a child I had heard of little else. They were Uncle Roy's obsessive theme, creeping into his conversa-tion however unlikely the beginning of a sentence might appear. Did Aunt Deirdre's friend Bunty, on a rare visit, allude to the petunias in the front garden? Before his wife had a chance to reply, Uncle Roy would have interjected with the one about Ursula Lampitt and the geraniums in her window-boxes. ("I thought we were going to have another War of the Roses on our hands" was how she concluded her debate with the Fellows of Rawlinson upon the matter.)

The world itself was divided in Uncle Roy's consciousness not as atlases divide it, into political regions or physical areas of mountain, sea, plain or river. It was a Lampitt world, in which other creatures, trees, elephants, Atlantic breakers, Australian deserts, served as a mere backdrop to Lampitt anecdotes. Mention the Grand Canyon and you would (of course) get old Grandfather Lampitt's visit to the United States in the late 1880s, or Angelica's "famous" misadventures with those railways shares. Speak of kangaroos, and that would be but a short step to Melbourne, and in Melbourne, naturally, you think of Richard Lampitt's ill-fated attempt to set up business there and his no less ill-fated Australian marriage, not a "suitable" subject for mentioning in front of a child, had it not been for the fact that Richard's father-in-law was destined to become the governor of Queensland. Africa? Well, you have an *embarras de richesses*. Vivian's phlebitis in Mombasa, Jimbo's unlikely and hilarious visit to Kenya ("Which way round do you point a gun, Fanshawe?") or, for variety, what of Mary, who married that banker in Capetown?

As the saying goes, I had had them until they were coming out of my ears; and if I had said that to Uncle Roy, he would only have been prompted to remember that time Sargie thought he was going deaf in that hotel in Torquay and summoned the doctor to syringe his ears—not once, but three times.

That is why when Volume One was published I almost liked Hunter. The book itself came as a relief to me: at last, a vision of the Lampitts so different from that of Uncle Roy, that I assumed it must be true. This silly family (as I by then thought them) were at last going to get their comeuppance. I was not rational about it; I did not consider the fact, for example, that they had not *asked* Uncle Roy to develop this obsession, any more than they had asked Hunter to write his book. At last, I felt, the record could be set straight. My uncle's Lampitt-mania, born as I cruelly supposed from sycophantic snobbery and hardly relieved by his so often making the Lampitts the subject of unamusing "funny stories," was at last going to be counter-balanced by the irrefutable printed word.

It was only after the publication of Hunter's book that other lines of thought opened up. I had not begun to question the whole morality of biography, its intrusiveness, its know-all claims, its essential vulgarity. I was immediately conscious, however, that Hunter's biography had hurt people, not least Uncle Roy himself. In its peculiar way, it had led to the severance of the most important thing in his life, his friendship with Sargie. The thought that I might become involved with a member of Sargie's family, that Uncle Roy might himself become a Lampitt in-law was heady stuff, and I was not sure how to break it to him, not least because the overwhelming Sibs obviously rather liked my uncle and because Anne was so irrepressibly anxious to make his acquaintance. The first meeting did not occur until several months after that lunch at Simpson's. Anne and I met Darnley one Friday morning in London, and we all travelled eastwards together as far as Cambridge. I forget if it was his last term there, or whether he was just hanging about.

All my worries about what Darnley felt about me and Anne had been put on one side—not because I had received any re-assurances from him, but because I was drunk with happiness, so delirious in my love for Anne that other people had very largely ceased to exist as real beings for me. I certainly would not have considered placing their feelings above my own in importance. How I felt—how Anne felt or how I imagined she felt—that was all that mattered. We were intoxicated by an *égoïsme à deux*. It is hard to behave unselfishly in such circum-stances. I did notice that the larky side of Darnley's nature seemed quiescent, and that he was low in spirits by the time we reached Cambridge. Given the environment, this seemed all too understandable—the grey brick courts, the howling winds, the ill-shaven dons in tweeds pursuing their mad way by splay foot or punctured tricycle through mean narrow streets. Thus Cambridge to a London eye. We were there to borrow Darnley's car, the Morris he shared with his sister. He kept it concealed down a side street of the Huntingdon Road. Perhaps he had rooms there. I remember his strange smile as he waved and we jolted off towards Norfolk. For Anne insisted that we should go and see my uncle and aunt.

Probably more than a year had passed since I had been back to Timplingham, but in a way all homecomings there were the same, the same sense that it was and wasn't home, the same unworthy feeling, born I suppose from my inability to recover from the loss of my parents, that the rectory was a joke, a mockery of home. These things were buried deep—too deep for me to understand them as a young man. I was always puzzled by my reactions to Timplingham. Like a child I would look forward to seeing my uncle and aunt, but by the time I had arrived, often within a matter of minutes, uncontrollably negative feelings would surface. Both of them, but particularly Uncle Roy, had a power to enrage me unrivalled by anyone else I ever met. "More coffee?" Uncle Roy always said this just before he finished his own breakfast. I have sometimes thought that he was actually risking his life by saying these three syllables. What was annoying in that? Any reader who needs to ask that question has never belonged to a family. The "causes" of why the remark was excruciatingly, sometimes heartrendingly annoying, were quite unanalysable.

On this particular visit everything would be different because Anne would be there. I did not quite know how my family would react to this new development in my life. At first I assumed Uncle Roy would be pleased. Then I wondered whether he would not be vaguely peeved, on the grounds that the Lampitts were his department, not mine. Would my bringing Anne to Timplingham stir up sorrowful old memories of his quarrel with Sargie? And, a different consideration, would he bore Anne to death? I never sufficiently took account of what a charming man my uncle was. Because he had this secret, familial power to irritate me and embarrass me, which by no means meant that I did not love him, I was in a poor position to see him as others

saw him. When they said they found him charming and delight-
ful (which in so many ways he obviously was), I always thought
they were "just saying it" rather than meaning it.

The large Norfolk sky brooded ominously over our heads and
the great elms which bordered the road were in bud. Momentarily there was a gap in the trees and hedgerows, and across
flat fields and meadowland one would make out the flinty oc-
tagonal tower of the parish church.

"That's it," I said.

Anne, who was driving, drew up by the side of the road. She
leaned over and very delicately kissed me on the lips. She had
a look of her mother when she said, with good humour, but
firmness (the school matron who had just slapped iodine and
plaster on one's cut knee), "Don't worry! It will be all right."

I held her for a moment. Had we seen the thing through, as
the Prayer Book says one must, till death, we should doubtless
have known a whole range of physical feelings for each other.
Because our marriage was of such short duration, this was not
so. I always felt her to be almost painfully attractive. Her large
laughing turquoise eyes, her big mouth and her chest touching
mine had their usual effect.

"What?" she laughed. "Here? Now?"

"Why not?"

"What if someone came along?" In a rustic accent (certainly
not of Norfolk) which was quite bad enough to have got her a
part on "The Mulberrys," Anne said, "Oi were cyclin' paarst
Top Meadow moindin' me own business an' what should oi
spoi but paarson's nephew cavortin' wiv 'is laars in fiel' yonder."

But even in this comic voice the prospect which she summoned
up was irresistible. We were soon lying in the fresh spring grass
behind the hedge. One can't write about such things—or, I can't.
Yet how well I understand the desire of other writers to celebrate
such joys, and to explore their meaning.

Returning to normal consciousness after such an experience,
dressing again, and wandering back to the car, dazed and hand
in hand, we found that Timplingham was the same old place,
and yet never quite the same again.

"We're going to be late for lunch," Anne said.

"There's Uncle Roy now," I replied, as the Morris scrunched up the rectory drive.

He was wearing his green golfing trousers and a tweed Norfolk jacket to match, a high, rather soft white collar (I wonder if Pilbright would have approved?) and a floppy white bow tie. Our lateness was bound to have disrupted that clockwork-run household. I thought it possible that he had been sent out by Aunt Deirdre to see "what on earth has happened to them." If so, he was endeavouring to be nonchalant, inspecting the jasmine near the front door rather as if he were a stranger to the place and had never seen it before. He turned with an actorly display of surprise and delight when we opened the doors of the car.

"Well, well!"

"We're frightfully late!" This was Anne, plunging straight in as always.

"Not at *all*," insisted Uncle Roy. "Not in the slightest degree. Though you remember lateness."

We both paused, puzzled by this superficially surreal question.

"Martin and the meetings of the railway board! He was a *byword* for being late, so much so that the secretary always told him that meetings were before lunch, in the hope that he would turn up to take the chair by half past two!"

"Is that my great-uncle Martin?"

"Uncle, uncle. But you are too young to remember him. Charming man. You, if I may say so, have grown since we last met, but since you were only two at the time that is hardly surprising."

He began to reminisce about the time when she and Sibs had come to Timplingham Place—"the last time poor Sibs saw her mother alive, I am sorry to say."

"I hardly remember my Lampitt granny."

"A great lady," said Uncle Roy, "a great lady."

As he led the way into the house, I realised that, beyond one short, airy wave in my direction, he had barely greeted me. He was not going to waste a second of precious Lampitt-time with Anne.

"As a matter of fact, we nearly met some three years later before you started at that school."

"Greencoats?"

"No."

"Frances Holland?"

My uncle smiled indulgently.

"Before Greencoats they tried you at a place called St. Werbergh's."

"So they did—we wore lovely little straw hats. But fancy you knowing, or remembering."

I had warned Anne of my uncle's interest in her family, but even so, his grasp of detail surprised and impressed her.

"Your grandmother, who was an exceptionally wise person, did warn your dear mama. I remember it so well at the time."

He held back a chuckle.

Uncle Roy could have performed such feats of memory with any member of Anne's family who had happened to turn up at his front door. Where they had been to prep school, early trouble with their teeth, no detail of their early biography (assuming it to be repeatable) would have gone unrepeated.

He led the way through the hall and then called out—the stage laird calling to the stage parlour-maid—"They're here!"

"Well, bring them through" came my aunt's voice, and a merry "Hallo!" from Granny.

With a shrug and rather a disloyal little smile ("The wife!" was what it said) he pushed through the kitchen door. As he did so he was still trying to clear up what seemed from his tone to be urgent matters: the exact date when he had narrowly missed meeting Anne the second time during her childhood; and her grandmother's exact views of the apparently dud Knightsbridge school which Anne had attended for a term or two. My aunt's coming forward to greet us (a peck on the cheek for me, a handshake for Anne) and Granny's lazy old wave from her chair seemed to annoy Uncle Roy. They were irrelevant intrusions into the urgent settling of Lampitt business.

Aunt Deirdre was shy with new people and blushed crimson when Anne took her hand. Granny, who was already seated at the table, laughed as she said, "What on earth have you been up to? You're *very* late!"

"I said they would arrive any old time," said Aunt Deirdre briskly. "That's why I did a shepherd's pie, doesn't spoil, hope that's all right." She added, by way of explanation to Anne, "We go in for plain food, you'll find."

Certainly no other impression could be derived from the steaming Pyrex bowl, which she transferred almost immediately from the Aga to the cork table mat.

"Roy," Granny persisted tactlessly, "was like a cat on hot bricks before you came; running in and out of the kitchen and wondering where you'd got to."

"I did nothing of the kind," he said genially.

"We are very late, I'm afraid," said Anne. "Julian said you liked to eat at a quarter to one."

It was now ten to two.

"Your uncle Jimbo used to madden his mother, I remember, by saying that the proper time for luncheon was half past one. Said it ate into the day if he had it any earlier. 'Yes,' your grandmother used to say . . ." My uncle Roy slowed down, signal that a Lampitt *mot* was to be enunciated.

"Whose day, we know," snapped Aunt Deirdre, to get the anecdote over as soon as possible. She had begun to scoop spoonfuls of grey mince and mashed potato onto our plates. "Now, Anne, do start as soon as you get your food. Don't stand on ceremony."

"Whose day," my uncle repeated. You could not hurry these things, any more than you could hurry a good wine. His face was wreathed in delight at the prospect of old Mrs. Lampitt's sharp words.

It was all new to Anne, like most of the Lampitt-lore which he unfolded to her that weekend. To say that she was "good" with them would imply that she made some kind of effort, which I don't think she did. She liked them and they immediately liked her.

After lunch, we washed up, and my aunt showed Anne to her room upstairs. There was a choice between the spare bedroom, occupied about once a year by Bunty, or my cousin Felicity's bedroom, which was very slightly more comfortable and a few yards nearer the bathroom.

By the time Anne had unpacked a small hold-all onto Felicity's bed, my aunt had emerged on the landing in her "gardening rig": thus designated, but to all outward appearance identical to what she had been wearing in the morning: blouse and tweed costume. We followed her into the back kitchen, where she assumed a sacking apron, and rubber overshoes, and took down the trug from its hook on the wall. It contained thick gardening-gloves, secateurs, twine and other necessaries of her craft. We followed automatically as she left the back door. It was the only moment of the day, in my recollection, when she lost the look of disgruntlement which otherwise played over her features.

Uncle Roy had begun to age; not so his wife. She still seemed the slightly overweight Girl Guide, no hint of grey in her mousy cropped hair, no lines on her large pink face.

"There's an awful lot to do," she said, leading the way into the garden. "Particularly since poor Mr. Gillard had his stroke."

Having delivered this information in the no-nonsense tone of her ordinary speech, she then broke into a quite different voice.

"Trot-ter! Trot, trot, trot-ter!"

This aria was addressed to a bouncy little wirehaired dachshund, a replacement for Tinker, who, as a sad letter had told me some fifteen months earlier, had been called to his eternal reward. When I last visited them, my uncle and aunt were dog-less, for them an unnatural condition. Trotter had arrived in the meantime. My aunt never allowed such a playful, semi-flirtatious note into her voice when addressing a human being as when she said, "What are you *not* going to do today, Trotter? What are you? No, you're not going to chew canes. No, you're not. No." She suddenly switched to a serious human tone again. "If you could help with a bit of the digging I should be so grateful. As you can see, it's all a bit of a mess."

I never saw a garden more orderly. The mess was all inside

Aunt Deirdre's head. The lawn, which had already been mown twice that year, sloped away to a sea of daffodils and narcissi under the huge copper beech. A wall of brick and flint, part of the old medieval priory in Uncle Roy's opinion, provided the background for the big herbaceous border.

"Everything's a bit dull at the moment, you see. If you came in six weeks, things would be much more interesting . . ."

She walked along the border slowly, every now and then bending her knees and sitting on her haunches, either to remove a weed or to inspect the condition of a plant.

"I'm so fed up with universal pansies," she said; a remark I could have imagined on Bloom's lips in different circumstances. "That *camellia japonica* at the back there provides a nice touch of colour, doesn't it? Funnily enough, I thought it had died in January."

"What are these dear little purple ones?" asked Anne.

"D'you mean the primula? Oh, that! It *is* nice, isn't it? It's a saxifrage—*saxifraga oppositifolia*. Again I thought I'd lost that one in the frosts, but it's doing well. Oh! Will the weeds never stop coming up!" She took out a fistful.

"But the rhodos are good, aren't they," she said. With a sweeping gesture, she indicated the great expanses of colour on the other side of the lawn, trees from the brush of Samuel Palmer, full of mystic light. "I'm glad I cut them back so firmly last year," she said. "Mr. Gillard said I was being too ruthless, but I knew what I was up to."

And she did, she did. I have seen and delighted in many marvellous gardens, but none have given me so much pleasure as hers.

"It's the vegetables which are going to be the real worry. "If we can't get a replacement for Mr. Gillard—I'm not quite sure . . ." Her voice trailed off.

The flinty brick wall was not the end of the garden, but a division within it. The path encircled the border to a small door which opened onto the walled kitchen garden, a scene which made one expect to see Peter Rabbit or Mr. McGregor stooped over his cucumber frames.

"Potatoes have done very well, and I'm pleased with my spring greens; but look at this—a wilderness! I suppose if one does a bit each day."

There was absolutely no sign of a wilderness. Already she had peas, sweet peas and two sorts of bean planted out in neat rows with arches above them. Beyond, in net cages, the gooseberry and currant bushes, having recovered from the vigorous short back and sides to which my aunt had subjected them at the end of the previous year, were putting forth their shoots. It was only in the comparatively small area of the garden where my aunt intended to plant out cabbages, carrots and lettuces that the supposed wilderness existed, a few scrubs of sorrel and the occasional dandelion disturbing the even brown surface of the earth, which she had evidently raked and sieved for weeks.

"I want to dig some compost into it before I plant it," she said. And then, desperately trying not to look as if she was saying something important, and looking away from us both, she said, "No, I'm only sorry that Felicity couldn't have come back this weekend to meet Anne."

She said it too casually. It was the sentence she had been planning to say ever since we left the back kitchen. She stomped off to hoe another part of the garden, leaving us with our forks. She had twigged that Anne was now to be part of our family. She wished that her only daughter had been here to welcome her.

"I think we should *tell* them," said Anne, when we were left alone with our digging.

"Leave it to me, though." I didn't want one of her frank outbursts. Mine wasn't a family for a lot of frank talk or discussions of "relationships" around the kitchen table. When such conferences had been attempted they had ended in quarrels. I didn't want Anne's happiness marred by a quarrel, by Granny telling us we were being rash, for example, or Aunt Deirdre asking practical questions about how we supposed we could live. It was typical of the unjust way I couldn't trust any of them. It seems extraordinarily cruel, from this perspective of time, not to have kept them better informed. There was absolutely no reason to suppose that they would have been other than kind to Anne. But I allowed the whole weekend to pass, hoping that the right moment would emerge and never actually finding it. As a family we were not great talkers. Certainly we were not given to the sort of talk which occupies people in great novels or plays. Whether, or with whom, we are in love, what, if anything, we believed about God or politics—these were matters which were never for one moment discussed at the rectory. The jabber which filled our silences was anodyne. In Aunt Deirdre's case it was largely concerned with the village or the garden. Uncle Roy only abandoned his pet theme if some item of ecclesiastical life was preoccupying him.

"I don't at *all* like the look of South India," he remarked that evening at supper. "No proper bishops." His facial expression would have been more appropriate if he had just told us that Indian bishops dropped their aitches. My aunt, conspicuously more and more fed up with church as years passed, looked quite aggressively bored.

"I'm jolly grateful to you both, anyway," she said. "That kitchen garden's almost respectable at last."

We were eating slices of corned beef, unadorned boiled potatoes and some of her early spring greens.

"I feel so glowing and tired," said Anne.

I felt worse than this, positively knocked up. My hands and back were aching and my neck muscles felt as if they might seize up. I realised that I had not done any work, real work, or exerted myself physically, since Aunt Deirdre last asked me to "help" in the garden. Life in the Bottle, and other pubs, and a heavy increase in the number of cigarettes smoked each day, were beginning to make a difference.

Was Aunt Deirdre trying to help us out, Anne and me, with the revelation about ourselves which she must have guessed we wished to make? Again, she reverted to Felicity, who had by now, between my aunt, Anne and myself, become a sort of code word for "Anne is about to become a member of the family and it is a pity that Felicity can't be here."

"Fliss is kept pretty busy," said Aunt Deirdre.

Uncle Roy repeated the name of Felicity's college at Oxford, in case Anne had been slow to recognise the significance of the word.

Granny who was moving into a phase of life where all manifestations of human behaviour were amusing, guffawed at the idea of Felicity being "busy."

"I asked her the last time she was home what philosophy *is*," she declared. "It isn't what I thought at all. I'd always thought it was your ideas about life, how to be—you know, a better sort of person."

She ate her corned beef hungrily; we all did.

"It's some years since I saw Ursula," said Roy, by now puzzled that Anne had failed to pick up his drift. Surely anyone hearing that Felicity taught at Rawlinson College, Oxford, would immediately think of the principal, Dame Ursula Lampitt?

"Mind you," said Granny, "it's all money, isn't it? Fliss gets paid for giving these what-d'you-call-'ems."

"Tutorials," snapped my aunt, who was clearly angered by her mother-in-law's implied contempt for the way Felicity spent her days. "She's very clever."

"Oh, we all know that."

"Only sometimes people don't always give her credit for it," said Aunt Deirdre, going very red. "Poor old Fliss."

I wondered if, like so many people in jokes and films, Aunt Deirdre hated her mother-in-law. Because I had always loved Granny it had never crossed my mind that anyone could find her any other than lovable. Now I could see that she was being almost deliberately provoking. On the other hand I could see the point of her deliberate unseriousness, whether or not it was valid. One couldn't imagine her common-sense friend Mrs. Webb having much time for such questions as the problems of knowledge.

"Dame Ursula—Felicity's principal," said my uncle heavily, giving Anne one last chance to knock the ball back over the net. She did just manage it, though it was hardly an impressive volley.

"Do you mean Dr. Lampitt? She's some sort of relation of mine."

"Second cousin once removed," said my uncle briskly. This established, he could proceed with his fund of Ursula talk at the leisurely pace it deserved. "I went back to Oxford some years ago for a college gaudy. The place is much changed, I'm afraid, since the war. I called in on Ursula for tea one afternoon. You will know her well enough to realise that this is a typical Ursula story."

Surrendering Anne to my uncle, the rest of us talked among ourselves until the punchline of this particular saga was accomplished.

"What about you, anyway?" said Granny, who had finished meditating on the strange fact that people *paid* Felicity for having her "weird ideas." "Been writing stories? And acting?" For some reason this was supposed to be funny; anyway, she laughed.

"It really looks as if the novel has been accepted," I said. The only reason for my sheepishness in that company was that the book was all about them. Nor could I talk about it much without revealing how extremely kind Hunter had been, more or less acting as unpaid literary agent, pushing the book Madge Cruden's way, securing a promise from her that she would at least send the typescript to one of their better readers, and, when the report was not wholly unfavourable, chivvying the firm to accept it. None of this could be told because Hunter was an unmentionable name at the rectory, since his love affair with Felicity.

I was prepared to let bygones be bygones. Hunter was becoming my enabler, an almost priestly figure in my life, if not a guardian angel, effecting my transition from one stage of existence to the next, from layabout and barman to someone whose existence could plausibly be defined as an artist, a writer. Bloom had begun the transition by getting me installed at Rikko and Fenella's. Hunter was to complete it. But I knew there was something disloyal in being so willing to entrust my destiny to Jimbo's detractor, Felicity's seducer.

My aunt said, as though putting Granny down, "If that's what Julian really wants to *do*. Different people are different."

Then with a girlish blush, she added, "And to think you really know Stan Mulberry. Is the actor at all like the real thing?"

This was how Aunt Deirdre phrased the question.

Stan Mulberry, a flimsy creation of radio drama, was, as far as she was concerned, far more real than Rikko Kempe. How far did Rikko measure up to the reality of Stan Mulberry? It was difficult to answer. Not the least of my difficulties was to know how far it was possible to tell the truth about Rikko (his hair, his mannerisms) without being malicious.

"I think he got the part because he's good at accents," I said.

"I'd assumed the *ee bah gum* was natural," she said, with some disappointment. "But I love Stan. He's such a decent sort. Take the way he helped out old Mrs. Humberbach with those hospital visits to her mother. That was Stan all over, even though it was in the middle of lambing."

There was something completely innocent about my aunt's fondness for "The Mulberrys," innocent about the programme itself, come to that. I felt rather sorry for her when Granny scoffingly remarked, "It's all rubbish." Then, after a pause, she said to me, "You should think of getting a part in it yourself one of these days."

"I think it would spoil it, hearing Julian pretending to be someone at Barleybrook," said my aunt.

"It's a good idea," said Anne. She would have seen nothing insulting in my grandmother's observation. She had none of my capacity for nosing out offence; and she was pathetically ready to believe in my talents. "Now he's got this agent, I'm sure parts will come along."

It was true that I had been taken on by an agent and that several small parts sounded as if they might be in the offing. The trouble was, I had begun to doubt whether I was cut out to be an actor. My sense that life's possibilities were infinite was receding. I no longer thought that I could act Hamlet, paint as well as Cézanne and write a literary masterpiece.

Granny, like Sibs, was scornful of the artistic ambitions because they did not seem very likely to make me much money. As I sat at the table wiping shreds of corned beef from my plate with a slice of bread, I felt rising within me some of the irrational furies of adolescence. The anger, doubtless, was partly prompted by guilt. I simply would not allow myself to see why Granny felt so strongly about my having left Tempest and Holmes. Her eldest son had worked there from the age of twenty until he joined the RAF. Had he lived, he would probably have returned, and would still be making his daily and dutiful way to the Accounts Department. Why not? Wasn't this the way in which most people earned their living? What was so special about me? In rejecting Tempest and Holmes, I was rejecting Daddy; but at the same time I was too insensitive to see that it was this which hurt and angered Granny. Tempest and Holmes were hallowed names for her. I wonder if she had so much as seen the place. For me, the shirt factory had no glamour at all. When I heard its name, I thought not of Daddy, whom I had never seen there, but of the tedium of my own routines. I heard again the clatter of the typewriters in the office pool, or saw again the huge workshops at the back where rows of women impassively supervised the passage of the shirts, in various stages of composition, into the sewing machines. I conceded that men wore shirts, so someone had to make them and sell them, and presumably some poor person in the middle had to enter the details of the transactions between the factory and the retailer into the company accounts. I wasn't proposing a shirtless universe, merely one where my contact with shirts was limited to buttoning and unbuttoning the things on my chest twice a day, and making sure that they were periodically washed and ironed. Let others do the rest.

"That Mr. Pilbright who worked with your father was such a nice man," said Granny. She turned to her daughter-in-law. "I remember him at David's funeral . . ."

She always said "David's funeral," though I believe that my parents had a joint service.

I could tell that Aunt Deirdre wanted to get the conversation back to "The Mulberrys." Uncle Roy, who found any mention of his brother's death excruciating, had taken a sudden interest in Trotter's bodily function.

"Yes, yes," he said to the little dog, who scurried about the stone floor of the kitchen much as Tinker had done in the old days, "after supper, I'll take you on a walk after supper."

"Mr. Pilbright, who worked with him, was so kind. I remember Mrs. Webb saying, 'Now, Thora, I call that a really kind gentleman.' You know, he said, 'If there's *anything* we can do' . . . and unlike some people, he really meant it. And he's always sent a card. Every Christmas since . . ."

"Just as soon as we've done the washing up," said Uncle Roy.

"Well," said Aunt Deirdre crossly, "if it wasn't Julian's line." The strain of life with her mother-in-law had led to a transformation in my aunt's views since I was last home; she was now a defender of my way of life for as long as Granny disapproved of it.

Only Anne gave Granny her complete sympathy and attention. The rest of us had heard Granny's views of Mr. Pilbright a thousand times. For Anne it was all new; and, with each unfolding detail, Mrs. Webb's remarks at my parents' funeral, Mr. Pilbright's formulaic offers of help on Christmas cards, the punctiliousness with which he always sent out these cherished objects "nice and early," Anne's large and infinitely kind eyes became more and more liquid. By the time Granny was saying, "Well, naturally I thought it would be nice if Julian followed in his father's footsteps," large tears were rolling in profusion down Anne's face. This, in Aunt Deirdre's book, would be another black mark against her mother-in-law; my aunt deplored displays of emotion, and no doubt thought that Granny was getting Anne "worked up," something she was often accused of doing to me as a child.

"It's like what Mrs. Webb often said when we were out in the country together, looking for, you know, a nice place to have a bit of lunch. 'Thora,' she'd say, 'we could go further and fare worse.' Well, it may be that Tempest and Holmes aren't exciting, but I think Julian could have gone further and fared worse."

Throughout this speech Granny, without stirring from her chair, was turning this way and that, forcing her body to make gyrations of nearly one hundred and eighty degrees. I knew the action well: it meant she was searching for cigarettes and matches. The more they eluded her gaze, the more she turned her head and shoulders. Anne, as much an addict of nicotine as my grandmother, offered her a Woodbine.

"Aren't they workmen's cigarettes?"

"Are they? I don't know."

"They'll be much stronger than my Craven A."

"I don't think so."

They lit up.

"Oh, you're a funny lot," said Granny, blowing her smoke in two very straight lines from her nostrils.

It was true. I knew that she had appreciated with embarrassing clarity, and without anything needing to be said, that my reasons for not continuing my work at Tempest and Holmes were almost purely snobbish. Without my wishing to do so, I had become the creature of Aunt Deirdre and Uncle Roy. There sat Uncle Roy, in his tweed knickerbockers, about to start another hour or two of Lampitt-talk. His fantasies were different from my own, but they were contrived with equal certainty of success to remove him from the taints of suburbia.

I lay awake most of the night. Partly, we had all gone to bed too early. I listened to the sounds of the house, so very familiar to me from early boyhood, the wind in the elm trees down the lane, soughing and rustling. The wind in the chimney, making a sibilant murmur to itself, reminiscent of that *sotto voce* musical accompaniment supplied at no extra charge by Mr. Sykes, the village barber, while he cut one's hair. And there were the sounds of the house itself. Quite of their own accord, floor boards would creak, though no visible step trod upon them. Water pipes gurgled and groaned. Through all the hours of darkness there were very few moments of silence. Lying there in the blackness I didn't like myself much. I was beginning to see how harmless and amiable my family were; yet I still reacted inwardly to them as if they were fiends.

All Granny's talk about my career was upsetting. I was actually despondent about getting anywhere with the writing. The black shadows of night brought only regret for the past, uncertainty about the future. I was totally sleepless, but my waking was unlike the waking condition of daylight when one moves, and is upright. Lying in inky dark, unable to see more than hints of shadow within shade on the ceiling, caused by the flapping of the curtains against faint moonlight outside the windows. I could have been anywhere. But the whole feel of the place was entirely unmistakable. Though I was able to see almost nothing, I would have had no doubts about where I was, even if someone had taken me there blindfold and put me to bed without telling me my whereabouts. It was not only the unmistakable sounds of the house; the whole feel of the place was tangible. I think it was the fact that I lay there seeing nothing, but feeling so much—a curious sensation—which lifted me from the present and carried me with such ease into earlier phases of being. In this very bed I had screamed and cried for Mummy to come and sit with me, night after night before I lost consciousness. I remembered it so clearly that it was almost as if she had returned that night, a silhouetted figure, stroking my forehead and singing "Golden Slumbers." These painful recollections passed into a time of darkness, of unknown duration, in which the mind went blank. Then, involuntarily, another phase of life would return, summer nights during adolescence, tormented by sexual frustration, or angry occasions when I had run to be alone in this room during some dreadful row in which things had been said, usually by me, sometimes by my cousin Felicity, which would have been better left unsaid. And then again, these images were supplanted by other periods of darkness, perhaps the most satisfying periods of the mind's life, when one is conscious of being awake but not thinking of anything at all. Then, the mind feels cleansed, emptied.

It was not long, however, before the emptiness filled with another image. Things returned to me that night which I had wholly forgotten. I remembered that at one period, perhaps when I was about fifteen, I was perfectly happy as Uncle Roy's companion. In all my conscious spoken memories of my uncle, there were tensions and difficulties. I found him embarrassing or boring or uncomfortable. Not here. As if somebody were showing me an old film of myself, I was conscious of a phase (I suppose it was only one four-week holiday from boarding school) when I positively rejoiced in Uncle Roy's company. I felt myself (a condition of mind wholly forgotten) exquisitely amused by Lampitt-tales. I felt no awkwardness about religion either, so it must have been when I was still quite young. This memory shocked and pained me more than any of the others because until that moment it had passed out of mind; and yet it should have been an important memory to which I had often returned. Relations with Uncle Roy had once been harmonious; the frictions and distances which had since grown up felt in that dark moment as if they had all been of my own cruel making. I felt that I had been offered love by my uncle and spurned it either for no reason, or for reasons which were unworthy.

This chilling thought made me need Anne all the more. I hated being alone in bed. Anne and I were at a stage where it seemed natural not merely to touch and hold each other but to be entwined in each other's arms all the time. In the company of others, we kept our distance from each other; one did not want to be silly in front of Aunt Deirdre. But when we were alone together we flew into each other's arms.

I rose and walked out into the blackness towards my cousin Felicity's room. The creaking noise on the landing when I trod on a loose board must have been loud enough to wake the household; but there were innocent reasons why I might have been pacing the landing in the small hours, and I had no fear. Instinct led me to Felicity's room. I did not even have to fumble for the handle. Then, when I did so, the oddest sensation came over me, lasting no more than a split second, but memorable thereafter. For that tiny fraction of time, I imagined that it was Felicity that I was going to visit, and found the prospect intensely exciting. Felicity and I, who had grown up together, had had our ups and downs. It cannot have been easy for her, an only child, to accept my arrival on the scene, as a permanency, when she was about ten or twelve. Never for a minute in all the time we lived together had I lusted after her or even thought of her in sexual terms. Now was different. The split second passed. I remembered that it was Anne and not Felicity to whom I ardently wished to make love. I turned the handle of the door.

Every movement which Anne and I made during the next half hour produced such creaking of the headboard, such *boing-boing* of bedsprings that we might as well have called out to Aunt Deirdre and told her what had happened. Afterwards we drew back the curtains, and the moon, which had climbed higher in the sky and grown brighter, shed enough light for me to be able to see Anne's pale thin shoulders in front of me. I stood with my chin on one of her shoulders, and put my arm around her breasts.

"I think you must tell them," she whispered.

"I will, tomorrow."

She giggled quietly.

"It is tomorrow. It was tomorrow ages ago."

"Anne."

"What?"

"I thought I was going to be one of those people who was never happy—I thought I'd never know what happiness was. I thought . . ."

"There's no need to say it." She kissed and then stroked my hand which lay across her breast.

"I know," I said. "There's no need to say anything."

In those strange moments of silence we watched the clouds racing across the sky. We stayed there until the last hour of night when there was a hint of sunlight dawning.

"But we must tell them," she repeated.

I knew that what she said was true, but Speaking Out had never been something we much went in for in our family, and Sunday was not the best of days for it. Uncle Roy and Aunt Deirdre both went to church at eight A.M. and returned to the rectory to cook Granny's breakfast. It never even occurred to me to attend church later in the morning, though afterwards Anne said that we should have. Instead, at the time of the sung service, we stayed in the kitchen and watched Aunt Deirdre prepare the treat luncheon in Anne's honour, boiled fowl. Aunt

Deirdre obviously welcomed company, but she did not want us to talk. The wireless was tuned in to the hour-long extended version of "The Mulberrys," to which she could listen without the irritating presence of her husband or the scornful commentary of her mother-in-law.

It was strange to hear Rikko Kempe's voice, transmogrified into that of Stan Mulberry, talking of the milk yield and the fecundity of sows; not normally Rikko's kind of thing. Odder still was the look on Aunt Deirdre's face, while Rikko was reading his lines. In all practical respects, for all it mattered, she believed completely in "Stan Mulberry." During an altercation with a recalcitrant farm labourer, she entirely took "Stan's" side.

"Oi caarn't shift all them bales on me own, Maaarser Stan."

"I wasn't asking you to shift them on your own," said Rikko, who managed to suggest, with his understated Herefordshire burr, a deep dependability and common sense.

" 'Course he wasn't," said my aunt, crossly holding a potato under the cold tap.

"Only with moi baark, Maaarser Stan . . ."

"Get off with your bother," said my aunt. "Your back's as healthy as mine."

"I'm sorry, Jos, but those bales have got to be shifted," said Rikko, with none of the agitation which came over his voice during real disputes.

"Good old Stan," murmured my aunt. "Don't let Jos get away with it, he's been playing on your better nature for too long."

And so on, for an hour.

By the time "The Mulberrys" theme tune had announced the conclusion of that week's visit to Barleybrook, my uncle and his mother were returning from church. It was a new thing, churchgoing, in Granny's life. I never recall her having gone to church in London during the lifetime of Mrs. Webb.

"Funny psalm," she remarked firmly, lighting her Craven A as soon as she had taken her accustomed place in the armchair by the kitchen range. "*I am become like a bottle in the smoke.* Whatever would that mean?"

My uncle, still in his cassock, was untroubled by the enquiry. "Old Mrs. Lampitt, bless her, was full of such difficulties. She was not a churchwoman, as you know."

"Never darkened the doors of the church," said Aunt Deirdre.

"Church is not the Lampitt thing. She did *occasionally* come—to Harvest Festival, for example. But I can remember her saying"—he nearly guffawed—" 'Roy, I'm not like a pelican in the wilderness, why should I say that I am one?' Typical!"

The skin round his eyes creased up as he laughed affectionately.

"You were cross at the time," said my aunt.

"And you haven't answered my question," said Granny. " 'I am become like a bottle in the smoke.' "

"It means you're browned off," said my aunt quickly. No doubt she wished to cut short any further reminiscences about the Lampitts, but I also strongly sensed that the Psalter was not to her taste. Its extravagant expressions of despair, elation, moral triumphalism, abject guilt, unspecified depression, spiritual ecstasy were not at all in Aunt Deirdre's mode. By all means get browned off, her tone implied, but why on earth go on about it?

"It wouldn't have been a glass bottle," added my uncle, at last stirring himself to respond to his mother's exegetical enquiry. "You've got to think of yourself shrivelling up like an old leather pouch too near the fire."

Granny laughed so much at this that she nearly choked on her cigarette.

"Thank you, I'm sure."

Her facial expression reminded me of the day when she and Mrs. Webb had taken me and Darnley out from school. Scarcely a dozen years had passed since that day, and yet, here I was with Anne. . . .

As we drove away down the old road out of the village in Darnley's car, Anne said, "You are a fool. That was the whole point of our visit, to tell them."

"You could have told them."

"Julian, they're *your* family."

"You don't think they sort of guessed?"

"Wouldn't they have said anything?" she asked.

"Not necessarily."

"Mummy will certainly have something to say when she sort of guesses."

This alarming prospect was all too believable.

But it was interesting that even Anne, who in most company was naively outspoken, had been reduced to diffidence by the rectory.

"I'll write them a letter," I said.

"They'll be hurt you didn't tell them in person. Particularly your grandmother."

"Oh, God, I *know*."

They were hurt, too. And it hurts to remember. At this distance of time I just can't remember why I found it so difficult to tell them that the day before our visit to the rectory, with Darnley and his sister as the only witnesses, Anne and I had been married at the Chelsea registry office.

five

"Joys impregnate," as the great man said; "sorrows bring forth." The next year was one of impregnation, and is a blur in my memory. I can't even remember the order in which things happened. It was a time of transition in my working life, but I no longer know which event preceded another. None of it matters much, or so it seems to me. Since reading Gilchrist (on Sargie's advice) I have always followed Blake's view that "the inner world is all-important; that each man has a world within, greater than the external."

The history of this world within, which I now shared with Anne, is distorted by too great Clarity. The outer things, I can hardly recall: the bar work at the Bottle, the novel being accepted by Madge Cruden, amateur theatre work leading to a couple of tiny bits of work. But the story of me and Anne, though now it only returns to me in the occasional vividly recalled episode, was life changing.

It was a year of blessedness.

Sometimes, when I was working behind the bar at the Bottle, Day Muckley would lean forward and say, "Don't let it spoil you, lad, don't let it spoil you." I now see that I must have been glowingly, transparently happy. There was tremendous wisdom in Day's advice.

"What do you know about happiness, toad's pus?" Cyril had genially enquired.

"I don't, I don't . . ." He drank from his beer glass and faltered.

"None of us is fucking happy or we wouldn't be drinking in your shit-hole of a pub," said Peter, addressing the remark to his favourite landlord but speaking into his gin-and-lime, like a priest speaking over the chalice at Mass.

As far as I was concerned, there were no lessons to be learned from the fact that everyone hanging about the place had made a mess of life, or alternatively, like Cyril or Fenella, had been born into the world as comic turns, "characters," whom I could enjoy like puppets in a show. I did not see the pathos of being a "character," of having a life no part of which anyone was prepared to take seriously. All I knew was that my life was to be different. I took its present blessedness completely for granted. I had been, on and off, abjectly miserable ever since Mummy died. Now I was acquainted with joy, and I did know the difference. There was so little excuse for throwing it all away.

Loving Anne transfigured existence, it changed everything. I found that all bodily sensations were quickened by loving her. Memory distorts, but I was so surprised and fascinated by this phenomenon that I jotted down very rough diary notes at the time. My eyesight, for example, became more acute than it was before. I don't mean that I was able to read farther down the optician's test card than in the days before I met Anne. But my appreciation of the way things looked was so profoundly enhanced that I felt in many respects that I had only begun to "see" since knowing her. Colours were perceptibly brighter. Sometimes when I left her in the morning and cycled into Soho, I would find myself dismounting and staring with wonder at quite "ordinary" sights, a tree, a bird on a window ledge, sunlight on a building which I had seen a thousand times but suddenly saw for the first time. It is hard to put what I experienced into words which do not sound as though I were experiencing some hallucinatory "high" of the kind which others have achieved through drugs. I certainly was not conscious of these experiences as metaphysical phenomena. They were deeply natural. I was not seeing a bird or a tree transformed into something else, but I was seeing trees and birds as if for the first time, and seeing "through" the eye, seeing into the life of things, so that the act of vision became a Vision, and a morning bike-ride an occasion for alleluias.

Unquestionably, all this was bound up with the energy and passion of my love for Anne. I have written that I left her each morning (and sometimes, even if the parting was only for a few hours, it would be almost intolerable); but it would be truer to say that we were never parted. When we were not together physically, we went on being together in an almost literal way. Not only did I carry about a powerful physical sense of her—we smelt of each other—but underlying all my thoughts and actions throughout a day apart from her, she was *there*. She had come to inhabit my mind as well as my body. We often, during our delighted evening reunions, would find that we had been in touch telepathically, thinking the same thoughts during our hours of separation.

That makes it sound solemn. At the time, it was all high spirits, laughter. Never for a moment did we seem "serious." Looking back from my present perspective, I now think that this was in fact the first truly serious, non-trivial thing which had ever happened to me. And it is this which makes it so hard for me to acknowledge that I did, in Day Muckley's phrase, "let it spoil me."

I think I must have assumed that this was just what it was like the first time you fell in love with someone "properly." I'm sure that's what I felt. Maybe I'm being too hard on myself, but I think I behaved as though these wholly unlooked-for sensations of well-being were my due. They were the reward for being young. I was aware that the world was now a different place. My love was quickened, not just for the world of nature, but for animals and people. Language, even William Blake's, is soppy when it tries to describe the unsoppy way in which love sees all creatures as lovable, all creatures and all people.

William Blake certainly played a part in my love story. Not

only had Gilchrist's life of the poet been recommended to me by Anne's uncle—and I had carried it frequently in my pocket during our courtship; I actually seemed, with Anne, to be experiencing many of the things which Blake wrote about:

> And we are put on earth a little space,
> That we may learn to bear the beams of love.

It was certainly reading Gilchrist, and Blake himself, which made me aware that one way of describing the universe is not inherently more rational than any other. What enables us to see the truth is the exercise of the Imagination, and not submission to some supposedly dispassionate or "scientific" version of things. Imagination in this context I take to be the same as love. Uncle Roy's version of the Lampitt story is infinitely richer, and probably truer, than Hunter's.

Hunter, who became a friend of mine at this date, once pointed out that Gilchrist's *Blake* stood in the greatest possible contrast to one of James Petworth Lampitt's mannered little biographies. It was different, too, I could have added (but didn't) from Hunter's own godlike poses in his biographical work, and his apparent belief that, having accumulated a lot of spurious "material," he had "understood." As a work of art, Gilchrist's book is nonexistent. It was not even completed by Gilchrist, but cobbled together by friends after he had died. The central figure, Blake himself, is always more important than the author. If James Petworth Lampitt had been writing the book, how sniggeringly anxious he would have been to cut Blake down to size. How easy it would have been to make a guy out of the son of a small shopkeeper who believed himself to be having regular visits from Julius Caesar or the Archangel Gabriel.

Doubtless, too, there was something inherently ludicrous, viewed from a worldly angle, in Blake's inability to make a success of things, to choose worthy patrons or tap the supplies of cash which are always available to artists who know how to compromise themselves. Hunter would certainly have despised that side of Blake's life. He would manage to popularise Mr.

Pilbright through the medium of television. Blake, however ardently he had desired that the world would take seriously his sublime engravings, poems and paintings, could not really have done himself justice on that essentially two-dimensional medium. Though he was abstemious, his attempt to sell himself on TV would have been as unsuccessful as Day Muckley's. Hunter, if he had taken Blake on as a subject of biography, would have wanted to establish at the outset that Blake couldn't draw (untrue) or that his prophecies were gibberish. Hunter would then have devoted three or four times Gilchrist's three hundred pages to a dissection of Blake's psychosexual nature. Was there not something odd about a man who could sit naked with his wife in their arbour, imagining themselves in the Garden of Paradise, but being unable to produce babies? What happened—or, if Hunter were asking the question on television, *just* what happened—between the Blakes in bed?

The fact that no one knows, no one could know, would not prevent Hunter from the dark suggestion that *he* knew. To sell the book, there would be a "new line" or what publishers sometimes call a "new angle." If no new "material" was forthcoming (and it almost certainly would not be there to be discovered), this would not prevent Hunter hinting at sensational discoveries. Copious extracts from Boswell's *London Journal* or the *Memoirs of Casanova* would provide a readable gloss on Blake's ability to hear "the harlot's cry from street to street." Or lengthy disquisitions from some psychologist would persuade Hunter, and his readers, of an indissoluble connection between visionary experiences and precocious exercises in masturbation.

And yet neither of these approaches, neither the neat Petworth Lampitt satire nor the ponderous know-all manner of Hunter, would have allowed Blake, as Gilchrist does, simply to be himself. There he was, in his black hat, simple breeches and stockings, short of stature, bright of eye, presumably cocknified of voice. Though he had been dead for a century before my time, when I became addicted to the book, Blake was as real to me as any of the other Soho characters who came to prop up the bar of the Bottle. I would come out into Poland Street and think of his five years' residence there, and of the wonderful things which he had produced while living in mean lodgings with his wife, a mere stone's throw from the spot where Cyril and I now dispensed their medicine to the Best Seller, Mr. Porn, Pete and the rest. "The now dingy demi-rep street," Gilchrist informs us, "one in which Shelley lodged in 1811 after his expulsion from Oxford, had witnessed the production of the *Songs of Innocence* and other poetry and design of a genius unknown before or since to that permanently foggy district." In addition to his incomparable lyrics, Blake had also produced some of his "Prophecies" here, and the "Proverbs of Hell," not irrelevant to my clients as they became hourly more imprisoned in the caricatures of themselves which drink had made.

Day Muckley had asked me where I had been.

"Where's he been?" Cyril answered for me. "Southend-on-Turd."

This was true: a fortnight in an execrable comedy during which Anne and I had lived as the guests of a seaside landlady.

"I once took a woman to Southend," said Peter.

"The thing about the English seaside is this," said Day Muckley, dewy-eyed with a whisky chaser. "It is fun, but it is fundamentally innocent, for Christ's sake."

"This one wasn't innocent. Next time I saw her, I said, 'It's just as well I'm not allergic to penicillin.' No subtlety, that cow, she didn't understand me. But she must have known what she'd given me."

Day Muckley was not interested in these consulting-room details. His monologue had half-congealed into one of those occasional *causeries* which he wrote for the *Yorkshire Post*.

"I still maintain, and never mind 'what the butler saw,' what I still say is never mind a bit of sauce. If it's still inno—it's still what I say."

"I've got a customer in Southend," said Mr. Porn. "A plain brown parcel goes off to him once a month. Anything with a bit of anal torture and he's happy."

"Really," said Bloom. "This pub gets more and more disreputable, with soliciting tarts in the saloon, and probably tarty solicitors in the Loo-loo Bar, one doesn't know where to turn."

"If forced to a decision, surely you wouldn't find it difficult," I said. "Besides, that isn't a tart, soliciting or otherwise. It's Fenella. She's just had her hair done, that's all."

The road of excess leads to the palace of wisdom.

I rather doubt whether William Blake would have got on with some of my friends in the Black Bottle. But certainly his proverbs were much in my mind during that first year of my marriage. *The lust of the goat is the bounty of God. . . . The nakedness of woman is the work of God. . . . The tygers of wrath are wiser than the horses of instruction. . . . Enough! or too much!*

Anne and I initially lived in two rented rooms a good way down the King's Road, more or less at Parson's Green. We were so far from what my mother-in-law regarded as the "centre of things" (i.e., Peter Jones in Sloane Square) that we were within perilously close hailing distance of Tempest and Holmes. Once I actually caught sight of Pilbright from the top of a bus going down the Fulham Road.

Anne was incapable of the subterfuge which was second nature to me, with my upbringing in the rectory, where everything was kept secret, from one another and from the village. As soon as she saw her mother again—it was about a week after our marriage—she told her the truth.

There was the predictable explosion, and the next time we saw her father he said in his tight-lipped manner, "Nothing wrong with your being married. There are ways and ways, that's all."

"Unpleasantness" of any kind was to be avoided at all costs as far as Sir Rupert Starling was concerned. Given this fact, there was something paradoxical in his having chosen (if that was what he had done) to marry Sibs. Perhaps marriage had changed them, made her more aggressive, and him more determined to be a high-ranking civil servant, both in and out of office hours. Thus, while wishing to avoid any sort of altercation about Anne's marriage to myself, he saw no harm in pointing out where procedural solecisms had been perpetrated. Two of his children, sons, had followed conventional paths and turned, by Sir Rupert's standards, into satisfyingly dull dogs. Anne, much the youngest child, interested in art, visibly a throwback to her Lampitt forebears, was acknowledged by her father to be something different. Fair enough, his manner implied; just so long as we all knew where we stood. The registry office wedding with no guests was in order. One felt that almost any form of nuptial ceremony would have been acceptable—a naked wood dance conducted by witches during the summer solstice—so long as Sir Rupert were not obliged to take part, and so long as he had been duly minuted and kept informed.

All he actually said when he heard that we were married was "Oh."

Some months later, Anne and I crept nearer the centre of civilisation as a result of her father increasing her allowance. We could afford three rooms in Lamont Road, several bus stops nearer the Starling family in Cadogan Square.

Sir Rupert was a tall, balding, red-faced man in his mid- to late fifties when Anne and I got married. Although his face was round and shiny, and seemed like the face of a fat man, the rest of his body was elongated and thin. His rather well-made dark suits hung from bony shoulders to bony ankles as though draped from wire coat hangers rather than worn. He always looked down when he spoke, unwilling to set eyes on his company. When I was in the room, this was understandable enough. He must have hated my guts. In so far as I was aware of this at the time, I put it down to his being lamentably "conventional" in outlook, rather than because it might be reasonable, given his obvious love for Anne, to be hurt that she had married without telling her parents, and chosen as her man a juvenile layabout with no prospects.

"Not there, darling," said his wife, watching him put down a very small glass of very dry sherry on the wine table by his plushly upholstered chair. "And not on the carpet either!"

Sibs in that moment appeared to possess absolute power. She was not remotely interested in where her husband put down his glass, but she could not resist pulling at the puppet string from time to time, simply in order to amuse herself and to remind Sir Rupert, as if he could ever forget, who was in control.

"But this is lovely," she said to us. "You're both getting on with things at last."

Anne had just been told by her supervisor that a chapter of her dissertation about Winterhalter was so original that she should think about publishing it. I, in addition to getting a novel accepted (and I didn't tell Sibs that it was through Hunter's influence), had various small acting roles half promised me. Moreover Hunter by some process had become our marital friend, though we never said anything about it to Sibs. All the strands of life seemed to be reaching a satisfying resolution. Sibs, a cigarette in one hand and an ice-cold dry martini in the other, stood by the fireplace pulling the invisible strings which made the whole puppet theatre spring to life. Her full but not fat legs supported her magnificent body with complete confidence. Her magnificent figure filled the dark blue cocktail dress. Her red lips stained the Du Maurier which she inhaled. Her eyes glistened with the excitement of so much activity. Although there was grey in her straight, well-washed hair she still seemed like a young person; certainly she seemed much younger than Sir Rupert, though they must in fact have been about the same age.

"If I can organise *you*, Julian, to pick up these boxes from Little Rat Hunter . . ."

"Don't be silly, Mummy."

"Anne, I can call Little Rat what I like. (Oh, dar-*ling*—don't put your glass on the floor . . . no, and not on the hearth either!) That really would be magnificent, because we can get the whole lot to the solicitor's office. I'm just so glad that I've made Sargie see sense at last."

"But Sargie isn't going to refuse Mr. Hunter the chance of quoting from the papers in his next volume."

"There won't *be* another volume!" she said triumphantly. "Everything's working out satisfactorily. I've got you your flat."

(She had, it is true, recommended the name of an estate agent.)

"Yes, Mummy."

"There's your being a success at last, Julian, and there's your thesis. (Darling, don't balance the glass on your knee, there's a pet. It'll stain his trousers.) Yes, there's your thesis, Anne, and now at last Sargie seeing sense about Jimbo's stuff."

Everything—my ability to write, Anne's knowledge of nineteenth-century art, Sargie's mood swings—was of course directly attributable to Lady Starling's force of character. One of her sons, Gavin, had reason to make fairly frequent business visits to the United States and it was he who had found out about the Everett Foundation, a curious institution in Manhattan. The chairman of a small oil company, one Virgil D. Everett Jnr., had decided to invest in a collection of literary manuscripts and rare early printed editions. He specialised in the late nineteenth and early twentieth centuries. Already, he had built up a considerable collection of Wilde letters (including one of the lost typescripts of *De Profundis* with marginalia in an unknown hand); he had a good Lionel Johnson archive, a certain amount of Yeats material, some Arthur Machen.

Gavin Starling had made the right inquiries and it transpired that Virgil D. Everett Jnr. was very interested in the diaries and literary manuscripts of James Petworth Lampitt. By the terms of Jimbo's will, all these papers belonged to Sargie, who could be relied upon to welcome the rather generous terms being mentioned by the Everett Foundation, while changing his mind at least twenty times about the advisability of the deal. Hunter had no claims on the papers and would have to surrender them. It was only because of Sargie's casualness that Jimbo's biographer should have been sitting on the papers for so long. Since Hunter was now our friend, Anne's and mine, the scheme to sell the papers would involve, on our part, an inescapable clash of loyalties. On the one hand, family was family. On the other, one questioned the wisdom of allowing Sibs absolute power in this or any area, not because she would necessarily behave with incaution or foolishness, but because of some natural instinct which makes us resist tyrants and their need to assert absolute control.

This scheme, to spirit the papers from Hunter's reach and

into the hands of a private collector on the other side of the Atlantic, had been vaguely discussed for months now. Anne had even hinted to Hunter himself that something of the sort was in the offing. He had merely shrugged. No one would suppose from his smile that the Lampitt family were about to deprive him of his life's work; there seemed at the time something noble and magnanimous in the slight curl of his lip. I came to feel that sexual jealousy must be the most distorting of all lenses through which to view our fellow creatures. When I first saw Hunter, he was embracing the art teacher, Miss Beach, with whom I happened to be in love. It meant that the next time I saw him, in Treadmill's dining-room at my later school, I was prepared to invest with sinister meaning the smiling geniality of Hunter's face. But surely the truth was that he was quite a pleasant fellow? And was he not taking this business of the Lampitt Papers, in so far as he yet knew anything, extraordinarily well?

There remained the possibility, which I now began to consider, that Hunter had in fact lost interest in the Lampitt Papers. He had other fish to fry: television, journalism, his wide range of important committees. Certainly, however, if he wished to continue his researches into the life of James Petworth Lampitt it sounded from what Sibs was saying as though access to the papers would be extremely difficult. Virgil D. Everett Jnr. was known to be stingy in his attitude to scholars; he did not allow material from his collection to be published on the sane commercial grounds that unpublished manuscripts were more valuable than those whose contents had seen print. There would be no chance for any mere literary sleuth to rifle through Jimbo's diaries once they had been encased in the well-padded air-conditioned strong-room in East Sixty-third Street.

"Mr. Everett is coming over in a few months and you must come to dinner to meet him," Sibs declared.

"So long as I'm not away, acting somewhere. There is a small chance that I might get a fortnight at the King's Lynn rep later this summer."

"Well, you must cancel it if you do. (Oh, darling, not on my

Times—you'll put stains all over the Births, Deaths and Marriages.)"

"No," said Sir Rupert.

Was the worm about to turn? Was he going to tell his wife that he would put his sherry glass where he damn well liked? Was it anger or dry sherry which brought the crimson to his weird spherical face?

"It seems"—he twiddled the glass in his hand awkwardly—"a very sensible provision, particularly since we gather that Mr. Everett is averse to the—er—publication of any papers in his possession."

"Oh, there could never be a published version of Jimbo's diaries now!" Sibs was exultant. "We'll just have to make sure that Sargie isn't an ass again."

The silent movement of Sir Rupert's shoulders and the faint suggestion of a smile which played about his lips indicated the equivalent in other human beings of a guffaw. Meanwhile, he stared at his sherry glass as others would have looked at an insoluble crossword puzzle. Clearly, he could not put it down, but nor, as his wife was now saying, was he meant to "fiddle about with it, there's a pet."

Perhaps the answer would be to put it in his pocket handkerchief, hammer it into small pieces, using the poker in the hearth . . . But then, what? Put the handkerchief in his pocket? Stir the powdered glass into his wife's next martini?

"We mustn't stay," said Anne firmly. "We've promised some friends we'd meet them before the play."

We were going to see Hubert Power's *Uncle Vanya*.

"I've heard it's superb," said Sibs. She spoke in tones which implied she had somehow been responsible for the play's success.

"Never got on with Chekhov," said Sir Rupert.

"Yes, but darling, you remember Hubert Power in *The Doctor's Dilemma* last year."

"I never remember actors' names," said her husband.

"If you are thinking of putting more sherry in that glass, don't. I don't want you upsetting your liver, and if you aren't going to fill it up again, do put it down, there's a pet."

She turned on me a sly grin, delighted to display to a young man how easy it was to tie a member of my sex up in knots.

Her husband was asking, "But isn't that by Shaw?" as she ushered us out.

Anne and I held hands on the Number 19 which took us from Sloane Street to Shaftesbury Avenue and on the way I talked about myself, how I couldn't make up my mind whether to be a great actor or a great writer; and I talked, too, about Jimbo Lampitt, and Hunter's biography of the man, and my increasing fondness for Hunter and how kind he was being, at that juncture, to both of us. Anne was silent, but I did not register her silence and sometimes she squeezed my hand, not as a lover would do, but as a mother might squeeze her child's hand in a dentist's waiting room.

It was only a short walk from the bus stop in Shaftesbury Avenue to the Bottle, and arriving there a little after seven, we pushed open the frosted glass door (emblazoned SALOON— LADIES ONLY) to see the familiar scene of greys and browns, overlaid at the top of the canvas by a smudgy haze of silver tobacco smoke and greasy yellow ceiling. Fenella and Rikko were standing at the bar talking with the Best Seller; or, as I framed it in my mind, they had "got waylaid" by him. For once, there seemed ample justice in Rikko's anxious consultations of his wristwatch, for breaking away from Muckley in mid-sentence was not always an easy thing to do and the curtain of the nearby theatre went up in half an hour.

Rikko was wearing a blazer, white trousers and what could have been a cricketing tie. It was not possible to guess why he (or more probably, why Fenella) had deemed this a suitable outfit for an evening at the theatre. It contrasted oddly with the gold lamé of Fenella's tight stocking-dress, a garment which unflatteringly revealed how extremely thin she was.

I felt that Fenella's fixed grin on this occasion was meant to display an aristocratic disdain for any bourgeois witness to the scene crass enough to suppose that she objected to Muckley's strong accent and evidently proletarian origins. The smile did equally well, however, to gloss over a probable ignorance of the literary matters under discussion.

"There's a limpidity in Chekhov," said the Best Seller. "It's all so sodding clear. You read something like the seduction scene in *The Lady with the Dog*, or the opening scene of *Uncle Vanya*, come to that, and you think, by Christ, life is this—it isn't like this, it *is* this."

He prodded some imagined opponent of the viewpoint with an ignited Sweet Afton.

"And at the same time," said Rikko, "as well as being so specific, I dunno. One gets this sense of a whole *society* behind the bleak lives he depicts. English writers can't write about societies. They can only write about families. Whereas almost every individual in Chekhov or Dostoyevsky seems able to suggest a world behind them. I dunno."

Day Muckley, one of the chief pre-war exponents of the English family "saga," looked at Rikko with considered belligerence. No doubt he was aware of his failure to match the Russian giants. At the same time, you got the feeling from looking at him that this would not necessarily restrain him from punching Rikko's face, if, as appeared to have happened, need arose.

"Don't give me all that sodding rubbish about *The Cherry Orchard*," he said. This must have related to another conversation, held with someone else perhaps, years earlier, about another of Chekhov's masterpieces. It was vain to speculate what the rubbish was, but Rikko obediently kept silent about it.

He hastily offered us all drinks. Mine was a gin-and-tonic, Anne's a grapefruit juice. Fenella relaxed her grin and said, "We want to see Hubie tonight anyway—he's very special to us."

Muckley emptied his straight glass of beer and mused on this desire.

"No," he said, "I wouldn't want to see Hubie Power or any other bum-boy pretending to be Vanya, for Christ's sakes."

"Doesn't that rather rule out any theatrical experience?" I asked. "Isn't that what going to see plays *is*—watching bumboys pretending to be someone else?"

"Cheers," said Muckley, taking most of his double whisky in one gulp.

"As a matter of fact, and I'm not sure why I'm telling you—

must be the drink talking." Fenella's coy smile heralded a true whopper. "My grandmother was practically a lady-in-waiting to the last Tsarina."

Rikko still had his back to us, since he was collecting his change from Cyril, but with one free hand he was able to pinch his forehead, and as he turned, I think he was muttering, "*Shut up, Fenella, just shut up, will you.*" But the Best Seller responded to the discourse. She might have hoped that he would be impressed that she was only a step away from the court life of old St. Petersburg, but Muckley's face showed no more excitement than if she had said that her grandmother once visited More-cambe Bay in the holiday season.

"I have no sympathy whatsoever, with the . . . no sympathy with the Tsar."

And that was the end of his chaser.

"And how's life down on the farm, then?" Cyril was proud to have a star of "The Mulberrys" propping up his bar.

I had begun to notice a certain smile creep over Rikko's face when people spoke of his radio work. It was the look of a man who was trapped. Rikko was doing the part really well, so well, in fact, that some radio critics were beginning to write about the programme in the same column as serious radio drama. But Rikko knew that he had opted for something safe, he had ceased to stretch up to the inaccessible, and, in so doing, he had killed something in himself. There was more pathos in his "success" as Stan Mulberry than there had ever been in his failure to get the big roles. While he was being a waiter or advertising indigestion tablets, Rikko's Hamlet, or Rikko's Vanya were still imaginable dreams. Stan Mullberry was somehow stronger than they. One knew that Rikko would never quite take himself seriously again.

"You should keep that drunken brother of yours in order," said Cyril. In spite of his totally cynical attitude to life, he clearly shared Aunt Deirdre's willingness to make an exception in the case of "The Mulberrys."

"They were so cruel," said Day Muckley, "and so fucking stupid, that they deserved it. They had it coming to them."

While Cyril topped up his Teacher's and gave him another

pint of Courage, Day Muckley spoke of the imbecile credulity of anyone who could trust Rasputin.

All kinds of conversational hazards loomed up. Peter and Mr. Porn had put down their racing papers and looked ready for a major set-to on the old religious question. On a more mundane level, I know we should be late for the play if we waited for the Best Seller, in his present state of sobriety, to make up his mind how to pronounce the word "haemophiliac." We stepped out into the summer evening. The plane trees near St. Anne's Church were in leaf, I saw when we came into Dean Street. Anne was on my arm, and such a variety of impressions assailed me that I did not notice, still less interpret her silence. I took her love for granted, just as, in that moment of quiet but intense happiness, I took everything for granted. I can remember an insane conceited grin which involuntarily stole over my features in those days. No doubt it came over my face as we all walked down Dean Street, as though I were the master of ceremonies and had organised all the things which at that moment gave me pleasure: my friends being so much themselves, whether in Cadogan Square or the Bottle; the anticipation of the play (I would never have admitted it during the conversation in the bar, but I had not read or seen any Chekhov and my smiles and nods concealed an ignorance deeper than Fenella's); even the physical conditions of the evening filled me with a conceited glee. I had more than a little of Sibs's egoism, the ability to behave, when things went well, as though I was partly responsible. I would not have thought it unreasonable if Anne had at that moment thanked me for the sunlight on the great branches which once again had come to life by the side of the little bombed church; for the Hogarthian ribaldry which the law still in those days permitted to the girls of Soho who called out to us from doorways and windows as we walked along, and who themselves cruised the pavements or hovered by lampposts in exaggerated poses; the crowds who outnumbered and largely ignored them, intent in some more generalised way on "an evening out"; the charabancs in Shaftesbury Avenue debouching the parties of old people and school children who had been driven up to town for an evening at the theatre. The whole happy world of London preparing for an evening of pleasure was so much part of my mood that I could almost have believed that I had created it.

We were only just in our seats by the time the curtain went up, and at first I did not settle. The evening outside was too bright and warm to be conducive to an evening enclosed in the dark fantasy-box of theatre. But, as everyone knows who saw or read about that production, it was one of the very great examples in theatre which do not merely redefine a work of art, but which stretch and enhance the human experience itself. No one who saw it will ever believe again in any other actor's Vanya. They will merely judge new performances by the extent to which the actor in question falls short of Hubert Power's interpretation. Likewise, any actress one sees attempting Sonya will merely remind one of Isabella Marno's definitive interpretation. I was electrified by the play. It was an evening which, as will become clear, began to change my life in more senses than one; but in spite of all its personal emotional dramas, it taught me for the first time what theatre *was,* what was the point of it all. Hitherto, either in my own feeble efforts to act or in the more or less competent theatre which I had witnessed, one never ceased to be aware of the fact that people were acting. The more I came to be interested in the theatre, the more expertly I felt myself able to judge the quality of delivery, stagecraft, timing; but I had more or less lost sight of the notion that theatre has a much greater power than a mere technical ability to pretend. If the alchemy is effective . . . Even to finish the sentence is to utter a commonplace, that the stage becomes a new world, the actors different people. But it is supremely rare for it to happen and that evening at *Uncle Vanya* was the first time it had happened in my presence.

As often happens to me in the presence of truly great art, my reaction was at the immediate level completely trivial. Without willing it, I allowed my own preoccupations to be interwoven with the realities of the play. Though the whole situation of the play was entirely different from anything which I had known, I allowed the dreary Russian farmhouse to become the rectory at Timplingham. The professor Serebrakov, most unfairly, was identified at this level of half-consciousness with Uncle Roy, and I, ever the hero of my own tale, was Vanya who shot him. All impure responses to art bring our own lives into the play, poem, picture under contemplation, and this is not because we are only half attending to it; rather because we are focussing our entire attention upon it, and are therefore unable to divest ourselves of our lives and feed solely on art with ear or eye or mind. By the end of the play, however, these crude levels of half-identification had fallen away, and the existence of those miserable people, miles from anywhere in a vanished Russian world, was more real to any of us than our own lives, and in the simplicity of Sonya there was something indescribably ennobling and touching. The last scene certainly had me in tears. In the actress playing Sonya, there was such transparent moral simplicity. She was so obviously an innocent, so completely a sexual and emotional virgin, so strong in her faith that "we shall rest." Her face, Isabella Marno's, was almost too real to have put on the stage. There was nothing pretty, nothing actressy, about it. And the simplicity with which she played the role of Sonya brought out the rugged manliness, and the bitterness and brokenness of Vanya himself. Vanya, one felt, had he ever come to London, would have found a welcome at the Black Bottle.

I see why those (my cousin Felicity among them) who dislike the theatre do so with such intensity. The combined genius of Chekhov and Hubert Power, with Isabella Marno's superb Sonya, had persuaded a packed theatre full of people that what we were watching was more real than our own lives. For a moment, those actors had held absolute sway over a thousand people. One could say that was all for the good, but Felicity the Platonist would probably have wanted to say that it could not be truly good because it was of its essence false. The tumultuous applause, the thousand hearts beating as one, the emergence from one's seat feeling that a truly important emotional landmark had been passed, all this could have been evil, not good. Crowd emotion, mass emotion, must always be suspect. It was for this that Shakespeare had given his life, out of this he had made his fortune, aware of the folly, and perhaps of the moral dubiety of making himself a motley to the view, conscious that a purer life would be possible only when the revels were ended and Prospero's staff thrown away.

These thoughts, if present in my mind at all that evening, were embryonic, the conscious emotion being a vast negative epiphany, a discovery that the theatre was not really for me. It took me a long time to act on this piece of negative information, but "information" is what it felt like, an absolutely certain diagnosis of my life and position. Without any humility, I knew I could never be an actor of Hubert Power's stature. The qualities which enable a good, even a great actor, to strip self of self and put on another being were ones with which I had been fascinated as a schoolboy actor and Treadmill my master had filled me with a literary interest in the drama as a literary form. But there was no longer quite room in my life for this psychological game. I more and more wanted to live in the world of the Imagination, less and less in the world of Let's Pretend.

Fenella's Let's Pretend was completely out of control that night. Over drinks in the interval, she had insisted on the importance of congratulating the performers in their dressing rooms after the show.

"It does so much for their morale," she honked. "We simply must go back and tell Hubie how much we enjoyed it. He'd never forgive us if he knew we'd been to the play and not come back."

It is true that such a convention exists, though I suspect that Hubert Power could have lived with the knowledge that we had been in the house without calling on him. To judge from the tumultous applause which followed the final curtain, lasting for at least a quarter of an hour, it was unlikely on that particular occasion that he positively needed Fenella's assurance that his performance had been satisfactory. However, I was quite anxious to meet him, and I believed he had been at the RADA with Rikko. The Kempes' claim to acquaintance with him was surely much less fantastical than Fenella's assertion of intimacy with the royal families of Europe. I noticed that Rikko could tolerate mention of Hubert Power without pinching his forehead.

While the audience were dispersing, we fought our way through the back of the house. Theatres (even modern, well-appointed ones, which the old Duchess of Kent's certainly wasn't) are almost rudely scruffy and uncomfortable once you step behind the facade of plush stalls and well-lit stage. Narrow corridors, peeling gloss paint, bare light bulbs, fire-buckets full of sand, induce an immediate sense of letdown. The place seems to crow over someone who has been credulous enough to believe in, or even to have enjoyed, the spectacle. It hurls your enjoyment and belief back in your face. It is like the postcoital sensations a man might feel when he had half persuaded himself, in the previous quarter of an hour, that a prostitute really loved him. The immediacy with which she breaks away from him when the deed is performed, the harshness of her smile, remind him that he has been tricked by a fantastic illusion. The knowledge that the illusion was all inside your head purely self-inflicted, that the theatre never pretended to be other than a theatre, or the street-walker anything other than a sensation for sale, only adds to the sense of disillusion a feeling of self-reproach.

We were not alone backstage in these corridors, Rikko, Fenella, Anne, I. Actors, theatre staff and visitors jostled about us.

"I don't want to be here," said Anne, rather desperately.

"We shan't stay long."

I tried to squeeze her hand, but she did not want to be touched. I merely thought she must be moved, as I was by the extraordinary last speech of Sonya. It was a moment for silence, aloneness, not for Fenella's charging forward saying, "I'm sure it must be down here!" in her deepest Camel-throated bass.

"Looking for the Gents?" asked a bright young spark, presumably a stage-hand.

"Hubie's dressing-room actually," said Fenella. "We're very close friends."

When we'd moved off in the direction indicated by this boy,

I heard him saying to someone else, "Wonder where Hube picked up that old faggot, real drag queen."

By now I had grown so used to Fenella's voice and appearance that I had forgotten how on my own first meeting with her (in spite of thorough preparation by Bloom) I had found it hard to believe she was truly of the female sex. Now, hearing the boys laugh at her, I felt protective towards her and sorry for Rikko, who had tried not to notice their talk.

"Now, Fenella, promise not to gush over Hubie," said Rikko.

"Hubie knows me too well for that," she said.

There were already a number of people in Hubert Power's dressing-room when we burst in. I'm not sure who they were. There certainly did not feel as though there was room for four more.

Anne repeated her anguished, "Oh, do let's *go*," as soon as Fenella strode ahead.

Fenella actualy spoke the line "Darling, you were marvellous." She put such peculiar emphasis on the words, however (like Edith Evans wanting to make the handbag line her own in *The Importance of Being Earnest*), that she managed to deprive the cliché of any meaning, stressing the word *were*. The oddness of the stress emanated from her croaking larynx with great gusts of Camel smoke, as from the nose of some Wagnerian dragon. Hubert Power, rubbing his face with cotton wool and vanishing cream, looked up at the reflection in the glass. The only visitors whom he could see were Fenella and myself. His face became tautened by fear.

"I don't think . . . ," he said.

Like the stage-hand whom we had just met in the corridor, Hubert Power must have supposed Fenella to be a man, perhaps myself her sexual companion, or merely her fellow-blackmailer who had cruelly selected an evening of particular triumph in the theatre to enact the vengeance of nemesis.

"Oh, darling!" Fenella repeated. "It's only *us*."

His first moment of shock over, Power was able to compose his features. He said, a little primly, "I'm afraid that you have the advantage of me."

Unabashed, Fenella continued, "I told them you wouldn't *forgive* us if we didn't drop in to say how absolutely brilliant you were, darling."

Conversation which had been in progress while we burst into the room had now stopped. The three or four other people there stared and faltered, and for a few terrible seconds one could see them wondering whether Fenella was actually a criminal or merely one of those poor deranged characters who are found wandering at large in any city, their minds possessed by some sort of nonsense or another, in this case the belief that she and Hubert Power were the best of friends. The moment was saved by Rikko, who had been hanging back in the corridor and who now pressed past Fenella.

"Hubie, we should never have come, we'll just shake hands and bugger off."

"Rickie, darling!"

Recognition between the two men was instantaneous. Greasy with remover, and with one hand still clutching a dirty piece of cotton wool, Power arose from his stool and enfolded Rikko in his arms.

"You've met Fenella—my wife," said Rikko.

"Dear boy, of *course* it is." Whatever he quite thought Rikko to have said, he had slightly misheard or chosen by this tiny piece of non sequitur to distance himself from the fact of Fenella's existence.

"And this is Anne and Julian," said Rikko.

"Not your babies? Not already?" Power's lips pursed. "Hers, then?"

"No, no, just friends," said Rikko.

"Well, do come in, and spread yourselves, dears, spread yourselves." He had resumed his seat and his rubbing with the cotton wool. "There's some bubbly. And darling Rikkie, I want all your news."

This was obviously not true—the part about wanting the news—because before Rikko could say Mulberry, a very rapid staccato postmortem of the evening's performance poured from the actor's lips. The magic, felt at the front of the house, was now being analysed trick by breathless trick. He examined each scene in technical terms from the point of view of how some other member of the cast had succeeded or failed in helping him to achieve some of the evening's more stunning effects.

"Billy"—that was William Landaw, playing Astrov—"comes in too fast, damn him, in the first act. It must be me saying, 'See him! Stalking across the earth like a demigod!' And then, *pause, pause* while Astrov thinks. But Willie never thinks, hasn't got a thought in his prick of a head, just bursts in with 'I believe you envy him!' and ruins my effect. I still hate the way Hayho"— Henry Mackenzie, the director—"is making us play that final bit of the first act, too. The placing on the stage is all wrong. I'm a mile backstage. 'How can I look at you otherwise when I love you?'—I have to bellow the fucking lines. And God knows Jan"—Janice Brunner, playing Helena—"is beautiful but the audience don't need to have her absolutely front stage, I mean, my dears, practically in the footlights while I'm languishing by the bloody French window."

It was strange that only two hours before, these words, when Vanya admitted his love for Helena, had struck me as deeply moving, more real than emotions which I had experienced myself. Now they had no more reality than puppets whose strings had been laid aside after a performance.

I found myself standing by Power at this moment, Anne having hung back by the door, shyly accepting a glass from someone else present. Rikko and Fenella likewise hung back so that I bore the full glare of Hubert Power's penetrating eyes. As he spoke of stagecraft (his face was clean now, and he had spun round on his stool to face the company) his hands fluttered like butterflies and his glance darted from me to Rikko and then back again.

His eyes strayed quite shamelessly up and down my person, as if the clothes I was wearing, possibly the limbs which inhabited them, were for sale. Feeling that it was probably the only chance I should ever get to be in the presence of one who was obviously destined for a great career on the stage, I lost my self-consciousness and felt that only simplicity could match the hour.

Power's sheer disappointingness of personality when met without the greasepaint didn't really diminish the achievement of
his Uncle Vanya, in fact the reverse. When one saw what a very
unprepossessing figure he cut, small and (Uncle Roy would have
perhaps wished to add) very much not the gentleman, the alchemy by which he transformed himself into the despondent,
maddening but wholly sympathetic figure of Chekhov's Vanya
was all the more remarkable. Sycophantic as it sounds when
written down, I simply blurted out the truth, that I had never
heard or read the play before but that tonight had been easily
the most moving and interesting evening which I had ever spent
in the theatre, and that this had much to do with his own
performance, and—of course—with Sonya's final speech.

He seemed quite genuinely touched by my essentially juvenile
sincerity. He stroked my wrist and murmured, "Dear . . . *dear!*"
as I spoke, and his eyes continued to dart up and down my body
and occasionally across to Rikko.

When, as it clearly seemed to him, I had diluted my praise of
his Vanya with kind words about Isabella Marno's performance,
his happy smile momentarily vanished (it was only the matter
of a split second) and was replaced by a much firmer, totally
artificial one, a chimpanzee's grin.

"You're *so* right, you're *so* right. Bella was fucking marvell-
lous. But then it's a marvellous speech, a fucking gift to an
actress, my dear. Where *is* Bella, by the way? Let's"—his hand
tightened on my wrist—"go and find her."

I attributed Anne's grumpy expression to an uncharacteristic
resentment at the fact that I was momentarily the centre of
attention. I must say that it crossed my mind that Hubert Power
was only asking me into the corridor to attempt some sort of
grope, but the idea that this posed a serious threat to my wife
was ludicrous. What had happened to her sense of humour? She
held up her own wrist and made signals that it was time to
leave.

"We're just going to see if we can find Isabella Marno," I
said. "Oh, come on, Anne, don't look like that. Surely you'd
like to meet her?"

Anne's face was not merely angry, it was positively murderous. I knew that I had said or done something to annoy her but I could not imagine what it was. There was little enough time to consider the question since Power was bustling me out into the corridor.

"My dear," he hissed *sotto voce* as soon as we had closed the door, "is that really Rickie's wife?"

I said it was, if he meant Fenella.

"But it's grotesque. What's it supposed to be, my dear? It's seventy-five if it's a day. I'd always heard that Rickie had made a mistake, and we've seen each other now and again over the years, but really! This is a very great shock. It's too much."

I felt a great wave of loyalty to Fenella as these quite unnecessarily merciless words were spoken. Her quite simple kindliness and goodness of heart to dozens of lodgers over the years, and above all her kindness to me, cancelled out, as far as I was concerned, any absurdity of which she might be accused.

"She's a friend of mine," I said.

"Of course, my dear, of course, but . . ." His voice trailed away. "Now where is *fucking* Bella?"

I regretted provoking this petulance, and the repetition of this disagreeable epithet. I could have no idea how accurate it was until he kicked open Isabella Marno's dressing-room door, without knocking, to reveal the actress on her dressing table, sitting in a petticoat, her legs wide apart, with a visitor standing between them with his back to us.

"Not now!" she said over his shoulder, I think to us rather than to him. Then, seeing Hubert, she said, "What is it, Hubie, darling?"

It was an intimate moment though as it happened not quite so intimate as at first appeared. The visitor at least was fully clothed. Indeed, the light grey suit which he wore was entirely familiar to me. Even before he turned I realised that it was Hunter who held Isabella Marno in his arms, the scene oddly recalling the important moment in my boyhood when I had seen him kissing Miss Beach. His expression on this occasion was noticeable for its complete lack of embarrassment and I took this to be the way that sophisticated people are supposed to behave when caught in positions which would make lesser figures blush. There was more to it than that, but I could not see what this *more* was. He was positively pleased that we had found him there, that was evident.

"Lordings!" exclaimed Hubert Power, "you were both invited to drinks with me. Now, come on! Do your duty!"

"Hallo, Julian," said Hunter.

"Ah, so you know each other."

"Bad luck, Hubie," said Isabella with, as I thought, real malevolence.

Hunter introduced me to the actress. I could not repeat to her the speech I had made to Hubert Power about the production; my version of "Darling, you were marvellous" therefore sounded a bit flat. She looked cross to be interrupted and in no mood to join the party in Power's dressing room, but he was insistent, and as he led them off down the corridor he began to explain in a deafening stage whisper that I had been brought along by his sweet friend Rickie, who, poor boy, had married his landlady long ago.

"No one thought it would last five minutes, but my dears, he has been landed—well, you'll see, you'll see, my dears!"

Fenella's croaky enthusiastic greeting when we returned to Power's dressing-room implied that it was her own place.

"And to think!" I heard her exclaiming, "these people"—she gestured to Rikko, myself, Anne—"were against coming backstage at all."

It was clear that she was preparing to have a whale of a time.

Hunter came forward and kissed Anne on the cheek. She gave him a funny look as she did so and then peered at Isabella Marno with an expression which I could not characterise; it seemed, unaccountably, like terror.

"Julian, you said we could *go*," she said.

"We won't stay long."

"Julian, *please*."

"It's not like you to be a party pooper."

In making this remark, perhaps a trifle irritably, I intended absolutely no rebuke. I didn't think of it as a serious comment. Probably my attitude to the whole scene was like Fenella's. I was looking forward to extracting every ounce of amusement and entertainment from it. At the same time in an egotistical way I was quite glad to find Hunter there because there were a number of small details concerning the publishers he had helped to find for me, about which I would have welcomed his advice. That he had been kissing an actress was quite unsurprising, given his "reputation," and it was no more than a source of mild amusement to me that traces of her red lipstick were now discernible on Hunter's own smooth, thin upper lip, giving his mouth an aspect of full-bloodedness and generosity which it was sometimes without.

I stood between Hunter and Isabella Marno. I felt absolute well-being. If you had said that I had left behind Tempest and Holmes solely in order to make such moments possible, it would not have been far from the truth. It gave quite disproportionate pleasure to contemplate Isabella Marno's fame as an actress, Hunter's as a man of letters. Whatever the snobbish implication of the word, I could not have been better described than as a parvenu. For I had arrived somewhere, in a place which I had ardently sought, without knowing its name or its whereabouts. In fact, I was merely standing in a small, overcrowded room talking to a lot of people whom I did not know, and most of whom I would never see again. The prattle was meaningless. Yet I felt an intense glow of happiness akin to the pleasure of love. I did not exactly feel that the pilgrimage was over, but I had reached the gates of the holy city and stood on the threshold of its shrines. It was therefore all the more astounding to me when Anne moved to the door and said quietly, "I'm off."

Hunter tried to exchange a sentence with her, but she pushed past him. The speed with which she did so made me, at first, misinterpret her action. It only made sense to leave a room in such a way if you needed a lavatory. Then I saw that she had her coat and bag with her and she was evidently intending to leave the room without saying goodbye to anyone. I felt embarrassment on her behalf and an equally engrossing rage. As soon as I twigged what she was doing, I followed her down the corridor. She was almost running.

"No need to follow me," she said without turning round. "Stay with them, if you'd rather."

Her words were angry and bitter in tone. One understood at once that staying would be about the least sensitive thing one had ever done. But why?

Once out in the street, she lolloped along at a pace where I could barely keep up with her, making herself the cross mother and I the child who had done something naughty, screamed or been sick in a shop. Her long Lampitt features which I had found so instantly irresistible when first met—and those large staring eyes—seemed for the first time lofty, mad and unreasonable. And her insufferable behaviour did not so much *remind* me of Sargie's absurd "leading Roy a dance" in my boyhood. It actually became the same infuriating farce. For me to kowtow and to put up with it was to place myself in the same toadyish position which Uncle Roy had, all those years, accepted vis-à-vis Sargie. This was just what Sargie would have done if he had not been enjoying a party—walk out, and give off powerful indications that his own unhappy whim was somehow everyone else's fault.

She stalked down Shaftesbury Avenue and crossed roads when she reached Piccadilly Circus without looking to left or right. It was pure luck that she was not mown down by traffic. At the bus stop in Piccadilly she had to pause and I had time to catch up with her, but I only saw her tail of dark hair, since she stared away from me in the direction of Burlington House. I tried to offer her one final excuse.

"If you're ill," I said.

She made a tutting, clicking noise with her tongue as though this imputation were simply moronic.

A Number 19 came. There were plenty of empty seats for two, but she sat down next to a woman in a headscarf, making it impossible for me to sit beside her. So I sat looking at the back of her neck, wanting very badly to take hold of it and strangle it. It was partly pity which inspired this desire. Pity and hatred are terribly close in my emotional barometer. I could not bear her misery, it made me angry. Also, I felt that my love for her which had begun as something so fresh and new was now doomed, forever, to be a mere reiteration of the Lampitt tragifarce. By implication, my own life itself, which I had pathetically imagined to be full of new and interesting freedoms, was programmed, it seemed to follow genetically ordained patterns. I was Roy without the knickerbockers. She was Sargie without the moustache.

She managed to get off the bus before I did, and we walked home separately; but she was still waiting on the doorstep of the house in Lamont Road when I arrived. I had half expected her to go inside, climb the stairs to our flat and slam the door in my face.

"Julian, I'd really rather be alone." I was silent. She added, "Without you hovering there."

"I live here. Perhaps you'd forgotten."

"Oh, *shit!*"

It was clear—again, it could be Sargie himself!—that she had lost her latch-key, come out without it. She was hopeless with keys and left spares with her mother, with Mrs. Wiley who did for us twice a week, and with Darnley's sister Elizabeth.

"Let us in." I sadistically enjoyed the moment. I intended to make her confess that she had forgotten the key. I had no intention of reaching into my own pocket and opening the door for her.

"I've lost my bloody key."

I had half a mind to open the door, walk through it myself and slam it in her face. Instead, I relented, and said, "Just as well I brought mine."

My hand felt in my jacket pocket where it should have been. Then with self-disgust I remembered changing into a suit just before we left the flat for drinks with her parents. What had I done with the jacket in whose pocket I normally kept the keys? Thrown it over a chair? Had I taken out the pocket book? Yes, I checked and felt it there just over my heart. But—in the right hand pocket, where I normally kept keys . . . nothing.

"Get on with it, it's cold." She hugged herself and still refused me even the turning of her head in my direction. Certainly she was not going to offer me anything so polite as a look.

I was speechless with babyish shame. It now appeared that to admit that I had been as absent-minded as she would be some kind of defeat in the great marital war which had apparently started. Strangely, as far as I was aware, the evening had begun quite well. She had been in a bit of a mood, but, without counting things out on my fingers, I guessed it was the wrong time of the month. Besides, seeing her mother always put Anne in a funny mood, and I knew she didn't like Fenella. A mood was to be expected, but this was like lunacy, her present condition.

"You've come out without your key, too."

It was the old, literal Anne, seeing the truth and stating it. I, less at home with truth, and badly needing to get my own back for the pain I now felt, wanted to construct a ludicrous fiction.

"I had it until we got to the theatre. Then, if you remember, I gave it to you. You had it. You surely remember?"

By now I was the husband in *Gaslight* wanting to drive his wife mad by pretending her memory was going. "You had my key as well as your own and you bloody go and lose them both."

"We could ring Mummy," she said, obviously deciding that my lies deserved no proper answer.

"Oh, that's right, ring bloody Mummy."

"Julian, it's nearly midnight. It would be better than ringing Mrs. Wiley, and I don't intend to spend the whole night pacing the streets. If you hadn't insisted on going backstage with that grotesque gang of people we wouldn't have been so late."

"It's your fault if it's anyone's," I said. "Don't go blaming me. As I said, I gave you . . ."

"Oh, God!"

She burst into tears and for the first time since leaving the theatre she turned her face towards mine. I still felt furious with her, but at that moment all I wanted to do was make love to her. This, I supposed, would solve everything. And yet something about her, something which I had not observed before, repelled my advance. I was to watch her unhappiness but I could not touch it. This instinct was confirmed when I reached out to put my arms around her and she stepped back to avoid me.

"It's all your stupid fault," I spat back at her. Seeing her face crumple yet more with tears, I renewed my attack. "You've behaved like a spoilt bitch this evening. Why couldn't you at least pretend to enjoy yourself? Do you think I *enjoy* some of the places you take me to? Do you think I *enjoyed* having sherry with your father? Christ!"

I railed and railed in this vein. At first, she moaned and through her streaming eyes she wore an expression of complete incredulity that someone whom she had loved and trusted could so wilfully inflict pain on her when she was already in a state of misery. Then, perhaps, her unhappiness entered further depths. She tried to say a sentence such as "I can't . . . stay here and listen to any more of this." But it all came out in jerky sobs, and then quite suddenly she turned and ran down to the King's Road where as it happened a taxi was free. She hailed it and before I had time to stop her, she went off. I learned later that she had gone to spend the night with Elizabeth, who had never much liked me, and I think thereafter had good cause to hate me. At the time, standing on the kerb watching Anne's taxi hurtle off towards Sloane Square I felt as close to despair as I ever felt in my life. I thought she was going forever, and perhaps it would have been better if she had done so. "Thought" is the wrong word for the whole jumble of totally irrational impressions which thundered and galumphed through my consciousness: fear that she would commit suicide, hope that she would, embarrassment that (as I was also certain) she had "run home to Mummy," heartbreak that she did not love me anymore, anger and fear, lacerating remorse for all the things I had thought, done or said since leaving the theatre.

I still hate myself for that evening. Not long ago it all came back with surprising vividness. I had been to dinner with some (rather smart, how things change) young people who lived in Lamont Road, and afterwards I stood on the kerb of the King's Road waiting for a taxi to trundle past. The dinner, where I had eaten well, met a number of old friends, been happy, evaporated at once into nothingness, as I found myself standing in what must have been almost the very spot where Anne and I had parted that night. Once again, I confronted that offensive and angry young man who stared after Anne's cab. Until that moment, I had forgotten the manic need which I had felt to press home an advantage in a non-existent battle, to fight Anne, though there was nothing to fight about. Nothing can ever quite cancel out these ghastly moments of truth about ourselves: not the passage of time, which in this case merely anaesthetised the pain for some thirty-five years, and then revived it with a pity for both of us, pity for our youth. It astounds me now how recklessly I risked and inflicted pain when I was in my twenties. The avoidance of pain, from middle age onwards, has been an obsession with me.

When Anne's taxi had gone, I realised that I wasn't quite drunk enough to be oblivious to all the tedious incidentals of the situation—seven or eight hours to be got through until breakfast, the flat locked up, the wife gone. Nor was I quite sober enough to reflect sensibly on what to do. Blundering up the road, I stopped in the first telephone kiosk which I reached, and dialled Sir Rupert Starling's number. He was an abstemious, regular man in his habits; I am sure he was in bed by eleven o'clock most nights, and probably asleep by the present hour of half past twelve. After a few trills of his telephone, I heard his voice, alarmed and at the same time deferential. Who did he suppose might be ringing at such an hour? The prime minister? It was not an impossible thought.

I pressed Button A and for a moment his voice was lost. Then I heard the deferential tone become crisper before being blotted out by the dialling tone. I had forgotten to put in a penny. I took out a few coins and felt, as I did so, the desire to smoke.

The next time I dialled, with fag alight, I had the coins ready and did everything in the right order. Complete certainty that Anne was with her parents possessed my mind until the very second when I actually got through to her father. It then occurred to me, not by any process of reasoning but by instinct, that his tone of surprise, and of just having woken up, would not have been right if Anne were with him, sobbing her eyes out. I realised that Anne would never have exposed her parents to the scene which had just ensued; she was too proud, too distant from them, too considerate.

"Hallo," said Sir Rupert's voice sternly.

I paused.

"Look, if this is some kind of practical joke," he added.

All at once, his disapproving tones brought back the world of school, of larks, of everything being a huge practical joke played against the grown-ups.

"You may not realise that you are breaking the law," he said with some pomp, but also with a tremble in his voice.

Quite near him, I could hear his wife speaking.

"Oh, Rupert, don't be such an ass."

Then there was a noise as of some great Atlantic roller bursting into a cave as she dragged the receiver across her linen sheets and then said into it, quite calmly, "Whoever you are, just bugger off."

The line went dead. The incident, momentarily hilarious, was of the kind which Darnley, or Anne in happier days, would have split their sides over. Having no one to share the joke with— indeed as cold air and increasing sobriety reminded me, it not being a joke—brought with it a bleak loneliness. I left the kiosk and walked. A bus came along, and I sat on it until I reached Victoria. I didn't sleep much in the cheap hotel near the station where I had found a room. Next morning, unshaven and with bad breath, I retrieved the contents of my trouser pockets which—incurable habit—I had scattered on the chest of drawers before undressing for bed. Coins, a match box, and inevitably, a front door key.

six

"Have we taken sufficient account," asked Anne's brother Gavin, "of the capital appreciation factor?"

"Rather difficult to do without the figures."

His father sniffed, and all eyes turned down the table towards Sargie.

Such a gathering of Lampitts would have kept Uncle Roy happy for weeks, savouring the memory of each "typical" utterance of every figure at the table.

They had assembled in Sibs's dining-room to hear the details of how Sargie intended to dispose of Jimbo's papers to the Everett Foundation, and we had all been given the printed brochure, drawn up by the Everett, listing its present holdings, and its ambition to become one of the "primary manuscript collections of Dowson, Pater, Wilde, two Douglases—Alfred and Norman—and Arthur Machen." The miscellaneous names collected suggested a very distinctive area of taste on someone's part, presumably that of Virgil D. Everett Jnr. himself.

One of the odd things which had emerged over lunch was that Gavin Starling had not in fact been the initiator of the deal, even though the Starlings knew the Everetts slightly and the phrase "World Bank" had been murmured to suggest a plausible link between Sir Rupert and the great American financier. The final approaches had been made by Mr. Everett's attorney in

140

New York to the Lampitt family solicitors, Denniston and Denniston of Lincoln's Inn Fields. Things had gone further than Sibs had realised, which was why she had convened this tribal pow-pow for the purpose, as she phrased it of "putting Sargie on the spot." Aware from early childhood of Sargie's congenital nervous imbalance, his inability to make up his mind, his capacity to be fussed by more or less anything, I felt sorry for him in his approaching ordeal. A Sunday luncheon had to be got through first to which Sibs had asked her cousin Vernon, the former Labour cabinet minister, and Ursula Lampitt, another cousin, principal of Rawlinson College, Oxford. Gavin Starling was there, a comically similar figure to his father in manner and appearance, only thirty years younger; Anne and I had been asked along, and Sargie had brought the elder of the two Denniston brothers. The implication behind this impressive *moot* was that they were all responsible for Jimbo's literary remains. As they now turned to Sargie, there was the strong sense that he was on trial, and needed to justify himself, or at least to explain how much of Virgil D. Everett Jnr.'s money he had taken, or intended to take, in exchange for the Lampitt papers.

One of Sargie's "famous sayings," endlessly repeated by Uncle Roy (it was the trivial sort of thing which no one else would have remembered), was that he liked to have a piece of dry toast on his side plate at every meal. "Not to eat, just to comfort me." "Typical Sargie," my uncle would add, and although he laughed at the saying, he treasured it. I thought of this "famous saying" at that moment, when I saw that Sargie had placed himself next to the solicitor. Sargie was not going to consult this dandruffy bespectacled figure, as it happened; but it was clear that the silent presence of Andrew Denniston would, like a piece of dry toast, bring its own mysterious strength. Something did.

I can remember, during the worst period of Sargie's depressions, that it had required in him, merely to decide whether or not he wanted to drive into Norwich, depths of heroic resolve which would have enabled other men to besiege towns or conduct *coups d'état*. Even nowadays, if one asked him over for the evening, one could expect six or seven telephone calls to alter, cancel, reconfirm arrangements. Psychosomatic symptoms would bombard him by the half hour, making it hard for him to know whether he could trust himself to go out without the descent of a migraine, muscular seizures, nausea, or simply overpowering, debilitating gloom. The present semi-formal assembly of his relations, not one of whom I had the slightest reason to suppose Sargie liked, was a sadistic idea of Sibs, who cooingly reiterated, when the dishes had been cleared away and we all sat with wine, brandy, or in Sargie's case watered gin, that we had only come together to help him.

Any sympathy which I had been reserving for Sargie was, however, completely wasted. He was sitting more upright than usual and the alcohol seemed only to strengthen resolution rather than make him vague. The smouldering Senior Service in his bone holder was held between his lips as he began to speak and occasionally removed for the chance of flicking ash in the vague general direction of Sibs's ugly Elkington's epergne. Uncle Roy had often remarked incredulously that Sargie had been a member of several government committees, and a powerful and effective figure on them. When my uncle spoke of this fact, none of us could quite picture the shambolic Sargie of Timplingham impressing his will on men of power and influence. But now one saw how it was done. Whether it was the money he was getting for the papers which thus emboldened him, or just the right amount to drink, or some feeling of atavistic rivalry with cousins and siblings, it was impossible to say.

Sargie ignored his nephew's overt enquiry about the price being offered by the Everett Foundation for the papers. With the sort of voice which might have been suitable for a public lecture, he began to speak.

"I think we have to recognise that there was no option here of standing still. At some time, and somewhere or another, these papers of my brother were going to pass out of my hands. That is a fact of mortality."

"You could have entrusted them to one of the children," said Sibs.

"But darling Sibs," said Sargie with a triumphant smile (and he obviously loved denying his nephews and nieces the ownership of the Lampitt Papers), "that raises all kinds of questions. I mean, I'm sure Andrew would bear me out . . ."

The Piece of Dry Toast (as I now thought of Mr. Denniston) lowered his head in assent. Clearly his readiness to bear Sargie out was unconditional, since he did so before Sargie had finished his sentence.

". . . when I say that once you get into that area you open up a whole lot of irrelevant questions. Obviously I should have to choose one member of the family to be the custodian of the papers. One can't have a lot of people deciding these things."

"Why not?" Lord Lampitt and Dame Ursula both asked at once.

"And if it went to the next of kin, I think it would almost certainly turn out to be one of Vivian's grandchildren in Nairobi or whatever flea-hole it is they live in."

"Mombasa," I chipped in automatically, unable, when these questions arose, to forget my childhood catechism.

"Then there are Rachel, and Michael, and there's all Ivo's brood, most of whom I haven't even met."

"Put the ash-tray nearer him, someone," said his sister wearily as the incinerated fragments of his Senior Service flew about the area of his chair. It was not avarice which was making her so cross. It was the knowledge that she could not exercise control over either Sargie or the papers.

"No," said Dame Ursula, "once we started offering the papers round the family, the situation would become completely chaotic."

She was a figure of whom I had heard much, but never met until that day. She had such a recognisably Lampitt face—a long beaky nose, a prominent chin, the Punchinello aspect of Sargie himself—that it was hard to think she was quite real, rather than being Sargie dressed up. A nervous laugh, totally devoid of mirth, revealed her false teeth to her company every time she spoke. She wore a funny old chintzy dress which could have been (and perhaps was) run up from a pair of drawing-room curtains. Over her shoulders she draped a lumpy maroon cardie.

"A library's the place for it." Giggle. "No doubt at all about this." Giggle.

"I agree with yer, Ursula, I agree with yer," said Lord Lampitt, leaning forward on the table with one elbow, flicking on a lighter over the bowl of his pipe with another. Vernon must have been by then between fifty and sixty. He had inherited his father's Lloyd George peerage "under protest" and abandoned his seat in the House of Commons.

As if to emphasise what he hoped we would all agree was the farcical inappropriateness of coronets or ermine in his own case, determined man of the people that he was, he had devised a curiously demotic pronunciation for himself bearing no relation to any discovered regional accent but differentiating him as strongly as possible from his own class, however that might be defined. He had a stupid but very amiable face, protuberant eyes, oval pink cheeks, reassuringly crooked teeth. A very few Lampitt genes seemed to have gone to his composition.

"If stuff's going to be preserved, let it be kept where yer ordinary bloke, yer researcher, maybe, or just yer interested enquirer can see it."

"But why should we want people to see Jimbo's diaries?" asked Sibs.

"Me old dad used ter say"—Vernon sucked on his pipe, and then came out with the *mot*—"it'll all come out in the wash."

I had heard this catch phrase before, but never known that it originated with the first Baron Lampitt. The thought occurred to me that if Vernon with his funny voice failed to get any further with politics there would probably always be a part waiting for him on "The Mulberrys." Barleybrook as yet lacked, for example, anyone directly classifiable as the Village Idiot.

"You can always" (giggle) "limit the access to papers," said Ursula. "There are many archives in the" (giggle) "Bodleian which the" (giggle) "public aren't allowed to read."

"But yer see, Ursula, with great respect I don't happen ter believe that's right." Vernon's manner was that of a patient teacher explaining something obvious to a backward child.

Sargie smiled at the chaos of views already presented by his kinsfolk. Then he continued.

"I think we all see the point of putting these documents in a library," he said. "I don't want a whole bloody archive in my flat. None of us live in places big enough to house such collections, except the very rich like Vernon."

Lord Lampitt shook his head as though his undeniably huge capital were a figment of our imagination, and Mallington Hall (like his other large house in Lord North Street) quite a modest little place really.

"The question remains 'Which library?' " (Giggle.) Ursula couldn't stop. "And a library like the" (giggle) "Bodleian . . .' "

"Of course," Sargie conceded, "we could put all Jimbo's stuff in some library like the Bodleian or the British Museum and place an embargo on it. Of course we *could*."

"But yer don't understand me point about the free availability of *information* for yer ordinary bloke."

"It would have to be a pretty *extraordinary* bloke who wanted to read Jimbo's diaries," said Sibs.

Sir Rupert loyally made a harrumphing noise which I took to mean that he had found his wife's intervention witty.

Anne and Gavin alone among the Lampitts seemed capable of sitting quietly and hearing Sargie out. Their elders, like naughty schoolchildren, had the compulsion to express dissent, amusement, agreement, quite instantaneously, and were unable to wait until Sargie had explained himself. Rather than being put off his stroke by this, Sargie seemed to appreciate it, and offer it as the very reason for the course of action which he expounded.

"And some of us wouldn't be happy to think of every Tom, Dick and Harry peering into them."

"Dear-a-dear," sighed his lordship. "Whatever happened to those socialist principles of yours, Sargie?"

"No, we don't want people peering at them the moment they're put on deposit. But this place in New York isn't a public library. Even scholars have no right of access to it unless they can persuade the chairman of the company, Virgil D. Junior

himself, that they are *bona fide* investigators. I'm sure we'll come
to a good agreement with old Virgil."

The Piece of Dry Toast once more inclined his head in assent.

"Ask again, Gavin," said Sibs.

"If the remuneration . . . ," my brother-in-law began.

But Sir Rupert silenced him with another harrumph.

"I suppose," said Rupert, "that the question exercising some
of us is how much this would affect the biography."

"That again, Rupert, my dear, is what is so ingenious and
pleasing about the present scheme. I know you all blamed me
for letting Lover Boy get his hands on the papers.

General murmurs of " 'Course not, Sargie," "Good heavens,
no." Ursula began a little lecture on the subject of Hunter's
book. "The trouble with Mr. Hunter's biography is that it starts
from a completely false premise . . ."

While she was speaking, perhaps to some imaginary audience
of undergraduates, Sargie continued, "On Jimbo's stuff, that is.
No, you all blamed me. But here, you see, is old Virgil, and
we've no reason to suppose that Hunter even knows who he is.
Now if it's all locked up in New York, Lover Boy isn't going
to be able to read it. And old Virgil D. Junior has given us
assurances."

Again the Piece of Dry Toast inclined his head. He seemed
to bow his head whenever Virgil D. Everett's name was mentioned, as some High Church people bow at the mention of Our
Lord.

". . . absolute assurances that no one will have access to the
Jimbo Archive without the personal permission of Virgil D. He
very much doesn't share your views, Vernon."

Vernon had taken his pipe from his mouth, and with its spitty
stem he was counting off the fingers of his left hand.

"Multimillion dollar oil conglomerates in California, one of
the biggest law practices on the East Coast, then there's 'iz art
collection—don't forget the Everett Dalis—and that's not to
mention all 'iz directorships of the big multinationals. No,
'course 'a don't approve, Sargie, nor would you uv done if he
hadn't offered you a thumping great cheque."

"Harrumph, which is really . . . ," said Sir Rupert.

"Come on, Sarge." Sibs was a little girl in the nursery once again. "How much is he offering?"

"Well, they were mine, those papers," said Sargie.

Having delivered the facts of the case rather clearly, he was now quite prepared to switch on the pathos. He became the Sargie remembered from my boyhood, a figure who seemed that he might burst into tears if you tried to "fuss" him.

"You always blame me," he said, with a sweeping gesture which sent his gin glass and its contents flying down the table. It was an "accident," not a tantrum, but it was hard to believe that it was not staged. In the ensuing muddle everyone got up from the table. Dame Ursula made things worse by shaking her sodden lap in the direction of Vernon, and the hostility between them, a theme on which my uncle Roy had often discoursed, became undisguised.

"Mind where yer going. Yuv sprinkled me best trousers, now, Ursula, yer clumsy . . ."

Giggle, giggle.

"And I suppose yer think it's funny."

The spilt gin glass provided the punctuation which we all required. There was no point in further engagements that day. The battle had gone to Sargie and the Starlings had been foiled. None of us knew at the time that Sargie had in fact, even as we discussed the matter, signed all the papers, handing over to Virgil D. Everett Jnr. the ownership and rights in all Jimbo's stuff. Sargie told Anne and me a bit about it, as we drove him home. Anne had bought an Austin Seven, so there was no room for the Piece of Dry Toast, who bowed his way into a taxi in Sloane Street not long after we drove out of Cadagon Square.

"I say, Robin, slow down unless you want to kill us," Sargie said automatically, as soon as she got into third gear. And while she was saying that we were only doing twenty, Sargie added, "Thank goodness we got through all that, though. I don't think your mother will bother us again. What is it your friend calls poor old Sibs? Lady Vulture?"

"You're sure you want to go through with this sale?" Anne asked.

"The thing is—look, darling Robin, I know I said slow down,

but I didn't mean a funeral pace—left, left bugger you, here."

"I can't turn left here now, Sargie. Not since they made it one way."

"Bugger one way."

By now it suited his purposes to appear pretty sozzled; perhaps he actually was in this condition. Before we got him back to his flat in Kensington Square he had persuaded us to promise to do the final stages for him. This no doubt had been his object when he accepted a lift in Anne's car.

"My only difficulty is how to get the papers out of Lover Boy," he said. "They really ought to be in Andrew Denniston's office in a week or two. Thing is, I can't specifically remember how much there was."

"Surely Mr. Everett has not bought the whole archive without looking at it?" said Anne.

"Trusting fella."

"There's something funny there," said Anne.

We never did quite find out how, in the first place, Hunter had come to be looking after the Lampitt papers. At one stage he and Sargie had been thick as thieves. Then later, for reasons which never became clear, Hunter fell from grace and Sargie began to share Sibs's unflattering views of the man. Sargie never bothered to explain any of this to us. Perhaps there was nothing to explain; he had always been capricious, and changes of mood about Jimbo's biographer were an inevitability. He had started out as one of that huge category of people who found Hunter charming. Like all members of the family, though, he was horrified by Hunter's biography of his brother. It was not that he had any of Sibs's humbug. He was not in favour of suppressing evidence if it was there. He simply failed to believe that Jimbo had led the life of a promiscuous and indiscriminate homosexual.

All this was awkward now that Anne and I had befriended Hunter. I wouldn't want to exaggerate the number of times he had been to our flat, but he was by now a fairly regular visitor. He always came at my invitation; he was not one to drop in. As it happened, Hunter was supping with us that very night, so, having left Sargie in Kensington Square, we had time to discuss the matter in the car as we returned to Lamont Road.

We had not had any major row since the terrible Night of the Lost Keys, but we were very much under strain. I was tormented by the thought that she had fallen out of love with me, and I couldn't imagine why. I still loved her, but there was so much hurt in my mind that I might as well have hated her. The eating and the living together and even the sex went on much as before. What had once been ecstatic now seemed merely routine, enjoyable on its own terms but almost impersonal. A deep, dark gulf had come to divide us.

We no longer held hands in the theatre or walking down the street. The expression "something has come between us" felt almost literally true. It was as if there was something which I could not see forcing us apart. I had thought that we were Nature's exceptions. We had broken all the rules and some kind angel or deity had, it seemed, spared us the sort of crabby non-relationship which appeared to be what most married couples of my acquaintance settled down to. Now, all Day Muckley's or Peter's bar-stool wisdom about marriage had a hideous plausibility. Both Anne and I had ceased to be happy. Before, our own company had been the source of the most ecstatic, semimystical happiness; now we did not really want to be alone together. When it was just the two of us, the misery was inescapable. Partings, such as saying goodbye to Sargie that Sunday afternoon, became painful little leaps from the world of friendliness back to one of gloom and togetherness. It was not that either of us planned to be in a particular mood once we were left alone together. It was more like entering a haunted house and not knowing what we should find there.

It puzzled me now that I failed so completely to read aright the signals of Anne's strange behaviour. Only a few weeks before the disastrous Night of the Lost Keys, we had seemed to be getting on as well as we had ever done. Or was that true? I now began to reassess the past and to admit to myself, or invent, the fact that Anne's breeziness had always caused me misgivings. It now appeared to me that she had never truly taken me seriously, whatever that was supposed to mean. It felt as if I had given her my besotted and whole-hearted devotion, but that she had only been able to respond with laughter. Sexual experiences which seemed at the time like journeys to a new stratosphere had perhaps for her been no more than jolly schoolgirl romps. Now, a spoilt youngest child and every inch her mother's daughter, she was bored, and she was not kind enough to conceal it. This was the sort of assessment I made of Anne's character and her changing relationship with myself. The chilling thing was the belief that on her side not much had changed, that she never had minded about me in the way that I so devotedly cared about her. Presumably it was because I felt so hurt and so frightened by her behaviour that I protected myself from any intelligent analysis of its causes. When contemplating the Night of the Lost Keys, I did not ask quite simple questions: What had that evening been like for Anne? Why had she been so unhappy in the first place? What was it about our visit to the theatre, and in particular to our going backstage, which had caused her such pain? Was she not by nature a killjoy? Anyone outside the situation would have asked these questions and found what I now see to be the obvious answers: but marital unhappiness has the capacity to stupefy, to stun to the point where right judgment is impossible. All that mattered during this particular phase of horror was that we should not be left too much alone together. This was, paradoxically, one of the only things which united us. We therefore spent so much of the time out. I was glad of my job at the Bottle, and even in periods when I was not being paid by Cyril to dispense drinks to the others, I spent more and more time in the place, on one side of the bar or the other.

Anne was often at the Courtauld. We never lunched together anymore. In the evening there was still the rigid convention that we met up. Sometimes we would visit Sargie or her parents or go to a restaurant with a third or fourth party. If at home, we nearly always tried to have someone to eat with us. We had the most miscellaneous string of people to suppers—never in large numbers since our table could not really seat more than five.

Fellow research students of Anne's from the Courtauld, Darnley and his sisters, William Bloom were regulars. Sometimes there was the social equivalent of a one-night stand, somebody we happened to have met in the course of the day and whom, in desperation, we had asked back so as not to have to dine *à deux*. There would have been plenty of such takers in the Bottle, but, understandably, Anne drew the line at my pub friends. Day Muckley had, on a number of occasions, said he would like to bring his mistress round to see us. I should have been pleased if he had done so because I did not quite believe in this person and was embarrassed that he should so frequently refer to her; but Anne, whose first glimpse of him had been on television, thought of him solely as "the man who puked"; she did not wish to risk the awkwardness of an encore on our rented carpet.

We ate almost entirely picnic food bought at delicatessens, which in those days seemed exotic. French or Italian cheeses, ditto bread, salamis, taramasalata, cole slaw—stuff which any English person can now go and buy in a supermarket—was something to be sought out in Soho.

Our entertaining of Hunter must be seen against this background. His visits belong to the period when we first started to get on really badly. It has to be said, however, that his visits were unlike those of the others. For one thing, we did not supply him with a picnic in which a piece of Dolcelatte or a Spanish sausage might be brought to the table in a brown paper bag. For Hunter, an effort was made. I polished our few glasses. Anne cooked simply, but always well.

It is painful to admit that we made so much effort simply because Hunter was now "famous." Speaking solely for myself, this had an extraordinary effect upon me. There was really no reason, on past form, why I should much like Hunter, though he had always tried hard enough to be charming when we met. The fact that he was now a face on the television screen, and a famous man of letters, worked on me, I am sorry to admit, like a drug. I hugged to myself, with delicious sensations of superiority to the rest of mankind, the knowledge that Raphael Hunter knew me, ate my wife's lamb chops, lolled in our rented armchair, drinking a glass or two (Hunter was always abstemious) of the best cheap wine we could afford.

My snobbery about Hunter was what blinded me to the situation and I blush for that. On the other hand, he had also become a sort of friend and over the matter of my novel he had been quite needlessly generous. Many people in his position might have put in a good word with their own publisher on behalf of a struggling young writer. But he seemed to have gone much further than that, talked Madge Cruden into accepting my novella for her list at Starmer and Rosen. Here again, I knew nothing at the time of the extent to which Madge doted on Hunter. She would probably have been prepared to publish any rubbish with which he presented her if thereby she could increase in his esteem. I believed the many stories about Madge being a powerfully formidable woman, nobody's fool, and it did not occur to me that so famously tough an individual might have taken on my book merely because she loved Hunter. On the contrary, I thought that it was my book and its brilliance which had broken through even Madge's iron resolve. Though I had decided that the stylish thing was to be modest about it, I inwardly believed that my novel was quite on a level with *David Copperfield* and Proust's recreation of Combray. I do not even possess a copy today but even if I did I know that I should be unable to read it. Something tells me that this barely fictionalised account of my childhood with Uncle Roy and Aunt Deirdre and their preferring their dog to myself was not in fact quite the masterpiece which I had supposed.

"Madge is very pleased with it indeed, anxious to see your next," said Hunter at supper. He was sitting in the cane armchair and sipping Chianti. By his side was a lamp which had been made out of a wine bottle. It had a red raffia shade.

Emboldened by the thought that I, a soon-to-be-published author, would soon be hobnobbing with all kinds of famous people, I said, "I'm sorry it's just the three of us again. We should really have asked someone with you. Isabella, perhaps."

I was becoming as bad as Fenella. The idea that we might actually entertain a famous actress like Isabella Marno, whom

I had met for about ten seconds, was a preposterous one. Hunter and I, luckily, were alone together when I said it, though to judge from a louder-than-average clatter of saucepans in the kitchen it is possible that Anne overheard the remark.

"I like coming alone, really," said Hunter. He made no attempt to pick up my cheeky allusion to Miss Marno. I even wondered whether he really knew her all that well. Perhaps he had gone backstage and met her that evening for the first time? Such a thing was by no means impossible. (Though as it happens, I should add as a footnote, untrue. Hunter had at this date been Isabella Marno's lover for about six months. They remained together, on and off, I understand, for about another year.)

My excitement at the imminent publication of the book, only a few months in the future, was intense and it must have revealed itself in every muscle of my face. For some reason, however, I thought it would be disgraceful for any pleasure to show. In consequence, I lolled with my Chianti and made some most injudiciously blasé remarks about the hideous dust-jackets used on Starmer and Rosen books, and then moved on to some very unwise jokes about Madge.

Everyone who knew about Madge made jokes about her. Like Fenella or Day Muckley, she was one of those people who had decided to become a caricature of themselves. Perhaps it is wrong to say that they decided on it. One naively wondered whether there was ever a time when they were less "themselves," when the persona so garishly thrust at the world had been rather less violently Technicolored. This is a question which I still have not resolved in my mind about those who set out to be "characters" and end as the prisoners of their own act. Madge was a by-word, not just among publishers but in London generally, for being a "battle-axe." Bawling out secretaries, throwing books around the office, spitting insults at literary agents down the telephone: these, legend had it, were her favourite games. If you wanted to appear discerning, it was usual to add, after some account of Boadicea-like office ferocity, that Madge had extraordinary literary discernment, a wonderful eye for a book. If my own case was anything to go by, she was not one of the world's great editors. I had spent an afternoon in her office while she chain-smoked Gauloises over my poor little quarto-leaved typescript, turning each page with rapidity and with no sign whatsoever of any enjoyment. It felt like taking work up to teacher's desk. The only things for which she seemed to be on the lookout were errors of spelling or punctuation.

Until that afternoon, I had sincerely believed that it was impossible to read my account of Uncle Roy (Uncle Hector in the book) getting tangled up in Tinker's (Smudge's) lead without laughter. Indeed, any normal person would, I considered, be in hysterics over this passage, as over the invented scene of Aunt Dolly (Deirdre) holding a meeting of the Mother's Union at the rectory and the Lady Novelist, loosely based on Deborah Maddock, who used to live in our village, introducing a frank discussion of sexual morals.

Madge read through these superb pieces of burlesque without the smallest flicker of amusement on her face. Her only comment on the Mother's Union scene was to squiggle her pen twice through the word *ciotus* and add the symbol TRS. in the margin.

"You've made that mistake twice, Mr. Ramsay."

"I thought it was funnier if Mrs. Sidebotham believed it was pronounced like that. It's a sort of malapropism."

"But it isn't the right spelling. *Coitus* is what you meant." She showed real impatience as she explained this to me.

"I did mean to spell it like that."

"Well, it was wrong."

She read on for some time, making innumerable tiny adjustments to the page with her blue pencil. At length she sighed and said, "Mr. Ramsay, where did you go to school?"

I told her.

"And did they teach you nothing about punctuation?"

"I think they did."

"One day you and I must have a word about commas."

I was saved by the bell on this occasion because the telephone rang and she was soon upping the decibels on account of the late departure of a recent title from the warehouse.

"I don't care what the shop steward says. . . . So am I a

member of the Labour Party. . . . That doesn't excuse pure,
bone idleness. . . . Look, I want those books in the shops, tomorrow!"

In Hunter's company I made the supreme blunder of supposing that no one took Madge quite seriously. The fact that
she had really made his career by zealous promotion of *Petworth
Lampitt* did not touch my imagination. Nor at that time had I
heard any gossip about her and Hunter which might have
warned me of the fact that she found Hunter heartbreakingly
attractive. But Anne was clearly aware of this.

"I'm not sure," I was saying, "that Madge is really any good.
Are you, Raphael?"

He sat forward earnestly in his chair, Rodin's thinker or a
man at stool.

"Madge is very . . ." He went red.

"She's publishing your book, damn it," Anne snapped out,
adding, "Raphael, come and help me with the washing up."

"Quite unnecessary," I said.

But he went.

This was part of the little routine. Hunter established his
essential ordinariness, the humility of the man behind the famous face, by clearing away the dishes and spending some time
in the kitchen with Anne while the coffee was being prepared
rather than enjoying the conversation in the sitting room with
myself. It mildly annoyed me that he did not wish to sit with
me for the whole evening; but great men must be allowed their
whims and I imagined that it meant a lot for Anne that he could
perform this little gesture of condescension. I always left them
to it on these occasions. There wasn't much room in the kitchen
and I was idle about all domestic tasks. While the coffee per-
colated (and our percolator took a very long time) I pottered
about, refilling my glass, or putting a record on the gramophone,
or did something Anne hated me doing, lifted up the table cloth
with all its crumbs and fragments and shook it on to the carpet.
By the time they emerged from the kitchen, I was hoping that
she wasn't boring him with talk about her research. I had been
planning the conversation with Sargie in his cowardice had shuf-

fled on to us, breaking to Hunter the news of the Everett Foundation's latest purchase.

"Raphael," I said, as Anne poured the coffee, "I'm afraid to say that something's cropped up."

"It's all right," said Anne, "I told him."

"You might have left it to me," I said.

"You had all evening to say something about it."

She now seemed incapable of concealing, even from an outsider whom we wanted to impress, that we were getting on badly. Instead of being able to smooth over this unpleasantness I was angered by it.

"I just hope you got all the details right," I said.

"Look," said Hunter cooingly. He suddenly seemed, though looking remarkably youthful and handsome, to be much wiser and saner than either of us. "It's very kind of you to have told me about all this."

"It isn't kind," said Anne. "Not if it's going to make your work totally impossible."

"You see," I said, "Sargie has actually asked us to . . ."

"I know, I know." Hunter sighed. Sympathy for us in our embarrassing plight seemed the dominant emotion on display. "Of course you must come and collect the papers whenever you like."

"Sargie doesn't always realise how busy other people are," I said testily. "I have my book coming out . . ."

"We *know*," said Anne.

"I just don't know when I am going to find time to come to your flat and help you move all those boxes to the solicitor's office. I still have a part-time job in this weird pub, you see."

"You mustn't think of doing anything," said Hunter.

"I've said I'll do it all," said Anne quietly and swiftly. "There's no need for you to be involved."

Although I protested great business, I in fact had almost nothing to do, and for some reason it had seemed obvious to me that I should be the one who supervised the transfer of the Lampitt Papers.

Talk was desultory after that. Anne did start boring him with thesis talk, and when I tried to stop her, he said he was finding it interesting.

I was jealous that Anne had been the one chosen to help. I should have valued the opportunity of seeing Hunter's flat: I should have liked to feel myself getting to know him better; for it was a curious feature of our relationship that though he had now called on us frequently, there was never any question of his returning our hospitality. This simply never crossed our minds as a possibility.

Anne's ability to persuade Hunter to part with Jimbo's diaries without fuss made me jealous of those powers of social competence which she so alarmingly shared with her mother. She was always able to get things done and to persuade people to do things for her: tradesmen who claimed not to deliver their wares were always willing in Anne's case to make an exception. Plumbers or electricians, if I implored their services, would refuse to come and mend overflowing cisterns or smouldering fuse boxes. But they changed their minds the moment she seized the receiver and said, "Let me talk to them." In the first year of marriage this superb efficiency had been one of the things which I loved about her. Now I rather hated it and I even allowed myself to wonder whether it was quite ethical. Hunter could scarcely have been aware of the family pow-wow, of the strength of feeling against him among Anne's relations. He seemed so calm and smiling that I wondered whether he realised the implications of Anne's effectual confiscation of her late uncle's papers. Had she been quite straight with Hunter? Was he aware that they were going to be locked up in some strong-room in Manhattan? It would surely spell the end of his career as Jimbo's biographer; and yet he was smiling. There was something almost pathetic about it.

"I'm afraid that the papers are in a state of some confusion," said Hunter. "It might require several visits."

"I'll come as often as it takes," said Anne.

"She'll enjoy hanging round your neck," I said.

Since I was cross with her for getting the assignment and so impressed by Hunter's sang-froid, I could only take refuge in the tired old banter of Anne being in love with him. This was a joke which we had never until that moment shared with Hunter. I helped him on with his coat and saw his features pucker as I said the words. I was then sober enough to remember that we had never told Hunter of my fantasy that he was Anne's "pin-up"; no more did he know of Sargie's nickname for him. His slightly puzzled frown soon vanished and by the time he turned, his blandly vapid smile was restored, an expression which was now so familiar on the television that one wondered whether in some strange way the face was not the invention of television lights and cameras, whether the smile, like that of the Cheshire Cat, was not disembodied from the smiler, hoicked out of the props department in the television centre and imposed upon him as a badge of his trade like the old masks of tragedy and comedy in Graeco-Roman theatre. It was not the first time that I had imagined Hunter's bland waxy face as a mask. The pained expression which I had glimpsed in the hall glass, infinitely brief and slight, hinted that if the mask of comedy were removed, a quite different countenance, perhaps a different character, would be found underneath.

Anne for her part looked mortified, furious, at my resurrecting this antique piece of marital banter. Hers was the kind of fury a child might have at school or at a party if a parent carelessly blurted out his secret family nickname. In the early days of our love she used to scream with laughter at the idea of having fallen in love with Hunter at the minute he was splattered by Day Muckley. Now, it appeared, jokes were out of order.

"As always," said Hunter, "it's been lovely."

He patted my arm and smiled. He had the air of one man encouraging another man. It was one *littérateur* to another. We saw together the obstacles which lay ahead: Madge perhaps being difficult, reviewers failing to see the point of the book. Together we would overcome, but there was nothing in his little gesture of patting my arm to suggest that this was what he meant. Touching someone's elbow is scarcely code for how to get on in the literary world, but at the time I was so certain that I knew Hunter's mind that his clasping my arm might have been a ritualised and universally (if secretly) recognised sign such as the Freemasons share with one another. I noticed with a certain childish glee that for all Anne's offer to help him with the papers he was really more interested in his friendship with me. He even forgot to give her the little peck on the cheek which he sometimes bestowed before leaving our flat. Indeed, I do not remember his even saying goodbye to her, whereas his farewells to me were on the verge of being effusive.

As soon as the front door closed I felt ourselves once more entrapped by the old sensations of intense unhappiness. Our feet crunched on the Cream Crackers which I had shaken onto the carpet.

"Oh, I've told you not to throw food on the floor," she said.

I felt a surge of rage against her for saying this. Keeping the flat clean was not my job. I was not her skivvy. What was Mrs. Wiley for? I wanted to clout Anne, but she moved out of range and lit a cigarette.

"I don't see why I should always be held responsible for keeping this place tidy," I said. "If it weren't for Mrs. Wiley the place would be a refuse heap."

She murmured something. It might have been "Oh, shut up." It was quiet, incoherent. With pompous slowness, an investigating magistrate's tones, I said, "You said? I didn't quite catch what you said."

I opened the bottle of cheap Scotch on the mantlepiece and poured myself some.

"Are you sure you aren't having too much of that stuff?" she asked, moving swiftly into the advantageous position of herself as prosecutor. The remark stung me. I was at the stage of being pleasantly blotto, but knew that one more glass would change this state into one of unpleasantness; and thereafter if I carried on drinking, I would be on the way to becoming blind drunk with all the dangers of the room spinning round, stomach and bowels emptying themselves, not necessarily at convenient time or place. These physical awarenesses arrived in the brain simultaneously with a hot, confused need to assert myself over Anne. Her arrogance was insufferable as she stood there on the other side of the fireplace, combing her hair with her fingers, pulling back her fringe to reveal her big pale brow. The gesture filled me with lust. I looked down at her legs. The sight of her calves in black stockings made me want to rip them off, her truculent fury with me only adding to her allure.

"Are you saying I'm drunk?"

"Don't be boring, Julian."

"Answer me."

She sighed a long sigh, blowing out smoke through lips and nostrils. Then, as she stubbed her cig she said, "I'm going to bed."

Gulping my whisky, pausing to refill the glass, I took this as the signal that I was meant to rape her. Perhaps I paused to refill the refill, because by the time I reached the bedroom she had already undressed and got in between the sheets. I noticed as I blundered into the room that my feet were not quite touching the ground. I sort of swayed about, not quite able to reach the carpet with my shoes; funny feeling. We had never gone in for pyjamas, so I knew she would be naked. She had turned off her bedside lamp and was lying on her side. Her eyes were closed.

I pulled back the bedclothes and saw that she was wearing a petticoat. What did she want me to do? Rip it off?

"I'm trying to go to sleep," she said. She did not open her eyes but her lower lip was trembling and she was on the edge of tears. I put down my drink on the dressing table and started to take off my own clothes, kicking shoes anywhere as I tore at shirt buttons. Had anyone observed me (and Anne, the only possible witness, had her eyes shut) they would have seen an almost infinitely derisory figure: the oldest joke in the world, a man with his trousers falling down to his ankles dancing like a clown to remove these cumbersome leggings. Within, by contrast, I was Blake's Tyger, tyger, burning bright. The violence but also the cosmic beauty of what I had to offer Anne made me feel like an embodiment of energy. Or so it seemed.

Without turning, Anne spoke through gritted teeth.

"*No*, Julian."

It was the first time in eighteen months that these words had ever been spoken between us and I refused to believe my ears. I leaned over the bed and took her by the shoulders.

"No!" she repeated.

Though in distress she was still in full command.

"Come here, will you." I grabbed her roughly. She sat up at once and clobbered me—hit out at my face with a fist. In spite of the violent fantasies which had flitted through my consciousness earlier, this was not a game I wished to play. I never wanted fighting to be part of the act of love, nor was it possible to mistake Anne's words or gestures as being anything remotely playful. She did not want me. That was clear; and the knowledge was sobering, painful, like being stabbed between the ribs with an icicle.

She sat up in bed, open-eyed. She looked at me with simple dislike. The course of action which I had been so brutally proposing some minutes before had been, throughout the last year, the central thing of my existence. All our spare time had been devoted to it; it coloured and made joyful the whole of life. We had done it everywhere, in open fields, on the bathroom floor, on hearth rugs, in bed, by night, by day. With this rapturously enjoyable accompaniment one felt that any pain life offered was superfluous, bearable. With this action "all losses are restored and sorrows end." There had never been any question before, even when we were quarrelling, that we were lovers, waiting sometimes with intolerable impatience to be left alone together so that we could resume the dance. It was against this background that my shock has to be registered. Anne was looking at me as if she had just received an improper advance from a stranger, as it were the window-cleaner.

"What the hell's going on?" I asked.

She burst into tears. She had pulled her knees towards her face and she hugged them desperately as she sobbed and moaned.

This sobered me up even more. I felt humiliated, cheated, deceived, and didn't know why. At the same time my heart was wrung by her misery and I too began to weep at the sheer pitiableness of it all. Instinct made me want to comfort her, to take her in my arms. I no longer wanted to force myself upon her; rather to cling to her myself for comfort. But even as I advanced and touched her, I felt her shoulder blades freeze and she shook me away. This rebuttal was worse than the first. I assumed that she had read all my unspoken signals exactly as I felt them. A small particle of unselfish common sense might have allowed me to see that there might have been some quite simple physiological explanation why she did not feel equal to the gymnastic rigours proposed. Now, however, she had rejected even simple kindness and sympathy. Her little shrug hurt and angered me terribly. Once more, I felt cheated. The clever, funny frivolous Anne with whom I had been in love had been a chimerical illusion concealing this, the real Anne, a congenitally moody, self-obsessed madwoman.

"Sargie, like many of the Lampitts, is very mildly barmy," Uncle Roy used to say. "And there was Angelica, of course."

"Oh, Christ," I said.

I got up and went over to the chest of drawers where I had left my whisky glass. After a swig, I asked, "It would help if you could tell me what I'm supposed to have done wrong."

She sniffed, a long, disgusting sniff.

"Oh, Julian, let's try to get some sleep."

"Why—that's all I want to know."

"I'm tired."

"I'm married to you—remember?"

"Good night, Julian."

The glass which had been in my hand hurtled through the air and smashed against the wall over the bed, its fragments flying everywhere. Splinters of glass were lodged like sequins in Anne's hair.

I wasn't in control. Any observer would have agreed with Anne's statement, repeated at various junctures in after time, that I had thrown the glass at her, and by any strict standards this was true. But it no longer felt as if I were doing things. My body was doing things in response to a wild pain which surged up inside me.

"Julian, put that chair down."

Her tear-stained face was now wide awake, and serious. She spoke slowly as to an animal. My eyes met hers, those great blue eyes which still had a complete and hypnotic power over me.

"Put it down, Julian."

Her head swayed about, momentarily becoming two heads. I was sober enough to realise that I was about to enter a phase of uncontrolled drunkenness. This little part of me which was still sober wanted to reach out to Anne's stern, calm voice and to look into her eyes for pardon. The chair was thrown aside. There was a terrible bang as this happened, but at least I did not throw it at *her*. Collecting myself with what felt like magisterial *gravitas,* I made for the door and on the second attempt I got through it.

Cold woke me, and the glimmerings of the grey dawn, which made the curtains of the sitting-room, hitherto an inchoate darkness, a discernible shape. I could make out the window between them. There was still a bit of spin left in my vision, whisky was still in the veins. The terrible physical sensations woke me. The back of my skull was pounding as I lay there on the carpet, my mouth and nostrils ached and reeked with too much smoking, a feeling which burnt its way all down my esophagus into the stomach. Even in this faint pre-light my eyes were terribly sore. I felt very cold underneath the blanket. It wasn't for an hour or more that I made sense of the blanket and realised that in all her anger and fear and grief, Anne must have tiptoed out of the bedroom to cover my naked and recumbent form as it lay stretched out on the sitting-room floor. Somehow this action, when I was awake enough to deduce what had happened, seemed the most heartbreaking thing of all.

seven

It hurts to remember how much pain I caused. Some of this pain was inflicted willfully, some of it was because I was young. Being in pain myself, I lashed out, heedless of where the blows would fall. But almost the most painful thing to recall is how stupid I was. The evidence was staring me in the face that Anne was in love with someone else; it was evidence which I was slow to piece together, slower to accept. The idea that she was really in love with Raphael Hunter was one which never crossed my mind. Even if I had recognised this staringly obvious fact, I still was not in a position to guess that he would exploit this situation.

But it was obvious that something was wrong, terribly wrong. Anne had changed. She was no longer the person with whom I had been so ecstatically in love. A great coldness had descended. Drunken quarrels of the kind which flared up after the supper with Hunter were rare. The anger which became habitual between us was without passion. It was dead and dull. Childishly hurt by her, I never asked myself why she was in this strange mood. The fact that she was different changed and destroyed me, but I saw the transformation as something which she was doing, or not doing, to me. There seemed no need to look for explanations outside the prison house of our own poisoned relations with each other. She was sullen and morose. I blamed her for being so unloving towards me, but I assumed that she had begun to find something amiss in myself, and therefore attributed all her stoniness to a puritanical distaste of my drinking, or a simple jealousy of my having had a novel accepted. Now, if I came into the room, she hardly looked up or she would make an excuse to get up and walk out. She did not always refuse me my "marital rights." In a ghoulish way she seemed actually amused by the continuance of this desire on my part, sometimes lighting a cigarette or even on occasion reading a book (*The Calderdale Saga*, as it happened) while the activity lasted.

"God, your friend writes badly" was her only comment at this supposedly ecstatic moment. The hungry, giggling little monkey-Anne of our earlier supremely happy conjunctions had become this *blasé* indifferent figure who, although lying there, seemed to be taking no part in the proceedings. All these were pretty definite signals, but of what, I would not allow myself to see. Anne is not a fundamentally unkind person. Perhaps she wanted me to dislike her, to make the sense of let-down easier. If so, she failed. I had come to hate her, but I remained passionately in love with her. Had I loved her less, had she been more of a friend and less of a mistress, I might have been able to sympathise with her, to guess at her predicament. If from the first I had known the cause of Anne's sorrow, I have sometimes wondered whether I should not have been able to "save the marriage." Since, in moments of terrible repining, I have supposed that I would have been able to set matters to rights. Time heals most things, but especially the wounds from which she suffered then. But I was far too hurt by her sudden withdrawal of affection to be able to see her as she was. I began to attribute it to some supposed small-mindedness which had been inherent in her character from the beginning but to which love had blinded me. The only new ingredient in our relationship, as I saw things, was the fact of my literary success. Therefore Anne minded my having befriended Hunter, made a success with Madge. She was prepared to love me when I was a pathetic figure, a part-time bar-man, the nephew of the village parson.

Now I had become someone in my own right, and it was a different story. Incoherent rage with Anne, and through Anne with all the tribe of Lampitts, welled up from atavistic depths. "They" had always despised "us." Anne had had her mind poisoned against me by her mother; perhaps even Sargie's lordly manner towards me had begun to brush off. They disliked me for knowing too much, that was it. Since childhood, I had had my eye unwillingly trained on the Lampitts by Uncle Roy and it made them uneasy. They wanted to send me back "where I belonged." The shirt factory was my proper place, following my father's footsteps. What had the likes of me to do with Cadogan Square? These thoughts were all totally preposterous. Even as they fixed themselves in my brain I did not quite believe them, but I said them to myself as we sat in silence on either side of the fire. Anne had given up reading at home. Sometimes she would have a newspaper on her lap, but more often she just sat, evening after evening, staring at the electric bars, smoking a lot, her once animated face transformed into a mask of sorrow. We gave up asking people to supper and little by little friends stopped calling. We must have been wretched company. Only Fenella was kind or stupid enough not to take account of this, but her visits were generally early in the evening, before Anne got back from the Courtauld.

Suppers with Hunter had fizzled out with the rest of social life. This fact puzzled me as much as the fact that Anne, who had now been weeks sorting and arranging the transfer of the Lampitt papers from Hunter's flat to the solicitor's office, found so little to say about it all. Normally, she was a good gossip, and would have found plenty to relate. If I pressed her about it, she was snappy.

But I wanted to talk to someone, and it was with half an idea of unburdening myself to an older man that I telephoned Hunter some weeks before the novel was published and suggested that we lunch together.

We had never had a social engagement *à deux* before, and on the telephone he sounded a bit harassed.

"Nothing special, is there, that you wanted to talk about?" His voice was nasal, conciliatory, his committee voice.

"Yes and no."

The truth was that after two or three very unhappy days with Anne I was desperate to talk to someone, someone sober, that is. Peter and the Best Seller were the obvious recipients of such marital confidences. That is one of the functions of pubs, the secular person's confessionals, the poor man's couch of analysis. I was frightened, though, of finding in Peter's unhappy experiences of marriage too many humiliating parallels with my own. If his vision of the universe was true, men and women were essentially enemies, and alcohol was the only way out. I was not strong enough to take such a view as my own. My unwillingness to sound out Day Muckley was based on a different delicacy, the fear of shocking him. He spoke habitually of the decadence of the age and deplored his own inability, blamed entirely on the outrageous behaviour of his wife, to lead a life of domestic rectitude—"as you do, Julian, lad, but then you are very happily married." The Best Seller used to say this so often to me that I simply felt unable to confront him with the reality of the case. He spoke eagerly of Anne and me spending an evening in a restaurant with himself and his mistress. I had not the heart to tell him that home life was miserable. An evening with him and Anne was anyway unthinkable. In the days when she liked me, Anne would have been in a perpetual state of schoolgirlish giggles because Day was the man who had puked. Latterly, she would have been truculent, as on the evening when I "made" her go backstage and see "a lot of grotesques." I could not begin to guess that the real cause of her unhappiness on that evening was that she had known of Hunter's liaison with Isabella Marno, hated watching her rival's triumphant performance on the stage, and hated even more being brought backstage to confront, with her own eyes, the intolerable knowledge that Hunter was, as gossip had related, hovering about the actress.

He was edgy, as I said, on the telephone.

"I thought you might ring, actually," he admitted.

"You did?"

There was such a silence that I thought we had been cut off.

"Hallo?"

"Let's talk in the restaurant," he said.

We ate at a Greek place in Charlotte Street, and for the first part of the luncheon he talked obsessively about his own professional affairs. The success of "Perspectives" was all very gratifying, but it made serious inroads into other equally important and weighty concerns. "Tom" and "Rupert" (not Starling, I think) had been marvellous in securing the future of the London Library, but Hunter somehow implied that it would have been too much to expect them to do so without his taking a much more active role on the committee. There was, he added with a ruthless glint in his eye, *dead wood* on any committee and it was part of a good committee man's function to get rid of it.

Then Madge had asked him . . .

"Oh, talking of Madge," I said. I was anxious to get on to the subject of my book, but Hunter was full of a major new literary prize which he and Madge were going to set up for a work of "literary" fiction. Then, as always, there were reviews to be written. There were some big international literary events which really demanded Hunter's presence. Yevtushenko had been over to England.

"I only managed to see him once. I feel bad about that."

I began to feel really sorry for Hunter that his television success was absorbing so much valuable time.

"Cyril should write an extra chapter of *Enemies of Promise*," said Hunter. The only Cyril I knew was the landlord of the Black Bottle, so this sentiment caught me momentarily by surprise until I grasped Hunter's drift.

"Television is a worse enemy than the pram in the hall," he added.

"And on top of all that," I said, "you've got to deal with the Lampitt Papers."

I never did know for certain how long it would take to transfer the papers from Hunter's flat to the lawyer's offices in Lincoln's Inn Fields. At a generous estimate, it must have taken the best part of one afternoon. At the time, I entirely accepted that this task was absorbing weeks of Anne's time, necessitating frequent visits to Hunter's flat. From the way that his face darkened at the mention of the Lampitt Papers, I now discern the fear of a show-down from the wronged husband; though I also realise that, even if this had been a card in my hand, Hunter, who must have met with variations of this problem before, would have handled things adeptly. During lunch itself, I interpreted his frown, his slight hesitancy, as irritation with Anne. Blood will out, I supposed. In her thoroughness with the papers, Anne was getting her revenge for the wrong that Hunter had done her family as well as showing herself to be the conscientious scholar who knew how archival material should be treated and preserved.

I now ask myself how it was possible for me not to see things as they were. I am tempted to think, because of what I subsequently knew about Hunter, that, during this lunch with him, I was mistaken to act towards him as I did. Yet, while obviously true in one way, it is surely false to suggest that people can be got right or wrong, like mathematical puzzles, rather than being entities in a state of endless flux who react so differently to each separate combination of circumstances or relationships that it makes no sense to define them. It is upon the fallacy of fixed personalities that biographers have made their trade, either by reinforcing caricature in Jimbo's dated manner or more often, like Hunter, parading themselves as fearless iconoclasts who are demythologising the "character" concerned. The exercise perhaps has a certain literary charm so long as no one supposes that it relates to the real, felt life of the individual under discussion. What shocks now in my surprise that I should have tried to unburden myself to Hunter, and share with him my marital difficulties, is the surprise itself. It is a clue to me that memory has hardened and ossified my picture of Hunter, and to a lesser degree of my earlier self. I am making them into stereotypes, which is why my vision of how they behaved is capable of surprising me. The real me, and the real Hunter, as opposed to these mythological projections, were figures of infinite fluidity, and even as they sat together in the restaurant in Charlotte Street they were many persons, possessed of many thoughts and aims. I have no way of knowing what a mixture of embarrassment and guilt Hunter felt, sitting with the husband of one of his current areas of female interest; nor whether his relations with women, which so obsessed me, had ever at any time played a large part in his consciousness; or whether they were always, if not a means to an end, at least subservient to his true aims.

Years later, during an indiscreet luncheon with Isabella Marno, I was astonished to learn, from the actress's own lips, the sort of details which lovers should never decently reveal to a third party. A general lack of interest on Hunter's side was what was conveyed. Throughout her period of most besotted devotion to Hunter, their secret afternoons and very few, very occasional weekends, he had been cold and languid. When in her company, his face had never been lit up, until he parted with her, to chair a committee or be interviewed by a journalist. I felt instinctively that Bella Marno's experience had been typical. Hunter's indifference to sex, while "allowing himself" to be involved with it (and this apparently was how it had felt to Bella), was part of the secret. It drove her wild, and it must have been what drove the others wild, too—the thought that if they loved him with sufficiently hysterical abandonment, he might begin to match with deeds the passionate colouring of his first, verbal overtures. So, perhaps, even as I sat there in Charlotte Street, unable to eat, and thinking that Hunter might be able to shed light upon the problem of Anne's unhappiness, his mind was really occupied with the edition of "Perspectives." And if this was the case, and if, as I now believe, he had only half-wanted Anne to be his lover (and that for mixed motives, such as we all might have), it is perhaps not surprising that I did not during that meal sense him as a rival. This is not to say that he was not my rival, nor that, only shortly after that meal, I came to hate him quite violently. But at that juncture, I saw him only as a friend, and also, ludicrously, as an expert on the Lampitts. It was in that capacity that I had sought him out; it was in that capacity, therefore, that I saw him.

From the many comments on his work already passed by Sibs, Sargie and the other Lampitts, it is a little surprising that I still thought of Hunter as the great Lampittologist.

"He just gets us wrong," giggled Ursula mirthlessly to me during a later phase of existence, dining at her austere high table. "The whole feel of us is wrong. We don't *smell* like Lampitts in his pages. And that sense that he gives off of Jimbo being the malicious sort of"—giggle—"bachelor, if you know what I mean. But it wasn't fair; Jimbo could be the kindest man in the world. Of course you only have to read his descriptions of Angelica to see that Mr. Hunter didn't have a clue! 'True blue'—for Angelica, who was almost as communistic as Vernon! And as for the suggestion that Angelica might have married Rupert Brooke! Well, one day, you must get me to tell you the story of her and Hilda Bean."

But most of us are slow, I certainly am, to dispute self-confessed expertise. I still believed in Hunter's knowledge and understanding of the Lampitts, and valued him precisely because he had considered the family from a dispassionate, academic viewpoint. He had an encyclopaedic knowledge of all Anne's relations. I myself had grown up with firsthand knowledge of what Sargie could be like if—in the surely unfair rectory phrase—"he chose" to be difficult. Choice was probably the last thing which came into play on these occasions; Anne's sudden mood swing against me could surely be put down to what Uncle Roy called "the very mildly barmy strain in the Lampitts."

On the other side of the table, Hunter disposed of a plateful of moussaka with clean, systematic forkwork. I had no appetite at all, and however much I played with my heaps of food they did not seem to diminish in size, or in nauseating unpalatability. "If in doubt give them mince": one of Aunt Deirdre's "mottos" appeared to be the view of the Greeks, if the limited menus of their nastier restaurants were anything to go on. I preferred my aunt's grey, rather watery shepherd's pies to this oily pile of cheese and gristle.

"I'm only sorry," said Hunter, "that I shan't be there for your party." He was reverting to the publication day of my novel. "Madge, as I'm sure you realise, likes any opportunity for a little gathering."

"I'd assumed you'd be there."

"I'd love to, but it's a 'Perspectives' night."

"Of course."

I had rather hoped that Hunter would invite me on to "Perspectives" to publicise the book, but presumably the decisions about who to have on such programmes was left in the hands of organisers other than Hunter himself. Now, rather than allow myself to nurse feelings of resentment at my non-inclusion, I began to feel that it was somehow clumsy of me to publish a book on a "Perspectives" night. I started to apologise, and say how much I owed him. Then I went on to say how much I had always enjoyed his visits to our flat, what a good friend he had always been to both of us, to Anne as well as myself.

Hunter ceased to look at me straight. His eyes, which were rather small for that round, pasty face, developed a narrow, weasely expression which at the time I read as telepathic concern for my marital problems.

"I'm a bit worried about Anne actually," I added. "She doesn't seem quite herself these days."

Hunter pursed his lips.

"You've no idea why?" he asked. Here his sidelong glance became so oblique that he stopped looking at me altogether; in fact, he turned and looked out of the window. The moment of possible intimacy passed by. From an intense desire to confide I suddenly felt embarrassed at myself and drew back from the abyss. Instincts of marital decency reasserted themselves. One doesn't speak of such secrets, even to a very close friend like Hunter.

"I think it may be that she finds it hard to be married"—there was a pause before I dared to finish the sentence with ponderous self-conceit—"to a novelist."

Visible relief had passed over Hunter's face when he swung round, faced me once more and laughed.

It stings me to contemplate what lay behind Hunter's laugh. There was something in it of whooping, almost obscene relief. He must have come to the restaurant with near certainty that he would be confronted by the young man he was cuckolding. At the very least, the man would expose him as a liar; but perhaps worse would follow—scenes of violence. These were still the days when such an incident could conceivably have cost Hunter his job at the BBC, an organisation which at that date resembled a large Victorian family, prepared to turn a blind eye to its children's lapses from propriety so long as they weren't found out. Had Hunter been cited as a co-respondent in a divorce case, it is not impossible that his future as the presenter of "Perspectives" would have been jeopardised. These and perhaps a dozen other fears explained Hunter's anxious looks. When my words made it clear that I was completely ignorant of his relations with Anne, it is hardly surprising that his mouth opened with such triumph. When it did so, I had a few seconds of surprise that his rat-like little teeth had gone quite black since I last noticed them. Then I realised that their sharp yellowish surface was coated with particles of the spinach which he had eaten as an accompaniment to his minced lamb. Recovering himself, dabbing his lips with a napkin, he was able to pontificate in general terms.

"I do believe that husbands and wives find it difficult to come to terms with their partners writing fiction, but then I am hardly in a position to say, never having written a novel, and of course"—He rubbed his plate with a piece of pita bread which he put into his mouth and chewed. When the bread had gone down, he finished his sentence: "I am a bachelor."

During his laughter, my desire to unburden myself to Hunter of my private sorrows left me forever. Hunter, instinct at least told me that he was not that sort of friend. It was something of a relief to both of us, I think, when a man whom I did not know came over from some other table in the restaurant and spoke to Hunter while he was signing the bill.

"Well, I've got a very full week, Dick," said Hunter.

"I know," said the man called Dick. "I know. I shouldn't bother you if I did not think it was important, but if we could meet for half an hour before the meeting . . ."

Evidently they were fellow members of a committee. Hunter's eyes had lit up at the prospect of some behind-the-scenes manoeuvering. Needless to say I remember very little of his conversation with the man Dick, but for the first time then since the beginning of our grown-up phase of friendship, I felt the difference between our ages. This committee chat was real grown-up stuff. I could not imagine a condition, nor a state of mind, when I might be interested in such things.

"I think it might be as well," said Hunter, "if I rang her *before* the meeting, actually Dick. I'm sure she'll vote our way, but I don't want her to be influenced by all that emotional blackmail that Jonquil can produce at times."

He was too remote from my juvenile difficulties to understand them. Perhaps, though, I had begun once more to be wary of him; the spell of enchantment which he had cast over me, really ever since I saw him on television, that night I fell in love with Anne, was beginning to evaporate; once more I became mindful of those occasions when he had been unscrupulous or manipulative.

"No, no, Dick," he was saying. "Don't whatever you do, do that! We don't want this as a named item on the agenda. It is the sort of thing we should spring on them during Any Other Business."

In a brief flickering one saw how he loved to exercise power, and instinct made me shy from allowing him to exercise power over us. Later, when I told Anne that I had lunched with Hunter, she received the information stonily.

"I thought you'd envy me," I said, never tiring of the worn-out banter. "Lunch with Raphael—what greater bliss."

There were two minutes of absolute silence broken only by the scratch and hiss of Anne's match against the side of its box as she lit up a cigarette. She had lately switched to du Maurier, her mother's preferred brand.

"You're smoking too much," I said.

She curled her stockinged feet beneath her haunches on the chair and opened a German grammar. Her only response to my observation about her smoking habits was to flick a bit of ash on to the carpet. I began another tack, and spoke of the publication of my novel, whether or not I should offer Madge dinner after the "small gathering" in her office about six o'clock on the day the book came out. In my mind, I had no doubt what one of Madge's "small gatherings" would be like. I had built up the party in my mind so much that my feelings of excitement and anxiety relating to this social event overshadowed my feelings about the book. Madge "knew everyone." This fact excited me, but it was also terrifying that she might have included among her guest list figures of such fame, or eminence, that I should be overwhelmed by embarrassment. I wanted a touch of *chic* on my great day, but I was anxious that Madge would wheel out the really big guns. At the same time, I secretly yearned for the greatest guns of all, and wondered, if she invited some of the luminaries with whom Hunter spent his time, whether or not I should soon be dwelling in unapproachable light, not merely in the literary world, but among such social divinities as Mrs. Eggscliffe or Lady Mary Spennymoor.

At the same time I was aware of this change in myself, the substitution of pure snobbery for artistic ambition. When I walked out of Tempest and Holmes, I had wanted life to contain more than pay slips and ledgers. I had wanted time on my own, not time doled out to me by an employer. I had been led on in part by a sense of life's sacredness, that it was too good to waste. These feelings had not been defeated by a half-fearful longing for social advancement; but there was the danger that, like Uncle Roy, I was going to use what imaginative gifts I possessed in building up a hierarchical vision of the human race fed by fantasy. In such a state of mind, the Lampitts themselves, and my marital connection with them, seemed to be a mere resting-ground before I pressed on to the higher reaches. And there was much less innocence in this than in Uncle Roy's highly localised and particular devotion to the Lampitts themselves. He genuinely believed that they were the most interesting beings in the universe. Mr. Attlee had been of interest not because he was the prime minister but because he had enjoyed the inestimable privilege of having Vernon in his cabinet. Had he been on terms with the Queen herself, Uncle Roy would have found the fact exciting only insofar as Lampitt connections could have been forced; Majesty, no less than any other individual, would have been treated to "appropriate" Lampitt tales, the extraordinarily amusing occasion when Vernon's father had been to the palace to collect his peerage from her grandfather George V, or the good fortune enjoyed by that monarch and Queen Mary to reside for some of the year at Sandringham, not three-quarters of an hour by car from Mrs. Lampitt of Timplingham, and nearer still to Lord Lampitt's residence at Mallington Hall.

But my mind was possessed of something less pure. It wasn't, or I told myself that it wasn't, respect for rank or blood for their own sake. It was the world of literate and intelligent London which with my baser self I dreamed of conquering; but the yearning itself, like some unwholesome erotic impulse, brought with it a sense of self-loathing so strong that I looked about for another person to blame, rather as an unhappy homosexual might blame the individual who first opened his eyes to the existence of the underworld where his tastes might be indulged. I had not been like this before I met Anne. That was a new stick to beat her with. She had corrupted me. Since, by now, we were barely on speaking terms, I could not choose to enter into the matter with her, but the case for the prosecution built itself up, silently, inside my head. Nothing could have been less fair. I don't believe that Anne ever cared "who" anyone was. As far as that circle of the heavens was concerned in which Hunter was a bright star, I do not think she even realised that it was meant to be important or impressive. When I first met her, she read little modern literature and I am sure that it had never occurred to her that one might be excited to meet the authors of books one admired. She found the newspapers and politics a bore, so that those hostesses who, like Lady Mary Spennymoor, had married newspaper proprietors and liked to entertain the more presentable members of the House of Commons, together with writers, musicians, or actors, would have carried no weight at all with Anne. That Sibs was a contemporary, and even a bit of a friend, of Lady Mary's (less friendly with Mrs. Eggscliffe) was hardly Anne's fault; nor was the fact that, all along, I had been more excited by these facts than I cared to admit.

The approaching "gathering" was supposed to precipitate me

into these worlds by my own steam, or, indirectly, by Hunter's smoke and wind. The very fact that I could, if I had been less shy of doing so, easily have asked Sibs herself to introduce me to these ladies gave me the savage wish to do it all on my own.

Can that really be right? I write these words, but the strange thing is, I can't really remember what I felt. Now, all these figures have passed into history. I never did belong to this world, which I found at that time so alluring, though many members of it came my way, and sometimes younger people will ask for my memories of the "famous." Newspaper articles and books have been written about the "circles" of Mrs. Eggscliffe and Lady Mary Spennymoor. Certainly as a young man I believed these circles to exist. If someone, such as Hunter, would take me by the hand, like Virgil leading Dante through the purgatorial regions, it would have been possible in my belief to know that you had arrived in a particular trough or domain of fixed beings. And what modern researchers into the period find so hard to recognise is that it was not truly like that; no world was ever as fixed as a Dantean circle; and even when these hostesses wished to make their drawing-rooms into *salons* along a continental pattern, few of their friends, one is almost tempted to write "their clients," took such ambitions seriously. Anyhow, it seems upon looking back and trying to remember the rare occasions when I was entertained by such figures that they introduced me to the very least interesting people I ever knew, not one of whom was as much fun as the Best Seller, or Pete or Cyril or Fenella and Rikko, still less interesting than Darnley, Bloom or Aunt Deirdre and Uncle Roy.

But I was different then. I can write that, but it is hard for me to recapture the reasons, the inner promptings which awakened this rather unworthy set of social aspirations. They mean nothing to me now, just as my love for Anne means nothing. All those feelings have gone. This narrative, this framing of the actions and sensations of an earlier self, has been for me a rediscovery of Blake's view that "the inner world is all-important . . . each man has a world within, greater than the external." If I had ever done anything which had merited someone writing the story of my life, the biographer would perhaps be able to tell my story at this juncture quite neatly. A short chapter would suffice to describe how, having left the shirt factory, I tried my hand at literature and drama. My novel and the date of its publication could be chronicled. As for acting, few enough roles came my way, and had it not been for Nicholas Gore (my agent) getting me a little work in radio drama I would not have been employed at all. The Black Bottle was still my main source of income. I now worked there two evenings a week as well as most lunchtimes. Such were the external facts. A more probing biographer might have been able to discover that this was the period when Anne was so in love with Hunter, and such a writer could weigh the pros and cons of whether the pair ever actually slept together. I can't make up my mind about that. When I found out about them, it was the thought of their lovemaking which obsessed me to the point of actual nausea. Visions of Anne, ecstatic as she had once been with me, her bare legs clasped behind Hunter's back, would send me retching to the nearest bathroom. But this lay a little in the future. What my biographer would never be able to convey (since there is no written evidence for it) is the fact that those particular weeks were dominated not by any outer shape of what was happening so much as by the feeling of interior desolation which gnawed at my heart.

"They change completely as soon as you get them back from the registry office and untie the gift wrapping," Pete used to say, stabbing an ash-tray with his Park Lane butt.

"My wife is the most selfish, the most voraciously cruel person I know," the Best Seller would say. "Old Karamazov"—pronounced "Carrer-marzoff"—"had nothing on her for naked, bestial unkindness."

"Why do you think they are all queuing up for punishment?" Mr. Porn would spit out. "So many happily married men—who would have thought it? It's because they are all bloody masochists. Believe me, there's no torture they could devise for you down at our place at Frith Street which could rival the horrors of an ordinary suburban marriage. Barbed wire? Chains? Dildos? Golden showers? It's nothing to the day-to-day, hour-by-hour knowledge that you're stuck with them, the bitches, with all their moods and their bloody relations and their . . ."

"They reveal sides of themselves"—Peter again—"you never saw until the marriage lines have been scribbled on. 'I hate the smell of cigarettes.' That's what Helen said to me."

"Wife number three," Cyril glossed.

"The very hour, the very fucking minute, we got back from the registry office, I lit up in the hotel where we were having the party and she told me she didn't like the smell of cigarettes. I told her, you've known me six weeks, you silly cow, and you wait till now to say you wish I didn't smoke. She told me she'd hoped I'd change."

"What I will never forgive my wife for is this"—with automatic hand the Best Seller held out his whisky glass for replenishment while with his other hand he raised the beer to his lips—"humiliating me, quite deliberately, in front of my children."

All the faces on the other side of the bar at the Bottle were telling the same story, whether it was the regulars, or other lonely characters who came in just once to echo the chorus. During all our spell of courtship and early marriage, it had never once occurred to me that these stereotypical expressions of disillusionment were anything more than a sort of comedy, produced like ribald jokes or salted peanuts as an inevitable accompaniment to pub drinking, but in no way relevant either to the human condition in general or to myself in particular. The discovery, now that I had myself belatedly removed the gift wrapping, that Anne had changed completely was by far the most important thing which had yet happened to me, and I listened to the old soaks at the bar with a growing sense of horror that they spoke from the heart. What they said corresponded to what I had suffered. When she was her old self, I had been totally incredulous that anyone could speak in this unenlightened way of women. Had they never been friends with a woman? Anne and I were the best of friends and surely always would be. I could not conceive of speaking about her in the way that Pete or Day Muckley described their spouses. That was before Anne became the truculent, cruelly silent chain-smoking companion of latter days. Day after day it went on. She was usually out when I got home. In the mornings she would leave early to go to the library or the Courtauld, her mind supposedly engaged with thoughts about Winterhalter. What went on, now always in darkness, in our bedroom, had started to become horrible, leaving feelings of unfathomable gloom. In daylight hours, our eyes hardly ever met. She was sadly remote, even a little mad. Already I began to understand the bar-stool confessions. In my early months at the Bottle it was a source of wonder to me that anyone could be so disloyal as to describe their most intimate relationships to strangers. Now, the impulse to tell someone, to find a sympathetic ear, simply to get help, was very strong. If help could by the nature of the case not be found, then at least I might find an ear. Hunter, in the restaurant, had obviously been the wrong choice of confidant.

Sometimes, when surfacing from the very worst pain of the problem and seeing that it was, must be, Anne's sorrow as well as mine, I thought of airing it with the family. As well as disliking Sibs and knowing that she disliked me, I also got on with her quite well, if the contradiction can be understood. I had more in common with her, in some ways, then I did with Anne. In retrospect I have come to share Uncle Roy's admiration for Sibs, even if his idea that she was of a submissive temperament remains unaccountable. If Anne had developed swollen legs, or glaucoma, or the symptoms of a duodenal ulcer, it would have been entirely unnatural not to mention the matter to her mother in the hope that the best medical advice could be procured. Might it not be that this slamming of doors, these long silences, this alternation of irrational anger and tearful frigidity constituted a problem that was in essence medical? No mother would relish being told by a son-in-law that her daughter was round the twist, and one risked the retort, if the diagnosis were accepted, "Whose fault is that?" But wasn't this an obvious source of help—even in Sibs's brisk way of comfort?

The trouble was, as I remembered on one of Sibs's impromptu

visits to our flat, that none of her offspring had any defects whatsoever. Where their characters showed variations from the normal which in others might have been a cause of disapproval, Lady Starling pursued one of two vigorous courses. The first, and simpler, way was to deny that the alleged fault existed. But her more usual tactic was to pounce on anyone (her husband included) who dared to see fault in her children. She would not deny, when in this mood, that they had the characteristics described; she would merely deny that there was anything wrong with the quality complained of. It is true that her son Michael (always called Youngmichael, as if one word, by Uncle Roy to distinguish him from his uncle Michael, who had been "one of the kindest men I ever knew") was notoriously stingy. Sibs's response to this would be to ask "if a young man in the city with a jolly good job and a jolly good income can't be careful with his money, where does that leave the spendthrifts?" This aggressively expressed viewpoint sounded almost like logic when Sibs said it, and certainly had the tendency to silence opposition if only by making your head spin. The ability of her other son, Gavin, to reduce dinner tables to silence, either by his own silences or by the unvarying tedium of his few chosen utterances, was hailed by Sibs as a positive social attraction. Hostesses should, his mother implied, be falling over themselves to get Gavin as a spare man at their table. "He didn't say one word all evening to the boring woman on his left, who should blame him, and to that absurd Amanda Harding he spoke only of Stocks and Shares. Mary was furious, but I think it was just a scream!" That was the last time Gavin was ever entertained by Lady Mary Spennymoor, and it was to be hoped that Mrs. Harding did not take his advice about the shares. When he gave detailed advice to Ursula about her college portfolio she involved her Fellows in a considerable financial loss. "I think it did those dons no harm at *all* to pull in their horns," said Sibs at the time. In short, we were living in a world where the moral absolutes had been abandoned, or in some cases actually reversed, for the benefit of Lady Starling's children. Logic did not come into the question, since Sibs felt perfectly free to criticise her children mercilessly and without stopping. But it was quite a different thing for another person to detect their faults. It was difficult then to raise the matter of Anne's near-lunatic manifestations of depression without implied criticism, and sentences beginning "I'm worried about Anne" died inside my head.

Sibs looked as ever rather magnificent when she called round. She wore a tweed suit with a little dark blue velvet collar and very good black patent leather shoes tied with ribbons in bows.

"She's never at home, that girl," she remarked of her daughter.

"Not often."

"Isn't that marvellous—doesn't do a bit of housework!" Lady Starling gestured to the brimming ash-trays and unfolded newspapers, clues that Mrs. Wiley was with her brother in Bridport, "and always at work on this thesis or whatever it's called."

"It is called a thesis."

"It's pure Lampitt, my dear, like Gavin working late at the office. Do you know the cleaners can't get in to do his carpet until nine o'clock at night sometimes? They wanted to knock off and go home without cleaning his office but he wasn't standing for that, lazy brutes. Then they had the cheek to ask him if he could just move out for half an hour while they did it. People's *cheek* since the war! Anne's a bit the same. Very single-minded."

This new explanation for Anne's behaviour, a purely genetic tendency to work at unsocial hours, became momentarily attractive, and my mind briefly seized on it as possible. I felt a few seconds of exaltation and relief, followed by worse sorrow than before when I realised that Sibs was talking nonsense.

The real reason for Sibs's visit was to announce the triumphant conclusion of her master plan. It had somehow become hers, even though she had had nothing to do with finding Virgil D. Everett Jnr.; no one had exactly asked how the contact had first been made, and all subsequent negotiations had in fact been orchestrated by Sargie and the Piece of Dry Toast. This did not prevent Sibs from seeing herself as solely responsible for the *coup* by which Jimbo's papers were delivered out of Hunter's flat and into the offices of Denniston and Denniston, as the first stopping post on their irrevocable journey to the United States.

"I think that's the last we'll see of that little man!" she said triumphantly, a Boadicea exultant over the Roman slain. Sibs took the not unreasonable view that Hunter's meteoric rise to fame was owing entirely to his having filched Jimbo's papers from Sargie and made out of his essentially innocuous life the scurrilous fantasy entitled *Petworth Lampitt: The Hidden Years*. At the moment of her visit to the flat, her opinion would have embarrassed me since I still thought that I admired Hunter; but I never specifically disbelieved Sib's version of things. Nor did the fact that Hunter's ambitions were puny and dull change the force of her argument. He had wanted to *get on*. No doubt, ambition should be made of sterner stuff than to be president of the PEN Club, or a spokesman for the arts on the less entertaining television programmes. But if that is the chosen field, then, however odd the choice, it is probably as good as any other in which to exercise power. Nor were Sibs's destructive views modified by the view taken by Sargie, and by myself, that if it had not been Jimbo's diary, it would have been something else which gave Hunter his leg up in the world.

"He'd have used someone else, my dear, if he hadn't used me, old Lover Boy would." Thus Sargie, and his sister would snap back, "Sargie, that isn't the point."

She was right. It wasn't. It was understandable, now that she had heard that the Lampitt Papers were in the hands of the lawyers, that she should rejoice.

"Mr. Everett is coming over to London in a few weeks' time," she said. "Mary Spennymoor knows him a bit and says he's an absolute sweetie, not at all the brash sort of American, quite nice suits, she says, and soft-spoken. We'll have a private dinner and you and Anne must come. We might even lure Roy to the capital. He'd like a real gathering of Lampitts."

"He'd love to come. Only wouldn't it be awkward if Sargie were there?"

"Feuds are so silly. I'm often wanting to ask Cecily to things and then can't because Sargie refuses to see her. He just walks out of the room if she's there. And now there's an embargo on Roy. Oh, I had the most divine letter from Roy the other day, and he really does know more about my family than I do myself. It's too extraordinary. I've got these cousins in Mombasa, haven't ever met most of them, and it's years since I saw Pam—when she was over in London before the war. My mother knew them all, of course, and since she died your Roy writes to them all. Well, he'd heard from Stephen—you know, Pam's eldest—the other day and it appears that Jimbo went to Africa. I never knew that. I bet Mr. Hunter never knew it." She really hissed the last sentence.

"I think I'd heard before from my uncle," I said. "There was a story about his not knowing which way to point a gun."

"Oh, and guess!" she said. "Rumours have reached Roy from Mallington that Vernon of all dotties wants to drop his peerage and go back to the House of Commons. Gavin says it's totally impossible, if you inherit a title you're stuck with it, and I'm sure he's right but apparently there are a number of the more Bolshie peers wanting to do it."

"Has Uncle Roy been over to Mallington?"

"Apparently. Vernon had a lunch for the Red Dean—well, you know he doesn't know any clergy, church was never the Lampitt thing. Rupert says that Vernon really wants to be the leader of the party. Our house'll become a commune. No harm in that, I suppose, but Vernon is extreme. And Sargie's as bad."

"I thought he'd given it up."

"Oh, he *says* frightful things about the Idiot People, but deep down he's the same as Comrade Vernon. Well, we *all* support the Labour Party, always have, always will."

I don't know why, but this came as a surprise to me. I knew that old Lord Lampitt was a Labour peer, and from Uncle Roy I had imbibed the view that uncomplicated Toryism of Aunt Deirdre's kind was vaguely common. At the same time, I had never supposed that Sibs had seen herself as a supporter of the movement. A house in Cadogan Square, sons in the City, a husband like Rupert did not to me suggest a particularly radical political standpoint. It was all the more surprising when she added, "Rupert's the reddest of the lot if the truth were known—which of course it can't be, because he's a civil servant."

This indiscretion had the appearance of being blurted out accidentally: but Sibs was an odd mixture of schoolgirl frankness and Machiavellian guile. One never knew, with what Rupert Starling called her gaffes, whether the information apparently conveyed by mistake had not been planted in one's mind quite deliberately; though it was hard to see then why she should have wanted me to know her husband's economic or political views, or indeed anything else about him.

"Isn't it marvellous, though, the way Roy keeps up with us all," she resumed her earlier theme, "hardly ever straying from Norfolk, but knowing everything. It's made all the difference since Mama died."

Mention of Uncle Roy occasioned pangs of guilt. It was months since I had written to him and Aunt Deirdre. If Sibs herself had not insisted upon it, the week after our wedding, I wonder if I would ever have got round to telling them that I was married. My guilt about not telling them during the weekend that Anne and I went down to stay should have spurred me into keeping in closer touch. Instead, it distanced me from them. It is so silly when I look back on it. I don't suppose that Uncle Roy or Aunt Deirdre would have wanted to see much of me. A regular letter and a visit every month or so would have been very easy to keep going. As it was, unable to aspire to some ideal of family intimacy inside my own brain, and full of self-reproach whenever I thought about them, I had more or less cut my uncle and aunt altogether. I also formed the view, based on nothing at all, that they violently disapproved of my marriage, thought it hasty, precipitate, juvenile. They had never said that was their opinion. Had Anne and I continued to be happy, perhaps we should have developed a regular routine of visits to Norfolk. As things turned out, I was anxious to keep secret the misery in which Anne and I were now engulfed. It was quite unmentionable by rectory codes. I had been brought up by them to keep things to myself, to play my cards close to the chest.

"There are some things we just don't talk about," Aunt Deirdre had said once. She was explaining, or not explaining, why she disliked the Wretched Woman, that is to say the novelist Deborah Arnott, who had for a while lived in our village and exercised no such conversational restraints. Politics or the secrets of emotional life (her own and other people's) were merrily and openly discussed by the Wretched Woman, in the course of shopping or queuing at the post office. For years, I accepted my aunt's belief that everyone in the village, the butcher, the sub-postmistress, the fishmonger, the man in the fruit and vegetable van, all disliked the intrusion of Deborah Arnott (Debbie Maddock in those days) into those areas about which One Didn't Talk. In retrospect I could find no evidence of this universal disapproval. Debbie was an open-hearted, intelligent young woman whom everyone liked and no one (that I could see) shared my aunt's ill-defined but sharply held sense of conversational boundaries beyond which it was improper to stray. The "things" not talked about included all the aspects of life which for most of the time occupy our thoughts—sex, religion, friendship, the behaviour of immediate neighbours, politics. It may have been one of the reasons why Uncle Roy developed his habit of making all conversations concern the Lampitts since this was a way of talking about forbidden subjects in a cipher. Over the Suez crisis, for example, I am sure that my uncle and aunt were divided. Aunt Deirdre had once blushingly agreed with Felicity when she said that she thought Anthony Eden the handsomest man in the world. This was years before the Egyptian crisis blew up, but I guessed that she vigorously supported British intervention in North Africa. When our troops set out for Egypt, she remarked that "the Yanks are always unreliable—look at all the girls in this neighbourhood who got led a dance by GIs." This seemed suggestive that the campaign should proceed in Egypt, regardless of international disapproval. And, more evidence, once when hearing Nasser's name on a wireless bulletin, a few minutes before "The Mulberrys" started, she had uttered the word "twerp."

Uncle Roy was really a pacifist and as a true Lampittite he was to the left of the political spectrum. He certainly viewed the Suez affair with dismay, but it was not quite safe to say so when sharing his house with so convinced a patriot as my aunt. The formula of the Lampitt anecdote here came into its own. Instead of saying, "I think such and such" (and any sentence which began *I think* was in danger of entering the conversational Out of Bounds), he could recount Vernon's view that Nasser was "in his way a perfectly good chap." The late Mrs. Lampitt's watercolours of the Pyramids provided their own oblique commentary on the international crisis, as did Sargie's knowledge of international law. On the worst night of the crisis, when it really looked as if world war might begin, I had come home for the weekend; it was when I was still working at Tempest and Holmes.

"What people always forget about the Canal," Uncle Roy said, "is that when Disraeli built it, one of the chief engineers they consulted was Roland Brown. Absolutely brilliant man."

I had not long since been discharged from the army and was dreading what seemed like the certainty, now that war had come again, that I should have to go back into uniform. I did not quite understand why Roland Brown's name was being raised. I had never heard of him; nor, I think, had Aunt Deirdre, nor Granny, nor Felicity as we sat round listening to the set. Brown's brilliance, with that of others, had provided a shorter trade route to the Indian Ocean from the Mediterranean. The wealth of Empire had grown up on it. Now, as we all came to terms with the fact that there was no Empire, it made a sort of emblematic sense that the Canal should be closed again by the Egyptians to show us our place in the world. But that wasn't what Uncle Roy had meant. Even as the excited news reader tried to tell us that Britain and France were in danger of fighting a war without the support of their other allies, my uncle's mind was fixed on more important things. There was a greater providence which brought to pass more wonderful happenings than the waxing and waning of empires, or the moving of great ships beneath a foreign sky. We did not during that bulletin catch the crucial bit of news about the failure of the campaign, because Uncle Roy was talking.

"Roland Brown. Brilliant man. I hardly need say that he married Hypatia, Sargie's great-aunt."

Sibs's great-aunt, too. I thought of the incident, a couple of years later, as Sibs stood there in my sitting-room.

"Well," she said, "I don't know what you're smirking at. There's nothing funny about the Labour Party."

"Oh, I don't know about that, Sibs."

"Well, if Anne's not here, I must love you and leave you."

Since becoming a member of her family, Sibs had taken to giving me dry little pecks on the cheek.

"I'll tell Anne you called."

"So I'd expect. Funny thing to say. You're not on No Speaks or anything are you? *Don't* be."

I resented her ability to get to the heart of the matter. I still hoped, assuming that our deep unhappiness, Anne's and mine, would blow over. The idea of it being known in the family became suddenly horrifying, not because it was embarrassing but because it made it all so much more real.

"She'll be thrilled to know that Mr. Everett is finally coming to collect Jimbo's junk," said Sibs in valediction. "No, I'll let myself out at the front door, don't bother to come down. All stacked and stored in nice Mr. Denniston's office."

She was still talking about the safe storage of the Lampitt Papers as she walked down the stairs. The fate of Jimbo's junk was of indifference to me, but it was not without importance in the short remaining history of my marriage. Later that evening, when Anne came home, I broke the silence by telling her that her mother had called and that Virgil D. Jnr. would soon be in London.

"I wouldn't mind seeing his art collection," she said. "He collects pictures as well as manuscripts. He's got Renaissance stuff (a Filippo Lippi), as well as nineteenth- and twentieth-century: some Henry Wallis, two Winterhalters, and a large number of Tukes."

"How d'you know what he's got?"

This provoked more silence. It was not a restful silence, but a jarring space in which one felt that terrible things could have been said, but were being held back for reasons yet more terrible. These sessions of non-saying caused such pain in the mind that they drove one's power of thought awry. The natural thing would have been to repeat Sibs's expression of delight that all the diaries were now safe with the lawyer. The Piece of Dry Toast had assured her of this. I certainly did not withhold the information from Anne. Considering the pain it caused in the next half hour, I should have done anything to spare myself the lie which then fell from her lips.

To my eyes she was looking more beautiful than ever before as she sat there on the uncomfortable sofa, her stockinged feet curled up beneath her haunches. Her eyes were always averted from me so that one saw her face in new three-quarter profiles which had not been visible so often in the days of our happiness when she looked me in the eye. Her mouth was perfect as it jutted out and said, crossly but calmly, "I've still got weeks of work on those diaries before I can move them from Raphael's flat."

A ghastly blush spread over her face as she said these words. I suspect that they were the first lie she had ever told in her life. She is so intelligent that I wonder whether she did not tell this easily penetrable untruth in order to be discovered. That was not how it felt, however, in the instant of her speaking. One talks of being stunned by information and it is assumed that mere metaphor is intended. On this occasion the experience of being lied to was almost like a physical blow. An instant before and I should have said that Anne was incapable of untruth. Now she was deceiving me. I knew that Jimbo's diaries were in Lincoln's Inn Fields. She told me that she would be occupied for weeks ahead, sorting them in Hunter's flat. The exact truth, so staringly obvious when one recalls it, did not dawn. I still did not realise that she was spending her time with Hunter. All I knew was that she had lied; she was providing herself with an excuse to be out of our flat for limitless hours. That could only mean that she was seeing another man. It makes sense to say that I was stunned because it really felt as if I had been hit. In one blow, Anne's mysterious behaviour all made sense, her distance, her bad temper, her dreaminess, the sense that she obviously did not love me anymore. She was having an affair.

I ran from the room and just reached the bathroom in time to kneel, abject and reeling, with my head in the lavatory pan. When I emerged, Anne was still sitting there in the same position on the sofa. Her hair was loose these days, she no longer had the pony-tail. The lamplight behind it made it seem as though her head was haloed. She was sucking a pencil and concentrating on German grammar. It was all the same scene which I had left, but now I looked out at it all from a cage of pain. The dull depression which had hung over me in previous months was nothing to this lacerating horror.

She looked up and said, "You look terrible. Have you been sick?"

I nodded some sort of assent.

"Julian, it's just *silly* drinking so much."

It is not quite possible to put into words what I felt for her then. It was because I loved her so much that she had such power to hurt; it was because she hurt me so much that I so hated her. My sense of rejection and humiliation was total.

"Where are you going?" she called after me; and, important afterthought, "Have you got a key?"

It was a good question, where I was going, and I can't answer it now. For the next few days I wandered about London and drank too much. Some of the time I returned to the flat to sleep. I don't think I ever slept rough, but I wasn't really bothered where I was. I did not contemplate suicide but I was in a state of mind where I was quite uninterested in self-preservation. When I began to sober up, the thing which caused most pain was having to admit to myself my complete ignorance. I had married a stranger, whom, it now appeared, I did not know in the least. It was now quite obvious to me that she loved someone else, but who that was I couldn't guess. Someone at the Courtauld, presumably, whom I'd never seen. I tortured myself by going back in time and adding up all the evenings and afternoons which Anne and I had spent apart, all the times when she had said that she had to be in the library or, latterly, sorting

boxes with Hunter. I had never questioned any of these asser-
tions. Now I questioned them all. Oh, why the shit had she
married me if she did not love me? How could someone who
seemed so nice, so tomboyishly decent have been prepared to
unleash pain on such a scale? From the perspective from which
I now survey it all, there seem many answers to these questions,
many ways of exonerating Anne, most of them covered by the
simple fact that she was young. She probably intended none of
it to happen. She, as much as I, was a victim. She could not
help being in love with Hunter, given the circumstances. If she
could have avoided torturing me, she would have. But it did
not seem like that at the time. I felt shock and fear. I developed
feverish symptoms, I couldn't stop shivering and I began to
think that I might become really ill. These symptoms never
developed into influenza or pneumonia, any more than alcohol
could numb my sense that everything, my whole life, was
torture.

I spent a couple of nights during this very bad patch sleeping
at Rikko and Fenella's house. Its noisy and over-populated
routines helped to swallow up my silent, miserable self-
preoccupation. Rikko was away in Birmingham recording episodes of "The Mulberrys," but there were never fewer than
eight at meals. The floating population of Fenella's lodgers,
friends, ex-lodgers jabbered comfortingly about their own areas
of gossip. The friend of a friend, a member of this group, I forget
names, I was drunk half the time that week, brought Elizabeth
Darnley to a meal one night. As a particular friend of Anne's,
Elizabeth was rather icy with me, but she told me that her
brother was living in London permanently now, working on a
weekly paper; Darnley had apparently remarked not long before
that he had not seen me in ages.

It was a saving remark, this of Elizabeth's, the first thing in
over a week of pure mental agony which lifted me out of myself.
I felt the genuine curiosity and affection of a friend, wanted to
know how Darnley was, what he was up to. Struck by my
interest, the next night Elizabeth came back to Fenella's table,
bringing Darnley himself, and it was as convivial as could be.

For a couple of hours I forgot my sorrows. He was very funny about all his colleagues on *The Rambler*, the weekly where he had landed a job, he was funny about the old days, affectionate about my grandmother. The only point of the evening where satire strayed into malice was when Darnley recalled Bloom in the army. Evidently, the two men were still on quite good terms, but saw each other as rarely as Darnley now saw me. This was one of the sad things which marriage had done, blowing old friendships, as well as happiness itself, sky-high.

The renewal of love for an old friend is one of the most—I should say *the* most—consoling of compensations for the rest of the dud cards which arrive in one's hand with such regularity as the game reaches its dull end. Why had I ever allowed my friendship with Darnley to lapse? "With thee conversing, I forget all time." With Darnley I did not want or need to get drunk. The morning after he had been to Fenella's was the first for weeks when I had not woken up with a hangover. I rang Darnley at his office and proposed meeting again that night. He suggested the French pub in Dean Street.

I suppose I'd decided in advance to unburden myself of marital troubles. After all, Darnley had been a witness at our wedding. Week had followed week and we had not seen him. In the first happy year, it was easy to let time pass without friends. By the time nearly a year had gone by, we had got out of the habit of meeting. But Darnley was my oldest friend, and he was the appropriate ear into which to tell my doleful tale.

I got to the pub first, having put in an hour dispensing their medicine to my clients at the Bottle. Darnley turned up at the French about nine, wearing that dark blue gaberdine which seemed almost a conscious allusion to the world of school, and a large brown trilby hat. Beneath the gaberdine were visible rather crumpled grey flannel trousers (again a schoolboyish touch) hitched too short, and revealing pale grey socks which could have been on the Clothes List which had to accompany our return, three times a year, to Seaforth Grange.

"Ginger beer, please," was his answer to what was he having. The previous night I had seen he drank water. The teetotalism, like the school clothes, was to be a constant feature of Darnley's life and personality from now onwards. Not feeling much like ginger beer myself I ordered a half of bitter.

When we'd found a table, never easy in that overcrowded pub, he produced from his pocket a battered Everyman which he put beside the ash-tray.

"Ever read this?" he asked. "I found it quite by chance the other day on a barrow in the Farringdon Road. Don't know why I bought it really, never been very interested in poetry or anything. But it's one of the most extraordinary books I ever read."

It was Gilchrist's *Blake*.

It is not a book so obscure that this coincidence demanded explanation in psychic terms. This book which had meant so much to me, and been my companion during the previous twelve months, had become a sort of lifeline to sanity. When plunged into drunken self-pity, or tempted by various manifestations of *snobisme*, the figure of Blake rose up in my imagination like a sort of prophet or redeemer. When I had read some pages of Gilchrist, it was like having a long, relaxing bath. Friendship with Darnley had, over the years, been like this, too. When one's footsteps seemed to be turning badly astray, he seemed capable of redirecting them, not by advice but by what he was. The sort of thing which Hunter, say, or in a different way Sibs took seriously never for an instant tempted Darnley. Though he might have had momentary sympathy with the Devil (as Blake did), he never had any time at all for the world or the flesh, which was why, I suppose, on the one hand he could be so hilariously funny, and on the other suggest disconcerting areas of seriousness. The clergyman's rig in which he had been dressed that night at Fenella's house was not quite as inappropriate as his sister supposed.

We spoke of Blake for about an hour, and found that we liked many of the same things, though Darnley was quite sharp in his distinction between what he called "the decent stuff and the absolute balls." I rather enjoyed some of the absolute balls, by which he meant the prophecies, but Darnley liked only the epigrams and the lyrics; yet we were agreed in liking Gilchrist and considering it perhaps the ideal biography. We also, and above all, liked Blake himself, and considered his supposed unworldliness, his lack of interest in anything which smacked of a good career or commercial success, as estimable and something to imitate.

The subject came to a natural conclusion when Darnley fought his way to the bar for drinks. When he came back, I plunged in at once.

"Miles, I'm in a jam."

"Move around, then, to my side of the table. It's more comfortable than perching on one of those little stools."

"No, I mean I'm in trouble. We're in trouble. Anne and I."

He looked down into his ginger beer, visibly embarrassed by this line of talk. Even as schoolboys, we had not gone in for "confidences." Anecdotes, yes; if a story about your private life would make the other person laugh, then it was worth telling; but not "soppy" stuff. I remembered him teasing me for being in love with the art mistress. "I hate love," he had remarked at a similar period. Perhaps this was still his position.

"You don't mean money worries?" he said, still peering into the ginger beer. "I mean, God, I'll give you a cheque."

Anything, it seemed, to get this embarrassing part of the conversation over.

"Anne's completely changed," I pressed on. "It's as if she's gone off her rocker. Do you remember that first evening, the evening you and Elizabeth brought her round to Fenella's house?"

For a split second, a look of sadness flickered over Darnley's features, which then creased into laughter. "Your friend the great novelist expressed himself rather vividly over that shit Hunter."

"Why d'you call him a shit?"

"Isn't he one?"

"Anne was so exuberant that evening, so bubbly. So happy. And now we've been married over a year, and she just sits there, staring into space. She's so miserable, Miles."

"Oh, Hunter's a shit all right," said Darnley.

I can't guess whether we would have got any further with our conversation had we not been interrupted. I was just about to have another go at telling him of Anne's dishonesty when my eyes became aware, at chair level, of a pair of black moleskin trousers and a little navy blue donkey jacket.

"My darlings," said Bloom, "a Cézanne, the pair of you hunched over the tavern table like that. All that is lacking is a clay pipe."

Had we needed to be private, Darnley and I could have chosen a less popular pub. It was foolish to be angry, as I was, at Bloom's appearance. He and Darnley did not really get on; and Bloom's determinedly frivolous attitude to everything would render impossible a serious unburdening of myself. Somewhat to my surprise, Darnley greeted Bloom with something like rapture, the ship passing the horizon after hours of standing on the beach of the desert island waving his shirt.

"What will you have, William?" he asked.

"Oh, he's in a mood to offer me things." Bloom cackled. "No, it's all right, darling, Mother's O.K." He held up a glass of Campari to prove it.

"What a day. What" pause "a" pause "day." Whether we liked it or not, we were going to hear about it, as he settled himself down on the stool beside me. "I've had sales reps all day, and not in the sense you might think." His eyes flew aloft and down again. "On top of which, Mother gets home and finds that Brucie"—his current, I seem to remember fairly temporary attachment—"has one of her stomachs. I said to her, darling, you can stay at home with a rice pudding. I'm going out. Just once in a while, Mother's going to enjoy herself. I say, did you ever see such a decorative creature?"

The figure indicated by William's sidelong nod was a rather clumsy-looking labouring man, unshaven for about forty-eight hours, leaning against the bar with a pint of beer in his hand. Blue overalls were spattered with dust and plaster. He was flabby, much addicted, if the double chin and the protuberant gut were reliable guides, to beer and fried potatoes.

"Gorgeous, isn't it," sighed Bloom, "but not looking my way, of course. But I say"—he touched Darnley's arm, and dropped the camp voice—"has Julian told you his news?"

"Well . . ."

"A book about to be published, even though it is with that bitch Madge Cruden. Oh, she's a bitch." He laughed, his tongue-out laugh. "And then you've had one or two little acting roles."

"One, and it was some weeks ago."

Darnley looked relieved that my "news" was limited to professional areas of interest.

"It's his real break," said Bloom in a too-perfect imitation of Fenella. He actually seemed to turn into her. Not only did he capture the timbre of her rumbling cigarettey bass; his face seemed animated by her spirit, and although they did not resemble each other in the least, he was able to suggest her winsome smile.

"Julian's multi-talented. It's just like what David Windsor said to me once when I was staying at the Fort . . ."

"Shut up, Fenella, shut up."

By now, William was both the Kempes, his finger and thumb rising to his brow in embarrassment, conjuring up Rikko with the same eerie exactitude with which he was able to be Fenella.

"I tell you I knew David *terribly* well, long before . . ."

And we all joined in the chorus of "Wallis Simpson came on the scene."

In my wretched condition there was consolation in this childishness. Darnley took no chances, and he rose to his feet while we were laughing in case the conversation swooped once more into a serious mode. He was gone, with a wave of the hand, before I had time to notice he was leaving.

Bloom had bought me some whisky, and almost at once I started to tell him of my marital difficulties. The whole tale poured out of me, Anne's silences and sulks, my feeling that she was no longer all there. I expect Bloom was as embarrassed as Darnley had been, and at first he tried to laugh me out of it.

"Now you know what I go through with Brucie when he gets his bilious turns. Come on, more whisky."

I laughed at the mention of Brucie because, of course, Bloom's life was comic whereas mine was totally serious. This was quite an achievement of Bloom's, to make his complicated and in some ways sad life an unending melodrama which the rest of the world accepted precisely on the terms presented to them. Viewed neutrally, Bloom's troubles with a difficult partner were no less sad than mine. Even if it had occurred to me to be sympathetic, however, Bloom would not have wanted my sympathy. This did not stop him being extremely sympathetic to me. I had always known instinctively that he was much more grown up than I was.

"Anne's well, physically?"

"She hasn't said. How should I know?"

"You haven't asked her?"

"We're no longer quite able to speak to each other."

"It's not Miles, is it?"

"What's not Miles?"

"I don't mean she's necessarily in love with him. She probably never was. He's probably still mad about her, but if people won't say, how's Mother to know what's on their little minds."

"William, what is this nonsense?"

"Oh, has Mother put her big foot in it again?"

"I'll be back in a minute," I said.

Standing in the urinals, I tried to meditate on what Bloom was saying. I'd put out of my mind, a year or so ago, the idea of Darnley being in love with Anne. Now I began to contemplate the possibility that they were having an affair. Surely he was too decent for that? I never did quite know what Darnley felt for Anne. Subsequently, it became quite clear to me that they had never been lovers. At the time, though, Bloom's gossipy, heedless remarks opened up new areas of discomfort in my mind which already throbbed with alcohol and terror.

When I emerged from the Gents, Bloom had left our table and was talking to the portly labouring man at the bar.

"Look, dear," he said to me, "would you think it frightfully rude of me if I abandon you. You see, Eric and I"—he touched the elbow of his new friend—"have things to talk about."

"I was on my way in any case," I said.

Stepping out into Dean Street, I felt hurt by Bloom's chumming up with the man in overalls. I saw it less as a harmless and inoffensive compulsion and more as a deliberate desire to shake me off. Unhappy marriage had made me into a bore.

The pavements of Dean Street were crowded with people, all pursuing pleasure and none of them caring about me. The lights of the restaurants, the smiles of the prostitutes, the gleam of street lamps on the wet paving slabs all seemed callous and hard. I wanted love, only love, and that hard-hearted street and the black night sky above my head were cruelly indifferent to my sorrow. It was raining gently. I stood for a while and looked at the tower of the ruined church, St. Anne's. The clock on the tower revealed that there were twenty minutes before closing time. With the air of a man turning for home, I retraced my steps to the last refuge of Soho's bores. They were all there when I pushed open the door of the Bottle, Day Muckley, Peter, Mr. Porn. Cyril was behind the bar. The saloon wasn't crowded like the French pub.

"You back, cunt face?"

"A large Teacher's, please, Cyril."

"You're getting to be as much of a piss artist as this lot."

"The marriage laws, as a matter of fact . . . the marriage laws of the Catholic church are irrev, irrel, bloody irrelevant," said Day Muckley.

"They didn't stop you getting a divorce, though," said Mr. Porn.

"Why do we promise for life?" asked Peter, pushing his empty glass towards Cyril and igniting his fiftieth Park Lane of the day. "If you make friends with a man, you don't promise it's for life. When you both get pissed off with one another, that's it."

"I got pissed off with you years ago," said Cyril, handing back the umpteenth gimlet, "but I'm still stuck with you week in, week out."

Day Muckley turned on me one of his genuinely beneficent smiles. It felt like the first real kindness I had received in months.

"I don't know what you're doing here with us, lad, I don't really. You're young. You're happily married, very happily married, as a matter of fact. You've got all your life before you. This place is meant for the likes of him and me—yes, you, you drunken bastard," he said to Mr. Porn.

"Not . . . pissed . . . as you," Mr. Porn tried to say.

"No, Julian," continued the Best Seller, "the thing about me is this. I've buggered up absolutely everything. My marriage, my writing, my life. Everything. I've buggered up the whole lot."

Peter looked across at us and smiled.

"That's very easily done," he said.

eight

I can remember that when, years after this particular phase of life was over, Granny lay dying, one was conscious of moving into a different time scale. The last phase, the death-bed, lasted about a fortnight, but we who sat with her, watching, waiting, no longer measured time by the rising and setting of the sun. Her life was over, and we knew that; but we were far from adapting ourselves to her non-existence. We still instinctively believed that there would be another time when she broke out into laughter at someone's tactlessness to her. ("He said, 'You sit there, love, your feet look as though they can't hardly bear the weight.'") Yet, in reality, we knew that she would never again shut her book using her folded reading glasses as a book-mark and then, two minutes later, ask, "Would some *clever* person find my glasses?" Never again would she shut her eyes and inhale a Craven A as she listened to "The Mulberrys," her taut, intelligent features concentrating so intensely that she might have been a musicologist determining the rival merits of two interpretations of an intricate violin sonata. (And then, when the programme was over, "What a lot of rubbish!") We had seen the end of all that made her distinctively herself, but it took two weeks of slow, stupefying resignation to accept this reality. We knew she would die, as we knew that we should all die; but this did not prevent the death, when it occurred, being shocking and almost as surprising as if she had been killed suddenly in the middle of an active life.

Granny's dying, which took place a decade after Anne and I split up, is the best analogy I can find for the stage our marriage had reached in that week of Madge's "little gathering" for my book. Hindsight makes it obvious by that stage that the marriage was over. At the time it was far from obvious. With the slow but strangely timeless acceptance of a watcher at a death-bed I came to accept, as presumably Anne did, too, that things would never be the same again. Life has such a vivid power to create routines, however, that we adapted to the new regime. We hadn't talked about The Situation. Anne wouldn't and I found that when I tried, I couldn't do so. It was a dark, lonely time for us both. I became acutely conscious (more so, I suspect, than Anne, who is far less vain than I, less interested in the figure she cuts in the world) of how it would all seem to others if they knew the extent of our severance and misery. Our families in particular haunted my fears. How could we break it to Sibs? To Uncle Roy? And, yet more chilling thought, what was it that we would be breaking? Was the marriage truly over? How did we not know that this was just what marriage was like? Plain sailing for the first year or so, and then unmitigated hell, covered up by various wheezes such as friendship with outsiders, or a shared interest in property and children. Maybe what we were going through was what they had all felt, Fenella and Rikko, Sibs and Rupert, Uncle Roy and Aunt Deirdre, only keeping it a secret because they chose not to make a display of it, as my friends down at the Black Bottle liked to do. Just as the figure on a death-bed continues to digest, to function at a minimal physical level, so did we carry on with life. There were a few, often cross, words at breakfast; most of each day we spent apart. If we could avoid doing so, we did not dine together, but it often chanced, still, that we did. Anne was often in a mood, tearful or cross. Largely because there was nowhere else in a small flat for us to sleep, we still shared a bed. Just as by holding the sick person's hand, saying his name, smoothing his brow, the watchers by the bedside half hope that they can bring the dying person back to life, I more than half believed that it would be possible to save the marriage so long as it did not quite cease to exist in carnal terms. Now, when I think of those two young naked figures lying together in the dark, she so unwilling, and he so wounded in his pride, so emotionally stupid, I feel an almost intolerable pity for them both. They do not seem to me like me and Anne but two figures quite separate from ourselves, strangers or even emblems of life's dreadful sadness.

Our daylight selves cannot be recalled without embarrassment. We were both behaving fairly badly, and if unhappiness explains this phenomenon it does not make it any less excruciating to summon to mind. I blush to remember how angry I was with Anne for not taking seriously the publication of the novel. At the time it was for me the most important event in the universe. The day when my six complimentary copies of the book were sent round by the publisher caused in me a frenzy of pride and pleasure.

"Not very big, is it?" Anne said when she saw it. The observation could not have been more humiliating if the organs of regeneration had been under scrutiny.

"Nor is *Candide*, nor is *Rasselas*."

"A hundred and thirteen pages," she said literally, turning to the back.

This was no way to judge a work of art. When she went on to say that it was a boring dust-jacket, I could have murdered her. Rosen and Starmer had a policy, congenial to the austere prewar ambience in which they came to birth, leftist, functionalist, economic, that they had no fancy jackets for their books. All Rosen and Starmer books looked the same, rather as I assumed (quite wrongly) that all books in the U.S.S.R. looked the same. The same pale green paper, the same Roman lettering in yellow picked out with black, the title, in this case *The Vicar's Nephew*, and underneath, the name of the author. The egalitarian and mean spirit in which this scheme had been drawn up meant that no Rosen and Starmer author was treated above the rest. My name, utterly unheard of, was printed in the same chaste characters as that of their more illustrious authors. For example, they had managed to lure away Bertrand Russell from his usual publishers for a short monograph entitled *Why Civilised Man Rejects the Atom Bomb*. This was produced in exactly the same format as the highly popular Duncan O'Rorke detective stories, or the first volume of Professor Wimbish's *History of the Labour Party*. There was a volume of essays by Lord Lampitt called *I Will Not Cease*, a Blakean promise which Vernon seemed intent on keeping.

There was no doubt that I had joined a pantheon, and I was certain that the little gathering in the offices in Coptic Street would project me into the stratosphere.

> Dream not of other worlds, what creatures there
> Live in what state, condition or degree

My old schoolmaster Treadmill had more than once quoted these words of the Archangel in Milton's epic, and ever since I had heard them I had known that, like Adam in the poem, I would disobey the advice.

Madge, my editor, whom I admired but could not quite like, had rung about a week before the "gathering" to enquire if there was anyone I especially wanted to invite. It struck me as rather short notice to put this question since the list of names I had in mind contained those who presumably filled up their engagement books weeks in advance. About the younger stars I was candidly uncertain.

"I don't want people just classifying me as another Angry Young Man," I said. "On the other hand, I suppose if you could get John Braine, Kingsley Amis, Colin Wilson. . . ."

"You don't understand," said Madge. I could hear her sighing into the telephone, the schoolma'am exhausted by the attempt to expound Latin syntax to illiterates. "Is there anyone you know whom you'd like to invite. Your family."

"I don't think so."

"Wouldn't they like to come and have a drink in my office?"

Madge, as I was to learn, had strong family feelings. My casual desire to exclude what family I had from the celebrations probably shocked her. Rightly, I now think. I could at least have asked my cousin Felicity down from Oxford. Uncle Roy and Aunt Deirdre had no reason to like the book but even they might have been less hurt by it had I asked them to the "gathering." They probably would not have come, but if they had, they could have stayed in a hotel, supped with Aunt Deirdre's friend Bunty, or seen a show. Sensing Madge's disapproval, I tried to read her meaning differently.

"It isn't that they wouldn't *like* your office."

"I didn't for a moment suppose they'd have an opinion on the matter." She sounded even crosser now. "I'd buy you both dinner afterwards but I have to get home to cook for a child. Still it will be nice to meet your wife."

I was silent.

"Your wife will be coming?"

"Probably."

There was an icy silence.

"Don't you know whether she's coming?"

"Sort of."

"We publish her cousin Lord Lampitt. Vernon and I have been friends ever since Spain. His volume of essays has just got a stinking review in the *New Statesman*, you probably saw it."

"No, no, I didn't. I'm so sorry."

"That rat Muggeridge."

"Oh, dear."

"There's no 'Oh, dear' about it, Mr. Ramsay. It's the best publicity the book's had."

It had been foolish of me not to realise that author and publisher could not have hoped for anything nicer than a "stinking" review.

"I hope I don't get a stinker," I said.

"We'll have a review here or there if we're lucky."

When she had hung up, the implications of this dispiriting forecast began to dawn on me. Until Madge said this, I had assumed that all the literary pages would be buzzing with excitement about *The Vicar's Nephew*. I had steeled myself for a few lukewarm comments from hasty reviewers who did not appreciate what I was up to. But if, let us say for the sake of argument, Harold Nicolson or Philip Hope-Wallace did not like the book, there would always have been Cyril Connolly, Philip Toynbee or Jack Lambert to sing its praises. I was hoping for a notice from Evelyn Waugh in *The Spectator*. Madge's prediction that getting any review coverage at all would be a piece of good fortune must have been intended as comic irony. I had no comprehension of how many dozens of novels poured into a literary editor's office each week; no idea that it was perfectly possible for books to be published and received in blank silence from the critics.

Certainly, on the day of publication, it was a disappointment that none of the newspapers carried notices; I was not at that point to guess that the novel would in fact receive only two reviews. *The Church Times*, towards the end of that year, had a round-up of fiction. It described my biting little satire as "a quiet comedy of rural life, set in a country rectory." It conceded that there was a certain "Old World charm" in my portrait of the eccentric parson and his crosspatch wife but wondered whether there was much originality in my "reworking of the tired old theme of English middle-class childhood." There was a more favourable notice in *The Rambler*. It was about two hundred words long and was signed with the initials S.K.C. For some weeks I persuaded myself that this was a dispassionate stranger who had found me "readable and funny." Though he never admitted it, I soon guessed that the review was in fact written by Darnley.

On the day of the "gathering" I had no idea that this would be the reception of a devastatingly incisive novella, which, in spite of the conventional setting, was in fact disturbingly "modern." Old World charm and vicarage comedy were not at all the effects at which I had been aiming; nor had it occurred to me until reading *The Rambler* piece that "one of the more pleasant aspects of the comedy is the way it rebounds on the narrator. He sets out to guy his clerical relations and only succeeds in writing himself down as an ass."

"Are you sure you aren't coming?" I asked Anne, one last time, before leaving the flat.

Silence.

"Anne—please?"

"I've said I'm not coming. I hate parties."

"Oh, *be* like that."

I slammed the door and walked—since there was so much time—all the way to Knightsbridge tube, taking a Piccadilly line train to Russell Square. There were plenty of minutes during the journey, in which to regret my *be like that*. It was so childish. Each time I expressed anger like that I was farther, as I knew in my deepest heart, from reconciliation. By now I felt that marriage had spoilt everything in my life; not just Anne, but marriage itself was to blame.

"Hebden Bridge is in a valley. You've got steep wooded hillside rising up all around you and if people come along there on a nice day in summer they say, 'Eee, isn't it luvly.' And what they don't realise, lad, is that Hebden Bridge for ninety-nine per cent of the year is swathed in wet fog. Living there is like being trapped under a bit of wet sack."

The Best Seller had once so described his hometown. Marriage cast a similarly dispiriting canopy over my skies. Every experience, however potentially pleasurable in itself, such as this publishing party, had to be snatched from a diurnal pattern of misery. Instead of walking calmly down to the offices of Rosen and Starmer, the literary man coming to meet his colleagues and admirers, I stomped along in a fury with myself for having lost my temper and a fury with Anne for having provoked it. "*She spoils everything*" was the phrase which kept recurring in my mind like a mantra.

I was early for the party. Madge had said to look in at about quarter to six and it was only half past five. I occupied myself by walking round the block, past the railings of the British Museum and into Bloomsbury Square. It was a muggy summer night with more than a hint of thunder in the air. The large leaves of plane and horse-chestnut rustled menacingly over my head. Then I stopped walking, and I stood still beneath that iron grey sky and bright green foliage, intending merely to notice, from a clock glimpsed through trees on the other side of the square, whether it was time to go in to the party. I was visited by a moment of great strangeness and stillness. It lasted only a few seconds, but it had power. In this brief period, as in a vision, I saw my own life. It is hard to put into words the absolute clarity with which I saw my existence as a contained, visible thing, a career or course on which I was running. Some people under anaesthetic and close to death on the operating table have experiences out of the body when they have felt themselves looking down upon the surgeon and their own prostrate forms and known themselves to be detached from their physical presence. This moment in Bloomsbury Square was analogous. In this vision, I saw myself, not as still, but as running, scurrying, after goals, such as fame and success, which did not in the least engage my emotions. As I surveyed my life I saw myself scurrying like this forever, in a hurry to move from experience to experience without considering whether or not it was what I wished to do. Something different lay at the core of what I truly needed and desired. I felt a tremendous sadness, like homesickness, but it was not an empty sadness. It felt populated, and my mother was there, reaching out to me to lead me home. When the split second of this odd sensation passed, I saw things only as a set of negatives. I did not really want to be an actor; I did not want to be married; I no longer cared about this book, though I felt the beginnings of a deeper desire to write fully, and honestly, not with the brittle surface of my mind, and not humorously or cruelly. This was the beginning of a simple, positive desire to record experience in prose as a homage to life itself, born from the certainty that I myself, before I was forgotten, would pass into forgetting, and owed it to experience, trivial or important, sad or joyful, to set down something of what I had felt. There would have been more wisdom to kiss the joy as it flies and live in Eternity's sunrise. But I had never felt sure about Eternity, nor about Art for its own sake, and I now began to wonder, in the middle of all my confusion about love and life, whether my only task would be to record; to see whether it was not possible, against the unknown chaos of nature, to at least map out a truthful picture of where I had been myself, and what I had seen, not with the aim of finding or imposing a shape as some stylish biographer might do with a more distinguished life, but merely in a spirit of reverence for the only thing given to me, life and existence itself. These thoughts came like a visitation, and although I have described the "homesick" sensation as a sad one, there was also a feeling of joy which, again, lasted only a few seconds. It was a joy with which I wanted to be alone, and the last thing I wanted was to go to Madge's party. The thought of that room, full of glittery and fashionable people, famed chiefly as columnists in Sunday newspapers, filled me with despondency. And yet it took almost no time at all for the purer vision to fade; and I realised that if I did not go to the party I should regret it. Seeing that it was nineteen minutes to six, I retraced my steps into Great Russell Street, and by the time I reached Coptic Street I had begun to form in my brain fantasy conversations with the famous people I was about to encounter, and to calculate which, or how many, Sitwells would be standing at the top of the stairs when I went in.

The offices of Rosen and Starmer were crammed into a small house between a shoe shop and a second-hand bookseller who specialised in Oriental languages. In those days, London front doors were left open during office hours. I pushed my way in and announced myself to the receptionist.

"Go on up," said the girl, who was painting her fingernails while reading the evening paper, and therefore couldn't look up. "Madge said someone might be looking in before we locked up for the night."

"There's a party," I said.

"Don't think there *is*," said the girl, with her eyes still fixed on the cartoon strip towards the end of the *Evening Standard*. I could not really see her face, just a fuzz of back-combed reddish-blond hair. "But I know she's expecting someone."

Madge sat in her office, a small square panelled room which overlooked the street, heavy with cigarette smoke, and piled high with proof copies and typescripts kept together with rubber bands. She had had her hair done. It was grey, hard and curly, more like an elaborate pewter helmet than hair. She was tiny, sharp, bespectacled.

"Come in, come in!" She removed her cigarette to say the words in festive tone. "Isn't it *hot?* Just wait a moment while I finish this page."

I stood there in the stifling little office and watched her peruse the typewritten page in front of her. To do so, she put her face very close to the desk. She did not look like a woman who was on the point of throwing a large party. I wondered if I had got the day wrong.

"I wonder if I'll ever meet an author who can punctuate." With fierce strokes of the diminutive blue pencil she attacked, rather than read, what was set before her.

"A difficult art."

"Not difficult in the least. I have quite enough trouble wading through the appalling prose of these individuals without having to put in all their commas and semi-colons for them. If I did not do so, however, they would be unintelligible."

Having established that she had a universally low opinion of her authors' accomplishments, she added, "Even dear Raphael isn't what you would call a stylist."

"Not what I would call a stylist, no."

Crossly, she raised one eyebrow; the expression appeared to ask if I were trying to be funny.

"Is that . . ."

"His book?" She smiled bitterly. "No, I wonder if we'll ever see that. I'm sorry he won't be coming. He's so busy, the poor dear boy, I'll say this to you, Mr. Ramsay, though I would not admit so much to Silas, but it is entirely because of Raphael that I bought your book. Entirely. Left to myself I should have said that you needed time. It is not necessarily a good idea to publish the first thing that comes into your head. People nearly always regret their early attempts, things perhaps which were of no great quality but which they wanted to get off their chests."

This was entirely typical of Madge's blunt way of expressing herself. I felt stung, almost tearfully angry that she could be saying such things, partly because I knew them to be true.

"Still, we shall say nothing of that to Silas. He has always taken the line and in my view it is an admirable one, that a publishing house should stand by its authors; that means standing by its mistakes as well as its successes."

She stood up. She was wearing a neat little blue dress with a ruby brooch just above her left breast. She was probably only in her mid-forties, but I reacted to her as if she were much older, and it astonished me that she had a child young enough to require its supper cooked for it.

"You haven't met Silas, I think?"

"No, I haven't."

"Come on, then."

She led me up the stairs to the room above her own which was twice the size, having been knocked together with the room at the back. It was furnished like a small library, as neat and comfortable as Madge's office was chaotic and austere. The walls were lined with books. There was a small eighteenth-century knee-hole desk, and a couple of leather armchairs on either side of the fireplace. Silas Rosen stood at the window, a small silver-haired man, bearded. His tininess matched that of his colleague. Indeed, everything seemed to be on a Lilliputian scale, and I felt clumsily large, standing between the two of them, neither of whom came up to my shoulder in height. He wore a bottle-green smoking jacket, grey trousers and slippers, said by some to have been embroidered by Madge herself, who was known to be a keen needlewoman.

"Come in, darling," he said to Madge in a quiet German accent.

"Silas, this is Mr. Ramsay," she said.

"What delayed you this morning?" he enquired sharply. "I waited until eleven-thirty, twelve, I think, what does this man think I am, with all morning to waste?"

"No, Silas," said Madge, "that was the young man coming about the job. Would you believe it, Mr. Ramsay, we said we'd interview this young man, he was sent over with a recommendation from another publisher whom it would be indiscreet to name . . ."

"A very old friend," said Silas Rosen. "You can guess who it was, I'm sure."

I did not then, as he assumed, have any idea who his friends were; nor did I know anything about the publishing scene.

"And he simply failed to turn up," said Madge. "Not that we need any more editorial staff. No, dear, Mr. Ramsay's written a book."

"Really? Well, show it to Madge. If she likes it, who knows—we may, I only say *may*, want to publish it."

"You did," I said. "This morning."

"I mentioned that novella to you," said Madge. "*Scenes from Clerical Life.*"

"*The Vicar's Nephew,*" I said.

"This calls for a little celebration, I think," said Silas Rosen. His voice never rose above the low monotone in which he spoke English. He had the fluent idiomatic speech of one who has learnt English as his second or third language. It was this, more than the very slight accent, which betrayed his foreign beginnings. Not that these were anything of a secret; he spoke of them at once.

"How long have I been in London, Madge?" he asked as he opened the bottle of ice-cold hock which stood on a table in an ice bucket. Had it been placed there for my benefit, or did they always conclude the office day by drinking together?"

"Twenty years," she said.

"Madge has been a tower of strength. I arrived in London as a penniless refugee. Penniless."

The story was a dramatic one and it put any sorrows or adventures which I have supposed myself to have had into a humbling perspective: the decision to leave Berlin, the anxiety of abandoning relations and friends whose maltreatment and ultimate murder at the hands of the authorities were matters of certainty, the financial ruin, the decision to set up a publishing house attacking fascism, the prosperity of the list, the making of a small fortune, the decision to buy old Gareth Starmer's backlist of respectable middle-brow novels, the birth of the firm of Rosen and Starmer, the death of Gareth Starmer, the rise of Madge from her position as Starmer's secretary to being Rosen's help-mate, colleague, sister, friend: all this was poured out in

Rosen's well-modulated educated tones. He must have told the tale, Ancient Mariner–like, to everyone who ever stepped into his office, but it came out that evening with all the freshness of a tale told for the first time. The last thing, evidently, which they wanted to discuss, was my book.

"I've asked one or two people to look in," Madge said to me. This was all that she had promised when the idea of a small gathering had formed itself inside my head. She had just said that she would ask a few people for a drink. It was I who had translated this into a full-blown reception. As soon as Silas had finished his summarised autobiography, Madge began to speak of the receptionist in the hall.

"I told her that if I saw that nail varnish in the building again, she would have to go."

"She was painting her *nails?*" He could not have sounded more incredulous if the girl had been daubing obscene graffiti on the office walls.

"And she doesn't answer the telephone correctly. *Rosena-Stormer.*" Madge was a good mimic and this was a plausible rendering of the way the girl spoke. "I told her, you must simply pick up the receiver and say, 'Good morning,' and perhaps the number, 'This is Rosen and Starmer,' quite distinctly. She should then ask the person concerned if they wish to speak to me or to you, Silas, dear. But then, not to go putting through every Tom, Dick or Harry who might wish to disturb our morning's work."

While Madge was demonstrating the difficult art of using a telephone, two figures entered the office. One was Day Muckley, who had had his hair cut. He wore a blazer and clean grey flannels and I snobbishly thought that he looked like a man on his way to a bowls championship. He was accompanied by a figure from my childhood, Debbie Maddock, now better known as the novelist Deborah Arnott. When she was first married and lived in Timplingham, married to a schoolmaster, Debbie had (probably unwittingly) occupied the unenviable role of my aunt Deirdre's bête noire. That Wretched Woman, my aunt's phrase for her, was how I still thought of her. She was no less handsome than I remembered her, and she did not seem to have aged.

Being in her thirties suited her better than being a harassed young mother in her early twenties. Perhaps the skill of a London dentist, or perhaps my own vision of things, made the teeth straighter now than in my memory of her earlier incarnation. They were very sexy teeth. They seemed to compel her to hold open her full cherry lips, giving her a film star's pout. Her mass of blond hair was thick and springy round her oval, intelligent brow. Her brown eyes were eager and alert. The low-necked blue-and-white-spotted blouse revealed that she had lost her slight tendency to scrawniness which I remembered from East Anglian days. I wondered why on earth she was accompanying Day Muckley.

He grinned amiably, and he was the first person that day to say the sentence which I had been expecting to hear a thousand times.

"A big moment, lad. And I wish you every success with the book, I do really." This was said with an affectingly transparent sincerity.

"Raphael said he thought you two were friends," said Madge. "The old writer comes to salute the young."

"Not so much of the old, thanks very much, Madge," said Debbie.

"I merely meant a well-established writer in an old tradition," said Madge self-importantly.

"You know," said Day, "when I was a very young man, Arnold Bennett said to me, 'They'll tell you a lot about how English you are because you speak with a regional accent.' " He certainly was doing so that evening, with inflexions which would have sounded exaggerated on the stage. "So they'll want to make you into a provincial genius."

"*A Man from the North,* in short," said Madge.

"I am from the North as it happens," said Day, who, if he had remembered the Bennett title, did not intend to show that he did so. "I've never denied coming from Hebden Bridge. But I'm forgetting my manners. Madge, I hope you don't mind my bringing a friend of mine, Deborah Arnott, to salute the man of the moment."

"You'll never remember me," said Debbie.

"Of course I do," I said.

"How's your auntie and uncle?"

I had never thought of Aunt Deirdre as an auntie, pronounced *anti*.

"They're fine."

"The auntie in your book is wickedly accurate," said Debbie. "Thanks." She took her tiny glass of wine from Silas.

It was embarrassing in some ways that my portrait of "Aunt Flo" should be so transparent. But here was someone who had read my book! She was saying all the right things about it; and, moreover, she was herself a well-established writer.

"But he said to me, Arnold Bennett did, as a matter fact, there is no such thing as an English tradition. And if you want to write good, realistic and above all *readable* fiction don't bother with English writers. Everyone says English writers have this tradition of realism, but all the best English writers have been fantasists—Swift, Defoe, Dickens even, in his way. Lewis Carroll."

"How's Isaac?" Silas Rosen asked Debbie. Isaac Zimmerman had been a (fairly friendly) professional rival to Rosen back in Berlin days, before they made their separate escapes to England. Zimmerman had brought out the last six or seven of Debbie's books, and she immediately began to tell Rosen about Zimmerman's latest dinner party, when Mrs. Eggscliffe had smacked the face of the Belgian ambassador.

"No, Bennett said read the French novelists if you want to see how it's done. Read Balzac. Read old Balzac, for God's sake. Read Floor-Butt."

He began to expound the merits of *Un Coeur Simple*, but it was evident that in a publisher's office such a literary line of talk simply would not do. Madge began examining the face of her wrist-watch and Silas, having shared the bottle of Tokay among the five of us, showed no sign of opening another.

Madge was snapping open and shut her handbag, checking that she had her car keys and powder compact.

"It has been very nice to meet you all," said Silas Rosen. "Darling, we shall have to talk some more about the painted-nails lady."

"He's too kind," said Madge. "What is there to talk about? She will just have to go."

For a moment it seemed that the five of us had been assembled in order to discuss the incompetent receptionist. Madge was extremely friendly as she shook me by the hand, but there was no ambiguity about the valediction.

"Goodbye, Mr. Ramsay," she said firmly.

She beamed at me, and I understood. I was not to come back unless I could write a better book than *The Vicar's Nephew*. It was eventually remaindered, and I don't think even those copies sold. Presumably they were pulped.

Outside, in the streets of Bloomsbury, it was hotter and muggier than ever. Clothes stuck to the body. The faces of Day and Debbie were glistening. I had now put two and two together and concluded that she was the person to whom he referred as his mistress. One tends when young to assume that people plan their lives or do things for reasons, rather than finding that in the right company or with the right amount to drink they have done things which they do not quite have the heart to unscramble. I therefore searched my mind for an explanation. Why should a beautiful, charming and successful woman have chosen to have anything to do with my collapsed old friend?

I did not know if they were trying to shake me off, or mutually wondering what to do with me.

"You'll be going to meet your wife now, lad, for a slap-up supper?" Day Muckley inhaled deeply, as if with energy he could make the air less torrid.

"No, actually . . ." It was hard not to allow an edge of pathos in the confession that, on this night of nights, I was entirely alone.

"Haven't you made any arrangements?" Debbie touched my forearm and the pressure of her hot fingers was more than sisterly.

"You'd think that bitch Match Cruden would have the decency to take you out to dinner," said Day. "It disgusts me. A young lad publishes his first book, for Christ's sakes."

"Anything to save money," said Debbie. "Come on, we'll buy you your dinner."

And she took my arm as we walked westwards where the sky over Oxford Street was an ominous gunmetal grey. The next hour, during which we made our way to Greek Street and sat at a table by the open window of the restaurant, was devoted to initiating me into the one shared emotion which binds together the majority of writers, a detestation of publishers. I discovered that Hunter's fondness for, even friendship with, Silas and Madge was highly unusual. The majority of authors, however successful in the eyes of the world, and however much on the surface they appear to like those who publish their books, in fact carry around a whole bundle of resentments against their publishers which it takes almost no more than a glass of wine to reveal. Rich or poor, bestsellers or failures, they nearly all have a story to tell, each one as tedious as the last, about mistaken royalty statements, shoddy proof correction, hideous dustjackets or simple failure on the editor's part to behave as if they were dealing with a genius. These compulsive and hate-filled Ancient Mariner tales occupied us until another bottle of wine had been consumed and some smoked fish had been toyed with on our plates.

"Mind you," said Day, "mind you, I will say this. Madge is in some ways very, very pathetic. She's never going to get Raphael Hunter, she's never going to get Raphael Hunter to drop, to drop his mistresses, for Christ's sakes."

"Let alone his trousers."

The wine must have been doing its work because this remark of Debbie's was enough to make us laugh loud and long. After about five goes, we even managed to remember, or think we remembered, Dorothy Parker's one about men making passes at girls who wore glasses. We made a terrific noise honing the quotation which Debbie had misremembered as "Men don't want sex with girls who wear specs."

"He's made a pass at one or two, any road," said the Best Seller, reverting to Hunter. It was news to me that even Madge was numbered with the elect, one of those adorers who found Hunter attractive.

"They don't, I mean you're not," I said. "Hunter and Madge aren't?"

"We never really know what Mr. Hunter wants in bed, do we, love?" said the Best Seller. He held hands with Debbie across the table, but the focus of his eyes was becoming indistinct. I did not know what he meant by this which, on one level, might have implied that Hunter had some curious *ménage à trois* with the pair of them. Day Muckley sat opposite us, holding Debbie's hand, while she and I were pressed close together on our chairs. Our thighs and calves touched. Far from being displeased by this I nestled up closer to her as the meal progressed. Since Day did not seem to notice or mind, my hand occasionally strayed beneath the tablecloth to meet her own moist palm which lay in the warmth of her lap.

"We know what Madge wants though, don't we, poor bitch," said Debbie.

"Isn't she married?"

"If you can call it being married. She never divorced Cruden."

"The poet?"

"It lasted about a fortnight, or so they say. Long enough to give her a kid and a chip on her shoulder. Can you imagine being married to Madge?"

I wanted to avoid a general discussion about marriage of the kind which dominated each evening at the Bottle, but inevitably as the main courses were dished up, Muckley began a rambling autobiography, most of which I had heard several times before, a wife who never appreciated his work, her extravagant ways, her need, after the success of *The Calderdale Saga,* to keep two servants, her prudish attitude to the physical aspects of matrimony. Eventually, after some row he had been thrown out and lived thereafter in rented diggings in North London.

"Of course, Julian, you knew me when I was first married," said Debbie. "Innocent days really."

"Apart from the fact that . . . apart husband, apart from the fact that you were married to a complete and utter bastard of a husband."

"Go easy love"; she stroked his hand. We were on our third bottle.

"Complete bastard, the way he treated you."

"Oh, marriage makes the nicest people into bastards," she

said. "That's why I'll only have occasional lovers from now on. I mean, what a crazy thing to do, to promise yourself to someone forever, to the exclusion of your friends, your profession, O.K and your lovers. We all fall in love more than once in our lives."

She pushed her beef olives to the side of her plate and lit up a cigarette. It was too hot to eat.

"I shall never . . ." Day Muckley's big frog-like eyes filled with tears. "I shall never be in love with anyone but you," he said simply.

I felt almost as moved as he looked by this testimony. I edged away from Debbie's thigh. As soon, however, as she removed her hand from his, as it lay there on the tabletop, it was evident that in some senses she had been holding him up. His weepy eyes were glazed, lifeless as marbles, as his thickset head cascaded towards the tablecloth and was cushioned by the picked-over remains of a bread roll and a very melted pat of butter.

"Oh, God," said Debbie Arnott, "here we go again."

A waiter came to ask if everything was all right. With some difficulty we pushed the Best Seller into an upright position, and Debbie solicitously wiped the butter and bread crumbs from his cheeks. We forewent coffee, not because some stimulant at that stage of the evening might not have been welcome, but because such a request seemed to offer too many risks—heads in broken cups, stains on table cloths. To my amazement and horror, the meal cost nearly eight pounds. Very generously, Debbie paid, with cash from her purse, in spite of my offering a pound note of my own.

"No, love, it's your treat tonight. And now I suppose we must get this old man home."

"You must let me help you."

She looked at me, her large brown eyes seeming in that moment very sad and very wise and very appealing. In that first glance I read many of the things which were to characterise our relationship, strong physical attraction, but also a desire shared by us both to behave well towards Day. We both knew that if I helped her get him home, it would not end there.

"If you're sure," she said.

In the compulsive bursts of marital autobiography during the coherent part of the meal, we had said nothing about my own marriage. When Debbie asked me if I was sure, I thought of Anne and momentarily missed her, felt homesick for her as I had felt so often homesick for my mother. But I wanted an Anne who no longer existed, an Anne who loved me as she had appeared to love me in the early months together. I knew that if I went home, I should either find it empty or full of Anne's new frigidity and anger and silence, full of her love for someone else whom I could not identify, but had begun to fear was Darnley. And I lusted after Debbie.

" 'Course I'm sure," I said. "You can't get him home on your own."

"I've done it often enough before," she said.

There is a knack to standing on a pavement with a man who is too drunk to stay upright on his own. We found a lamppost and took it in turns to hold underneath Day Muckley's arms while the other scanned the street for a taxi.

"Perfectly all right, all right really . . . ," he muttered as we shovelled him into the back of the cab. At several points of the journey, he murmured, "Sorry, love. Sorry, lad . . . wanted it to be so . . . nice this evening."

"It's all right, pet, it doesn't matter." She had one arm on his shoulder and stroked his head as she spoke, a mother comforting a sad child. Her other hand was clasped in mine. I did not quite know by this stage to whom her words were addressed.

There was something inherently squalid about the three-quarters of an hour which followed, but Debbie's kindness deprived the scene of much of its indignity. Mercifully, he more or less woke up as we got him out of the taxi, and with both of us holding an armpit we got him through the front door of the house. We were in Pooter-land, spiritually if not in fact: Leighton Road in Kentish Town. Nowadays only a stockbroker could afford such a residence. In the 1950s it seemed pathetic that a man who had once written *The Calderdale Saga* should be in such reduced circumstances. He occupied two small rooms on the ground floor. It was to the back room that we propelled him. As we did so, he began to chant, a phlegmy, gurgling,

> "I am sick o' wastin' leather on these gritty
>   pavin'-stones
> An' the blasted English drizzle wakes the fever
>   in my bones . . ."

No song could have been less meteorologically appropriate. The heat in Kentish Town was positively tropical and heaving Muckley made us even hotter. But in the song's melancholy longing for escape from life's ordinariness, he had perhaps hit on an appropriate ending to our revels.

"Shush, love, shush."

"Is that door open?" I asked.

"Just push it," she said. She was obviously an old hand at this exercise.

> "Though I walks with fifty housemaids outer
>   Chelsea to the Strand
> An' they talks a lot o' lovin', but wot do they
>   understand?"

A door opened on the landing above us and a female voice, disembodied as far as I could see, said sharply, "Would you mind being a little quieter?"

"Very sorry," said Debbie.

"Is that a young woman down there? You know I won't have young women visiting after ten."

"We're just seeing Mr. Muckley home," I said.

"On the road to Mandalay!"

"Shush, shush, my baby."

We did get him onto the bed, and as we pulled at trousers and shoelaces, he was quieter, but not asleep. He lay now with his eyes open, staring at the ceiling. It was a room of heart-rendering dinginess. The bed took up most of the space, an ugly Edwardian thing with mahogany headboards. There was a towel-rail from which depended a few grey rags which might once have been towels and a number of damp items which, earlier in the day, the Best Seller must have been attempting to wash: some odd socks, a string vest. Three or four metal ash-trays, purloined from pubs, were dotted about the room, balanced on the chipped white chest of drawers and the wobbly bedside table, and on the washstand in the corner, which was ingrained with dry shaving soap, some of it black with filth and a hundred semi-successful attempts to shave. The only adornment in the room hung above the bed: a picture of Christ, revealing his Sacred Heart. Underneath the picture was the legend SACRED HEART OF JESUS HAVE MERCY UPON US.

There was an absolute simplicity about the way Day Muckley gave himself up to being undressed and prepared for bed. He did not resist. He was like a baby, or a man who had never known the use of his limbs. His lips were moving. At first I thought he was cursing or continuing to quote Kipling.

"Oh, my God . . . Oh, my God," he said. And then his prayer came fluently from his lips: "I love Thee with my whole heart and above all things and am heartily sorry that I have offended Thee. May I never offend Thee anymore. O, may I love Thee without ceasing and make it my delight to do in all things Thy most holy will."

"Come on, pet."

He was down to vest, socks, pants, and by lifting him we were able to get him under the appalling sheets.

"You'll be too hot with a blanket," she said, stroking his head.

"Stay with me, my darling girl, stay with me."

"Not now, love, it's after ten and Miss Whatsit's getting angry."

"Sod Miss Whatsit."

"Good night, love."

It didn't feel right to be the witness to such a scene of intimacy and tenderness. I tried to creep from the room unobserved, but he said, "See her home, lad. I'm very, very."

"Good night, Day," I said.

"I'm tired," he said. "I'm very pleased for . . ."

In that moment I vainly wondered whether he was not saying that he was pleased to have reintroduced me to Debbie. Or was he pleased for me on the day of my supposed publishing success? Or was it something else which pleased him?

As we crept out of the door he was muttering, "Pray for us sinners now and at the hour of our death."

The unseen woman on the landing above was still hovering there. One could sense her and see the light from her door which was ajar, and which opened farther as we came out into the hall. In every sense I felt a trespasser. As soon as we were out on the pavement I took Debbie in my arms. In later months I ungallantly told myself that I had never really been in love with Debbie, as though the word "really" in such a sentence meant anything. We waited for a taxi, but when one failed to appear we walked home to her house in Dartmouth Park Avenue. We did not sleep that night. Compared with the absolute harmony of my lovemaking with Anne, it was all very fumbled, but at a moment which could not have been more fitting the bedroom was illuminated with lightning and an almost instantaneous thunder clap. We were still tight in each other's arms, silent with the strangeness and beauty of the moment as rain began to beat hard against the windows.

"You really made the sky move," she murmured, though I knew that I had given her almost no pleasure at all.

Then began the conversation which we had in various forms over and over again throughout our affair. Because it was a ritualised conversation we took it in turns to take an opposite viewpoint. One would argue that what we were doing was crazy, that we were playing with fire, that it would desolate Day if he ever found out about it. The other participant in the debate would assert that it did no harm so long as no one knew, so long as we had something to give to each other, that life was short, that we wished Day no ill, that we did not want to upset Debbie's children, nor Anne if she was capable of being more upset than she was already.

Peter one day at the pub had said, "It's when you go off and screw someone else that a marriage has finished. It's such a fucking stupid thing to do. It ruins it. Once you've done it, you never make love without looking over your shoulder. Don't give me all that cobblers about affairs enhancing your marriage. I know. I've had three of the fucking things."

One never listens to advice.

Lying there in the thunderstorm it was not of our folly that I thought. In that particular moment, Debbie and I simply needed each other. She told me "all about" her love affair with Muckley, and I tried to tell her about myself and Anne.

I must have said that I thought Debbie was kind to Day.

"Don't be such a patronising sod. I love him."

That was the real reason why our affair had no future.

"Some people probably think I spend my two days a week with him because I'm sorry for him. Just because he gets pissed—well, I admit, that's boring. But they think, because he's an old wreck and he hasn't got any money . . . ."

I was also on the point of adding that Day Muckley could be quite thunderingly boring, but I'm glad I didn't. She was squeezing my hand as she said, "I love him because he's a real man. We first met at some awful party and he was half plastered, not so bad as tonight, but pretty far gone. I remember Bridget Hewlings"—another novelist—"saying, 'Day Muckley's here, drunk as usual, hands wandering over every skirt in sight,' and what Bridget said was true and of course when we met he tried to grope me within about ten seconds. He probably would have done it to absolutely any girl, but I just felt ten feet tall."

"But there must have been other men . . . since your husband?"

"You mean I'd go to bed with anyone."

"You know what I mean."

"Oh, there were other men, yes, with poncey southern accents, or wives, or problems with bisexuality, or all three. Sorry, love." She squeezed my hand again. "But with Day I knew I'd met a real man."

Since I had no right to be in her bed, I had no right to be jealous, which I was. I knew, though, that she spoke with absolute sincerity when she said that she loved Day Muckley and explained to me the rather curiously rigid regime which she and the old man had devised, never meeting for more than two days in each week.

"But Debbie, if you love him—why me?"

"Don't ask, love, don't ask. I don't know. I could ask you, if you love your wife . . ."

I went very quiet.

"Do you love her? Anne? You must."

I did in that moment very much miss Anne. It was like spending Christmas Day with the kindest family in the world, and realising that though they offered me turkey and presents and pudding, they weren't *my* family.

"Let's be honest with each other, Julian, always. Don't let's pretend anything. The worst thing about what we're doing would be if it made us think we had to pretend to hate Day and Anne. That's what so many insecure people do when they have affairs; to justify it all to themselves, they pretend they have been more unhappy than they really were with their regular partners. You don't need to pretend to me, love."

And the rain fell against the windows and we made love again. After the silence which followed, she leaned over to the bedside table and lit two cigarettes, putting one between my lips, as she asked, "Are you happy?"

With my hand on her stomach, I said, "What do you think?"

"I don't mean now, here, silly. But perhaps you don't want to talk about it."

I did want to talk about it. I had been wanting to talk about it for weeks, months, but unable to find the right person, the person with whom it did not seem disloyal to reveal the depth and extent of my marital wretchedness. The moral paradox of the situation was that having committed the ultimate act of infidelity with Debbie, it was only with her that such conversational infidelity lost its wickedness. I no longer felt it was a betrayal of Anne to describe what had happened between us in recent months. By talking about it, Debbie was helping me regain my lost respect for Anne, or so I was believing until she dropped her bombshell.

"I know it's hard for you, love. I remember how shattered I felt when Derek had his first affair. And he felt so guilty he had to take it out on me and the kids."

"You married very young."

"So did you. Julian, I know it won't make it hurt any less, but it won't last, you know, Anne's affair. They never do."

Starting at the base of my spine and rising to the back of my head, I had the chilling knowledge that Debbie knew more than I did, and that perhaps everyone knew more than I did. Perhaps Anne's emotional life was the subject of gossip—but how had it reached the "literary world" which Debbie Arnott inhabited?

"They never last."

"Derek's affair lasted. He married her, didn't he?"

"That was different."

"How do you know?"

"Because she was pregnant. And Mr. Clever never gets his girls pregnant. That poor cow Bella Marno thought she'd got him, but he was two-timing her all along with Anne. Or so it seems."

I had the strange sense of something popping inside my ears, and with the pain, which was so strong that from its first inception I did not know how it was to be borne there came a grim relief at last to have arrived at the truth. Such puzzles as why Anne had been so furious that night at the theatre now became explicable.

I now realise that Hunter and Anne probably drifted into whatever it was they had drifted into. At the time I imputed to them motives of pure villainy. Hunter must have planned every stage of my betrayal, softening me up by getting Madge to publish my rotten book. He had only wanted Anne as a notch on his totem pole, a name in his catalogue of conquests. The mind raced back with horror to the first evening of my meeting Anne, and her jokey little comments about Hunter's handsomeness. Had the *whole thing* been a falsehood, all my love for her, all her professions of love for me, all our happiness and trust—all false, all meaningless?

"What are you saying?" I asked quiveringly. I had to be sure, now, even though I knew what she was saying, and it all made sense—her frequent visits to his flat to sort the Lampitt Papers, his preparedness to eat supper with us. Oh, damned, smiling, villain. "You're not saying that Raphael Hunter . . ."

"Oh, darling . . ." Debbie propped herself up on the pillow and looked down into my face. "I thought you knew. I thought that was what we were talking about."

"No . . . no . . . no . . ."

"Oh, poor pet. It's always the one who's most affected who's last to know. Oh, my poor boy. It does you good to cry, pet, it does you good to cry."

Debbie's kindness to me then probably explains why I was still able to look on her as a friend long after our short affair came to an end. Not since childhood had I so given myself up to grief. Probably the weeping only lasted half an hour, but it felt as if we lay there like that for half the night, me sobbing, Debbie comforting me. When morning came, she said, "Hey! You've got to go, love."

"No, Debbie, don't kick me out."

"I've got to, love. The kids will be awake soon." Brisk, no-nonsense talk now. "If this is going to be more than a one-night stand you've got to realise that the kids come first. I'm not putting any man first in my heart again. So long as you understand that I love the kids and I love Day."

Weeping for a long time is a bit like heavy drinking. It works you into a kind of frenzy which you need shaking out of. This line of common sense shook me out of my tears. So did the sight of her nakedness in the dawn light.

"Hey, *gerroff!*"

"You're irresistible."

"No, I'm throwing you out."

Which she did. As I left the house, one of the twins was shouting to her that he could not find any clean socks. The twins were in their early teens and needed to be got up early for the journey across North London to their school. I walked down towards Kentish Town, retracing our steps of the previous night, and then sat on top of a bus which wove its slow way southwards into London. To the east, the sky was a blaze of gold. The thunder of the previous night seemed to have washed the air itself and I thought of Blake's famous remark about those who saw the sun as a golden disc in the sky the shape of a golden guinea. No doubt, in the previous twelve hours, my life had become more complicated, sadder. But it had also been re-touched by a glimpse of glory. I thought with great tenderness of Debbie during that bus journey and of Day Muckley, who would soon be awakening to the rays of the sun, and of Anne and of Hunter and of myself. For months I had been angry with Anne, without understanding the reason; and now that she had broken my heart, I was not angry with her. I breakfasted at a café patronised by those who had to be at work by eight o'clock. It was the sort of scene well evoked by Mr. Pilbright. In one Pilbright it is through the roof of just such a café, with Formica-topped tables, sauce bottles, ash-trays and plates of baked beans, where customers wore overalls and headscarves, that his friends were lowering the paralytic man to the feet of Christ.

"He was completely paralytic," the Best Seller was to tell me, the next time we met, complaining that the "other Day Muckley had been up to his tricks again" on the night of my "publication party."

I ate black pudding, eggs, bread, the complete fry-up, and drank mug after mug of tea. It helped to counter the effects of having been awake all night. When I was fairly sure that Anne would have left the flat, I turned for home.

nine

"Really," said Anne, "you do like the most awful people."

It was true. I had begun to notice it myself. No explanation occurring to me, I pretended to be puzzled.

"Do I?"

"The Kempes and their filthy dogs."

"I don't really like the dogs."

"And there are all those slobs from the Black Bottle. And now Day Muckley's girlfriend. They say she's the last word in awfulness. All the same, she *is* becoming rather famous."

"Not so you'd notice, surely."

"*The Melon Garden, My Mother Said, Man About the House.*"

I was silenced by this display of knowledge. She had never been aware of modern literature before, nor responded with the faintest interest when I had tried to speak about it. I concluded that Hunter had been initiating her into the somehow guilty knowledge of who was who. When she had first seen Hunter on Fenella's television set, Anne had regarded his encounter with Day Muckley as a purely comic turn. Later, when she first met Hunter, and, come to that, Muckley, she had shown no more excitement than would a child who had been shown the Punch-and-Judy puppets after a show. Now a version of her mother's beady-eyed snobbery seemed to be at work in her. She had picked up all the right opinions about everyone in the literary world. I am sorry to say—and I set it down without malice—she is still lumbered with them. Long after she was done with Hunter, I found, on the occasions when we met, that she had been permanently affected by his habit of viewing contemporary art as a variety of London-based fashion parade. Instead of thinking about new books, films or plays, she seemed only capable, when we discussed them, of sniffing out the prevailing view of them; the view prevailing, that is to say, among the comparatively small number of people whom Hunter and his kind esteem. I do not think she was ever a great reader; such people seldom are. But she always knew what to say about the latest books. Manifestly boring or ill-constructed novels always earned her highest praise if they had been well-reviewed in the Sunday newspapers. She even spoke in reviewer's clichés. How I blushed for her when, at some family obsequies long after our marriage was over, she told me that she thought Debbie Arnott's latest (*A View of England*) was "a *tour de force.*" As it happened, that was the book which marked Debbie's transition from the warm-hearted, if gushing, chronicler of young married women and their emotional problems to being the rather pompous narrator of her later books. "Undoubtedly a great step forward," Anne added.

Even in her own field of expertise, painting, she never again showed anything which one could distinguish as taste. About her nineteenth-century subjects—Winterhalter in particular, Landseer to a smaller degree—she became more and more of an "expert," though I seldom heard her explain the merits of these painters, merely the facts which, in copious profusion, she had established about them. When it came to judgement of what was happening among contemporary painters, however, she spoke like any old colour-supplement reader. Her statements about modern art were no more than echoes of that dull, parochially English way of looking at things which has dogged most of the London critics in our lifetime. She was tepid in her praise of anything happening in Europe or the United States and was happy to speak as if L. S. Lowry, Pilbright, and, in after days, Hockney represented to the *dernier cri*. She would probably have been astonished to think that anyone judged her opinions as unoriginal, because they were always expressed with great conviction, just as a pious person, taking the church catechism for his own, might say the Creed as though he alone had thought of it. She would have been even more astonished to hear that anyone attributed this dogged conventionalism to Hunter's corrupting influence.

Her pleasure in my new friendship with Debbie Arnott was the first sign of this tendency. It crossed my mind that she guessed what was happening between us, and even felt some relief, as if this somehow let her off the hook with regard to Hunter. Years afterwards, I discovered that this was a false deduction and that she had known nothing of my affair with Debbie. I told her that we had met at Madge's "party," taken Day Muckley home, drunk too much. I allowed Anne to believe, without saying so, that the Best Seller and Debbie had been with me all the time, and I omitted a description of our putting him to bed in his lodgings.

"You want to watch Debbie," she said. "They do say she's rather a one for men."

Again, "they," in this sentence, could only have meant one person, since neither Anne nor I moved in circles where Debbie Arnott had been heard of, let alone discussed. (The fact that she was a "famous" novelist only meant "famous" to the circle of people who esteem such novels. She was not famous as Agatha Christie or Somerset Maugham was famous.) When Anne dropped these hints that she had been absorbing all Hunter's dispiriting views of the world, I suppose I should have challenged her, and accused her of betraying me. Since, however, I was anxious not to reveal all the secrets of my own heart during that period, there seemed no point in a "showdown."

I have spoken of an "affair" between myself and Debbie, but this is rather a big word for something which occupied only a very short interlude in my life. In the next fortnight I met her a number of times. I visited her house during the middle hours of the day. We were both deceiving Muckley, and my wife, but the association was strangely consoling. As far as relations with Anne were concerned, I suppose that my going to bed with Debbie was decisive in finishing the marriage. I am not naturally monogamous but, like the weighing machine speaking to the fat man in the joke, I want only "one at a time, please." Since Anne had shown no willingness of late in the bedroom, this seemed the moment to bring that side of things to a close. Nothing was said, but after Debbie, things were over between Anne and me. In the short term, however, I felt buoyant. I went through a shortsighted phase of believing that the affair with Debbie would enhance, or even heal, my relations with Anne. Certainly I was better humoured during those weeks. Some of Debbie's volubility and desire to be amiable had perhaps been absorbed.

Amiability was certainly required of me at that period, since, *faute de mieux*, I had been adopted by Sargie as the man who drove him about, provided companionship at luncheons, kept him supplied with cat food and library books, or met him for "snifters," when mood took him, at his club in Mayfair. This had all happened gradually, so that I did not notice it creeping up on me. He asked no questions about me and Anne, but since he had himself been estranged from his wife, Cecily, for years, I hoped that it would not scandalise him to know that I was fast approaching an analogous position. In fact, if it left me freer to be involved with his needs, all the better as far as he was concerned. He was cunning enough to spread the duties around, and since the breaking of his friendship with Uncle Roy, he never relied upon one individual to be his sole companion and slave of his whims. But now I took it for granted that, whatever happened between me and Anne, I would somehow be stuck with the legacy of looking after Sargie, at least for some of the time.

At the approach of Virgil D. Everett Jnr.'s visit to London, to meet the family and celebrate his purchase of the Lampitt Papers, Sargie became more and more excited, and summoned me one day to his club at twelve to hear about the final arrangements. The habit of very early luncheons, I remembered from childhood, was one of Sargie's ways of breaking up his mornings, and the mornings of anyone else whose time he wanted to waste. The selection of this particular venue had its own appropriateness in my mind since it was outside the Savile Club that I had parted from Sargie on the very day of Jimbo's funeral, not long after my twelfth birthday. Uncle Roy had conveyed me to Paddington Station, where a train waited to take me back to another boarding school term, though not, as it happened, any old term, since I was then on the threshold of a new life; I was about to fall in love with Miss Beach and to experience all the torments of jealousy when I saw her in the arms of Raphael Hunter: my first glimpse of the man. The story, in some ways, had begun on the steps of that club.

Few of these associations could have been present in Sargie's mind. He must have known as little of my inner life as I of his, though I did wonder whether he remembered that he and Uncle Roy had lunched at the Savile on the day of Jimbo's funeral, and whether, if so, he thought it was a setting fit to celebrate, as he saw it, the salvation of the Lampitt Papers, and with them, the salvation of the Lampitt name. The sale was final, complete. A sum, undisclosed to the rest of us but said to be absurdly generous, had been paid, via Denniston and Denniston, into Sargie's bank account. It only remained for Virgil D. to arrange for their final transport to the Everett Foundation in East Sixty-third Street, and the ultimate triumph would be complete.

"You see, the beauty of the scheme is that Virgil D. Junior has bought the whole collection *and* the copyright. Rather unusual, that," said Sargie with a gleam. "In fact, Andrew Denniston had never heard of such a thing!"

"Why does he need the copyright? Surely he's not going to publish the Lampitt Papers?"

Sargie laughed aside the very idea.

"I wondered, but Andrew has put my mind at rest. Let's be bloody frank about this, Julie, my dear, Jimbo's old boxes of junk are completely valueless as far as we are concerned. Virgil D. has bought a pup, an absolute bloody pup!"

I laughed because Sargie laughed, and because we had already put away an unwisely generous dry martini apiece. All the same, I could not help asking.

"How d'you know, Sargie, if you never read them?"

"What's that, dear boy?"

"Well, when your brother died, Hunter almost immediately homed in and took away the papers, didn't he?"

"Not quite right. I hung on to them for a couple of years."

"And you read them?"

"Turned over the odd notebook. Quite amusing some of it— old Jimbo met everyone, you know, in that early phase of his success after the Prince Albert was published. Conrad, dinner with Joseph Conrad. He even went down a few times to see old Henry James, in what's the name of the bloody place?"

"Rye."

"That's the boy. But none of this filth that Lover Boy dug out. Don't know where he got it—made it all up, Sibs thinks, bless her. I mean, can you imagine Jimbo, aged twenty-something, same age as you are now, and Henry James, who never laid a finger on anyone else as far as we know . . . Look, let's have another drink."

"I still don't see how Virgil Everett buying the copyright will help you."

Sargie ordered more drinks and then he lapsed into a little doodle which was so familiar to me that it almost antedated memory. I can remember perching on a tiny beaded footstool at Timplingham Place—Mummy must have been present, and Uncle Roy as ever would have been in attendance, and Sargie would suddenly relapse into a semi-nonsensical fashion of speech. When I was a little boy, and instructed to call him "Uncle Sargie" by my actual uncle, we had called this particular gabble "talking Chinese." It wasn't a sign of drunkenness, it was deliberately done, and it involved muddling all the consonants in a word and blowing raspberries between each syllable.

"Ben-er-lubber-lubber-ph-phpston-Dennis-blubber-lubber-velly clebber-phph-st-velly clebber fella."

I believe that the habit of talking Chinese went back to Sargie's childhood, and was something which he used to do with his brothers.

"I do wish that Sargie wouldn't do that silly kind of talking," Aunt Deirdre once said crossly one afternoon during the war, when we were all on our knees lifting a row of carrots which she had patriotically intruded into the herbaceous border.

"Oh, but it's *funny*," Mummy remonstrated, "and it makes Julian laugh."

"And then before we know where we are, he'll be talking like that all the time," said Aunte Deirdre. "Now how did that get there?" She yanked furiously at a fistful of greenery, and then surveyed its roots. "Thank goodness. For a moment, I thought it was hogweed back again."

"How has Denniston been clever, Sargie?" I asked, to break the reverie, and destroy the memory of my mother in the garden on that perfect summer day. Sometimes even nowadays, the longing to be with my mother is so intense that I feel it will kill me, and it comes at just such inconsequential moments—sitting in a club with Sargie, or in the middle of a meal when all around me are quite unaware of the mental agony which has suddenly descended, the panic, the sheer childish need to be in her arms, a longing which can never be satisfied.

"Well, apparently these collectors aren't so interested in owning a manuscript if it's already been published."

"So the manuscript of Keats's *Ode to a Nightingale* would interest them less than a letter from, say, F. Locker Lampson?"

"Point taken, clever clogs. But on the whole, collectors of literary manuscripts like unpublished stuff. If we'd only sold Virgil D. the manuscripts themselves, but retained the copyright, we could technically have allowed someone like Lover Boy to quote from them, you see, publish great chunks."

"In his first volume, he hardly quotes at all. He *refers* to the papers, but his narrative is chiefly based on paraphrase."

"Sibs said we should have sued him, but you're right. He'd done his work very cleverly. All innuendo and hints and very little, if any, quotation, for which he would have needed our permission, legally. I think we were powerless. But, you see, now that Virgil D.'s got the stuff we are actually in a much stronger position. That's what Andrew Denniston thinks. We won't have any control over the family papers, true. That's been handed over, lock, stock and thingummybob, to Virgil D."

"Do the others realise this?"

"What others?"

"Sibs? Vernon? Ursula?"

"Virgil D.'s a wily old bird by all accounts," said Sargie. He looked shifty. "He's not going to let the likes of Lover Boy into his strong-room."

"Well, let's hope not."

"I say, drink up, my dear. If you sit there dawdling, we're not going to get any lunch."

The abrupt transition from the leisurely, lolling self slumped in a leather chair in the bar into a panicky figure who was being delayed by my own procrastination summoned back many incidents in Uncle Roy's word-hoard of Sargie stories. Sargie's desire to speed up or to slow down the pace of things was sudden and irrational, always an occasion for blaming whoever he happened to be with. He pulled himself quickly out of his chair, looked at his watch and flicked ash off his waistcoat with petulant gestures. Then he led the way upstairs to the dining-room. It was by no means late—only about quarter past one—but by some chance the place was packed. It soon became clear, when Sargie buttonholed the head waiter, that he had failed to reserve a table.

"I'm sorry, sir. If you'd like to wait in the bar, there might be a table for you in half an hour. Rather a lot of members have . . ."

"Oh, this is hopeless."

Sargie looked angry and crestfallen at the same time. All his exuberant excitement at the sale of the Lampitt Papers had deserted him. I could see that it was vexing—he had hoped to give me lunch at the Savile, and now he would be unable to do so. But this was not the end of the world. His manner suggested no such sang-froid.

"I'm sorry," said the waiter.

"I don't mind waiting," I put in feebly.

"Well, I *do*," said Sargie. "The *buggers!* It's a disgrace. I'm going to write to the committee."

Presumably those referred to, whether or not sexual inverts, were those members of the club who had had the cheek to lunch at the place on the day when Sargie wished to entertain me there.

"I am sorry, sir."

"Don't keep saying you're sorry. Anyway, you're not sorry." We had moved into a near-tearful nursery bate. "What are we going to do? Look, what about that table? Here's a free table, Julie."

"I'm afraid that table is reserved, sir. Reserved for a member who booked."

"Oh, death!"

"Come on, Sargie," I said. Heads were starting to turn in our direction.

"It amounts to turning a chap out of his own club."

"I'm happy waiting," I said. "Truly. Or we could go somewhere else."

"I'm not waiting about here for this man." Sargie was glaring at the waiter with almost murderous hatred in his face. His tone suggested that the word "man" was the deadliest insult which could be imposed. None of Cyril's inventive rudery at the Bottle ever sounded more devastating. He turned his back on the *man* while the waiter was repeating the profusest apologies.

"I don't have to stay here," said Sargie. "We'll go to Claridge's and eat oysters."

It was hard to see how this was supposed to be skin off the waiter's nose, but a look of childish triumph illumined Sargie's face as he had come up with the idea.

"That'll show *him*," he said, as he led the way downstairs once more. "We'll go to Claridge's and see how he likes *that*. This club has become horrible anyway. Full of shits."

This last was said not to me but to two club members who were just climbing the staircase as we came down it. I followed at a discreet distance, hoping that it might not necessarily be assumed that I was with Sargie. He could see their faces, which were impassive as they walked past him, as though they had not heard. Because I was several paces behind Sargie I could see that as soon as he was past them they smiled in a resigned, conspiratorial way which suggested that these little tirades were a regular feature of Sargie's club life.

In the hall, he was an excited child.

"We'll go and have oysters at Claridge's," he repeated. "That ought to show them."

It was certainly a relief to be out in the street. Not until that moment had I ever fully appreciated the nobility of Uncle Roy's character. Extreme nobility, or an intense fondness for Sargie, would have been required to put up with this sort of thing over repeated occasions over so many years. It would not have taken much for this Saga of the Luncheon to be worked up into one of Uncle Roy's anecdotes. And as he finished telling it, and wiping away the tears of laughter, he would add, "Good old Sargie."

That was the saddest thing about the estrangement between the two of them. Others in future might be kind to Sargie, and keep him company as I was doing at the moment. When the "moods" darkened to the point where medical attention was deemed appropriate, there was no question that his family would stand by him and do all the right, humane things. But no one except my uncle Roy would say "Good old Sargie." No one would positively love in Sargie the very things which made him annoying, which is perhaps a way of saying that no one else, quite, would love him. To be able to love other people as they are, rather than as we wish them to be, is rare. Perhaps this was what prompted me to take Sargie's arm as we teetered down Davies Street to our palatial destination.

Claridge's had always been used by Sargie as a place of healing. I don't think he was much in the habit of staying there, but discreet luncheons in the dining-room had often been his way of molly-coddling himself when the rest of the world seemed indifferent or positively hostile. The waiter recognised him as he shuffled in.

"Good afternoon, Mr. Lampitt. A table for two, yes?"

"If it doesn't mean waiting all bloody day."

"But of course not. This way, sir."

"See?" said Sargie to me defiantly. Some point had been scored against the head waiter at the Savile.

As soon as we were seated at our table, he called for oysters and his own particular favourite Tokay. Sargie was not a sybarite. So long as he could be half tight during waking hours, and so long as he had something to smoke, I do not think he thought much about food. The "treat foods" with which on such occasions he wanted to supply himself and his friends had a purely emotional function and status. Lobsters. Salmon. Oysters. *Crème brûlée*. I have no reason to suppose that he liked to eat these things more than cottage pie, but they were ordered as gestures of defiance, kindly lights amid the encircling gloom.

"*En mangeant les huîtres, toujours on soupire la mer*—the sea air itself seems to come out of them." It was one of Mme. de Normandin's phrases.

There is that strange moment just before the oyster goes into your mouth when you inhale what seems to be the very essence of the sea, followed by the sensual experience of putting the oyster into your mouth. The soft moisture of this creature on the tongue could almost be another tongue, fishy but willing, so that even as one is about to swallow one has the sensation of kissing, perhaps kissing a mermaid or a siren.

Mme. de Normandin had a passion for oysters, and they were often at her table. I had not eaten them much since, *huîtres* for some reason hardly ever being featured on the menu at school, or in the NAAFI, or at the cafés where, in Tempest and Holmes days, I had exchanged my luncheon vouchers, or at the Black Bottle. "It's a mistake," Aunt Deirdre liked to say, "to give people food that's too rich." It was a mistake she was studious to avoid in her own cuisine and I am certain that an oyster never passed her lips. It is hardly surprising, then, that the gleaming porcelain plate, with its dozen grey coracles of shell whose touch recalled the rocky purlieus of our *petite plage* at Les Mouettes and whose very aroma reminded me of the Atlantic

Ocean pounding against the shingle, should have summoned up an earlier phase of life which now seemed very innocent. All that guzzling, and those secret assignations on the beach with Barbara, Mme. de Normandin's maid. Since then, what compromises, what acceptance of the unacceptable, what bleak discoveries about one's own lack of single-mindedness. When pain cannot be avoided, it must be accepted. It is only when we think we have found a remedy or a cushion for unavoidable pain that we diminish ourselves. Pain can be embraced without morbidity. Its sting does not always bind us. Pain is not the worst thing in life. But I did not know that then. I looked for consolation in a situation where there was no consolation, and succeeded in making more unhappiness, not less.

The only good thing to emerge from this is that it deprived me of the temptation to play the role of the "wronged" husband when, as eventually and inevitably happened, our marriage came to an end. (Though even being deprived of the temptation did not stop me on occasion from yielding to it.) The first time I had been to bed with Debbie it had seemed like a blessing, a balm sent to heal a broken heart. After half a dozen times, it threatened to become a habit, and I found myself becoming coarsened by the experience. In moods when I wanted to disguise this fact from myself, I expressed it in a cliché—I had joined the human race. By this phrase I meant that life is punctuated by emotional calamity. If your wife falls in love with someone else, hard luck; but maybe she will fall out of love, or maybe you, too, can find consolation. I assumed that it had begun from Debbie's point of view as a piece of harmless sensuality, or simple kindness. For me, it represented a fall. Secret bedroom assignations in the middle of the afternoon. Returns to the bar where Debbie's lover sat getting drunk, or to my flat where my wife had perhaps been working or perhaps spending the day in a fashion similar to my own. This is the stuff which makes us cease to believe in life. It was the use of sex, and of people, to console. I did not know that we cannot be consoled, by people, by alcohol, by anything.

Sargie, it may be said, was only a more privileged version of what I encountered on a bar-stool every hour in the Black Bottle. His nervous disorders were peculiarly his own. In his attitude towards Cecily he could have been Pete or the Best Seller.

"It'll be good to know that Cecily will never get her hands on Jimbo's diaries," he said between mouthfuls of brown bread and butter. His manner was genial once more, with food inside him.

I had never met his wife, who was still quite a friend of Sibs's.

"Did she want them?"

"Lord, yes. Cecily even tried to make out that Jimbo would have wanted *her* to inherit the papers. They were thick as thieves, you know. Ganged up against me all the time."

"How?"

"Tales out of school to Mama—naughty Sarge is in debt or drunk, or failed to give one of his lectures. I was a don then, when I was married to Cecily. Norham Road. Oh, Christ."

I had never visited Oxford. I did not know whether Norham Road had any significance beyond the fact that it had been Sargie's marital address.

"Two years of absolute bloody hell I had with Cecily," he said, repairing to his glass of Tokay. I now half wanted to join in with his marriage talk. Sooner or later the Lampitts were going to have to know that Anne and I were estranged. Sargie might have been a sympathetic ear. On the other hand, it was by no means safe to take this for granted. Those who have felt no obligation themselves to struggle on with matrimonial difficulties are capable of violent disapproval of the comparable misfortunes of others, particularly when their own flesh and blood is in question. Experiences which for themselves have been harrowing, pathetic, even tragic become immediately disgraceful in their minds if undergone by other people. Sargie had walked out on Cecily because, as he told everyone, he no longer liked her. There was no certainty that he would forgive me for doing the same to Anne. Nor could I be sure, were she eventually to be the one who did the walking, that the Lampitts would regard me in any more sympathetic perspective. In such a case, they might reasonably wonder why she had walked out and conclude that I was simply impossible to live with.

"Some people aren't strong enough to be married," he added. "Now you are. I can see you are, my dear."

He dabbed his moustaches with a napkin and smiled at me. There was something a little cruel about the smile. If I told the truth I should have denied this assertion. It felt as if he were taunting me to deny it. If I accepted it, however, this was to consent to be placed in the crudely insensitive class of those who did not get on one another's nerves. But I didn't reply because Sargie's head had gone out of focus. Drink was not responsible so much as an involuntary concentration of the optic nerve towards a table on the other side of the dining-room which now came clear into view as I allowed Sargie to become a fuzzy shape beside me, a colourless blob eating the last of its bread and butter and feeling sorry for itself.

There were three figures at the table I was staring at. Anne's was the first to arrest my attention. Anne had a way of wearing quite simple clothes and looking dazzlingly smart. A black skirt and a striped-black-and-white blouse could have been the clothes of a school prefect; but on her the effect was sophisticated. She was her mother's daughter. A great self-confidence lit up her appearance. She was animated, smiling, gay as she had been when I first met her. I had begun to assume that she was now incapable of gaiety, but here she was keeping her company in high spirits.

The two men with her were Hunter and a man in a large double-breasted suit of pale grey. The suit was large for the very necessary reason that the man was large—fleshy but also huge. Hair of a similar silvery grey to that of the suit was swept back from a big brow. The hair was much thicker than in most men of his age, which must have been between sixty and seventy, and much longer than was fashionable in those days.

The vision was interrupted while a waiter took away the oyster shells and prepared to bring tournedos. Another waiter was asking Sargie if he would care to taste the Château Margaux. It must have been years since Sargie's palate, perpetually overlaid with gin and cigarettes, had tasted anything, but he sipped the wine and declared, probably truthfully, that it was very nice.

242 · A. N. Wilson

The meal progressed. Sargie's mood of good cheer was restored. He began talking Chinese again—"Clabbages vebby
clebber men"—as he packed away the forkfuls of meat, mounds
of broccoli, sprouts, potatoes. I suppose he wasn't properly
speaking an alcoholic because he hardly ever abandoned the
habit of eating. When out, and eating food for which he was
paying—that rather mean strain in the Lampitts—he ate greedily
to get his money's worth. Sibs was much the same. I ate, too—
you couldn't not, it was so good—but without much relish. I
felt I'd spent a lifetime looking across restaurants to see Hunter
with women he had no right to be with. In fact it had only
happened once before, but it was one of the moments where
my dealings with Hunter seemed fixed, almost destined.

The certainty that he was my wife's lover had of course
changed my attitude to him completely. I wondered how I could
possibly have been taken in by him. One now had the sense
that behind his seemingly expressionless and almost boring face,
there lay depth upon depth of hidden motivation. He had been
nice to me in order to seduce Anne, that much was clear. But
one also got the impression, though it was impossible to prove,
that he had seduced Anne (I was sure that he had done so) for
some further ulterior purpose. But what? And why did we all
let ourselves be used in this way? Presumably, none of us would
have known much about Hunter had he not been able to practise
his wiles on old Jimbo, for it was as a Lampitt expert ("Petworth
Lampitt's close friend and personal assistant," it said on the
blurb of the paperback) that Hunter rose to fame. In so far as
he had crossed my path, I had watched him use people and then
discard them with complete ruthlessness. My cousin Felicity had
first helped him sort the Lampitt Papers. Sargie had fallen under
his spell and in the aftermath of that, we had all been changed.
This was just the Hunter *we* knew. It was hard to suppose that
there were not dozens of such sad stories of exploitation lurking
behind his pasty countenance. (There was, for example, the
whole pathetic story of Madge's unrequited passion for him.)

None of these considerations, however, weighed so heavily
as the desire to get out of Claridge's without actually encoun-

tering the trio at the other side of the dining-room. Sargie's mood had been restored to an acceptable level of good cheer. He was not embarrassing me in front of the waiters. After the histrionics at the club, I could not face any sort of public show-down between Sargie and Hunter; nor could I quite work out how I would behave during such an encounter. I had not set eyes on Hunter since Debbie had given me an explanation for all Anne's strange behaviour. The fact that Debbie had told me in bed might be thought to have deprived me of all right to hold a view, but I was not rational on the subject: not even rational enough to reflect that Debbie could not possibly have known, not exactly, what went on between Anne and Hunter. I was convinced that Anne spent all her available spare time in acts of fornication. Such thoughts, when entertained of a spouse, induce something like lunacy. I now consider it on balance unlikely that Anne slept with Hunter. She was obviously in love with him. But from what I know of him, he could achieve his effects without the trouble of undressing, and he would have been happy to leave it at that. Besides, her miserably inarticulate "It's not what you think," spoken to me at a slightly later date, hinted at her innocence if I had only allowed her to finish the sentence. One of the Rothschilds in the early days of the family fortune is supposed to have remarked that any fool can make a million but it takes genius to keep a million. I suspect this truth (if it is one) has its parallels in the emotional life.

At various stages since my marriage ended my old love for Anne has flared up again. My self-reproach has taken the form of incredulity. How could I have been so stupid as not to cherish her? How can I have not seen that her fundamental niceness, decency, honesty, would have helped me through if only I had been more patient? The passion for Hunter might have lasted for months, or for at most a year or two. Instead of waiting, I had to walk away and blow it all. Without seeking it I had landed a million, and within a year it was spent; the account was empty. That in sentimental terms was what had happened.

"I call that a jolly good lunch," said Sargie to the waiter. It must have been, for with rather surprising moderation, he waved

perhaps lasted about twenty seconds, and we probably all re
alised that there was nothing any of us could do to alter
situation of which Hunter was completely the master. Perhap
it was just the sense of our powerlessness which made us stan
there in stupefied silence, broken by Mr. Everett expressing hi
sense of honour at having become the owner of these trul
fascinating Lampitt items, and his hope that as many member
of the family as possible could be his dinner guests the follow
ing week.

"No, no, you must be our guest," said Sargie. He was almost
leaning on Virgil D., patting his arm. They looked like fellow
mourners at a funeral.

Hunter advanced on me, shameless at being found in Anne's
company, and bared his increasingly brown foxy little teeth by
way of substitute for a smile.

"I saw Madge the other day. She's very pleased with the way
The Vicar's Nephew is going."

"She's not said so to me."

Again, his indulgent smile as though I were the one stepping
out of line.

"In fact," I added, "I don't believe the book has sold at all."

"*Succès d'estime,*" said Hunter. I got the strong impression
that he would like to indulge his patronage further, and perhaps
welcome me into his brood of unjustly neglected authors, names
he sometimes brought into reviews or broadcasts, reputations
for which he laboured with paperback publishers. "Literary
reputation is a matter of luck as much as of merit," he had once
written in a Sunday paper. "The historians provide us with, as
it were, a governing cabinet, but those of us who have read in
the by-ways of literature know that there is a shadow cabinet
waiting in the wings who could, had things been different, have
occupied the seats of power now held by Thomas Hardy,
W. B. Yeats or Joseph Conrad." It is not really a tenable point
of view, but I was struck by it when I read it. There was a
generosity of spirit here, and, for Hunter, something almost
elegant in its manner of expression. Not until later, doing my
own researches in the Ann-Louise Everett Collection, did I find

the original sentence almost word for word in a notebook of Jimbo Lampitt's.

"I'm sure Madge is looking forward to your next," said Hunter. "Not that I'm one to talk! She's been promised my next for years now."

"Your next—volume?" I could not quite bring myself to ask, "Of the Lampitt biography?"

He just shrugged and gestured towards Mr. Everett, as if things were all in the hands of the gods. Anne disappeared into the Ladies and re-emerged to collect her coat. When she came out, the men, too, dispersed. She was the one member of this small group with whom I had not exchanged a word.

"See you later," I said to her as we stepped out into the street.

She just smiled, and waved, as she set off alone in the vague general direction of Piccadilly. It was not long before I had seen Sargie back to his club, where we had left our coats, and where there had been all the kerfuffle. We had somehow said goodbye to Hunter and Mr. Everett without noticing it; the moment had simply passed.

Coming out of the club, we managed to hail a cab. I saw Sargie into it and promised to meet him again soon. It was nearly four o'clock. I had had an arrangement to call on Debbie at her house at three. I went for a walk alone in Hyde Park, and across to Kensington Gardens. White clouds flew rapidly across a blue sky. The leaves of all the trees, noisy in the wind, were on the turn, yellowing but not yet brown. By the time I had reached the Round Pond, I had decided that my adulterous liaison with Debbie must come to an end.

ten

The moment in the park, the moment of the Āwakening Con-
science, was a bit like the ending of a great Russian novel. The
hero walks along beneath the trees and feels at one with the
world of Nature, the sunlight and the wild sky. His life is
changed, and he no longer wants to live in the old way. He
would put away the sins which beset him, in this case afternoons
with Deborah Arnott, and aspire after a purer soul. Crestfallen,
overbrimming with emotion, the hero will find consolation in
loving one good woman and thinking simple thoughts. Amazing
how these images appeal to men. My momentary impulse to
regard Debbie as a bad habit, something like booze or cigarettes
which I was trying to give up, was dignified in my mind as a
high moral decision. Just as she was beginning to get a bit fond
of me, just as there emerged a reason for me to be gentle, I
started to regard her as an obstacle to personal goodness, or
perhaps merely as a distraction. Perhaps Hunter felt this when
he sailed on to new destinations, leaving another Dido sobbing
on the shore.

I just dropped Debbie. Didn't turn up on the agreed afternoon.
Didn't write. Didn't ring. In the meantime, I had several amiable
encounters with Day Muckley. One day in the Bottle he told
me that he had been visited by a strange sense of blessing, a

sense of well-being not experienced since the days of his young manhood in Yorkshire.

"We all know the reason for that, you filthy old goat," said Cyril.

"No, no, though relations with my mistress are as happy as ever. They're neither more carnal, neither *more* nor less."

"Early senility," said Cyril and wandered off to the other end of the bar, a sort of *palais de glide* of a walk. Before he delivered an insult to a harmless middle-aged stranger who had made the mistake of coming into the pub for a drink (asked the man if anyone had ever told him he had a face like a badger's bum), he turned to the Best Seller and shouted, "Sorry, forget I said *early* senility; just senility."

"You see, I'm writing again, lad. After about ten bloody years in which I couldn't write at all. People who aren't writers don't understand the torture of that silence. But now I feel like a traveller setting out again, old Ulysses turning again for home. In fact, that is what the novel will be about—after a very long journey, and making an absolute bloody mess of life, a man comes home. You'll have guessed that the man is in fact . . ."

I assumed he was going to say himself. At that point, Pete enquired, "Don't we get served anymore in this place? I mean, why does Cyril still employ you?"

By the time I'd topped up Pete's gimlet, the Best Seller was expanding on his theme.

"My Ulysses figure is of course Clive Pendlebury."

My bluff was not quick enough. There were a few seconds during which it must have been abundantly clear that I had not the first idea who Clive Pendlebury was. Since he was the main character in *The Calderdale Saga* it was therefore obvious that I had not read Muckley's masterpiece. He smiled, summing me up. It was the expression of a man who had just come across an uneducated fool—not to know Clive Pendlebury was like not having heard of Ulysses himself. More stomach churning than this was the thought that Day, as I was, might have been racing back in his mind over the many conversations which we had had in the past year in which the subject of *The Calderdale*

Saga had come up. How much, implicitly or explicitly, had I claimed knowledge of the book? I couldn't remember. Because he assumed that everyone knew the book, there would never have been a possibility of admitting that I had not read it. But his nerve was no stronger than my own. He was not prepared, in the silence which followed, to risk my saying anything which would make clear that all my expressions of sympathy for his falling sales, of amazement as his hard-luck stories about obtuse publishers, of admiration for him as an author, had been based on sheer wind. How could I ever say now, without crushing embarrassment on both sides, that it was for himself that I liked him, not his books? (This is as deadly an insult as could be delivered to an author, who, when in the grip of authorial self-conceit, would sacrifice the love of a spouse, family and friends for one flattering sentence, perhaps from someone he did not know or did not like, about his writing.)

"Clive Pendlebury from *The Calderdale Saga* will be the Ulysses, and there will in fact be several figures from the other Calderdale books. Like I say, an Odyssey, a homecoming. A confrontation between this man who has totally wasted his whole life, thrown it away, and his wife, and the wife's suitors who have been betraying him. Oh, ay, lad, they'll have done it in my version. No Penelope's web for Lettice. Lettice Pendlebury. That's Clive Pendlebury's wife."

"I know who Lettice is," I said hotly, wondering with sweaty horror, because he smiled at me when I made this confession, whether he hadn't tricked me, whether no such character as Lettice Pendlebury occurred in the Muckley *oeuvre*. I also wondered whether Muckley knew about me and Debbie. If so, I was causing him the same sort of pain that Hunter had caused in me.

"The world divides as a matter of fact—no, thank you, I'm all right"—he had made a pint last half an hour and showed no inclination to overdo things—"no, the world divides between those who think the *Odyssey* is the archetypal story of human life and those for whom it's the *Aeneid*. The Odysseuses wander through all kinds of hazards and adventures entirely by chance, or so it seems when they can't see the gods who guide them. But their journey is always in essence a homecoming. Aeneas, now, he's a very different bugger. He knows where he's going, all right, and he's going to get there however many people he tramples all over. The New Troy, the Roman Empire, is vividly present to his imagination all the time, and that's what motivates all his journeys, all the lives he ruins, all the hearts he breaks. But he's a man of destiny, too."

"What'll it be for you?" asked Cyril. "Ulysses or Aeneas?"

"Are they cocktails? How too thrilling, darling."

It was Fenella, unseen, or so it felt, since the Dawn of Time. She greeted all around her with condescending smiles. She, like Muckley on that particular morning, seemed on the up and up, basking in the regular money brought in by Rikko's impersonations of Stan Mulberry. Rikko joined her in a moment—he had been in the Gents—and so there was no chance of developing the Best Seller's Odysseus and Aeneas idea. Cyril whistled the "Mulberrys" theme tune and for a split second (absurd idea) I imagined he was going to stand Rikko a Babycham on the house.

"That'll be two and nine, you ponce."

"Our producer's joining us here for lunch," said Rikko, "and he's bringing along one of the script-writers. You remember Rodney, I expect, Rodney Jones."

"Terribly important to remember directors' names," said Fenella.

"He came here for lunch when he offered you that job on 'The Mulberrys,' " I said.

"Well, before my audition."

"I don't really"—the Best Seller was toping now in earnest and there was a large whisky in his hand—"I don't as a matter of fact listen to the wireless at all."

"Alexander said to me—Alexander Korda—'Darling Fenella.' "

"Shut up, Fenella, shut up."

"And anyway," said Mr. Porn, who was there somewhere in the middle of it all, "this chap comes into the shop and says

would I have a use for soiled—soiled, mind you—ladies'
knickers."

It was hardly the most propitious moment for resolving the
complications of my life. As it happened, however, life was to
be changed in the next few minutes. First Cyril told me—"Why
should slags ring you at fucking work?"—that I was wanted on
the telephone.

"Julian, it's me, Debbie, Julian."

Her voice was all trembly. She had not normally repeated my
first name in that manner.

"Hullo."

"Where have you been?"

"A bit busy."

"Julian, I've got to see you."

Long silence.

"Julian, I said . . ."

"I know what you said. It's a bit difficult just now."

"Julian, just tell me what's happened. Just tell me what I'm
supposed to have done. Tell me what's changed, love. That's
all I want. Just tell me, and I'll be able to accept it. Really, I
will, Julian."

"I can't talk here. There are people listening."

"Too fucking right they are. And paying you to serve at the
bar, not talk to women."

"Julian, are you still there?"

"Yes."

"If it means everything's all right again between you and
Anne . . . I just wanted to say that's fine, I'm really glad for
you." She was crying now. From where I stood, way out of
earshot, I could see the Best Seller shaking hands with the men
from the BBC, and accepting a drink from Rodney.

"Look," I said impulsively, not being able to stand the tears
and realising in the same instant that instead of behaving sensibly (as I had hitherto believed) my attitude since the park
éclaircissement had been about as morally admirable as a belch.
"I'll come and see you. I'm sorry, I'm really sorry. I'll come."

"When, pet?"

"I'll come this afternoon."

"You're lucky," called Mr. Porn. "I've not come since the Blitz. You don't in my trade somehow, it's the last thing you want to do."

"Oh, Julian, will you really? You've made me so happy, pet. Oh, Julian."

" 'Bye."

When I came back to the bar I was astonished to see my old schoolmaster Treadmill standing between Rikko and the Best Seller. The man from the BBC was with them, too. I wondered whether Treadmill had come deliberately to see me or whether he had wandered in by chance.

"Val says he knows you," said the one called Rodney, the producer.

"My dear Julian."

At school, while pretending to mock Treadmill, we'd all been in awe of him, his range of acquaintance, his experience of the world, the fact (for example, his left-wing views) that he wasn't like the other masters.

Meeting him in the real world was potentially embarrassing. In fact, the slightly two-dimensional persona which any successful teacher must present to a classroom is not unlike the sort of "character" which gets built up in pubs. Now I summoned back to memory some of the names dropped by Treadmill at school. Wasn't there some story about Dylan Thomas having cadged money for cigarettes and a taxi? Treadmill had worked it into the lesson in the way he did. The beginning of the sentence probably had to do with Chaucer. Then, by some curious sleight, Treadmill would have told us about Chaucer's known riotous and bawdy behaviour in London taverns, which would have led on quite naturally to our sonorous Swansea bard. Not long after wondering whether he would ever see his ten-shilling note again, Treadmill would have intoned, " 'Do not go gentle into *that* good night!' " which of course none of us had heard of, though it instantly became one of the many poems, first heard on Treadmill's lips, which passed into the repertoire.

"Dylan said he would willingly come down and read his poetry to the Lampitt Society"—Treadmill's small literary club for older boys—"but Pamela Hansford Johnson, sitting indeed in that very chair, advised against it." The significance of this statement was lost on a room full of sixteen-year-olds, though one grasped at once that it contained a significance. Treadmill's, in some ways morally dubious, method of teaching was to whip up a yearning to belong to the in-crowd, as it was always implied that he did himself. Unlike us whom he once dismissed as bourgeois bores, he had fought in Spain for the Republic, been to Oxford, and, now I came to think of it, done a bit of sound broadcasting, mainly talks between concerts on the Third Programme, but also a couple of plays. And there was the ten-shilling note lent to Dylan. As he had declaimed, *Et in Fitzrovia Ego.*

So here he was being introduced as Val, and rather than feeling that Treadmill was diminished or that his schoolmasterly poses made him seem from grown-up perspectives ridiculous, I found that I moved at once to accept this different, new adult Treadmill on his own terms, and that must have been a tribute to him somehow. Yet I could not forget that he was my teacher, and I was ashamed, after all he had tried to teach me, that I had found nothing better to do with my life than pull pints for Cyril. Something of this must have been said or hinted, I forget the details, before Treadmill was kind enough to say that I had been one of the best schoolboy actors he had ever known.

"That's what we came to see you about actually," said Rodney, who had a rather unsatisfactory beard. He stroked it, less out of love, one felt, than to see if it was really there, and in some lights it was hard to know whether it was or wasn't.

What was I to call Treadmill? "Sir" was an absurdity which could hardly be continued in grown-up life; "Val" was too matey, even though this was what Rodney and Rikko both called him. I settled for calling him nothing.

"I'd absolutely no idea that you wrote 'The Mulberrys,' I said, immediately aware that this was a potentially insulting remark.

"It's not my only source of income or employment—as you may know."

The last phrase, added with heavy irony, was preceded by an infinitely slight non-verbal vocalisation, a sort of *mm*, little more than a closing of the lips. When as children we all imitated Treadmill, this mannerism was exaggerated into a strangulated *Yeair* sound. So much in memory did I recall the imitations of Treadmill, my own chiefly, that the Real Treadmill's voice seemed almost toneless. For the others, he was just perhaps any shambolic figure of the kind who might drink in Soho bars and do odd bits of work for the BBC. They could have no conception of what this man had been to me, what worlds he had opened up. It was just one of those many instances in life where one is confronted by the mystery of our different views of one another. The extremest case is when we are in love. When I was most in love with Anne, I would be astonished that she could enter a room and not produce in every bosom present some of my own feelings of worship. Had everyone felt as I did, then each time she walked into a pub, library, drawing room, would have been like the Exposition of the Blessed Sacrament to the faithful. Every knee would bow, every tongue confess her. Yet, mysterious fact, she made her effect on so comparatively few. In her case, sexual attractiveness and stunning prettiness made a few heads turn, but that is not what I am talking about. She did not engage the imagination of others as she had engaged my own.

"I'm really an understudy," said Treadmill. "When P.J.—you must know P. J. Barnes by name?"

"Not, I'm afraid."

"Val's wonderful," said Rodney. "Whenever P.J. wants a few weeks off, Val is prepared to step into the breach and keep the show going. Quite often, we find that it is during Val's period as—with great respect, Val—caretaker script-writer—an awful lot has happened in the series."

My knowledge of the intricacies of "Mulberry" politics lay in the future. I did not know that Treadmill's nickname among the regular cast was the Angel of Death. If Rodney did not like actors or actresses, it was often during P.J.'s absence that they were irrevocably removed from the scene. It was Treadmill, for example, who had scripted the episode when Mol Mulberry drowned in Barleybrook Pond, a tragedy not unrelated to the fact that the actress playing Mol had a violent temper and had upset most of the cast by her uncontrolled ego. When another actor had a lover's tiff with Rodney, Treadmill was hired to arrange a family tragedy among the Swills. When two or three other members of the cast said that they would resign if Timmy were got rid of, the dread pen of the Angel of Death ordained that motor accident on the way to Silchester. Len Swill's pig van, originally destined to career into a stone wall, found another target when his "little friends," as Rodney called them, had rallied to his aid: the vicar's Austin Princess with Nora Tilehurst at the wheel. There were complaints from Equity, but once the characters had been killed, there was not much that Treadmill could do to resurrect them.

"There's a borderline between keeping listeners interested and straying into—melodrama," he said.

"But we are thinking, aren't we, Val, of a new story line," said Rodney.

"When did you last hear 'The Mulberrys'?" Treadmill asked me a little sharply.

My truthful reply was that I was now only an occasional listener to the programme, my chief period of addiction having belonged to my teens. Cyril, though, was a devoted "Mulberry" fan and he came up and leaned on the bar next to me, quite deliberately ignoring all the signals from Rodney, myself, Rikko, that a private conversation was in progress.

"You can't come and join us at a table, I suppose?" Rodney asked.

"He can't, he's serving," Cyril said, smilingly.

"I don't know"—Treadmill's voice sank to a whisper, and it was clear that what he was muttering was classified information—"if you've kept up with old Harold Grainger."

"The silly old blacksmith?"

"It is evidently some time since you listened," said Treadmill shortly. Apparently this was a less than adequate description of

Harold Grainger, the strongest comic character of the drama, and a source of wry wisdom, country lore, old songs and a lot of other things which might in a happier world have been kept under wraps.

"What we're really thinking of," said Rodney, "was to give old Harold a bit more depth; add, not tragedy exactly to his life, but well, that other dimension."

"You want to fucking well leave him as he is." Cyril volunteered this advice spontaneously and with real vehemence. It was the sort of reaction found in those who feel some beloved monument of their imaginative world threatened by change. New dimensions in the life of Harold Grainger were of the same order of turpitude, I could see as, for analogous devotees, the Ring at Bayreuth in modern dress or updatings of the Book of Common Prayer.

"Look, this is all very private at the moment," said Rodney.

"Then what are you talking about it for in the middle of a public bar, you stupid blob of snot?"

Ludicrously, Rodney responded as though he had to justify himself.

"This was the only day we could both manage to come to London. Val has to see a specialist at four."

"Nothing serious, I hope," I asked.

Treadmill held up a scaly hand, purportedly to forbid any anxiety on the score of his health. The rhetorical effect of the gesture was to suggest stoicism in the face of terrible difficulties.

"I've all my life had duodenal trouble, it's no more serious now than it was when you first knew me, Julian." And then, perhaps displeased by the expression of relief on my face, he added, "Not *much* more serious anyway. As Rodney says, we were hoping to do a short voice test and audition before I take myself along to—Devonshire Street."

"What's this, then?" asked Cyril. "You cunts offering him a part in 'The Mulberrys'? That's the second bloody bit of casting you've done in this bar. I'll set up as a theatrical agent if you carry on at this rate, you arse merchants."

He was glowing with pride as he walked back to Mr. Porn's

end of the bar where conversation concerned the dog races at White City that night.

"Have you noticed?" asked Treadmill. "That extremely rude man, whom I take to be mine host, bears the most extraordinary resemblance . . ."

"He does," I said.

"Resemblance to whom?" Fenella asked.

Cyril had surmised at once what was slow to dawn on me, that Rikko, Treadmill and Rodney had come to the pub to try me out for a job. The bucolic, innocent wiseacre Harold Grainger was getting a bit bland even by the standards of the BBC Home Service. They recognised that he had become a national institution and that hordes of listeners like Cyril would protest if Harold were killed off or worse, revealed to have some unexplored side to his character, such as an interest in art or dishonesty as treasurer of the Parochial Church Council. But it was perfectly legitimate and indeed added a faint touch of tragedy to old Harold's nature if he were to be landed with a relative who was a black sheep. They were still toying with the idea of making this figure a younger brother of Harold's who had been in Australia and now turned up like a bad penny. The alternatives were that the figure should be an East End Cockney woman, foisted on Harold's household as an evacuee during the war and now exploiting his good nature, or, as was finally agreed, the figure should be that of old Harold's son.

Cyril let me off work at the bar as soon as it became clear what was in the offing, and, saying goodbye to Rikko and Fenella, and waving to the Best Seller, who was by now sitting with the dog fanciers, I turned towards Langham Place and Broadcasting House with Rodney and Treadmill.

The collection of a visitor's pass from the uniformed official at the door, the journey down long subterranean corridors in the bowels of the Corporation, the fiddling with tapes and machines in a recording studio: these seemed to me that afternoon no more than a pleasing diversion from the main business of life itself. I gave very little thought to what I was doing, and, when they gave me passages of script to read into the microphone, I felt no nervousness.

"We had thought of making Jason speak in the same accent as his father," said the producer, "but—what do you think, Val? I think that supercilious pseudo-posh accent is very good, Julian. Jason has risen above old Harold, left the nest, excellent."

The supercilious pseudo-posh voice so much admired by Rodney had been, until that moment, the one I regarded as my own. Soon, listeners all over Great Britain would be getting used to it and hating it, hating Jason for all the trouble he was causing his poor old dad. Among the heinous crimes lined up for Jason to commit were conning his father out of his life savings, a little blackmail, and possibly getting the barmaid into trouble.

"But we have to play down those sorts of elements," murmured Treadmill, "for obvious reasons."

"Cards on the table," said Rodney, "it's an idea. It might work, it might not work. We'll give Jason eight weeks. If it doesn't come off, well, none of us are losers. P.J. will have come back then as our regular scriptwriter, and we can always force Jason to leave the village, go back to the Smoke, perhaps even get arrested by the police."

Since the offer of a role in "The Mulberrys" was made in these very tentative terms, it did not feel like a serious step when I accepted it. I shook hands with Rodney and we parted in the vestibule of Broadcasting House. Treadmill and I walked northwards together, in the direction of Devonshire Street.

"I'm sorry you have this awful stomach trouble," I said.

"Oh, I've had it ever since Spain. The school doctor, strictly *entre nous,* is an incompetent. He made me drink barium meal, which guaranteed that I should be constipated on the actual day of the Inter House Seven-a-sides. He said the X-rays showed me to be fit. That merely showed that he did not know the truth of something Johnson once said: 'Sir, sensation is sensation.'"

"Well, we shall probably meet quite often in the next couple of months."

Treadmill beamed weakly. This was only the first of dozens of conversations I had with him about his health. He raised his hand in that strangely effete limp gesture and disappeared behind the polished mahogany of his specialist's front door.

Human faces—it is one of the things which distinguishes them from supposedly lesser creatures—acquire a particular look of totally concentrated absorption when they are about to indulge themselves without regard to the needs or requirements of others. A glutton peruses the menu in his favourite restaurant. The roué eyes up the girls in a brothel and selects one to his particular taste. The old Breton women in the church near Les Mouettes edged nearer the confessional. Their turn would soon come to bore the priest with an account of their own lives since the previous Friday. Just such a look had come over Treadmill: in prospect, a professional man's undivided attention while Treadmill talked about his digestive processes.

I did not realise it, but Treadmill had just solved for me the problem raised by Granny when I left the army: what was I to do with my life, for the time being at least. Jason Grainger was a figure who was waiting to take me over. In the next month I made two or three visits to Birmingham to record perhaps a month's worth of life in Barleybrook. These improbable rustic adventures were then snipped up by Rodney into ten-minute episodes of "The Mulberrys." Having discovered that what acting talent I once possessed had entirely deserted me, I was not prepared for any of this. Nor was I prepared for the powerful magic of broadcasting. I was, wasn't I, acting, when I read the lines apportioned to Jason Grainger? And yet Jason's return to the village, his inability to tear himself away from old Harold, whilst landing his father in any number of scrapes, felt like a fantasy projection of the relations I had had over the years with Uncle Roy. Not for the last time, I wondered whether it was possible to escape the drama of our own childhood and adolescence, whether in fact we only ever relate to our families, whether all subsequent friendships, love affairs and emotional adventures are not programmed repetitions of our infancy, or, which amounts to the same thing, attempts to react against it. All journeyings into the uncharted seas turn out to be a voyage home and the only story we are able to tell is our own story. If Day Muckley's set of contrasts was a plausible one, I was a Ulysses and not an Aeneas.

Doubtless, had I tried out this idea on Aunt Deirdre she would at once have smelt a rat.

"Isn't that psychology?" she would have asked. Shudder. "A friend of Bunty's had it once. Wouldn't let them near me, electric shocks and a lot of, well, *silly* ideas."

Yet silliness would keep on bursting through, in my life at least. Looking back, I should almost say it had been my vocation.

"Surely you could spare me a fiver, Dad, to help your own son out of a difficulty?"

"It baint thaart, son. Truly it baint. Only, Constable Brayley 'e bin raarnd askin' 'bout that car you've em said you'd bought. Stolen proputty 'e said it were."

"Really, Dad. Constable Brayley is a man of very limited sensibilities."

" 'E mebbe uv limited sensib-whatjuma callems, but the law's the law 'e sez."

"That itself is debatable," said Jason snootily.

I hated Jason, almost more than I had hated anyone, as I sat and listened to his pseudo-posh.

" 'Ow much longer is yer goin' ter stay, son? It baint that I don't wantcher, yer knows thaart."

"Poor old Harold," said Aunt Deirdre, when the inevitable climax had been reached at the end of the programme (Constable Brayley knocking at the door of Harold Grainger's cottage). "Pity they had to make you into quite such a villain, old thing."

"It's to give themselves the option of getting rid of me," I explained.

"It spoils it for me when you say things like that."

Tender towards her illusions, Aunt Deirdre was, in the years that followed, a mixture of curiosity and caution whenever we spoke of "The Mulberrys." If I had to earn my living by pretending to be someone else (and from the start, I conceded that this was a frivolous thing to do), then there was no drama in the world which would have more occupied my aunt's attention. "The Mulberrys" had been her favourite programme, almost her vicarious existence, for as long as I had known her. At the same time, precisely because she loved "The Mulberrys" so much, she wasn't sure that she wanted to be told all the secrets. The idea that Rikko was different in kind from Stan Mulberry was something which she had long ago excluded from her mind and if I attempted to say anything of Rikko and Fenella (a rare enough occurrence because I knew that my uncle and aunt would have disapproved), it was always greeted in silence. Happily at that date there was no bad news to relate about Rikko, but had I told her that some personal calamity had befallen him she would have received the news with unshakable indifference. She was capable, however, without much whimsy, of a genuine empathy with Stan and would often ask after him. I was not sufficiently a professional "Mulberry" actor to be able to play up to such enquiries by imagining the world of Stan outside the scripts written for him. Normally I answered these questions with some reference to Rikko himself, Fenella's cough, or Rikko having recently splashed out on new lampshades at Peter Jones, or a possible palliative having been found for the Afghans' bowel troubles. Aunt Deirdre would look bored and say, "No, Stan works himself too hard, I'm afraid, and Gill isn't all the support she should be. I mean, I ask you, taking her mother to Lyme Regis during harvest week, just when Stan needed her most."

There was nothing very unusual in Aunt Deirdre's need for vicarious living. Uncle Roy had been doing it for years, only the serial drama was not coming out of a radio loudspeaker but was going on inside his head and was called not "The Mulberrys" but "The Lampitts."

I'd gone back to stay at the rectory for a few days, and after the customary non-conversations, I felt strongly on my last day that I should say something about me and Anne. The three of us were in the kitchen having washed up lunch. Granny was upstairs listening to the wireless in her bedroom where she spent more and more time. Uncle Roy, who was to hold a ruri-decanal chapter meeting that afternoon in his study (he was rural dean now) was dressed in his version of clericals, a white bow tie, white shirt and grey flannels.

I had made up my mind to tell them calmly and fully, and not to blame Anne or myself, but simply to say that after an initial period of great happiness we had both come to realise that the marriage had been a mistake. I would go on to say that

I fully respected their religious and moral principles and did not expect them to approve, but that I was going to divorce Anne. In trying to frame this difficult narrative in my brain I was preoccupied with my own feelings, to a lesser degree with Anne's. What justified the divorce, made it inevitable and even desirable, was my certainty that there was no virtue in two people making each other unhappy. That my uncle and aunt disapproved of divorce I took for granted, but I had not been home often enough to appreciate what my marriage meant to Uncle Roy.

The fluent and sensible speech did not come out as planned. I blurted out, "There's something you ought to know," and then wasn't able to finish the sentence. After a very long silence, I said, "It's . . ." And then another long silence, at the end of which I said, "Anne and I." Then more silence before the single word "divorce" escaped my lips in a whisper.

"She's asked you for a divorce?" Aunt Deirdre said.

"No, but we just aren't happy."

"Nothing's happened, has it, old thing?" I think this was Deirdre-ese for wondering if adultery had occurred.

"No, nothing's happened exactly. Just—don't get on." Long pause: a pause so long that the world could have ended. "Miserable, both of us."

"I often think there's no point in two people staying together if they're miserable," she said decisively. Often? When did these thoughts come to her? As she was stooped over the flower beds yanking at weeds, presumably. I hadn't expected her to be understanding. She looked very sad, but kind. My uncle's face was a picture of desolation.

"This can't be true," he said.

"I'm afraid it is."

"Many people live apart," he said. "Sargie and Cecily hardly ever lived with each other. But a divorce is unthinkable."

"If we don't want to be married . . . ," I feebly began.

He was staring away into nothingness.

"Poor Sibs," he said quietly.

I tried to take in the significance of those two syllables, but

I couldn't. Only later did I realise what my brief, careless marriage had done to my uncle. For a little over a year he had enjoyed what he had always dreamed of having, a family connection with the Lampitts.

"It would hit Vernon very hard," he said, coming to grips with himself. "The Labour Party can be very prudish about such matters."

We had re-entered the region of sheer fantasy. That Vernon's "career" as a Labour peer should have been changed one way or another by the marital status of a first cousin once removed was not to be believed.

"And Ursula. The Ladies' Colleges, again . . ." His voice trailed away. Perhaps Felicity's life had shown him that Ladies' Colleges were occasionally able to accept the ups and downs of an imperfect human condition.

"But poor Sibs," he repeated.

"And poor old Julian," said my aunt, patting my shoulder with her fingertips, an extremely demonstrative gesture for her.

My uncle looked up sharply. He was angry.

"I think Julian is being very selfish," he said. And he left the room without another word. There did not seem much more to say. Not long afterwards I got into the car and roared back towards London. Poor Sibs. Not poor Anne, not poor me, but poor Sibs. I had made the mistake of supposing that life was an occasion for pursuing personal fulfillment and I had forgotten that its true function was the contemplation of the names, doings and sensibilities of the Lampitt family. No wonder that my uncle was shocked. By his standards, the step which I was contemplating was insane. A philatelist watching a child stick a Cape Triangular into a book of Green Shield stamps could not have reacted with more horror than Uncle Roy when he saw me throwing away my Lampitt bride, almost my claim to *be* a Lampitt.

I drove the car, Anne's car, dangerously, my mind entirely detached from the driving, focussed with obsessive intensity on the drama of my interior life. I felt the need to go back to Anne, to talk, to sort things out once and forever. One has this sense when very unhappy that a crisis can be resolved by doing or saying one more thing. One loses the sense of life as an idling hilly landscape of long vistas which we get through whatever happens and which will not be altered much by one big conversation, or one big decision. Oddly enough, the certainty that I must see Anne, settle things, talk of lawyers, was accompanied by a great dread of the conversation itself and of its finality. I was not truly certain that I knew what to do and I found, as the traffic got heavier in the streets of the City, that I was continuing westwards with some reluctance. What if her mother were to be in the flat when I returned?

The answer, obviously, was that I would postpone any big conversation until Anne and I were alone together. I did not think of this answer. The thought of "poor Sibs" was enough to determine the path which the car took, nosing its way down Oxford Street and the familiar left-hand turn into Soho Square. The square was full of people—office girls sitting cautiously on benches; shy men, some in uniform, wondering about a tart before their next engagement; tarts themselves, as well as many people just wandering and enjoying the heat. It was the last day of summer. Autumn weather was on its way. I parked in Poland Street and looked at my watch. It was only about six-thirty. Not many would yet have arrived in the Bottle. Indeed, the Best Seller himself had not yet arrived, for even as I was locking the Morris, he came shambling towards me, a determined smile enlivening his big frog-like face.

"Well, Julian, lad, this is a very pleasant surprise."

"You're looking very pleased with yourself. The writing is still going well?"

"So, so, lad, so, so." I didn't believe him. There had been no mention of his modern *Odyssey* novel since the first time he had told me about it.

"I thought perhaps you'd won some money on the dogs."

"The dogs?" His mock outrage, his little attempt to put on a posh voice, did not quite come off. "Young man, are you implying that I gamble? On the dogs? How very socially . . . inept!"

He was very smart. His hair was smarmed back with bay rum, his collar was stiff and clean, the blazer and trousers were just back from the cleaners. The tie was the Bradford Rotarians'.

"No, as a matter of fact, I've just been to confession," he said. "Wiped the slate clean again, lad. It does you good, like a real dose of syrup of figs. Cleanses you. Empties it all out."

"I get the idea."

"I feel twice the man."

"They say it's good for you. What I find difficult to believe is that past deeds could ever be undone."

"They're not undone, lad, no one believes that. No, the difference between Catholics and the rest of you is this. We all want to forget, we all want to pretend it didn't happen, we all want to put it behind us for Christ's sakes, and we all want forgiveness. But the difference between a Catholic and someone like you, Julian, is that a Catholic knows forgiveness. You could confront the worst sides to your nature, the most horrible things you ever said or did if you knew you had the forgiveness of God."

"Maybe God has less to forgive than we have. Maybe we hurt Him less than we hurt one another."

"That's where the crucifix comes in," said Day Muckley. He said it on the pavement outside the Bottle. He said it as we crossed the saloon and he said it again when we reached the bar and he asked me what I'd have.

"I'd better have a very large Scotch," he said.

"Glad you got a large something, apart from a mouth," said our genial landlord.

"I'll stick to beer," I said.

Hardly anyone was there yet. The little man haloed by a trilby and the two old women smoking and drinking brandy, and Mr. Porn who had abandoned his literary endeavours for the day. In spite of the warmth of the evening, he still wore his bowler hat, his black shirt, thick black suit and black tie. Sweat cascaded down his smooth red face as he sipped his gin-and-water.

"I heard you say crucifixes were coming in," he said. "Very interesting. I mean, I've known for years in my business about the kinky appeal of all that stuff. What else are all those High Church nancy vicars except transvestites? Convent girls with rosaries knotted around their tits, monks with hard-ons under their habits, group sex on the High Altar, it's all got its market."

"Shut up," said Day Muckley. He had gulped down his first large whisky and was holding out his glass for more.

Pete said, "Jesus, not another religious discussion, if you please. I thought we'd all agreed to keep off the fucking subject. I'll ask you all the question which is a bloody sight more interesting than theology."

" 'All questions are ultimately theological.' Cardinal Manning said that," the Best Seller informed us.

"Well, he must have been a prat. What's theological about women? And don't let's have another go over the Virgin Mary, please. There was an Irishman in here one day . . ."

"Why don't they go to one of their own fucking pubs?" wondered Mr. Porn. "God knows, there are enough of them."

"He told that one about the Virgin Mary and the camel," said Cyril. "Oh, dear, you'll be on to the Jews next. I don't care what religion people are so long as they spend money."

"I warned you," said Day Muckley. He had started to sweat and to go red.

"My point is," said Peter, "where do we get our ideas about women and sex? Maybe the Virgin Mary does have something to answer for, come to think. I mean, when a man's been unfaithful, he's a shit."

"You may have been," said Cyril.

"No, he's a shit. It's all 'Where in hell have you been? Get out of my life, you horrible man, you've ruined everything.' But when a woman goes and screws a bloke . . ."

"Then it's 'You whore, you've ruined everything.' " This viewpoint of Mr. Porn seemed at least to strike a balance.

Seeing the Best Seller subside into his customary evening stupor prompted thoughts of "poor old Debbie," as she had become in my thoughts. I felt guilty about not seeing her, as I had promised to do, when she had so obviously needed cheering up. I had no intention of reviving or continuing our affair, but I was conscious of owing her at least some kindness, and the image of Day Muckley's inebriated face gave me an acute sense of what she must have suffered. I finished my drink and said I must be getting along.

"It's always 'Poor girl, I don't know how she puts up with him,'" said Peter. "Always them having to put up with us, isn't it? Never a word about what they make us suffer."

"I'll be going then," I repeated.

Day Muckley did not even reply. He was just staring, staring, too vacant to contribute to the Marriage Debate which was in perpetual progress at that bar. Driving northwards towards Tufnell Park, I pictured the scene upon which I was to intrude. Debbie would be giving an early supper to the boys, perhaps to some of their teenage friends. It would be a good time to call. Not long thereafter the boys would go to their rooms and Debbie would make coffee. I would apologise for having stayed away and explain that it was the best way of insuring that neither of us became too fond of each other. She would understand, and then I could go back to Anne. A mood of benevolent optimism overcame me. I was not drunk; indeed, I made a firm resolution not to drink any more that evening. In this new mood, when I thought of Anne, it was not of the truculent Anne of recent months but of the happy, beautiful girl I had married. What if Uncle Roy's reaction was not the right one? Had I been too quick to despair? We were both sensible people. (What on earth allowed this idea into my head?) We might after all work things out happily. Debbie would go on being my friend. Anne might pass through this phase if I could only tell her what she meant to me.

The days were drawing in. It was dark by the time I drove downhill into Dartmouth Park Avenue. Walking up to the house, my feet scrunched on fallen leaves and the shells of horse chestnuts. I rang the doorbell, rehearsing a pleasantry with Simon or Jon, or whichever twin were to open the door. In fact, Debbie stood there alone.

"Hallo, stranger." It was unmistakably a reproach.

"Hallo, there."

"Julian, it's been weeks."

"I know, Debbie, I know."

"What do you want?"

"Can I come in?"

Her cross expression was mollified by a toothy smile.

"Why do I put up with you? Come on, I'd been looking forward to a quiet evening with my proofs. Day said he'd ring, the sod, and he hasn't."

"And the boys?"

"It's one of their weekends to be with Derek. They just hate going there, Julian. They have to share a bedroom and there's nothing for them to do . . ."

We walked into the kitchen as she spoke compulsively about the legal arrangements relative to Derek's access to his sons.

"There's a bottle of wine opened. Chianti."

"No, thanks."

"What's the matter with you?"

"Oh, all right, then. Just a glass."

She filled up a big tumbler of the stuff. There was a longish silence after I'd taken my first sip and sat down. Her kitchen was very modern, with red and white fitted units, coated in plastic and Formica, strip lighting in the ceiling, fitted cupboards, and, on top of one of the units, a food mixer.

"I've been busy," I said. "I've some work at last."

"Day told me. You're wasting yourself, Julian, you know that." Was she drunk or just emboldened by disappointment? "Acting in crap on the wireless instead of getting down to a proper book."

"Writing isn't everything."

"It is to me."

"Everything?"

"That and the kids. And the few people I can rely on."

Another punishing silence during which there was nothing to do except drink up my wine in nervous gulps. When my glass was empty, I said, "Debbie, what we had together, it was fun, it was lovely, but it wouldn't have lasted."

"I wasn't asking for it to last, Julian. Just for a bit of sympathy, when I needed you."

Her lower lip trembled and she began to cry. I rose and went over to comfort her. She was not sobbing, just crying quietly with tears coming out of her great brown eyes.

"I wasn't kidding myself you loved me," she said, responding to my caress by stroking my hands as they lay on her shoulders. "I just missed you."

"I missed you, too."

Why did I say this? It was almost completely untrue. She stood up when I spoke these words and put her arms round my neck.

"Still, you're like all the others, the selfish sods."

It was just reaching the point where it would be bad manners not to respond to these endearments. Our lips were meeting. Hands were straying up and down each other's backs.

"Debbie, I . . ."

"There's no need to explain, pet, no need to explain."

Perhaps there wasn't. What harm was being done? At length, having opened another bottle of Chianti, and given me the three-quarters-finished one to carry, she led the way into the sitting-room. The lounge was as lavishly modern in style as the kitchen, no expense spared. Three walls of ochre paint were contrasted with the fourth which was covered in a heavy bold wallpaper, midnight blue with splashes of orange to match the contemporary Scandinavian sofa on which we sank down.

"You're just lovely," I said.

"You're wicked."

"Just a bit."

We drank up the first bottle of wine and smoked a bit and then we went on to the second bottle. I took off my jacket before resuming our embrace. She put one hand inside my shirt, and I began to unbutton her blouse, and to undo the awkward straps and hooks which I found inside. While I was thus engaged, she froze, and asked, "What's that?"

"What?"

"Was that the front door?"

"But the boys are away. You said."

"Yes, but." She did not need to explain what she meant because the lounge door opened and Day Muckley lurched in.

She had said he might call. My hand was instantly withdrawn from Debbie's chest, hers from my trousers. Evidently, he had a latch key and came and went as he chose. Was it conceivable that he would suspect nothing, or suppose that there was an innocent explanation for the two of us to be sitting on the sofa, I with tousled hair, she with blouse unbuttoned to the waist? Was it possible that he was too far gone to notice? I dreaded his wrath, but more I dreaded his hurt, and it would have been an impossible insult to them both to suggest that what was taking place on the sofa was entirely without seriousness as far as I was concerned.

She began to button herself decorously and he just stood there, staring. He was pale, and his eyes were more than ever marbly behind thick lenses.

We were frozen in that terrible scene for some moments. Debbie began to shiver. Then she said, "Hallo, love. Day!"

He said, "My God."

His voice was gravelly, flat, despondent. I do not doubt that he did appreciate what was going on. He could not have failed to put the worst possible interpretation on what he saw.

"Love, it's not what you think," said Debbie.

I said, "I'll go."

I had not thought how to manoeuvre my way round his figure as he stood by the door. Even drunk, his short, stocky body looked massively strong. He could do damage with a punch.

"Day, Day," said Debbie. Her voice fluttered. She was anxious. Her third "Day?" was interrogative.

"My God."

His pale, impassive mask-like face now creased with pain and a huge hand came towards his lips. Was he going to weep, or belch, or repeat his celebrated television performance?

"My God, I love thee with my whole heart . . ."

He was not talking to Debbie, he was talking to God, but his sentence got little further, and became a deep groan. He bent double and clutched his stomach.

"Oh, no, love, not here," said Debbie.

He did vomit, but what came out of his mouth was a torrent

of blood, and he collapsed onto the carpet, dragging a table over as he fell. When we knelt beside him, we saw that blood was dribbling from his nose and continuing to come out of his mouth. His brow was already that of a corpse, white and damp, but he was breathing in bursts. Blood was coming out of his ears.

We tried to lift him and found that he was squelching in blood from behind, and his light mackintosh was crimson and sodden.

"Where's the telephone?"

"Oh, Day, Day, love." She stroked his head and wept.

"The *telephone*."

"In the hall. Oh, Day. It'll be all right, love, it'll be all right."

I dialled 999 on the hall telephone and came back into the room when the ambulance was ordered. Debbie looked up at me. Her face was quite changed. All its innocence was gone.

"Oh, he's not going to, he's not going to, is he?"

"The ambulance will be here soon."

"Oh, my God."

Her hands and cheeks were stained with blood. She fell on him, clawing and crying in uncontrolled grief.

We both felt instinctively that our act of casual betrayal had precipitated if not actually caused this terrifying effusion. Certainly in my own case (though all Debbie's feelings must have been proportionately more painful in so far as she loved him) I felt like a murderer. In the discussions we were to have after the funeral, Debbie told me that Day had often been to a doctor complaining of stomach pains. Unlike Treadmill, he had not taken his disorders to a specialist and his doctor had done no more than prescribe an occasional palliative, dismissing the very idea of ulcers. I knew nothing about the condition and insofar as I knew of people suffering from duodenal or gastric complaints I had associated ulcers with hypochondria, or with those who were pushing themselves unattractively hard. Ulcers were for thrusting business executives. If I had had to name anyone of a literary bent who would have been a likely sufferer it would have been Hunter, not Day Muckley. I certainly did not know until I witnessed it what a burst ulcer, a haemorrhage on a gigantic scale, could do. Nor until I watched over Muckley's bloody and recumbent form had I thought how tenuously the human body contains itself. The line in *Macbeth* is so right: who would have thought an old man could have so much blood in him? And only when the blood starts to come out, and un-controllably, when all the orifices are opened and the polite arrangement by which we are parcelled in with skin and muscles to contain our liquid constituents breaks down, does one realise what a mess we are physically, and how little it takes to destroy us. He wasn't dead. His eyes were shut, and he was deathly pale and his breathing came very irregularly. When, quite soon, the ambulance arrived, Debbie recovered her composure; and when Day had been lifted onto the stretcher she became aware of the minor practical difficulties of the situation.

"How will you get to the hospital? Oh, look at that car-pet . . . If I stay behind and you go in the ambulance . . . Oh, no, look, if you . . ."

It was one of the ambulancemen who resolved things for us. Debbie went with Day in the ambulance. I stayed behind to clear up some of the mess, saying I would come to join her in the hospital, the Royal Free.

When she was gone and I had the house to myself, I wondered how conceivably I could have found myself in a position socially so painful, morally so shabby. In the ordinary course of things, had it gone unwitnessed, what had passed between me and Debbie on the sofa that evening would have been harmless, though it was not what I intended and it certainly muddied the situation between me and Anne. And now Day Muckley was dying under the impression that a friend of his had deceived him with the woman he loved, which would have been bad enough if it was true: but it wasn't really true, or I didn't think it was true, believing at that age that actions took their moral colour from how you felt when committing them rather than from their effect on others. Perhaps this was Hunter's criterion of behaviour, too; and perhaps this was how he was capable of causing so much pain in others while appearing to suffer none himself.

I must have made between ten and twenty journeys between Debbie's sitting-room and kitchen with a bucket and mop. The carpet was not merely stained but sodden. No one would ever get rid of the stain but with enough diligent rubbing and sponging I could clear up the worst of the mess and leave it to dry. Having a grim practical task to do was particularly consoling. While I worked I thought of Day Muckley, as I was often to do in the months and years that followed. He was not destined to die immediately. In fact he lingered for several days in a coma before the end, which was, I remember, on Michaelmas Day. I had grown fond of him for reasons which could not be put into words and when in afteryears I spoke of him others would be puzzled that I had liked him. All stories about him, or nearly all, made him sound coarse or boring; and he could be these things. But I was fonder of him than I was of Debbie, particularly in the years which followed his death, when her devotion to literature seemed increasingly bound up with a desire to get on in the world. Day Muckley had wanted desperately to get on. He had none of Blake's self-confident otherworldliness. He wanted his books (which I didn't like much, when I read them) to make him rich and famous. But he had helped to develop in me what he held as a genuine creed for himself, the sense that literature was something to be intensely grateful for, almost something worth living for. I doubt whether he would have been much fun before the war, in the brief period of his triumphant success, when he had liked to waste money on showy cars and to mix with the more famous practitioners of his craft. (How he had envied Arnold Bennett's yacht.) My Day Muckley was a collapsed man in a pub, no longer convincing anybody, given to anger and confusion and plausibly, though incomprehensibly, at one with his God.

(At his funeral, we sang a belligerent hymn called "Faith of Our Fathers," said to be his favourite, whose jaunty trivial tune was at variance with the suffering of the martyrs it described.) If God were like Stalin, as Day had once averred, then there was nothing surprising about the way He had dealt this last blow to His loyal old supporter. ("Did He smile His work to

see?") Just such a bloody end awaited those in the U.S.S.R. who
had kidded themselves that they had got on the right side of the
Kremlin mountaineer. Yet Muckley's church taught a different
doctrine, that God when He walked the earth had turned His
feet to places where He could eat and drink with sinners, places
like the Black Bottle, in fact.

When I'd done all I could for Debbie's carpet, I drove to the
Royal Free and found her, tearfully waiting in the corridor
outside the intensive care unit. His wife had been sent for, and
the last piece of torture which Debbie had to suffer during those
final few days was to be compelled to make herself scarce while
Mrs. Muckley brought a priest to her husband's unconscious
body. I forget what the doctors did to him, if anything. There
was some talk of an operation if he was strong enough, which
he wasn't.

Debbie and I sat on a bench together.

"I'll never forgive myself," she said.

"You shouldn't feel like that."

"I do, I do."

"If it was anyone's fault, it was mine."

"Julian—how could we?"

She blew her nose. Then she said in a determined, brave voice,
"He'll pull through. I know he's going to pull through. And
when he does it will all be different. I shan't limit his visits to
two days a week. He needn't go on living in those horrible little
rooms. He can come and live with me. We'll make a life.
Together."

"Of course."

"I'd rather be alone now."

"I see."

"Can you understand? I want to be alone."

I touched her hand, got up, and walked away down the corridor. There was no more to say. A clock on the wall said five
past twelve and it conveyed nothing to me. I had no idea what
sort of time it should have been, and no consciousness of
whether it was the middle of the day or the middle of the night.
Because it was dark in the car park, I remembered it was night,

and that six hours earlier I had been on my way home to see Anne.

London was curiously empty, so that the journey from Hampstead to the far end of Chelsea took less than half an hour. My mind was no longer full of Debbie, or of Anne, or of my work, the things which had haunted so much of the last year. Nor had I framed into any rational cliché the notion that in Muckley's end I had witnessed a horrible version of what we were all journeying towards, whether in a stately genteel manner (the car was passing Cadogan Square) or in the more unvarnished mode of my friends at the Black Bottle. I thought rather of Muckley himself and how sad I was that I'd never see him again, talking nonsense with his pint of bitter in his hand or swaying out into the afternoon light of Poland Street. And I wished I could tell him the truth about what he'd seen on the sofa, wished I'd been able to explain that I had meant no harm by it, certainly no harm to him. But I knew that such wishes would never be fulfilled.

The car sped down the King's Road. Just by the Town Hall where Anne and I were married, I saw Hunter standing alone by a lamppost. He appeared to be doing nothing. He was some way from the nearest bus stop and did not seem to be on the lookout for a taxi. I supposed that he had been at our flat, and the thought made me angry, but I slowed down to check that it was truly Hunter, rather than someone who looked a bit like him. I have a tendency when much preoccupied with a person to "see" them all over the place and to recognise them in perfect strangers. It was possible that this was some other man, not Hunter at all. As the car slowed down, Hunter looked up and peered through the side window with a strange smile. It infuriated me that he should be trying to ingratiate himself after all that had happened. But when our eyes met, the smile vanished and his face revealed genuine surprise. Who had he supposed it was? Our eyes met only for a second; I had merely slowed, not stopped the car, and I immediately drove off, leaving him there. In the driving mirror, I saw that he had turned and walked briskly up in the direction of Sloane Square.

The lights were all off in the flat when I got in. I switched on one of our raffia lamps in the sitting-room and sat on a cane armchair. One last cigarette before bed. As I lit up, Anne appeared at the bedroom door, bleary-eyed. Either she was becoming a good actress or I had woken her up.

She had on an old dressing gown of mine left over from schooldays.

She yawned and asked snappishly, "Where in hell have you been?"